Stea[illegible]y

Other Books by Lexi Blake:
 EROTIC ROMANCE

Masters And Mercenaries
The Dom Who Loved Me
The Men With The Golden Cuffs
A Dom Is Forever
On Her Master's Secret Service
Sanctum: A Masters and Mercenaries Novella
Love and Let Die
Dungeon Royale, *Coming Soon*

Masters Of Ménage (by Shayla Black and Lexi Blake)
Their Virgin Captive
Their Virgin's Secret
Their Virgin Concubine
Their Virgin Princess
Their Virgin Hostage
Their Virgin Secretary, *Coming Soon*

CONTEMPORARY WESTERN ROMANCE

Wild Western Nights
Leaving Camelot, *Coming Soon*

URBAN FANTASY

Thieves
Steal the Light
Steal the Day
Steal the Moon, *Coming January 2014*
Steal the Sun, *Coming 2014*
Steal the Night, *Coming 2014*

Steal the Day

Thieves, Book 2

Lexi Blake

Steal the Day
Thieves, Book 2
Lexi Blake

Published by DLZ Entertainment, LLC

Edited by Chloe Vale and Kasi Alexander
ePub ISBN: 978-1-937608-21-7

Acknowledgments

Thanks to the team that helps keep me going. Thanks to my editors, Chloe Vale and Kasi Alexander. To my lovely beta readers, Stormy Pate and Riane Holt. To my friends, Kris Cook and Shayla Black who keep my spirits up. And to Liz Berry and my husband, Rich who have championed this series from the beginning.

Chapter One

I stretched as I rolled out of bed, trying not to wake the man next to me. I caught sight of Devinshea Quinn and couldn't help but stare. It didn't matter that I'd seen him naked a hundred times before. I always had to stop and sigh. His tan skin made a stark contrast to the white sheets. His dark hair was mussed from our activities, and though his face was relaxed, there was no way to soften that perfectly shaped jawline. The sheet was around his waist, leaving most of his lean, muscular body on display. Everything about Dev Quinn was perfect, from his washboard abs to his cut chest, to those ridiculously sensual lips.

I felt a smile cross my face as I sat there and just watched him sleep.

He shifted, rolling over in bed, and I decided it was time to go. As much as I liked to look at him, I really didn't want the argument that was sure to come when he realized where I was going.

I stood up and was finally able to get out of the Christian Louboutins Dev had given me earlier in the evening. I flexed my feet, trying not to groan. The shoes were ridiculously gorgeous. My eyes had widened when I opened the box, and my heart fluttered. It hadn't taken Dev long before he had me in the shoes and nothing else. Those shoes were exciting and sexy, and just the slightest bit uncomfortable. They were a little like my relationship with Dev. The sex was incredible and, while I was in bed with Dev, I didn't think about anything but him. The minute I rolled out of bed, I wanted to get out of those shoes and put on a pair of Converse. That was our problem.

Well, that and my husband.

I walked through the grotto, collecting stray clothes along the way. Dev's apartment was at the top of a building he owned in the middle of downtown Dallas. The bottom of the building housed his club, Ether, the hottest club of its kind. It isn't the kind of club that shows up on the Best of Dallas lists. It's an underground club where the bouncers zealously guard the entrance. I'm one of the only humans to be permitted inside.

Ether is the place where the supernaturals of the world go to mix and mingle and do a little business. It's an official place of peace despite my best effort to burn it down several months back. I hadn't meant to, but then I never do. Trouble just follows me. That had been my first date with Dev, my first date of any kind in years, really. I had been sadly single for a very long time before meeting Dev.

I slowed, unable to rush through. Dev's "condo" took up the whole top floor of the building and was the most decadent space I'd ever seen. The first time Dev had taken me up the private elevator from his office in Ether to his penthouse, the doors had opened and I'd gasped.

I call the whole place "the grotto." It's something like an indoor forest, complete with a brook that runs through the various rooms of the apartment. When the sun is out, the whole place lights up with soft, natural light. In the dead of night, moonbeams stream through the overhead windows, shining down and making the room seem magical.

It's odd for a faery to live year round in the city. They don't like the feeling of being enclosed. It goes against their nature, but Dev is mortal. He's the only of his mother's children who didn't take after her and, because of his mortality, he'd chosen to leave the *sithein* and cut off ties. Since the day we'd met, I could remember two conversations we'd had about his family.

This place made me think he missed them.

I walked into the bathroom that was bigger than my entire living room and turned on the shower. The splendor of Dev's home put in stark contrast our relative differences. Money wasn't a problem for Dev. The same couldn't be said for me. I'd recently finished a job that gave me enough money to buy a little fixer-upper in the country, but I was starting to hurt for cash. My account was down to the low four digits, and I didn't have more money coming in.

Of course, I would have given up all the money I made on my

last job if I could have changed the outcome of it. Some jobs aren't worth the payday.

Tossing my clothes on the counter, I stepped under the rainfall of deliciously hot water. The water stroked over my skin, and I stretched again. Sex with Dev was inventive and exciting, and required a certain level of flexibility. I could see yoga classes in my future.

Suddenly two big hands came from behind and cupped my breasts. I sighed for two reasons—one because it felt so good, and two because there would be no getting out of a fight. I let my head fall back against his chest, his body nestling against mine. If we were going to fight, I might as well enjoy the first part.

"Zoey." Dev breathed in my ear, his voice the sweetest of seductions. His hands moved across my skin and despite the fact that we'd made love earlier, I responded to him immediately. Everywhere he touched, my skin seemed to flare to life. "I sincerely apologize. I have treated you poorly."

I smiled because I knew what was coming next. "I disagree, Dev. I was treated incredibly well. At least three times."

One hand played with my breast, plucking at my nipple, pinching and lighting it up. "Three times isn't enough. I want to watch you come all night long."

It wouldn't be the first time he'd done it. Dev seemed to have a never-ending appetite for sex. On some men it might have been annoying, but Dev was part sex god. It was his nature and somehow, even when I thought I couldn't possibly want him again, the minute he looked at me with those emerald eyes, I melted. He could get me hot and wet and ready for sex with just a glance.

He got to his knees, his mouth at my breast. The warmth of his tongue covered my nipple and I was done for. I could already feel anticipation building, a fire he stoked to the perfect heat.

"Have I told you how fucking pretty you are?" His voice was a low growl, the very tone hungry.

I couldn't help but smile. He was liberal with the praise. "You might have mentioned it."

He nuzzled my breasts with a sigh, kissing them sweetly. "Hush. I'm talking to your breasts."

And he could make me laugh. I threaded my fingers through

that black silky hair of his and let him completely take over.

His big hand made its way lower, his fingers sliding over my clit. "I'm crazy about this, too. Such a pretty pussy."

I nearly cried out when he ran his tongue there. I protested with a little groan as he got to his feet.

Dev pressed himself against me, his cock hard and willing. "No. You be patient. If I had done my job properly earlier, you would have passed out. The fact that you can move means I've got work to do. I didn't even get to the part where I tie you up and we play."

Dev liked to "play." He liked to play with handcuffs and toys. He had a whole closet full of naughty little devices, like an FAO Schwarz for kink. With a low growl, he shifted, turning me toward him. His mouth took mine in a luxurious kiss. His tongue plunged deep, rubbing against mine in a silky glide. I could taste just a hint of my own arousal on his tongue.

This was what Dev and I did best.

He lifted me up, settling me on the ledge of the shower. I was sure the contractors who had built the place thought the wide shelf was to store shampoo and soap, but I knew better. Dev designed it with sex in mind. He moved between my legs, the ledge placing my pussy at the perfect height for him.

My hands reached out as though they just couldn't stand to be this close and not touch him. Whenever I was close to him, his hands running across my skin, I felt a little drugged.

"I can't get enough of you. I fucking crave you." He'd come prepared. He slipped a condom on and worked his way in, his cock stretching me wide. His chest nestled against mine as he pushed deep inside. I held on to his shoulders and wrapped my legs around his waist. We fit together perfectly. It wasn't long before my back was up against the natural rock of the shower and I was screaming out number four.

He hugged me even as the pleasure still pulsed through my system, his hands stroking me, cheek rubbing against mine. This was when I felt closest to Dev, when he treated me like I was precious.

"Let's dry off and go back to bed," he whispered as he helped me to stand. He held me up because my legs weren't quite working yet. It wasn't easy keeping up with a man whose grandfather had been a fertility god. He leaned over and dropped a kiss on my nose.

"I'll tell Albert to send up breakfast for two in the morning."

I hugged him close to me hoping that my affection would make the next few minutes easier. "I can't. I have to go. I have a meeting with a client."

Dev stopped, a grin crossing his face. I suspected one of the reasons he liked me was my unusual job. I was pretty sure he'd never dated a thief who specialized in procuring objects of an arcane nature before. Stealing from supernaturals made my job one of the riskier fields. It was thrilling when the job ran well and completely terrifying when anything went wrong. Dev had run one job with me and he'd been bugging me ever since to let him go again. He'd gotten off on the adrenaline rush.

He winked down at me, his hands smoothing my hair back. "That's great, sweetheart. I'll get dressed and go with you. I promise to keep my mouth shut and be good eye candy. Should I take the Ruger or the Glock?"

I pulled away from him because no amount of affection was going to fix this. "Sorry, but I have to go alone."

His deep green eyes formed suspicious slits. "Alone? You never go alone. That's your first rule." He took a step back, his mouth turning down. "So if you're not going alone, you're going with Daniel."

And there it was, the one name that could wreck our day. "He's my partner."

"He's your husband." Dev spat the word out as though it was poison. He stalked out of the shower, leaving me with an incredible view of his preternaturally glorious ass.

Yep. And just like that our nice night was wrecked. I picked up a bottle of something Dev liked the smell of and then put it back down in favor of plain old soap. I told myself it was because I needed to be professional. I didn't want to go into a client meeting smelling like a woman who had just had sex four times.

If I was honest with myself, and I tried not to be, I didn't want to hurt Daniel.

I finished up in the shower and turned it off, wrapping a warm towel around my body. Dev was sitting on the sink when I went to retrieve my clothes. He'd slipped into silk boxers and looked at me with a sad smile, his shoulders slumped.

"Sorry," he said. "I know I'm being an ass. I'm just jealous."

"You have nothing to be jealous of." It sounded like a reassuring lie even to my ears. I still saw Danny almost every day. It had to bother Dev. "If I could get a divorce, I would."

I'd come to accept the marriage I'd been tricked into. It wasn't like I had much of a choice. Tricked is a harsh word. Daniel had been trying to protect me at the time. It was kind of his excuse for everything. I didn't resent the protection. I resented the fact that he'd left me ignorant. I had to find out from a demon that we were married.

There'd been no vows of love and devotion, no white dress or fabulous reception. There had been blood and sex and a transfer of ownership between Daniel and myself.

And there was no divorce when you were married to a vampire.

"I guess I should be happy my head's still on my body." Dev shrugged negligently, a boyish gesture. "When I found out Daniel was back from Paris, I kind of expected to become one of those 'bodies in a dark alley' stories."

"Oh, babe, they would never find your body." Daniel would be far more careful than that. I slipped back into the dress I'd worn earlier. It was wrinkled from sex in the elevator on the way up. I looked very "walk of shame." "He won't hurt you. He promised me. It's one of the reasons I didn't kick him to the curb when he came back."

There were many other reasons, but I didn't go into those with Dev. I didn't mention that it was difficult for me to even imagine my life without Daniel Donovan in it, no matter how pissed I was at the time. I didn't mention that it was becoming increasingly difficult to just be friends with the man I once planned a life with. Months had passed and my anger was softening.

"Where are my shoes?" I'd worn a comfortable pair of boots with a smaller heel in deference to my meeting.

It was a nice fall night and the boots would be warm. The peep toe heels Dev had bought were not the best fit for the season. And the way some of my client meetings went, I might be running for my life before the night was over.

"I think you left them in the limo. I sent the driver home, but I can call him back."

I glanced at my watch as I clasped it on my wrist. “Damn it, I’m going to be late. No, I’ll go in the heels.”

I winced inwardly at the thought. They hadn’t bothered me at all when they were wrapped around Dev’s waist, but I didn’t think tonight was the night to break in a new pair of shoes.

Dev smiled, and I wondered if I had really left the shoes in the car. He looked satisfied as I slid my feet into the four-and-a-half-inch heels. I could guess what he was thinking. There was no way I bought those shoes for myself, and Daniel would know it.

I kissed him anyway. It was a sweet kiss and made me remember that Dev and I had fun. It was easy to be with Dev. With the exception of my marriage, we never fought. We satisfied each other, and that was enough for now. He never told me he loved me, and I tried really hard to not even think the words about him. Loving Devinshea would be very dangerous, but I couldn’t seem to walk away, either. I wasn’t his destiny or his last remaining tie to humanity. He liked me. He wanted me. That was enough. It was what I needed.

Dev walked me to the elevator, his hand in mine. “Hey, could you try to find out something for me?”

“Sure. What’s up?” I was willing to do just about anything now. He wasn’t forcing the situation with Daniel so I could definitely do him a favor.

His eyebrows drew together as he looked down at me. “It’s about the new regulars at Ether. Have you not noticed? Is there a vamp convention in town or something? Normally I get one or two a month in the club. But lately, I’ve seen a couple of new fangs in almost every night. They’re odd, too. You know how normal vamps act, right?”

“Sure.” Vampires weren’t big on individuality. They tended to dress the same and act really cool and standoffish until they needed a snack. It was the way Daniel acted until he started taking my blood on a regular basis. In the last several months, he’d come out of what I termed his “long, dark broody period.” He was behaving more like the Daniel he’d been when he was alive.

Dev held the door open, his face thoughtful. “These vamps don’t dress alike. One of them was wearing jeans and a Cowboys jersey, and he was hanging out with a female wolf. I swear, Zoey, I thought he was human. I was about to kick him out of the club when I realized what he was."

It was curious. Wolves, especially the local pack, had never been friendly with vampires. It was one of the reasons my roommate, Neil, severed all ties to his family. Neil wasn't welcome in the pack due to his blood oath to protect Daniel. There was something very odd going on if wolves were suddenly buddying up to strange vamps.

"I'll ask around." I stepped into the elevator and realized I had another problem. Dev had sent a car for me. I opened my mouth to ask, but Dev was already tossing me the keys to his Audi. I caught them with a smile. "Thanks."

"Don't destroy it." He shook his head because he knew I was perfectly capable of doing just that.

I took the elevator straight down. The doors opened directly into Dev's office. I had to walk through Ether to get to the parking garage where the car was parked. I opened the door to the office and was assailed by the full-time rave that is Ether. The throbbing beat filled the air as I descended the steps as quickly as my shoes would let me.

A large red demon stood at the bottom of the stairs, dressed in an elegant suit. He tipped his horns forward in acknowledgment. Albert. Dev's all-in-one, go-to demon. He acted as Dev's butler, his bouncer, and his second in command. "Mrs. Donovan."

I was going to try pleasantries but simply snapped my lips shut and started to walk around him. At one point, I thought Albert and I could be friends. Now, he just viewed me as the harlot who was leading his precious master down the wrong path. Seriously, no one can be as judgmental as a demon. They really do know their sin.

"Zoey," he called out as I tried to get around him.

I turned because he hadn't called me by my first name in several months. "What do you need, Albert?"

"A moment of your time."

"If you're going to give me another lecture on adultery, you can save your breath. Daniel and I have an open marriage." The open part wasn't Daniel's idea, but then the marriage part hadn't been mine.

Albert ignored me. "Did my master discuss our worries with you?"

"He mentioned something about new vampires in Dallas. I think he wants me to figure out where they came from." I had to strain to hear him over the noise. I was sure he could hear me. Sometimes it's difficult to be the only human in the room.

"Yes, we've had several new vampires in the club." Albert raised his voice and inched closer to me when he realized my difficulty. I was happy for the heels because Albert was at least seven feet tall. With the extra four inches, I was all the way up to five eight.

"And Dev said they had been seen with werewolves?"

Albert nodded. "Several of them were seen with weres and shifters. The two-natured were all female, and the vampires were all male. It did not seem like a business relationship."

Curiouser and curiouser. If vamps and weres didn't typically do business together, then they really didn't have relationships. It was more about the weres than the vampires. Vampires have no problem coupling up with anything they find attractive, and were blood is particularly rich. If a vamp could get a pretty were to agree, I was sure the vamp would be thrilled. The werewolf, on the other hand, would be outcast. "Do you have any idea how many new guys we're talking about? One? Two?"

"I have reports that state at least five new vampires have taken up residence in our city," Albert explained.

My eyes widened at that bit of news. I really had been spending too much time alone if I hadn't heard about that. Since we lost Sarah, our witch and my friend, in the last job we'd run, I'd spent a lot of time restoring my house. I'd retreated from the world, but it seemed to move forward just fine without me. "Five vamps have moved into town? There are eight vampires in residence? Can the city even sustain eight vamps for long?"

"You aren't hearing me, Zoey," Albert said. "The vampires haven't moved here. They rose here. Or if they didn't have their turn in our fair city, then they got here as quickly as they could. None of the vampires appears to be over thirty human years old, and I suspect that is their true age. These are new vampires. I am almost certain of it."

I shook my head at the thought.

My husband had an awful lot of explaining to do.

Chapter Two

I steered the Audi through downtown traffic, glad that I could make it to Daniel's with a blindfold on because I wasn't thinking about the drive. It was difficult to concentrate on anything except what Albert and I had discussed.

Why was the Council sending new vamps to Dallas?

It didn't make sense. Vampires are very rare. In the course of a decade, maybe five will rise. Almost all of these vampires will be located in the First World. The genetic mutation that causes vampirism seems to be more prevalent in males of European descent. Advanced medicine and health care in the wealthier societies have had an effect on vampire society. In the past, many would die on the battlefield or from disease. Now they mostly died of old age. Old age and vampirism is not a good combination. The thought that five new vampires had risen, and that they had died as young men, was too much of a coincidence.

If such a thing had happened, the Council would certainly not send their precious new fledglings to the same city as Daniel Donovan for training. Quite the opposite. The Council would try to make damn sure Daniel didn't taint them with his outlaw presence. It was only because of his patron's influence that the Council hadn't written an order of execution on him about seven months ago. They should be glad they hadn't written out that order because Daniel wouldn't have met the dawn quietly. He would have gone down—if they could take him down, and that's a big if—in a blaze of glory.

Daniel is the vampire who scares the shit out of the other vampires.

Albert had to be wrong about the vampires being new. It just didn't happen. If the Council had sent the vampires, then they were here for one reason and one reason alone. They had come to fuck with Daniel.

I pulled the Audi into the parking garage of Daniel's building, parked and started for the entryway.

"Mrs. Donovan," the doorman acknowledged as he held the door open for me.

I smiled briefly. I couldn't get used to the deferential treatment I got whenever I entered vampire society. I'm a companion. It's the vampire word for wife, dinner, and addiction all rolled into one. Apparently the only thing rarer on the Earth plane than vampires are companions. No one has ever explained to my satisfaction just what it is about me that makes me a companion. There's something in my blood that makes a vampire stronger, smarter, faster than a vampire without a wife. The flip side is the vampire is completely addicted to companion blood. Even though Daniel and I weren't living together as man and wife, I donated blood every week to feed him. Many people would love to see Daniel Donovan in a permanent grave, and though I was trying to live apart from him, I could never be the one who made that happen.

I strode to the elevator and pushed the button for the floor that held four large apartments. As far as I knew, only three of the rooms were occupied. The entire undead population of Dallas was supposedly housed in those rooms.

There was Daniel, the youngest, but without question strongest of the three. Michael House looked to be an affable man in his twenties, but he'd died on the battlefields of World War One. And then there was Alexander. Of all the vampires I'd met, Alexander Sharpe was the creepiest. Daniel had reason to believe Alexander had been Jack the Ripper, so I kept my distance.

God, I wished I'd been able to find my shoes. Daniel and I had settled into a nice sort of friendship, and I didn't want to wave a red cape in front of a bull. Though we had agreed to work on being friends, he still managed to make me feel like a cheating wife sometimes. It wasn't so surprising. Up until seven months before, I would have done anything to be Daniel's wife. We'd known each other most of our lives. We fell in love as teens and were engaged at twenty. Before we could get married, he'd died in a car accident. The upside? He'd turned out to be a vampire. The downside? The craptastic Council had taken him away from me for three years and sent him back as a distant stranger with more secrets than I could handle. We'd only gotten intimate again months before, and that was when I discovered all the things the love of my life had been hiding from me.

My blood calls to his, but then it does the same with any vampire. If I'm in a room with a vampire, you can bet his eyes are on me. He doesn't have to know me to want me. It was only luck that I hadn't met up with one before or I would have been taken off the street, flown to the catacombs of Paris, and sold to the vampire with the most money or clout. Daniel's patron, Marcus Vorenus, had assured me he would have paid top dollar. Daniel, in his post-turn fumblings, had managed to protect me. When the Council had come for him, my blood had been in his body. It was enough to make a claim but not a marriage. That had come later.

I had discovered that the person I loved beyond life, beyond death, returned my love because I tasted good.

Dev might not love me, but I wasn't actively pursued by every faery I met. He slept with me because it felt good, and he liked me. I was Daniel's obsession, and that was a heavy burden to bear.

The elevator doors opened, and I stepped out into the quiet hallway. I used my key and opened the door to Daniel's apartment. I was going to sneak into his bedroom and change clothes when I heard a burst of masculine laughter.

I peeked into the small dining room where five men sat around a table. At first I thought they were playing poker. Dev's club had lively poker rooms going all hours of the night. Then the dice came out, and I knew I was wrong.

"Take that, dragon lord," one of the men, and I use that term loosely, said.

I shook my head, looking at the table in front of me. "Seriously, you're a vampire with unbelievable power, and you spend your nights playing Dungeons and Dragons?"

Daniel smiled up at me, his longish hair in desperate need of a trim and completely perfect for its shagginess. His blue eyes were lit with mirth as he looked over at me and I tried, I really tried, to not let my heart break a little bit. "I'm immortal, baby. Do you have any idea the kinds of campaigns I can run?"

I had to smile back. "Nerd."

"Back at ya," he replied. "Gentlemen, for those of you who haven't met her, this is my lovely wife, Zoey. Don't let her adult-like disapproval fool you. She's thrown the dice in her time."

Yes, I had. I'd played with Daniel. I looked at the men around the table. "He's pulled you in, too, Michael?"

Since Daniel had come back, I'd had several nice conversations with the WWI veteran. He enjoyed talking about his time in the army, and though he didn't remember much about the sixties because acid apparently works on vamps, too, he was a veritable fount of twentieth century history. He'd even managed to stop staring at me like I was a particularly juicy steak.

Michael shrugged. "It's fun. It's just nice to have some friends."

I knew it was nice for Daniel, too. He'd spent an enormous part of the last several years keeping everyone at arm's length. He sat there in his Spider-Man T-shirt, and there was nothing I wanted to do more than go over and sit in his lap and hold him close and show his friends that I was his girl. It was an impulse, and now I knew it had nothing to do with what I wanted and everything to do with blood and biology. So I forced myself to stand there.

Besides Daniel and Michael, there was a vamp I didn't know and two other males of undetermined species. The vamp I recognized because of the glazed look of desperate longing that had hit his face the minute he got a whiff of me.

"Justin," Daniel said evenly, reaching over to touch the other man's arm.

Justin shook his head and forced his focus from me to Daniel. "Yeah?"

"She is mine." The words were said with no real threat behind them, which was surprising. In the past, Daniel had threatened wretched death on any vamp who looked at me twice.

"Of course." Justin sighed as though some pressure had been released. That answered one question I had. Justin wasn't a newbie. Baby vamps struggled with control. It was why the Council ruthlessly handled their training. "I'm sorry."

Daniel cut him off with a wave of his hand. "You didn't know."

"Well, I don't get it," said one of the non-vamps, a scruffy looking guy in his mid-twenties. I would bet he turned into some sort of canine. "She's all right and I wouldn't kick her out of bed or anything, but I don't get the drool thing. Dude, you should wipe your chin."

"You aren't a vampire, Blake," Daniel pointed out needlessly. "Think of a really hot alpha female. Would you do just about anything to mate with her?"

Blake's eyes got heated for a moment. "Oh, yeah, especially when she's in season."

"More info than I needed!" I felt myself flush.

"I was just trying to give him a point of reference." Daniel looked very amused at my embarrassment.

The last male smiled, an open, honest grin. He was the smallest man at the table, with a boyish physique that hadn't quite filled out to the man he would inevitably become. He looked to be in his late teens, definitely the baby of the group. "Well, I'm a sad-sack human, and I would totally do you. I mean, if you would and if it didn't mean my horrible death and stuff. I got to be honest, though. I wouldn't be too flattered if I was you. I don't have real high standards."

"You have a human in here?" I stared at Daniel, waiting for a damn good explanation.

As I said, I'm usually the only human in a room. I survived because I'd been surrounded by powerful protectors my whole life. My father, Harry Wharton, was important in the supernatural world and Daniel, well, no one messed with Daniel. I now had the added protection of being considered the property of the Council. To the Council, I was an asset, a plaything to be coddled and protected and sheltered. No vampire would try to take me from my master. To do so would invite a duel, and Danny was far too badass to risk that. That being said, if Daniel wasn't around, another vampire would be duty bound to provide the ass kicking. It was a testament to my hold on Danny that Michael and Alexander hadn't tried to take out Dev. It was their instinct to protect what they considered vampire property. It generally meant I could go where I wanted and no one messed with me.

To be a human in our world was to be vulnerable. Without protection, most would never survive.

"Oh, my name's Nathan," the human, who would probably be

dead soon because he hung out with vampires, said. "It's totally cool. I know they're vamps and Blake's a shifter and you're a companion. I grew up in this world. You're totally the first companion I've ever seen. My brother and sister will never believe me."

Michael laughed, and it was such a human sound. It was the sound men make when they're fucking with each other. "You grew up trying to destroy this world, dude."

"He's a freaking hunter?" I practically screamed the question. Daniel had brought a teenaged hunter into his gaming group?

"Ex-hunter," Nathan corrected me. "I just kind of did it 'cause it was the family business. Then I tried to hunt and kill Daniel here, and he convinced me I should probably take a different career path."

I bet he had. The poor little boy had probably tried to come after the most powerful vampire the world had seen in millennia with a stake and a clove of garlic. It should have been a bloodbath that ended with little Nathan as a snack. But as Nathan continued his story, I learned that Daniel had chosen to take the idiot out for a pizza.

"That's when Daniel got me a job at a comic book store," Nathan concluded his tale. "I like it. It's way more relaxing than hunting, and I get a twenty percent discount."

The shifter, who in my experience shouldn't be here either, pointed at me. "Hey, you look just like that club owner's girlfriend. Not exactly, of course. She's way hotter, but you look a lot like her. You know that guy who runs Ether?"

Michael was the only one who looked uncomfortable besides Daniel. The other three men were trying to decide if I was hotter than me.

"I don't get that guy," Blake said, shaking his head.

"What don't you get?" I wanted to know because Dev didn't seem to have any male friends. He spent all of his time with me or his half-demon butler. "He's gorgeous, rich and successful. What else do you need?"

Justin shook his head. "I don't get what women see in him. How much time does he spend getting his hair to do that? I know he looks all cool and shit, but he's that guy who all the other guys think is a douche."

Nathan pointed at Justin and nodded. "I know just the type. I hate that guy."

I looked at Daniel, who was smiling under his hand but chose not to comment. "Gentlemen, I'm afraid my lovely wife and I have some business to deal with tonight. I'm going to have to call the game."

As the boys got together their various pieces of equipment and decided on the next time they would meet, I watched Michael and Daniel exchange a look. I think Michael was trying to make sure his friend was okay.

Daniel showed his group to the door, and I walked down the hall to his bedroom. It was such a change from the way it had looked months ago when Daniel had first brought me here. While it wasn't a wreck, there was a certain messiness that let a person know the space was lived in. And he'd added a bookshelf. I walked around the room picking up his clothes because they would lay there until I decided to do laundry. I couldn't stand the thought that he was wearing something he'd picked up off the floor and sniffed to make sure it wasn't too offensive.

I opened the drawer where I kept a change of clothes. Living in the country could be very inconvenient. I loved my house, but I had to spend time in the city, too. It probably would have made more sense if I had left my stuff at Dev's, but nothing about this made sense. I had a drawer at Daniel's, and he had the third bedroom at my house. We'd gotten him light-tight drapes, and I planned on putting shutters on the windows. He didn't stay there most nights, but it was always there for him.

I eased into blue jeans and a dark T-shirt. I didn't have any sneakers here. I would have to do this in the heels that Daniel hadn't noticed yet. I opened the closet because Neil kept a few things here as well. Sure enough, I found a stylish blazer that was only a smidge too big for me. It was perfect to fit around the shoulder holster I put on. When wearing an armory, one really has to consider the fit of one's clothes. Too small and said armory is easily discerned by bulges and wrinkles in the clothes. Too big and you might find yourself wading through layers of fabric to get your gun. If I'd had to wear something of Daniel's, it would have devoured me.

When I shut the bedroom door behind me, I heard Daniel

walking around in the kitchen. I listened to the opening and closing of the fridge. I stood in the doorway and watched as he squeezed blood from the bag into a mug. He carefully sealed the bag and placed the mug in the microwave. The whole time he was waiting for the microwave to finish, he watched that mug go round and round while his right hand shook slightly. I could only guess what he was thinking. He couldn't wait to get that blood in his mouth, couldn't wait to taste it, to feel it slide down his throat and start to work on his body.

The oven dinged, and Daniel poured the contents down his throat. It was over so quickly, and then Daniel used his index finger to scoop out the last bits. It shouldn't have been that hard for him. Marcus promised me if Danny had a regular supply of blood, he wouldn't be this way. He should be calmer, more in control.

"Do I need to give more?" I would give a lot to not have to see him so desperate.

"Nope," he said firmly. I watched as he forced himself to put the mug down.

"Danny, you aren't getting enough," I replied. "It's obvious. Please, I'll just let the nurse know you need more. It's not like it'll kill me. I barely notice it now." I'd been taking vitamins and a horse pill I was assured would keep my iron level up.

Daniel steadied himself against the counter. His hand tapped on the granite, and he dragged in a long breath. "I don't need any more. I'm trying to get off the shit."

"What? You can't." I walked to the refrigerator and pulled out the donation bag. This late in the week it should have been almost empty, but it was half full. Anger started to flood my system. What the hell was he doing? "I can't believe this. I need you to be strong. Do you remember where we're going?"

He turned on me and flashed his fangs. "Of course I do, Zoey. I know exactly what's on the line, but you have no idea how hard this is. You don't know what it's like. I crave it. I'd do anything for it. I fucking hate it. The first time it took years before I could stop thinking about it every minute of every day."

"You didn't hate it when we were together." Even as I said the words, I regretted them because we were both thinking about what it had been like. I'd never been closer to a person in my life than when

I shared blood with my Daniel. If only it hadn't turned out to be a lie.

Daniel's blue eyes were hot with the memory. "That was different. That was love and intimacy. It meant something. This is just an addiction. I have to be stronger."

"You want to go back to what you were before?" He'd been cold and distant. I couldn't stand the thought.

"I don't think it will come to that." He frowned, his mouth a stubborn line.

"But you can't be sure."

"Zoey, let it go," Daniel warned, and if I had an ounce of sense I would have. Unfortunately, when it came to Daniel, I'd never been known for my sense.

"No, I'm not going to let it go. You need blood and I have it."

"Then take off your clothes and meet me in bed," Daniel said harshly. "Start being my wife, and I'll take the blood. I'll open a vein and let you suck me until we're both high. You ready to do that, baby? I didn't think so. So if you're not my wife, stop bitching at me like you are."

I felt my face flush with anger and no small amount of shame. I was his wife, but I didn't act like it. I was openly having an affair with another man, and I knew Daniel thought I was just fine with that. He couldn't understand how torn up I was about the whole mess. Sometimes I felt like my own stubborn rage had put me in a corner, and I had no idea how to get out of it.

Yelling at Daniel wasn't going to solve anything. I leaned against the fridge and let the worst of my anger go. "I'm just worried about you, Danny."

He shoved a hand through his hair and turned away from me. "Don't. I'm a big boy. I can take care of myself. I'm not going to slide back into what I was. I just need other coping mechanisms. That's what my shrink says. I spent too many years denying myself. I've started indulging certain other hungers, and I've found it helps."

I didn't think he was talking about D&D. Daniel spent his first years as a vampire denying his own wants and needs. He'd only taken as much blood as he'd needed to function, and for the most part, he'd avoided my blood like the plague. He'd also denied himself sex. I got the feeling he wasn't denying himself anymore, and I couldn't exactly play the offended wife. But I suddenly wanted to. God, I wanted to. The idea of someone else letting Daniel sink those delicious fangs into her smooth neck made me want to kill.

"I thought we were trying to be friends," I pointed out, wanting desperately to defuse the situation. "I can't be worried about you?"

He shook his head. "Well then, friend, if you want to worry about something, worry about the fact that I'm almost out of cash. We need a paying job."

My eyes widened because unlike me, Daniel didn't have to worry about things like a car payment or rent or food. "You went through a hundred and twenty-five thousand dollars in seven months?"

Daniel smiled what I've come to think of as his "big jerk" smile. He crossed his arms defensively, and I knew what was about to come out of his mouth would be nasty. "Well, baby, I don't have a sugar daddy and hookers cost money. I've downgraded to the cheap ones, but papa needs to get paid to get laid." He didn't seem to mind my pissed-off stare and grabbed my keys. "I'll drive. We need to pick up Neil." He stalked out of the kitchen, but not before he got in a parting shot. "And, Zoey, nice shoes."

I shook off the need to punch him in the face. We really were going to be late if I didn't get a move on. We had a guy to see about a one-way ticket to Hell.

Come to think of it, maybe we should upgrade to a round trip.

Chapter Three

Daniel pulled the Audi into the parking lot of the Church of the Immaculate Conception with ruthless accuracy. His hands were steady and strong on the steering wheel, displaying none of his normal casual elegance. He was feeling the lack of blood, and I needed to figure out how to break through his wall. I really couldn't deal with his self-destructive tendencies right now.

Neil chattered on in the backseat, talking about our new neighbor who he was sure liked boys. Neil thinks all hot guys really like boys underneath their thin veil of heterosexuality. "His name is Chad, and he's so hot. He was jogging and wearing these teeny tiny shorts." Neil sighed, and maybe he was right about this one. I didn't know a single hetero who would be caught dead wearing short shorts. "You should meet him, Zoey. I think it would be a good idea to invite him over for dinner."

"You invite him." I pulled off one shoe and bit back a groan. My toes weren't made to curl like that. "It's your house, too."

It wasn't like he paid rent or anything but occasionally he would chip in for food.

Neil appeared to think about it for a moment. "I don't think so. That would put me at a disadvantage. I need to play this one cool. You should invite him, Zoey, and then we can all be there, you and me and Daniel."

Why Daniel would want to sit down to a meal he couldn't eat and meet a dude he could never really be friends with since he couldn't let him in on the whole "blood sucking vampire" secret, I had no idea. Daniel was silent as he pulled the car into a parking space.

"Holy shit! Is that what I think it is? Is that Christian

Louboutin?" Neil pulled the shoe out of my hand, rubbing it against his face lovingly. "God, there are days I wish you didn't have such freakishly small feet. This is the most beautiful twelve hundred dollar shoe I've ever seen."

That got Daniel's attention. "Those shoes cost twelve hundred dollars?"

"Well, I guess technically it's only six hundred a shoe." Six hundred sounded so much better.

Daniel wasn't buying it. "He bought you twelve hundred dollars' worth of shoes?"

I pulled the shoe out of Neil's clutching hands and regretfully forced my sad little toes back into it. "Neil, you'll have to excuse Danny. He's thinking about how many hookers he could buy with twelve hundred dollars." Neil laughed, but I saw the thought go through Daniel's head and I couldn't help but punch him in the arm. "Asshole."

Danny's frown broke and a chuckle rumbled from his throat. "Well, Dev only bought one. Someone needs to give that guy a lesson in frugality. Hey, if I'm getting hit for thinking things, I might as well say it."

Daniel got out of the car with a smile on his face. I was so glad calling me names could lighten his mood. I slammed the door, cursing when I realized the grass in front of us was wet. My heels were going to make it feel like I was walking through quicksand.

Daniel checked the clip in his gun and settled it in his holster. Before I could protest, he scooped me into his arms. "You should have worn boots. It's this or you'll slow us down." He bent down and kissed me swiftly before I could stop him. "I'm sorry, Z. Be patient with me."

"Hey, friends don't kiss," I said disapprovingly, even as I relaxed in those strong arms. He could carry me all day and never notice the weight. It felt so good to be in his arms.

Daniel started across the lawn. "They do in Europe. I'm trying to be more continental."

I snorted but held on. Danny was the least continental person I knew. He had that slow Texas drawl I found comforting. When he was alive, he liked beer and burgers. He was not a man of sophisticated tastes. He set me on my feet when we reached the steps but took my hand.

"I don't want you to break an ankle," he said before leaning close to my ear. "And just for the record, if I had twelve hundred dollars to blow, I would totally buy you flooring, hand-scraped hardwood in Brazilian cherry."

"That's romantic," Neil huffed behind us.

But it was. I really wanted that stupid flooring. I hated my carpet. If I knew Danny, he would have installed it, too. When he wasn't playing D & D or working on mysterious jobs for the Council, he was usually at my place fixing something. I bought my house for a song, but it would have been a money pit without Daniel's free labor.

"Ah, you're here." The voice came from the steps above us.

I looked up and put a name to the voice I had only heard over the phone so far. Father Francis had been the one to set up this mysterious meeting. He'd called this morning and insisted we be here at the church at midnight. He said he'd been contacted by people who could solve my little problem. He'd tried to convince me to come alone, but I didn't do alone. Alone was stupid. Alone would get my ass killed.

"And you've brought company." The good father stared down, shaking his head.

The trouble with clients is they often try to get the upper hand. The motto "the customer is always right" might work at Macy's, but I'm not selling handbags. I'm an artisan, and far too often, I suffer for my art. I get shot. Sometimes I get shot by things that aren't guns, and I'll take a freaking bullet over an arrow any day of the week. The client is paying for a service they know nothing about, so while I am willing to listen to a client whine and complain, I will not allow a client to dictate how I run my business.

The first line of my mission statement, to put it in terms the good father can relate to, goes something like this—thou shalt not go into the night alone.

I knew what was out there, and sometimes the sweetest face turned into something with a bunch of teeth really fast. The good news was I had a vampire and a werewolf on my side, and like an American Express card, I didn't leave home without them.

"This is my crew, Father. We're a team, and if you don't like it,

I'm sure you can find someone else." I was really hoping he wouldn't just refuse us entry.

The father shook his head and sighed. "No, I'm afraid they're very insistent. It must be you, but I don't think they will be happy about the men. Come in."

I started up the steps with Daniel at my side. He didn't look happy, like some supercool vampire sense was tingling, but he remained silent. Neil took the steps two at a time and got to the door before we did. Neil's senses were even sharper than Daniel's, so he was our reconnaissance man. Father Francis held the heavy wooden door open but stared at Neil suspiciously as Neil did his thing. He let the air around him wash over his senses.

It was the first time a client had ever wanted me to meet them at church, and I hoped this wasn't a prelude to some "save my soul" lecture. Over the last several months, I'd met with many people who had promised me they could help me with my particular problem. Every lead turned out to be a dud. Most of them presented solutions I'd already thought of but discarded for practical reasons. A few of them wanted something from me and promised way more than they could possibly deliver, and one had been a dumbass vampire looking for a mate. That particular meeting didn't end well. It had been a frustrating couple of months as I was ready to do the job, but I couldn't find the right tools.

I have stolen from many a dangerous place. I've broken into houses sealed with magic and locks and protected by some really scary things. I've been shot at, stabbed, attacked by more animals than I can count, and felt the awful effects of magic. But I was scared of this job. I also knew I couldn't back down.

Ever since I watched Lucas Halfer drag my friend to Hell, I'd been sure of one thing. I was going to get her back. I was going to do what I did best. I was going to steal.

"If you would please follow me," the father said, his dark eyes imploring. "They are very impatient."

Neil held up his hand. He wouldn't be hurried.

"What is it?" Daniel asked, taking in a deep breath to see if he could figure it out.

"There's one human, that's you," Neil said to the priest. "I can smell the remnants of many humans, candle wax, incense, and someone used a steam cleaner a couple of hours ago to cover up…ewww, vomit."

The father took a step back, his eyes wide. "The Peters boy apparently has the stomach flu. They shouldn't have brought him to mass."

But Neil was continuing his litany. The harder he tried, the more his eyes took on a distinctly wolf-like stare. "You had macaroni and cheese for dinner, probably microwaved, and then some cognac, but that was the good stuff. Oh, and the faintest whiff of troll. Bet you didn't know you had that in your congregation."

"What is it?" the father asked, looking at Neil like he was something deadly. Neil might look like a sweet little club kid, but I'd seen him rip apart an enemy and eat the remains. He especially liked the second part.

"He is no concern of yours, Father," I said with an emphasis on the "he" part. I don't like my friends being treated like freaks even when they act like freaks. Besides, it just showed how little the father knew when he was terrified of Neil but had paid no real attention to Daniel.

Of course, the father was probably under the mistaken impression that vampires couldn't enter a holy place. It was one of those myths vampires had started themselves to put humans at ease. It gave the false impression that one could identify a vampire because they followed certain rules. As Daniel pushed his way into the vestibule, I felt bad for the little priest. Vamps rarely followed any rule they hadn't made themselves.

"That's weird." Danny sounded slightly disturbed, which sent a chill through me. If something spooked Daniel, it was usually bad—really bad.

"Yeah, you're getting that, too?" Neil stood beside Daniel, both staring into the building.

"What?" I asked, trying to keep a professional demeanor. What I was really wondering was "when do we start running?" A thousand things ran through my head. When you live the kind of life I do, you can call up some real nightmares when you try hard enough.

"Nothing." Daniel crossed his arms over his chest. "I'm getting absolutely nothing."

"Not nothing, exactly," Neil qualified. "More like an absence of something."

"And the definition of nothing is?" Daniel replied with a sarcastic zing.

"We really must go." The priest's hands fluttered restlessly, gesturing down the hall and then clutching at one another. "They will grow angry."

"You're afraid of nothing?" I ignored the priest. Danny and Neil were still trying to figure out what was at the end of that hallway.

"I know something's there, but it's like there's a hole in the church." Neil pointed down the hallway. "About a hundred yards that way, my senses stop and pick up again a few feet later."

"It's weird. I think we should go, Z," Daniel said. "Let's take you home and Neil and I will come back and figure out what we're getting ourselves into."

I just stared because that was the stupidest thing I'd ever heard.

Daniel sighed because he knew when I looked at him like that, I wasn't going anywhere. "Just stay close to me."

"If you will please come this way." The father walked, taking short, jittery steps. I felt kind of bad for the little guy. Even over the phone he'd seemed uncomfortable. I wondered what these people had on him to force him to act as a go-between when he so obviously didn't want to. He didn't seem like the type to be involved in anything unsavory, and I didn't say that because he was a priest. I've met some badass priests who could chop the head off a demon without dropping their rosaries. And then there were those nuns…

The father stopped in the middle of the vestibule, right beside the holy water. He absently took some and made the sign of the cross. "You wouldn't be armed, would you? This is a house of the Lord. There are no weapons allowed in the church. I must insist on it." He looked nervously at the three of us as though he expected a fight.

Why fight when a lie will work?

"Nope." I was comfortable that my Ruger was hidden under Neil's blazer. I had two extra clips in the pockets, but I doubted the padre was going to pat me down.

"I'm a pacifist," Daniel replied with a predatory smile. He was carrying at least two guns and probably a few knives, but he didn't really need them. Daniel was a weapon.

Neil, the only one of us who never carried a weapon, simply smiled.

Father Francis nodded as though he didn't really believe us, but he wasn't going to press further. He held his small hand out, gesturing toward the sanctuary. It was a typical Catholic church. The sanctuary was dominated by a statue of Christ on his cross looking down on worshippers. Down the long row of pews, standing in the middle of the aisle in front of the altar, was a couple. From a distance, they looked nice enough. It was a man and a woman, both in their early twenties. They were both blond and had bland good looks. She was in a slim skirt and pink sweater while he wore slacks and a button down. They could have been parishioners checking out the church.

I glanced back at the father, who was sweating though the church was cool. His hands shook as he pointed to the couple. "There they are. Please do whatever they say. Please."

And then the father ran.

Chapter Four

Neil and I watched the priest run down the hall, but Daniel never took his eyes off the figures in the sanctuary.

"Where is he going?" Neil asked.

"I think he's going anywhere they're not." I turned and looked into the sanctuary, wondering what the hell had the little priest so spooked.

Daniel sighed, seemingly resigned to whatever was going to happen. "Are you sure you want to do this? You're sure she's worth it? Sarah did shoot you."

I remembered. It hurt like hell, but nothing hurt more than the look on her face as the demon sank his claws into her body and pulled her to Hell. It might have been different if I thought she was comfortably dead, but that's not the way demon contracts work. There's no parole and no end to time served. Death would have been acceptable, but what Sarah had to endure, I couldn't live with.

"I'm sure." I didn't see or sense whatever had the boys in a tizzy, and I decided to let ignorance be bliss. Or rather bravado. With my trusty handgun snug against my body, I strode down the aisle toward the nice suburban couple who scared the shit out of my badass boys.

Daniel cursed behind me, but he and Neil caught up easily. Daniel would prefer I follow behind him, but I just wasn't that girl.

"Hello," I said as the female made a move to meet me.

She stepped into a shaft of light, and I had to stop. Had I thought she seemed bland from a distance? She was lovely. Blonde, with alabaster skin that practically glowed, she was delicate and fragile and everything feminine. She smiled gently, and I had a sudden urge to please her, to do whatever she requested so I could keep that smile on her face.

"What the hell are you?" My question came out harsher than I'd intended. I didn't like the way she made me feel. If I hadn't had so much experience with magic, I probably would have wondered if I was maybe more bi-curious than I imagined, but I knew what this was. This was a very strong, well-placed glamour. It wasn't crazy and out of control like Dev could get, so I didn't beg for her love or anything, but it was there. She obviously wanted me able to think, but she definitely wanted me willing.

A glorious smile crossed her face, lighting up the room. "I'm so pleased to meet you. I am Felicity Day, and this is my brother, Oliver."

I forced my eyes away from the shining beauty and glanced at Oliver Day. He obviously didn't give a shit whether I was willing or not. He scowled as though he disapproved of the entire meeting. I had zero desire to please him, so I knew he wasn't working any mojo on me.

"If you don't turn down the glamour, I'm going to pick up my wife and leave here, and there won't be anything you can do about it." Daniel put a hand on my shoulder as though he would pull me away at any moment.

Oliver snorted behind his sister and looked at Daniel with arrogant disdain. He seemed to want to dispute Daniel's assertion. His sister turned in a flash. For a moment, it seemed like they were having an argument the rest of us couldn't hear. Oliver finally nodded shortly, his face a grumpy mask. Felicity turned back to us with an apologetic smile.

"Please forgive my brother." Her voice was light, almost musical. "He will be more amenable from this point on or he can keep silent. It's his choice. Now, Mr. Donovan, you're angry about a glamour? I don't understand."

"He's talking about the magic you're working," I explained. Her face was so open, I found myself believing her. "I don't know what plane you're from, so you might not understand the terminology, but here we call it a glamour. It makes you more beautiful, more attractive on every level. It doesn't work on Daniel. I'm not sure about Neil, but it's definitely having an effect on me. I would appreciate it if you would turn it off. I can't take a job if my head isn't clear. And it makes my husband nervous."

I looked over at Neil, who was watching Felicity like an eager-to-please puppy. Yep, the glamour had to go.

She laughed, an enchanting sound. "I apologize. I didn't realize I was doing it. I'll try to tone this down."

The need to please dimmed, and she was merely beautiful. Daniel relaxed slightly behind me.

"Thank you," I said, enjoying the return of my complete free will. "I would appreciate it if you don't use any more magic."

"What's she's saying is if we get another whiff of witchcraft, we walk," Daniel said irritably.

Oliver took a step forward, but Felicity merely nodded, stepping in front of her brother.

"No witchcraft, got it. Is he always so testy?" she asked me with a conspiratorial grin. It was the kind of thing one girlfriend said to another, and I was suddenly aware of how much I missed Sarah. There was so much I hadn't told anyone because she was gone.

"He's a nightcrawler, sister," Oliver stated flatly. "What did you expect, manners?"

"The correct term is vampire, Oliver." Felicity didn't bother to look at her brother. "He is also a king, a very rare creature, so some amount of respect is due."

"No, I'm not," Daniel replied quickly.

He didn't like to be called by that particular name. Like many parts of Daniel's vampiric status, I'd had to learn this tidbit from other sources. Apparently, once every couple of thousand years, a superstrong, über-vamp rises, and some sort of hell breaks loose. Daniel had been holding that lucky ticket when he punched out. Honestly, I didn't think it could possibly be that great a thing since the last king was no longer in the building and hadn't been for a long while. I'd promised myself that the next time Marcus Vorenus was in town, I was going to ask him what happened to the last vampire king. I was betting it didn't end with "and they all lived happily ever after."

Felicity considered Danny with soft, almost sympathetic eyes. "Whether you choose to wear the crown or not, it changes not one whit of your nature. You are what you are, and your destiny will play itself out."

Oliver scoffed. "The king of a dung heap is still full of shit."

And Daniel being Daniel actually laughed at that. I did not.

"And he is possibly the only one who can get into where we need him to go," Felicity said, finally showing some temper. Even with her brows slightly furrowed, she was stunning. "If you cannot keep the contempt from your voice, please be gone. I will take care of matters on this plane. I'm sure you can find something to contemplate at home."

Oliver scowled but held his tongue.

I'd had enough of the introductory chatter. I was anxious to get to the meat of the matter. "The priest said you could handle my little problem. My question is how do you even know about my little problem?"

I'd been extraordinarily careful in my investigations. I put everything in hypotheticals, and even then they weren't hypotheticals that anyone could trace back to the reality of the situation. I hadn't walked around asking for a guide to Hell. The last thing I needed was someone talking about the crazy chick who was planning a heist on the Hell plane. I wasn't interested in warning Halfer of my half-baked plans. As it was, my plan was probably doomed to fail spectacularly even without the mark finding out I was coming.

"I'm very well informed," she stated simply.

"I doubt that."

She chuckled a little. "Correct me if I am wrong. You lost a very close friend to a demon contract a little over seven months ago. A witch named Sarah Tucker. Her contract was written as a legacy. She was the daughter of a witch who was heavily into dark magic. To strengthen their coven, Sarah and her sister, Lily, were given as offerings to the Hell Lord Brixalnax. The Tucker sisters were conceived with the help of demon kind, making them extremely strong in certain forms of magic. The contract was due to be active on the girls' twenty-fifth birthdays, but Sarah made a contract of her own to try to save her sister. She was contracted by Brixalnax to ensure you failed in completing your own contract. But the demon wasn't really interested in you. He needed you to get around the Vampire Council and force the king to be his willing assassin. When you very cleverly managed to find a way to fulfill your obligation, the demon took your friend. Now you wish to get her back. Please feel free to fill in any details I might have missed."

Fine. She knew a little bit. Maybe she knew way more about certain parts of the episode than I did since the information about Sarah being part demon was news to me. It didn't put me at ease. It just made me wonder. How did Felicity know everything? And why the hell did she need me? "You have your facts correct. Sarah Tucker is my friend. She was a member of my crew and that makes me responsible for her. I want to break into Hell and bust Sarah out."

"By the way, we were very pleased you didn't end up on Halfer's leash, Mr. Donovan," the blonde said. "It would have gone poorly for all of us. He had certain plans for you that would have been counterproductive. It was good that your companion was so quick-witted. It is this cleverness that I wish to use. I think you'll find that my brother and I are also facing a dilemma. But if we put our particular talents together, I believe you'll discover we can all get what we want."

"And what is your particular dilemma?" This had to be interesting.

Even Oliver managed to look a little sad as Felicity began her tale. "Our brother, my twin, Felix, was also taken by Halfer. He went missing over six months ago, and it has taken a while to discover exactly what happened. You must understand that Felix is very special."

My eyebrows rose because "special" made me think not politically correct things.

Felicity sighed. "It's not that. He's a kind soul. He loves the world around him, and that is possibly his downfall."

"Was it a contract?" Daniel asked.

Oliver laughed, an ugly sound. "Halfer wouldn't dare try to contract with Felix. It was a weakness that left Felix vulnerable. He was always too concerned about the beings on this plane, and it cost him mightily."

Felicity placed a hand on Oliver's shoulder. "What Oliver is trying to say is Felix was kidnapped by Halfer and taken to the Hell plane where he is being held and, I fear, tortured."

"Do not fear it, sister. Fear the unknown. Avenge what we know is happening," Oliver swore. "Felix is being tortured by the demon.

There is no other reason for him to have been taken from us. The demon is feasting on his blood. He's is gaining strength by draining our brother."

"So you want us to get Felix when we pick up Sarah," I surmised. "Not really seeing the upside for us. I mean, I'm sorry about your brother and all, but it's going to be hard enough to get one person out of Hell. If I start trying to fill a truck and cross the border, I'm going to get caught. I mean, in this case, one really is easier."

"And how do you mean to get to the Hell plane?" Felicity asked.

That was something that had figured itself out. In one of those wonderful coincidences, this was the year that demon kind and the Vampire Council renewed their treaties. Like anything involved with the two tribes, there were many rituals that took place as the contracts were renegotiated. There was a particular clause that would come up about uninitiated companions, and I really hoped they called it the Zoey Clause. Apparently after several days of arguing, all the demons and all the vampires got together to party. The party was held on the Hell plane, since reality didn't really have to come into play there. It was a no-holds-barred free-for-all, and this year Zoey Wharton would be attending.

"Let's say I have an invitation," was all I offered.

"Of course, the vampire king would be invited to the ball," Felicity reasoned. "It's a way onto the Hell plane, but once you're on there, how do you intend to navigate?"

And so the blonde woman neatly summed up problem number one with my whacked out plan. Hell isn't some city laid out with neat roads and street signs. And I was pretty sure that no GPS would lead me to the building where Lucas Halfer was most likely to house his bitches.

"I haven't figured that one out yet." I was open to suggestions.

She leaned forward, the shaft of light that seemed to follow her illuminating her face. "What if I told you I know of a particular artifact that will help you find your way around the Hell plane?"

I would probably dance around like an idiot doing that whole "the roof is on fire" thing. To Felicity, I merely gave her a cool, "I would be interested in such an artifact."

"It is called the 'Revelation.' It's a very odd piece of jewelry."

Felicity leaned close to me as though she wanted only me to hear. I could have told her she could whisper straight into my ear and the boys would have heard her loud as day. Instead I leaned in because I wasn't going to burst her bubble. "It was fashioned by an alchemist to find his true love."

"You mean the guys who thought they could turn everyday metal into gold?"

Felicity laughed and pulled back. "They didn't think, dear. They took objects and fashioned them into gold and other precious things. This particular alchemist worked in Italy during the Renaissance. He met a woman and fell in love, but she was different. She would change form on occasion, and he needed a way to find her without using his eyes."

"She changed forms?" Several options floated through my brain. There were many creatures that could change form and many creatures who would be more than willing to take a human lover.

"A shifter?" Neil leaned in like a child eager for a bedtime story.

"Nothing so common, little wolf," Felicity said, and there was a certain amount of affection in her voice. She actually reached out and touched his hair, ruffling it like a loving mother. "This creature loved the alchemist, but it went against her responsibilities to be with him. Though it tore out the heart she didn't realize she had, she forced herself to hide from him. He was in her charge, you see, but as sometimes happens, he was more beautiful than the others. He made her wish she was alive in that way."

"So he made some jewelry and found her?" Daniel asked tersely. I made a face at him. It wasn't his kind of story since no one had mentioned laser guns or spaceships shaped like fireflies.

"Ignore him," I said.

"The alchemist was clever, like you," Felicity continued. Behind her I saw Oliver roll his eyes. He might not like Daniel but they had a lot in common. "He knew that if he was in danger, his love would appear to save him. He threw himself from a bridge, and right before he drowned, she came. As he clutched her, he managed to steal a single strand of her hair. He kept it hidden. It was still in his hand when she vanished later. It was this single strand of hair that the alchemist used to fashion the Revelation."

"So the dude took a trophy and it's supposed to get us through

Hell?" Daniel asked.

"Do I need to give you the same speech she gave Ollie back there?" I shot back. "Feel free to wait in the car if we're boring you with details. I'll call you when the killing starts."

Daniel tossed up his hands in submission. "I just don't see how a piece of some chick's hair is going to guide us to Sarah."

"It won't," Felicity said. "It will, however, guide you to Felix. Well, not you, Mr. Donovan, but rather your companion. It actually won't work at all if you're around."

"You're impure," Oliver pointed out, malice dripping from his words. "Too much demon in your blood, vampire. The Revelation will only work on the purest of souls."

Neil burst into laughter, to my everlasting regret. "You've got the wrong girl. Pure? Do you have any idea what she did for those shoes? Let me tell you there was nothing pure about it."

I kicked him solidly with my twelve hundred dollar torture devices before returning my attention to Felicity. "What do you mean it won't work around Daniel? And why will it guide me to Felix?"

Felicity shot Oliver a nasty look before explaining. "It won't work around your mate because Oliver is right. He is part demon, as all vampires are. The Revelation was fashioned to find a very particular creature. The alchemist was careful and put in certain safety features. One of these features is the amulet doesn't work when too close to demon kind. I am afraid your husband's blood is too strong. You'll also find it won't work in close proximity to your wolf friend."

Daniel shook his head, anger evident in the straight line of his jaw. He didn't like to be reminded of his close DNA relationship to demon kind. "Well, then you've wasted our time. I can promise you I'll never allow my wife to walk into Hell without me. It will not happen. I might be willing to let her go with Neil, but I won't allow her to go alone. Besides, you seem to have forgotten that Hell is sort of full of demons, so I don't know how that's going to work."

"The Hell plane isn't some city," Felicity countered. "It's actually quite large and the population is spread out. There isn't a demon on every corner. I assure you it will work on the Hell plane. But not if you're close to her."

Daniel shook his head. "You can take your amulet and shove it up your ass. Let's go, Z."

He took my hand, and I was willing to let him because like I said earlier, alone gets you killed in the regular world, much less on the Hell plane. I cared deeply for Sarah, but I wouldn't be much help to her when I got caught trying to navigate Hell with a magical compass.

"It will work around the faery." Felicity's words echoed through the church.

Daniel kept walking, but I stopped. I turned and ignored Daniel's muttered curse. "It'll work if I'm with Dev?"

"Devinshea Quinn is pure enough for the Revelation to work." She looked almost sad, like she hadn't wanted to reveal that piece of information. I had a feeling Dev was her last resort. She would have preferred I'd gone alone.

"Again, I'm not understanding the definition of pure," Neil said, shaking his head in confusion.

"Why Dev?" I didn't understand her version of pure either. Dev was absolutely the filthiest man I'd ever met, and I meant that in a very affectionate way.

She stepped forward. "You and Devinshea are closer to what the Revelation was meant to find than the others. The amulet will work, and Devinshea can be your guard. It is a solution that should satisfy your vampire."

"You don't understand my definition of satisfaction, lady," Daniel shot back. "I told you it's me or Neil. I don't trust anyone else. I'm not sending her in there with some douchebag lothario who'll get her killed because he has no idea what he's doing. How is he supposed to help? If I need a fucking DJ, I'll call Dev."

"He would die for her," Felicity said quietly.

"He still might," Daniel swore.

Daniel was missing several points of the conversation due to his emotional outburst. I wished Dev hadn't come up, but if he was the solution then I would deal with it. It was time to bring the conversation back to business. "How does the amulet find Felix?"

"The amulet will point the way to where Felix is." Oliver stepped up. He seemed to be giving his sister time to recover. "The amulet is worn on a chain by a pure soul. When used properly, it will light the way to the one you wish to find."

"But the one we wish to find is Sarah," Neil pointed out.

Felicity nodded. "I believe she is with Felix. From our reports, she is housed in the same area."

"What are you not telling me?" I asked because she was suddenly blank.

"I believe your friend is being used to torture my brother," she said quietly.

My stomach took a dive. The thought of Sarah, who loved men and having fun and dying her hair silly colors, being twisted into something evil killed me. It had already taken longer than I planned. I was worried if I waited too long, what we found wouldn't even resemble the girl we'd lost. I was running out of time and options.

"So Dev and I could use the amulet to find Felix, and Felix should lead us to Sarah." If that was true, and I had no reason to believe this Felix was going to lead the way to the woman who was torturing him, I still had other things to deal with. "I still have problem number two."

Problem number two was even worse than problem number one. If I was good enough to bust Sarah out of Hell, there was nothing I could do when Halfer found us, and he would find us. Her contract was iron clad. There was no clause that stated she could go free if her crazy-ass friend managed to bust her out. Halfer would simply show up and drag her back, and no one would try to stop him.

"I can take care of that," Felicity said.

"Great, and how will you do that?" Demon contracts weren't easily broken. They were almost never broken. It was far easier to find a creative way to fulfill the contract, but Sarah had already lost at that game.

"Trust me," she said with a glowing smile. "I will see her redeemed if you bring our brother back to us."

"Bullshit," Daniel spat with a deep cynicism that had become a part of his core. "They're cons, Z. They can't redeem her. They're playing us. It's a simple setup. 'Hey, we've got this magic amulet that will solve your problems but it won't work if you keep your muscle around you.' They're trying to cut you off from your major resources. They're trying to get you into Hell with only Dev as a backup. Now they claim they can break a contract? What does that sound like to you?"

I knew what it sounded like. It sounded too good to be true, and too good to be true usually went really bad.

"They're working for Halfer," Daniel reasoned. I was inclined to agree with him. If Halfer knew a weakness of mine, it was that I got impatient and was willing to try some crazy things. He also had a definite beef with me. "If he can catch you on the Hell plane, he has us right where he wants us. These two are nothing but cons, pure and simple."

"You insect!" Oliver shouted, his fair face turning red with rage. "How dare you? I could extinguish you with a thought, yet you insult me?"

I rolled my eyes because Danny's beast was already close to the surface, and Oliver was waving that red flag. Daniel's fangs had popped out, and his hands were twitching like he needed to wrap them around something. His eyes were already bleeding blue.

"You should start thinking then, asshole," he growled, but held his position.

Oliver squared off like he was ready to go ten rounds with Daniel. "Do you understand how it pains me to stand in the same space with you, nightcrawler?"

I got close to Danny. Felicity took up the same position next to her brother. Oliver might talk a good game, but I was betting Daniel was meaner, and he'd been itching for a fight since I walked in the door earlier tonight.

"Oliver, please," she begged.

But Oliver plunged on. His eyes seemed to darken, proof he wasn't human. "You disgust me. All of you. If it were up to me, I'd send you to the Hell plane myself. You belong there, you perverted animal." That was said to Neil, who shrugged because he really couldn't care less what anyone thought of him. Oliver turned back to Daniel. "Blood sucking, junkie low life. You did not wish to be Halfer's attack dog, but you are the Council's assassin? How many innocents have you sent to their deaths, but you dare to stand before my glory?" He turned to me. I sighed because I've found, when running down a litany of sins, you usually save the best for last. "And you, you're the worst. The blood that runs through your veins is pure, yet you whore yourself to the demon."

That was when my gun made an appearance because I was betting this was just his opening salvo, and Daniel was about to blow. I eased the Ruger into my fist, clicking off the safety. I didn't really care if Daniel killed Oliver Day, but later on he would feel bad about it, so I might have to put an end to this little battle.

Oliver didn't seem impressed by my firearm. "You could be so much more, but no, you choose a life of crime. You steal from those weaker than you. You can't even be faithful to your demon husband. You have to whore yourself to another man and your husband stands by. Does he know the things you've done with the faery? The things you never let him do to you?"

"Daniel," I said, knowing as the word left my mouth I could do nothing to stop him.

Daniel closed in on the other man. He didn't bother with a weapon. He wanted to feel the flesh tear and smell the blood run. Daniel roared as he reached his target, the sound visceral and all encompassing. I nearly closed my eyes because I didn't want to watch as he killed my only path to success.

Then, just as he was about to tear Oliver Day apart, he went flying backward, hard and fast. I watched helplessly as his body flew past me. He was flung across the sanctuary and smashed into the wall, the wood giving way and cracking under the force of his impact.

"You want to know what I am?" Oliver asked as I started to back away, the gun in my hand forgotten.

I suddenly really didn't want to know. I had an idea now, and it scared me more than any demon could, but Oliver was no longer playing with us. It was like the air in the room rushed to be around him as his wings unfurled. I had an awful glimpse of righteous wings and monstrous rage. Then there was nothing but the thought that I had to get to Daniel. The light was blinding, and it was starting to fill the church.

Here in this old structure, in the middle of the night, the dawn was coming for him.

Yes, this was the part I'd been waiting for. This was that moment of the evening when we started to run for our lives.

Chapter Five

Daniel was already trying to get to his feet when Neil and I started to sprint toward him. I could see blood running down his forehead, a stark red arrow shooting down his face. It was just sheer luck the wooden panels hadn't pierced any important parts of him.

Neil was faster, but I did my damnedest to keep up. The light coming from the angel followed us like a tidal wave, threatening to crest. I ran faster to try to get to Daniel before that light did. I wasn't sure the light wouldn't hurt me, but I knew damn well it could kill him. Neil hit Daniel and knocked him to the ground where he should have stayed if he had any sense. Given the fact that Daniel had just angered an angel from the Heaven plane, I doubted he had any real sense at all.

I heard Felicity yelling at Oliver to stop, but it didn't seem like he was in the mood to listen.

Neil rolled with Daniel, who finally seemed to understand the danger he was in and was willingly letting Neil maneuver him toward the relative safety of the pews. It didn't offer a ton of cover, but we couldn't make it out the door. I felt the minute that light hit my back. It didn't hurt per se, but I was filled with it. It scared me more than anything I have felt before. That light was real and had mass and motion. I closed my eyes because they didn't seem to work anymore and leapt toward Daniel and Neil.

"To your left, Zoey," Neil screamed because a loud hum had filled the room until it was bursting with the sound.

I twisted as hard as I could to my left and hit Daniel's big body with a thud. From here, we had a little cover. I could see Neil as he tried to shield Daniel with as much of his body as he could. Though Neil was strong, he was small-framed and Daniel was not. Even as I tried to cover the parts Neil missed, I could feel my husband's flesh charring, the smell sickening to me. Daniel gritted his teeth and shoved his head into my shoulder in an attempt to keep his eyes.

I covered his head with my hands. I've never held onto anything the way I held onto Daniel, but it wasn't working. That light was finding its way into everything. I could feel him coming apart in my hands, his skin burning beneath me. His face was in my neck, and I had the horrible feeling that this was the way I would lose him. I would hold him so close to my heart, and he would fall apart until there was nothing but ashes in my hands. There was nothing I could do.

"Feed." Neil looked over Daniel's body into my eyes. I squinted, trying to see. "He needs to feed. His body will try to heal itself if he can feed!"

I pulled Daniel's head away, alarmed at how weakly it fell back. Neil was right. It was our only shot. If we could just keep him alive through the onslaught, his body would heal eventually. "Danny, you have to feed. You have to feed now. Do you understand? No bullshit. Don't you leave me like this."

He let his head slump forward again, but I felt his fangs trying to find a good place to penetrate. With flawless accuracy, he found his sweet spot, and I felt him bite down. For the first time, it hurt. All I'd ever known from the feeding process was pleasure. The blood was entwined with sexual energy until the two didn't exist without the other. When Daniel fed, we made love. It had never been different until tonight.

I winced against the pain but held him to me. Tears pricked my eyes, the pain was so bad, but I wouldn't let go. He began to draw against the vein, his strength steadying. His hands tightened on my waist. His will was back and though his flesh continued to char, I knew he would make it. Me, that was another story. I was used to donating for the cause, but he was drawing heavily off me, and I couldn't keep it up forever.

"Are you all right?" Neil shifted, covering Daniel's burning arm. "I can pull him off. He won't like it, but I can feed him, too."

Neil was very sure of his physical strength, but I doubted he'd ever tried to get between a dying vampire and his companion. He had no idea what was going through Daniel's mind as he drew the blood from my body into his. In these times, I wasn't his friend. I wasn't the girl he'd grown up with and loved and explored everything with. I was *his*. I was a possession, and he would allow no one to take what was his. He would surely kill Neil if he tried to move me. There would be no thought behind the act. Daniel would regret it later, but he was one large ball of primal instinct right now.

"No, I'm fine." I forced myself to say the words even as I felt myself weakening.

And then just as quickly as that righteous light had flooded our world, it winked from existence.

Neil sprang up, giving us cover. Daniel took one last long drag from my neck, but this time it started to resemble something like pleasure. He was back in some semblance of control. He let his head fall back, his eyes rolling to the back of his head before he closed them. Even though his flesh was still burning in places, he looked blissful, like a man who'd had his first full meal after days of starvation. He reached up to touch me, but his hand fell back, exhausted.

Neil held a gun in his hand, one of Daniel's. I'd never seen him with one before. I sat up and pulled Daniel's head into my lap, smoothing back that sandy hair of his while he shook slightly. I tried not to think about the agony in my neck. I could feel the blood continuing to trickle out and knew when I looked in the mirror I wouldn't see the twin delicate holes he left when he was careful.

"Look, bitch, I have no idea if this will do anything to you, but I am willing to try." Neil's voice was harder than I remembered it ever being. He held the gun properly, and I wondered if Daniel had trained him.

Felicity Day approached, her feet moving with caution. She looked very apologetic, and I did not give a shit.

"You stay away from him." I pulled my own gun, hoping I wouldn't have to hold it steady for too long. It wouldn't do any good, anyway. I doubted an angel could be taken out with a bullet. I knew that, but my empty gesture made me feel better. I felt very vulnerable with a half dead vampire shaking in my lap and nothing but useless metal between me and that light.

"I do not mean him harm. I am so sorry Oliver did that. Please believe me. I didn't come here to harm any of you." Felicity held her hands out as if to prove she wasn't armed. It didn't make me feel better since apparently she could call the freaking sun to her defense.

"Then I'd hate to see it when you mean to do damage," I muttered as Daniel tried to wrap himself around me. This was one of those times when I was everything to him. His higher brain stopped functioning as every cell of his body concentrated on healing what was burned. I smelled like home to Daniel. I smelled like healing and safety. He wrapped his arms around my waist, and I pulled him close.

Felicity took in the scene, and instead of disapproval, I saw a longing on her face as she watched us. "I'm truly sorry. If I had any idea my brother would react like that, I would never have allowed him to accompany me. You have to forgive him. It is his nature to be judgmental. He serves a particular function, and with Felix away, he has lost his balance."

"I really don't care about the whys or the wherefores, lady. I will not help you. You'll have to find someone else." And I would have to find another way because I wouldn't put Daniel in that position again. Had I known what we were walking into, I wouldn't have even taken the call.

"But there is no one else," she said beseechingly. "It must be you."

"Too bad." I had no sympathy for her. I could still smell Daniel's charred flesh. The burns were trying to heal themselves, but I feared he was going to need more blood. He'd made himself vulnerable by cutting back on his intake. He would need to gorge himself if he wanted to heal. Felicity Day's problems were no longer any concern of mine.

"I can help." She took a tentative step forward.

My arm shaking, I raised my gun. "You touch him and I'll find a way to kill you. I will be very clever, and I'll make sure it hurts."

"All right." She backed away, her face a mask of worry. "I'll contact you again. I'll find another mediator. You won't find anyone else who can help you as I can."

"Don't bother. I won't take the call."

"You will, Zoey," she said with serene certainty now. It made me nervous, as if she had figured out something I hadn't yet. "I'm the only one who will help you. I'm the only one who can answer your questions. You want to know what you are and why. I'm the only one who can make you understand."

She turned and walked down the hall and, in a blink, she was gone. One minute her petite figure was walking away, and the next there was nothing.

I let loose a pent-up breath and stared down at Daniel. He was breathing, but it was a shallow thing, a shaky rattle of his chest. "We have to get him out of here."

Neil clicked the safety on the gun and shoved it in his pocket. He walked over to us, his eyes searching the church for more trouble. "He needs a doctor, Z. He's not the only one. You're very pale. Your lips are almost blue."

"I'm fine," I assured him, the world around me swimming a little. "Just get Daniel to the car."

Neil grunted as he lifted Daniel's two twenty frame. He moved quickly and was back for me before I managed to get to my feet. My hands shook, a combination of blood loss and adrenaline.

"Stop there, sister." Neil swept me up in his arms. "No more walking for you. Hey, those shoes held up nicely."

"I'm never wearing them again." I sighed, letting my head rest against his shoulder. Neil smelled clean and like all the really good parts of a Dillard's men's fragrance counter. He would take care of things now, and that was a good feeling. I didn't exactly lose consciousness. I kind of drifted as Neil drove. I heard him make several calls. One was to Michael House. He was to bring the rest of Daniel's supply of blood to my father's house. The next call was to my father, Harry Wharton. His house was closest, and as much as my father annoyed me on occasion, he was good in a crisis.

Neil was cool and collected as he drove through the streets of Dallas. In no time at all, we pulled up to my father's large home in North Dallas. I opened my eyes and saw the house was lit from what looked like every room. There was a dark Council-issued Benz out front. Michael had beaten us here.

It was Michael who opened the back door of the Audi and hauled out Daniel. "What the hell happened to you, man?" he asked under his breath.

He tossed Daniel over his shoulder and started for the house.

I heard my father curse as he passed Daniel. "Neil, you better start talking. I want to know what happened to my daughter and my son-in-law."

Neil opened the door, and I stubbornly tried to get out on my own. It didn't work. My legs felt like Jell-O.

Neil picked me up. "She's fine, Harry. She just lost a lot of blood. We need the doc to look at her after he sees Daniel. If we can get enough blood into Daniel, maybe he can help her."

"From what I just saw there might not be enough blood in the world to help our Daniel," my father said, jogging to keep up.

"What's wrong?" I asked, suddenly perking up. "He was fine back at the church. He was healing."

"He just needs more blood. Your father likes to exaggerate." Neil entered the house and walked straight to the living room. He settled me on the plush leather couch and my father's assistant, Christine, was there to wrap a blanket around me. She was dressed for bed in pajama bottoms and a T-shirt. I didn't like to think about where she was sleeping. She was a year younger than me, but she was also my father's girlfriend and a fairly decent witch.

She pressed a mug of something warm in my hands. "It will help until the doctor gets here."

I didn't ask what it was because I didn't want to know. It was bitter, but I felt warmer. I forced myself to sit up, looking for Daniel. He was a few yards from me. I could see him through the door that led to the kitchen. Michael and Neil were both trying to hold him down, but his big body bucked and convulsed. Michael cursed as he tried again to force Daniel to the floor. I suddenly found the strength to move, throwing off the blanket.

"Get his legs," Michael ordered.

"I'm trying," Neil yelled back. He looked up and saw me in the doorway. "Damn it, Zoey, get back. Who do you think he's trying to get to?"

Daniel suddenly scented me. His head cracked around to get me in his sights. He was all fangs and those alien eyes with no irises, just sapphire blue spheres of his will. "Come to me, companion."

I shrank back. I'd only met this version of Daniel once before when he was close to death. Then he took what he needed and managed to not kill me. He was even further gone now, and I worried he wouldn't stop if I let him start again. Unfortunately, he'd taken enough of my blood to get his strength back, and Neil and Michael were losing their battle. If Daniel managed to get off the ground, there would be no holding him. He would come for me and take what he wanted. My father cursed, walking past me to start up the stairs. I knew where he was going. He would get the crossbow, and if he had to, he would put an arrow in my husband's heart before he would allow me to die beneath him. I didn't have very long if I wanted to save him.

Over the vigorous protests of the two men trying to hold him down, I kneeled at Daniel's head and started to stroke his hair.

"Zoey." He immediately calmed when I touched him. I noticed physical contact with Daniel could sometimes quiet the beast that raged from time to time. A companion was not without her talents. "Zoey, I need you."

"And I'm here," I said soothingly. Daniel was no longer fighting but rather trying to bend me to his will with persuasion. I certainly preferred seduction to force. I didn't break eye contact but held out my hand. "Give me the bag, please."

Neil let up just enough to pass me the bag I'd seen in Daniel's fridge earlier.

Daniel shook his head, his hand covering mine. "I don't want that. I want you. Let me have you and it'll be good. It'll be so fucking good. Baby, you know how it feels when we're together."

I felt him try to assert his will, but I was better at ignoring the effects now. I held the blood above his mouth. "You've already had me, baby. You had too much of me. This is all you're going to get. Now take your medicine like a big boy or I'll leave. I'll get in the car and drive away and leave you alone."

It wasn't the nicest thing to do, but I knew if he was this out of control, there was an edge of fear. He wouldn't want me to leave. He needed me close.

I put the bag to his lips and watched him sullenly concede. His fangs punctured the bag and he began to suck. I held his head in my lap and stroked his hair until I watched the beast finally leave, and he was Daniel again. I motioned to Michael and Neil to leave us, and they got up to go. Even my father put his crossbow down.

"It's all right now, Danny," I said, quietly satisfied that he was going to survive.

Danny drained the last drop and tossed away the package. He twisted until he could get his arms around my waist, holding me tightly. He just sat there breathing in and out and letting me rock back and forth. It was the way I held him when we were children, after his father died. That first night he'd been so bereft. He'd cried because he was worried no one would take care of him. He'd been thirteen at the time so it was a reasonable fear. Now I felt him trying not to cry, and I wondered why. It wasn't the first time he'd come close to death, and now his wounds were visibly healing. Pain wouldn't make Danny cry. Pain just pissed him off. This was something else.

"What is it, baby?" I asked, falling easily back into endearment.

His eyes opened, a brilliant blue that kicked me in the gut every time I looked at him. "That was an angel, wasn't it, Z?"

"Oh, yeah, that was an asshole angel."

"I burned, Zoey," he said quietly. "I stood in front of an angel of God and I burned like I was nothing. I wasn't worthy to stand in the light."

My heart ached for him. "Danny?"

"I don't have a soul anymore."

There was such sadness in those six words that tears came to my eyes, and I held him tighter.

"That's not true." I knew he had a soul. I'd seen it. Soulless creatures didn't care about the people around them, didn't sacrifice for them.

His grip loosened, and he went limp as he settled his head on my lap. "I think Heaven would disagree with you, baby. I'm tired. So fucking tired."

"Then sleep," I urged him, trying to keep control of my emotions. He needed to rest. He didn't need to deal with my angst.

"I love you, Z. Soul or no, I love you." His voice was quiet and sleep overtook him.

"The doctor's here, darlin'." My father leaned down and kissed my forehead. "He's got a soul, Zoey. Don't let him forget it. Now let the doctor have a look at our boy, and then he can take care of you."

"My, is this my patient?" a cultured British accent asked from the doorway. Alexander Sharpe looked down on us with a superior smile. His body was lean and elegant, reminding me of a predatory insect, all arms and legs and black as night eyes. He carried an antique doctor's kit. I really hoped it wasn't fully stocked with leeches. Alexander was that old.

"Not a chance," I said because the vampire always made my skin crawl. "Get another doctor."

Alexander scoffed, his shoulders shrugging negligently. "I'd like to see you try, Mrs. Donovan. There isn't another doctor in three states who knows as much about vampire physiology as I do. I believe the nearest with any competence at all is located in Los Angeles. I'm afraid I'll have to do. Trust me, the Council would insist. Can't have our prodigal son passing away now, could we?"

"It'll be fine, Zoey," Michael said. "He really is an excellent physician."

"Would you let Jack the Ripper examine you?" I shot back.

Alexander smiled, not even attempting to hide his fangs. "I find that accusation offensive, Mrs. Donovan. No one has ever proven that allegation. At least no one who lived."

Neil came over and helped me up. Alexander examined the now unconscious Daniel. He looked at Neil and me with a curious gleam. "If I hadn't seen him earlier tonight, I would accuse the two of you of all manner of crime. He looks like he was staked out to meet the sun."

"It was an angel," Neil explained.

The doctor's eyebrows raised in surprise. "You don't say? You're keeping curious company. How did he manage to survive? No, don't tell me. The wayward companion did her duty and fed her master. It looks like you fed him well, too. Your lips are blue. I'm surprised you're still standing."

"I'm tough," I replied, though I found myself leaning against Neil.

"Well, you're going to need a transfusion," Alexander stated flatly. "Your master will survive thanks to you, but he can't help you. In fact, tomorrow he'll need more blood. You, wolf, you'll do. Werewolf blood is rich. It's not as good as companion blood, but she can't donate for a day or two."

I leaned back against Neil as the vampire got uncomfortably close and sniffed me in a vulgar fashion. "Hey, has anyone explained the idea of personal space to you?"

"O neg," Alexander said, pulling back. "No wonder he craves you. You smell delicious. Unfortunately, that's very rare. The wolf won't work unless you would enjoy doing it doggy style once a month."

"Pass." I looked back at Neil. "No offense."

"Don't knock it 'til you tried it, sister."

"The humans here aren't the right type, either. Michael or I would greatly enjoy donating to you, love. I assure you we would find the task immensely pleasurable right up to the point that your master cut our heads off. What we need is the supernatural equivalent of a universal donor. You're lucky, dear. There happens to be one species who can donate to any blood type."

"And where would I find this magical creature?" Why wouldn't he just get to the point? I was tired and cold. I had donated a great deal of my blood volume, and no one had even offered me a cookie.

Alexander's face lit with menace. "It's faeries, of course, dear. Faery blood is so vital and versatile. I think you won't have any trouble finding some. From what I hear, you have a faery willing to donate other bodily fluids. I doubt he'll deny you a little blood."

"No, don't you call him," I said, but Michael had already pulled out a phone and I was betting he'd dialed the number to Ether. The last thing I needed was the utter chaos that would happen if Dev walked through the door. He would be so mad at me. Everything had gone wrong. I didn't want a fight with Dev, too.

And then it was all just too much. My vision narrowed in that strange way it does just before you pass out. I felt Neil's arms go around me, and I hoped it was all just a dream.

Chapter Six

"You're playing a dangerous game with that one. And I certainly would like to know why we have so many visitors in town." Alexander's voice was the first thing I heard as I slowly came back to consciousness.

I couldn't have been out for too long. I was on the couch and someone had covered me with a blanket. I tried to stay as still as I could because I wanted to know what dangerous game was being played and by whom. What can I say? I'd had a rough night and I like good gossip.

"It isn't a game." Michael's words sounded careful, almost wary. "They aren't here for any reason other than to get to know Daniel."

Now I was really listening. In all the chaos of the evening, I'd never gotten around to asking Daniel about the new vampires in town. Michael seemed to think they had come as some sort of group hoping to socialize with the vampire of the moment.

"Well, he is an interesting chap. I will admit that. Wish he dressed better, though. He's having a bad influence on you, as well. I don't see the point in blue jeans," Alexander admitted.

The table beside me rattled as the doctor placed something on it. He was more than likely getting ready for my inevitable introduction to nineteenth century blood transfusion practices. I doubted it would be as nice as it was when I took blood from Daniel.

Alexander huffed a little, his British accent crisp and neat. "I just find it difficult to believe there are five vampires I've never met before. It's a rather small world."

"William says he met you a couple of years back," Michael offered.

"Funny, I don't remember him."

"He says you were in Seattle and there was a rash of unexplained killings," Michael said, disgust plain in his voice. "Prostitutes, I believe. William was working with the police. Night shift, of course."

"Now that does sound like me." Through slitted eyes, I could see the smug smile on Alexander's face. I really didn't like him. There was a small part of me that wished he would do something, just anything that would justify Daniel killing him. Unfortunately, he'd had centuries to perfect his techniques, and the Council didn't care what he did as long as he didn't get caught. "Well, that explains it. I was distracted at the time. Ah, you're awake, Mrs. Donovan."

I gave up the game and opened my eyes. "Is Dev here?"

"Do you hear accusations and righteous indignation? No, he hasn't made it yet. Apparently you have his vehicle. He had to get his driver up," Alexander stated blandly. "That club of his shouldn't pay so well. Makes you wonder what he does on the sideline."

He held a piece of weird medical equipment. At least I thought it was medical equipment. I winced at the sight. It was a metal and glass tube. On the top was a plunger with a circular handle. Tubing came from both sides and each was tipped with the largest, nastiest needle I'd ever seen. I got a little nauseous at the sight. Give me fangs any day.

"Can't we go to a hospital? Or maybe I could just rest and everything will be all right in the morning?" I could last a day or two, right? Blood builds back up. Maybe a few days of bed rest and I'd be fine. My DVR was backed up anyway.

"Not at all, dear," Alexander said, smiling his creepy grin. "You'll be dead by the morning if we don't get some blood in you. I believe it's the residual effects of sharing blood with your husband that's managed to keep you alive and talking this long. I'm surprised. I didn't think you shared blood with him. The gossip is you donate but choose not to receive."

"I haven't taken Daniel's blood in months." Seven months to be precise.

Alexander stared at me, for once his mouth closed in shock. He looked back at Michael. "He really is a bloody king, isn't he?"

"I told you," Michael said.

The door opened, and Dev's voice rang through the house. "Where the hell is she, Harry?"

"Ahh, let the recriminations begin." Alexander smiled, obviously enjoying the drama. "Your lover is here, dear."

My father stalked into the room, a fierce frown on his face. He didn't like Dev, and he certainly didn't approve of my relationship with him. Daddy was firmly on Team Daniel. I'd been asked several times in the last few months when I was going to stop "fucking around with that faery." Dad was just one more person who didn't understand how I felt. In his view, Danny and I had been planning to get married and Danny had finally come around, so I should fall in line with the life plan that had been laid out when I was seventeen. It didn't matter that I'd been lied to. It didn't matter that I had questions no one seemed willing to answer.

I pushed Felicity Day's promises firmly out of my mind.

Dev followed my father. He'd gotten dressed in a hurry, it seemed. His clothes were usually immaculate, but now his slacks were slightly wrinkled, and I recognized the dress shirt he'd worn earlier in the evening.

"Well, I don't need to ask how the meeting went, do I?" Dev asked, looking down at me.

Gosh, he was tall. He towered over me, six foot five inches of pure disapproval. His green eyes didn't look sexy now. Anger had replaced his natural sensuality. I was glad the blanket was up around my neck. I'd pulled it up because I was so damn cold, but now it offered a certain amount of protection from his disapproving eyes.

"There might have been a few minor problems." I tried to look as cute and vulnerable as possible, hoping to tap into his softer side. I didn't want another lecture, especially not in front of company.

"Let's see it, Zoey." He braced himself for the sight, his feet planted on the floor, his shoulders squared. "There's no point in putting it off. I'm not an idiot. I get called in the middle of the night because you need a freaking blood transfusion. I can put two and two together, sweetheart. Let's see how stupid you got tonight."

"Hey, you treat her with respect," Michael demanded, to my surprise. "Watch your mouth around her."

Dev turned, his eyes flashing and ready for a fight. "Asshole, I'm not the one who caused her to need a blood transfusion. You want to get pissed off at someone, talk to her husband. Trust me, buddy, when I fuck her she doesn't end up needing a doctor."

"Dev!" Even in my weakness, I wasn't going to stand for that.

Ugly claws popped out of Michael's hands, a particular talent of his. He pointed one at Dev, who proved he had a death wish. He moved aggressively toward the angry vampire. It was one of those testosterone fueled gestures that no female can understand.

"If my mas…my friend hadn't forbidden it, I would kill you here and now," Michael proclaimed. "I would kill you and it would be a righteous kill, you understand. You live on his sufferance."

Dev smiled that sarcastic grin I was sure would be on his face just before he died. "Don't let Daniel keep you on a leash, Mikey. Since when did you become his bitch?"

"As much as I enjoy a good bloodbath, and make no mistake Mr. Quinn, it is your blood I refer to since Michael could gut you before you thought to scream, I have to ask the question," Alexander said, his voice a little island of creepy calm. "Are the two of you going to allow my patient to expire while you work out your differences?"

Michael took a deep breath, and his hands shifted back to normal. The tension in the air went down a notch.

Dev turned back to me. "Not until I see it, Zoey."

It was nice to know his cooperation in saving my life came with ultimatums. I was just pissed enough to pull the blanket back and twist my neck so he got a really good view. It hurt, but I turned into the pain because I didn't want him to miss an inch of what he'd come to see.

If I expected a sudden onslaught of sympathy, I was disappointed.

"Nice." He bit off the word before settling into the seat beside me. He unbuttoned his sleeve and started to roll it up. "Any other places he decided to chew on?"

Alexander was busy tying off Dev's arm with a rubber band. I wore a thin T-shirt, Neil's blazer long ago discarded. I pulled up the blanket until just my arm was outside its warmth. I looked forward, trying not to watch as Alexander prepped Dev.

"Make a fist, please," the doctor ordered.

"You don't want to answer the question, Zoey?" Dev asked.

"I'll find out later. If I have to strip you down and examine you, I'll find out every bit of damage he did." There was a pause as I stared sullenly straight forward. Dev huffed a little before continuing. "Seriously? You want to shove that in my arm? That's not a needle, dude, that's a drainage pipe."

Christine pressed a glass of something cold in my hand. "Drink it up, fast as you can."

"Witchcraft?" I asked, hoping it would knock me out.

"Vodka." It was Christine's go-to medicine of choice. I swallowed it before Alexander could stop me.

Alexander's head shook. "That's going to go straight to her head. It's not a good idea."

"It'll go straight to her head and maybe she'll forget you're shoving a…whatever that is you're about to shove up her arm." Christine took the glass from me and refilled it.

"Good point," Alexander replied as he placed the needle in Dev's arm. There were several curses in languages I didn't speak. "Perhaps a dose for this one, too."

"Just give me the bottle," Dev demanded.

Christine passed it over and sat down beside me. She took the hand that wasn't attached to the arm Alexander was working on. "It's going to be all right, Zoey. Just watch me and listen to my voice."

She rubbed my cold hand between her warm ones. I felt a great debt of gratitude for the sometimes annoying witch. She started intoning something in Latin in a pleasant sing-song, and I found my world narrowing to the sound of her voice.

"Done," Alexander said. I was startled by the pronouncement, and when I looked, sure enough, there was a large-bore needle taped securely in my arm. The doctor pulled up on the plunger and bright blood began to flow from Dev's arm. "All right, get comfortable. This could take a while."

Dev cursed again and took another long swallow from the bottle of Grey Goose. I laid back and let Christine's voice soothe me, and before long I was feeling warmth flow inside me again. I don't know how long the process took, but I was grateful when the needle was sliding out of my arm and the wound was being wrapped. I was ready to fall asleep on the couch when Dev slid his arms under my knees and shoulders and lifted me against his chest. I was completely limp in his arms.

He looked at the assembled room, which now also included Neil. I guessed he'd gotten Daniel settled in the room my father had built for just such an occasion. It was a solid, interior room, with no possibility of that pesky sun finding its way in. Dev turned his gaze to my dad.

"All right, do I go upstairs or bundle her up and take her back to Ether? It's your choice, Harry, but understand I'm not leaving her here alone with three vampires, even if one of them is incapacitated." Dev looked to the vampires. "By your own laws, I have the right to care for her. My blood sustains her. At least for tonight, she is mine by right of law. If Daniel has a problem with that, he can get his ass up here and we can handle it here and now. Stay or go, Harry?"

"Upstairs, second door on the left." My father gestured toward the hall, a grimace of anger on his face, but he allowed Dev to carry me.

Dev turned his back on the room and whisked me upstairs. My old bedroom had been redone as a guest room and now boasted a king-sized bed. Dev laid me down on the bed and stared at me. It looked like he was going to make good on his threat to inspect every inch of me. Normally, I would have gotten a little excited at the prospect, but right now it just pissed me off.

"I didn't sleep with him, Dev." I tried to put some fire into my words, but I failed. Though my blood volume was up, I was so tired. Still, it was all he really wanted to know so I decided to put the truth out there. It was good to know my lover wanted to make damn sure my husband wasn't getting some.

"Right, Zoey." Dev's hand found the waist of my jeans. He was an expert when it came to undressing a woman. "I'm supposed to believe he gets his fangs in you for the first time in seven months, but that's all he impales you on?"

"He was a little concerned about the fact that he was on fire, Dev." I pushed my hips up because fighting him wouldn't help. "I doubt he was thinking about how to get in my pants."

"You would be surprised, sweetheart. I would be thinking about it." Dev ran his hands up and down my legs before he pulled the T-shirt over my head and dispensed with my bra. His hands smoothed over my skin. Even though I was angry with him, the touch was sweet. He seemed satisfied there was no further damage or evidence of vampiric possession. "On fire, huh? Did the client have a flamethrower?"

I shook my head as he placed me under the covers. Dev stepped out of his slacks and tossed his shirt aside.

"We got surprised. Didn't know what we were dealing with." I'd been stupid. I should have never taken that meeting without knowing what I was getting into. I was obsessed with this job, and it almost cost Daniel his life.

Dev was down to his boxers and slipped into the bed beside me. He pulled me into his arms, and I let my head rest on his chest. I was still mad at him, but he felt safe and warm and the events of the day just slammed into me. Tears started to run down my face. I wish I was one of those tough chicks who never cried, but I always do. Dev pulled me closer, his hand tangling in my hair.

"What was it, Zoey?" He laid a sweet kiss on my forehead, his voice gentler than it had been all night.

"Angels. They were angels, and they nearly killed him."

"Real angels? From the Heaven plane?" Dev asked, his voice hushed with awe. Dev might have contact with all manner of supernatural creatures, but angels didn't frequent Ether. "Jesus."

"Yes, those angels," I agreed. "It was horrible. The light was everywhere, and he was burning."

"Well, he's fine now, Zoey," Dev said with more sympathy than I expected since we were talking about Daniel. "These angels, were they gunning for Daniel or you?"

It was a question he had to ask because I'd had fairly nasty things come after me before. He also knew that if anything wanted to come for me, it would have to get through Danny. I shook my head against the firm muscles of his chest. "Neither. I think Danny just managed to piss one of them off. It doesn't matter. I won't have anything to do with either of them again. I think I made myself very clear. I'm only taking straight jobs from now on. Get in, grab some stuff, and get paid."

Dev sighed. "Yeah, I'll believe that when I see it."

Chapter Seven

When it comes to my chosen career, Tom Petty is totally correct. The waiting really is the hardest part. There's no Monster.com for thieves. We don't have a social network where we can put out the word we need a little green. There are several reasons for this omission in the modern world of networking, the first being thieves tend to not like one another. It's a competitive world, and let's face facts, thieves tend to not be really good people.

Unlike some IT guy who calls up old friends when he gets laid off, a thief is probably trying to hide from his old colleagues. I don't know what it's like in real-world thievery. By that I mean guys who steal paintings that don't bring about the apocalypse or cars that aren't inhabited by their former magical owners. The real-world guys might refer for each other every now and then. They might get together for a beer years later, but that's not the way it tends to go in the arcane world. If your crew splits up in the arcane world, it's probably because someone tried to screw someone else.

The idea of waiting was heavily on my mind for the whole two days I was forced to lay in my father's guest room. Despite the success of Dev's donation, the doctor had convinced my dad and my boyfriend that I should lay around doing nothing for a couple of days. Dev made sure I was inundated with flowers, movies, and books but refused to allow me out of bed. For a man who didn't like vampires, he was certainly willing to listen to Alexander. Dad had tried to bar Dev from the house, but one way or another he showed up every night and climbed into bed with me, holding me to his chest and threatening me with all manner of torture if I didn't follow doctor's orders. Not even the promise of sex had moved him this time since he decided I was too fragile. To my father's surprise and

Neil's delight, Dev even sent over a chef to make sure I ate well.

All of that was nice, but I really had work to do.

I needed a job. I needed to make some hard decisions about the way my life was going to go. The past seven months had been spent in a strange waiting pattern, allowing the way I felt after Sarah was taken to keep me in limbo. Dealing with the angels was a wakeup call. I couldn't just sit around and hope for some magical solution to fall in my lap. I wasn't giving up on the idea of saving Sarah. I just had to start living my life again. The morning after my meeting with the angels, I told my dad I wanted to work, needed to work. Daniel needed cash, and I was sure Neil had gone through most of his. I was the leader of this crew. It was my job to bring in the clients, and no one could find a job faster than Harry Wharton.

I was hoping he would find something soon as I let myself into my house the afternoon I was sprung from my comfy jail.

"So, don't get pissed," Neil said as he graciously held the door open for me.

"What did you do?" I prepared myself to get really pissed.

I threw myself down on the couch. Alexander had been right. I was still really tired. I tried not to think about how Daniel must feel. His wounds had been grave, ultraviolet rays being one of the only things that can really cause a vampire some serious downtime. Coupled with the fact that he'd weakened himself by trying to detox, he was taking his time healing. He was still being held in the safe room. If the doctor proclaimed him healthy, he would get out tonight. I knew I should have waited to see him, but I didn't want to deal with it. I knew how it would go down. Daniel would feel guilty, and he would undoubtedly pull away for my safety. When he found out I needed a transfusion, well, I was just hoping he didn't decide to leave town.

"Okay, I got tired of waiting and invited Chad to dinner," Neil said with a look of hopeful anticipation on his face.

I let out a deep breath. Chad I could handle. "Please tell me you don't expect me to cook, and I'll be fine with it."

"As if. Honey, you can barely microwave soup. I will be thrilling our audience with my amazing manicotti *al forno*, a spinach salad, garlic bread, and I made a raspberry cheesecake."

"This is why I let you live with me." My stomach rumbled at the thought.

"Let me? You couldn't live without me." Neil sat down on the couch next to me. He was wearing neatly pressed jeans and a lavender polo. He sat closer than I would have felt comfortable with any other male friend, but that contact was necessary to Neil, and I had come to find it soothing. I let my hand find his. "So, are you going to ask or should I just tell you and we can pretend you don't care?"

"How is he?"

He sighed, clasping my hand in his. "He's all right, Z. The first day was touchy, but he's going to be fine. I think Alexander was wrong about keeping you away. Daniel wouldn't have attacked you. He was so weak, but he was back in his right mind. He wanted you, Zoey. Not the beast. Daniel wanted you. He looked so sad."

"It's the guilt," I replied, Neil's account verifying my worst fears.

"I don't think so. I mean, it's in there, but it's more than that. He loves you."

"He craves me."

Neil pulled away, his eyes rolling. "What the hell does it matter? I don't get it, Zoey, I really don't. You have this guy who would do anything for you, who loves you to the bottom of his soul, and you go sleep with Dev. Don't get me wrong. If Dev was gay, I'd be in his pants in a hot minute. He's spectacular, but he's not the guy you spend a life with."

"I don't think what Daniel feels for me is love." That was my deepest fear—that neither one of us could trust our feelings.

"It feels like it. If this isn't love, then screw love, I'll take this." Neil took a long breath, tears in his clear blue eyes.

"What are you talking about?"

A rueful smile crossed his face. "I fed him for two days, Z, and there's not a mark on my body. I feel fantastic."

"You took his blood." I remembered how good just a sip of Daniel's blood could make me feel. It made me feel younger, faster, and stronger.

"More than I've taken before. The effect was stronger than ever." Neil was Daniel's servant. He'd taken a blood oath to serve the vampire years before. In exchange for his loyalty, Neil received weekly blood from Danny. That blood had taken Neil from werewolf runt to badass. "Did Daniel tell you how I was when Harry found me?"

I nodded. Daniel needed backup after he came home from his training with the Council, and my dad found Neil living on the streets. In the normal course of the world, werewolves and vampires rarely mix. The were community is insular by nature. Even the different species tend not to date or be friendly.

But Neil was different. He was rejected by his family because he liked boys. There is no GLAAD—werewolf chapter. He was an embarrassment to his family, and they kicked him to the curb. Perhaps if they left it at that, he would never have accepted Danny's offer but no, they had to get mean. Neil had become the pack's whipping boy. My father found him after a particularly brutal episode.

"You don't know what it's like living on the street, wondering where you're going to get your next meal and which of the people around you is going to try to kill you next. I wasn't strong then. I did things I don't like to think about now. I did them to survive, but it didn't make me hate myself less. I sold myself, Zoey."

I leaned forward and took his hand. I didn't give a shit what he'd done. I was just glad he'd made it. "I don't care."

He laughed a little. "I know. It's one of the reasons I love you, but there are others. I was shut down before I met Daniel. I didn't care about anyone or anything except surviving to the next day. I told Daniel I'd be his whore if he'd just save me. Blood, sex, whichever way he wanted it, I offered it all."

I smiled because I was sure that had been an uncomfortable conversation for Daniel.

"Obviously, that wasn't part of our agreement," Neil continued. "But that blood of his, god, Zoey, you know what I mean. I was a different person after a few weeks. I was stronger in every way. I was confident. I liked myself again. I didn't really understand what was going on until the day I met you. It was then I realized how important it is to love a person. I take Daniel's blood once a week. We have a connection. When I saw you for the first time, I felt my heart open up in a way it never had before. For a minute, I thought I'd found the one woman who could make me straight. Then I realized it wasn't me. It was Daniel. I felt an echo of what he feels when he looks at you. God, Zoey, you're the sun in his sky. If that isn't love, then I don't know what you want."

My heart hurt just thinking about it. "He's programmed to feel that way, Neil. A vampire wants a companion. It's as simple as that."

"We all have our addictions." Neil shook his head, obviously disappointed. "I hope you wake up soon, Z. I don't say that because I think Daniel won't wait forever. I say it because I'm pretty damn sure he will."

Neil walked back toward the kitchen, and I wished I could give him a better answer. This ache in my heart was what had sent me to Dev in the first place. Daniel spent two years pushing me away, and I finally understood why. He hadn't trusted his feelings then any more than I trusted mine now.

"Hey, go make yourself presentable," Neil commanded from the kitchen. "I laid out some very nice clothes for you, and for god's sake, put on some makeup. Oh, and a scarf around that neck of yours, please."

I groaned because I thought it would require more than makeup and a scarf to make me look good tonight.

* * * *

"Dinner was delicious, Neil." Chad pushed his plate away. He was an affable man of twenty-seven, dressed in olive slacks and a silk shirt. He'd obviously worn a tie at some point in the day, but had discarded it in favor of a casual chic this evening. He was well-groomed and well-manicured. His haircut was on trend and probably required more product than mine. If he wasn't gay, then he was one of the most metro guys in Dallas.

"I'm glad you liked it," Neil replied with a smile. "I like to cook. It's a particular talent of mine."

"Yeah, that Neil is a great cook," I said, playing my assigned part. My part was to make Neil seem like a domestic god. "There isn't a night that goes by that he doesn't come up with something fabulous."

It wasn't true. Neil was a great cook, but I didn't mention that he was also incredibly lazy and preferred to order in most of the time.

Chad smiled across the table at Neil, definitely impressed with his skills.

The dinner conversation revealed a lot about Chad Thomas. I couldn't remember the last time I'd met an actual, plain old ordinary human guy. If I met a human in any capacity beyond talking to someone while in line at Starbucks, they were usually in the life. They were thieves like me or looking to hire one. They didn't sit and talk openly about their lives. They didn't talk about their careers as lawyers or how much they liked dogs. Neil was particularly happy with that last tidbit Chad had dropped. If he'd been a cat person, that might have been a deal breaker.

Neil stood up, gathering plates. "Let me go grab dessert."

I glanced at the clock, and my heart sank a little bit. I shouldn't have expected anything less. It was almost a full hour since the sun disappeared. Part of me hoped Daniel would come out as soon as he was released. He was, undoubtedly, locked in his apartment sulking. Or maybe he'd found those cheap hookers he'd talked about.

"Wow," Chad said, his brown eyes widening. "That looks like it hurts."

My hand flew to the scarf I'd tied around my neck. Without Daniel's blood, I healed like an everyday person, and the holes he'd left were transitioning from horrifying to merely disgusting. My fingers quickly redid the knot, and I blushed as I tried to find a good excuse. What was a reasonable explanation for the black and blue monstrosity that was my neck? There wasn't one so I gave him a creative piece of crap that should let him know it wasn't his business. "Bugs, man they get big out here in the country, don't they?"

"That's a bug bite?" He leaned forward, trying to get a better look.

"Oh, yeah, and let me tell you those suckers hurt," I replied with a smile as Neil brought forth the raspberry cheesecake.

He'd barely set it down when the front door slammed open. Daniel stalked through the doorway carrying four long boxes on his shoulders. It was way more than even a built man like Danny should be able to carry. He put them in the entryway and walked back outside without a word. It took less time than it should for him to be back with more.

I had to catch his attention or he might scare our guest, who wasn't used to super speed. "Hello, Danny."

He caught sight of the three of us and stopped, finally letting his senses tell him what they should have told him long before now. "We have company?"

"This is Chad," Neil said and introductions were made.

"Nice to meet you, Chad," Daniel managed. "I have some more boxes to bring in. Don't let me interrupt your dinner."

Chad's eyes were wide as Daniel turned. Oh, yeah, no question about it now. He was gay. "Who was that?"

Neil didn't seem bothered by the fact that Chad was nearly drooling. "That's Zoey's husband, Daniel. If you think he's hot, you should meet her boyfriend. I practically stop breathing when he walks in a room. He's sex on two legs."

I gave Neil my best "you're going to die later" stare and got up from the table to follow Daniel outside. Stepping around the boxes littering my foyer, I made my way to the front yard.

"You bought my flooring," I said with a happy smile. He was here, and he wasn't telling me to stay away. It was progress.

"Yeah, well, turns out Visa works at Home Depot and hand-scraped hardwood is supposed to be good at alleviating the gut-gnawing guilt I feel at nearly draining my wife." His eyes slid away, but there wasn't any bitterness in his words, just a sheepish regret.

"You don't take the same lessons from these episodes that I do." I picked up his tool box from the back of the truck he was driving. He'd traded in his Benz for a truck after I'd pretty much destroyed it earlier this year. The truck was more useful anyway. He ducked into the cab and came back with a small thermos. I didn't have to ask what it was.

Daniel handed me the cup of the thermos. He held it out, and I could see he was hoping I wouldn't fight him on it. "And what do you take from the times when I nearly kill you?"

"That you never do." I took the cup and drank it down. I didn't have any desire to spend weeks waiting for my neck to heal. I tried not to sigh with pleasure as I felt the blood start to work. I suddenly wasn't as tired as I'd been before. "That you always find a way. We always find a way."

I untied the scarf around my neck, feeling the smooth skin there.

Daniel stopped on the porch and smiled, leaning the last box against the wall. "All right, Pollyanna, we'll play it your way. Maybe it's time to trust ourselves. Did I bother to thank you for saving me? You know, I'm supposed to be this big bad vampire, but I get my ass saved by a girl an awful lot. What does that say about me?"

"That you're fortunate in your choice of companions?"

He leaned forward and kissed me swiftly. This time I didn't really try to get away. "I am that, Z. Now, I need to go pull up that god-awful carpet of yours. Who installs lime green carpet?"

"You don't owe me anything, Daniel." I might have saved him once or twice, but it didn't even start to equal the tally sheet he'd run up saving me.

He held up a hand in protest. "You let me work this out my way. You said I'm not allowed to run and hide, and I'm not allowed to act like an asshole to cover up my guilt. So I'm left with installing flooring. Besides, after the last couple of days, I need to do something manly, baby. I was stuck in some homoerotic nightmare where dudes held me down and forced me to feed from another dude."

I couldn't help laughing. Vampirism was forcing Daniel to look at his sexuality in a whole different light. "Neil's very effeminate," I pointed out. He was. Sometimes he stole my underwear.

"Not helping, Zoey." Daniel walked back into the house. He was moving furniture around when I followed. He looked over at me and slowly stripped off his T-shirt, revealing that magnificent chest of his. It was ripped and tapered into a six-pack that made my mouth water. He shrugged, satisfied I'd noticed. "I know you like a show with dinner, baby," he said, then went back to his work.

"So that's your husband?" Chad stood beside me, watching the way the muscles of Daniel's back bunched. I couldn't blame him. It was an enticing sight.

"That's him." I let my gaze slide down to Daniel's very nice backside.

I saw he wanted to ask about my boyfriend, but he was far too polite. "Well, Neil said we should retire to the back porch. It's a lovely night. He would like to serve dessert al fresco. He's making coffee. He said he'd be out in a minute."

Chad held his arm out in a courtly gesture, and I allowed him to lead me through the house toward the back door. I loved my backyard. There was no fence, just two acres of land lush with trees. It made up for the commute I had to make into the city. It was peaceful and I felt a calm out here that I could never get in Dallas. I'd taken particular pains to make the back porch of my sturdy old farmhouse inviting. There was an entire set of plush patio furniture to lounge on while I watched the sun set or rise, and I tried to do at least one of those a day. But what I loved more than anything else was the antique porch swing Daniel had refinished and installed. I let Chad lead me to the swing and contentedly started to rock.

"Hey, what happened to the bug bite?" Chad asked, leaning forward to inspect my now perfect-looking neck. "It's completely gone. That's amazing. How did you do that?"

I hadn't really thought about that when I'd downed the blood Daniel handed me. All I cared about at the time was clearing up my bruise and not having Daniel feel bad every time he looked at me. This was why we didn't date everyday humans. In the course of one evening, we'd had to hide or explain away too many odd incidents. As I looked at Chad, I knew what Neil wanted but I wasn't sure it was ever going to work. Neil was a werewolf. He couldn't hide that forever, and I was pretty sure he didn't even want to.

"Yeah, I took some Benadryl," I lied. "Clears it right up."

Chad shook his head and sat back. He looked out over the porch and into the night shrouded trees. "This place is strange. I guess I lived in the city too long. I'm not used to all the nature. I decided to move out here after my parents died. It's so cutthroat in the city. I wanted something more laid back, you know?" He looked up as though surprised he was talking so much. "Sorry, I'm completely dominating the conversation. You're very easy to talk to, Zoey. Odd, but easy to talk to."

I was glad he found me easy to talk to because that way I didn't have to talk back. There was a brief lull, and I wondered where the hell Neil was. How long did it take to make coffee? I tried to continue the small talk. "I like the whole wide open spaces thing. I lived in a tiny apartment for too long. I like the fact that I can come out here in the morning and there's usually a fluffy bunny jumping in the yard."

"It's not so much the fluffy bunnies I have a problem with." Chad looked out into the night, his eyes narrowing as though he was trying to spot something. "It's the larger wildlife that kind of freaks me out. Did you know there are wolves out here? If I didn't know better, I would swear I'm being stalked by a big white wolf. I've seen it three times when I'm jogging. It's weird. It looks almost intelligent."

Oh, it wasn't intelligent. That white wolf was really stupid, and Chad was lucky Neil hadn't come up and humped his leg. I was going to have a talk with my roomie about not freaking the locals out. This was the country, and the locals had shotguns. They probably had torches and pitchforks, too. I was thinking about all the weapons the locals might use on us when Chad suddenly reached out and stroked my hair.

"God, you're beautiful." He stared at me, and there was a languid heaviness to his words. I was stunned as Chad leaned over and pressed his lips against mine.

"You trying to take on a third, sweetheart? Or would he be our fourth?" a very sarcastic voice asked from the back door. Dev stood there, looking down on us with a predatory smile. He had on his black slacks and a form-fitting T-shirt. It was what he wore when hanging out at Ether. I stood up as quickly as possible and realized the situation was even worse than it looked because Daniel and Neil were watching, too. Dev, of course, couldn't let a bad situation be bad. He had to go for really awful. "Seriously, little boy, you can't handle her. You have no idea the exotic things she likes, and quite frankly, her schedule is a little full as it is."

Chad looked horrified. Neil looked hurt and Daniel…well, Daniel looked curious.

"I have no idea why I did that." Chad's eyes shifted between me and Neil. "She's not my type. I don't like girls. I'm one hundred percent gay. I have been my whole life." He looked Dev up and down. "God, you're the boyfriend aren't you? That's my point here. I don't want to do her. I want to be her doing you."

"That's not what it looked like from here," Neil said bitterly as he turned with his coffeepot and stalked back into the house.

Chad sat back on the porch swing and let his head fall to his hands.

I tried to go after Neil. Dev stopped me. "He won't want to talk right now, sweetheart. Don't make it worse."

"I didn't do anything." It wasn't my fault the new guy decided to be bi-curious.

Dev rubbed a hand on my shoulder. "I know you didn't. I wasn't accusing you. You would never do anything to hurt Neil. Now, that one over there obviously has control issues."

"Yes, he does." Daniel's eyes hadn't left Chad since the whole incident had begun. "Zoey, Dev needs to talk to you, and I think you should go with him. I can handle things here. Don't worry about Neil."

"You want me to go with Dev?" Daniel never wanted me to go with Dev. Daniel would come up with a thousand excuses for me to not be alone with Dev.

"Absolutely," he replied. "Dev said he has a line on a paying job."

"And you don't want in on the conversation?"

Daniel smiled, but it was a distracted thing. "Hey, we're working on trust, right? I trust you to make the right decision. So go, spend the night in the city and get us a job. Those hookers aren't getting any cheaper."

I let Dev lead me away while Chad tried to figure out what had gone wrong and Daniel…I think Daniel was trying to figure out Chad.

Chapter Eight

I glanced around Ether, trying to figure out which of the women was my potential client. Dev had chosen to be difficult during the drive from my house to his club. He'd evaded my questions about the client, saying only that he thought she was legit. Dev dealt with enough people who weren't legit to know what he was talking about. The nightclub industry isn't known for its upstanding business practices in the human world, and it's probably worse in the supernatural world. Dev's staff dealt with numerous incidents on a nightly basis.

The bartender shook my Cosmo into a cocktail glass, and I accepted it with a grateful sigh. No one stood out as I surveyed the club.

Dev came up behind me and placed a possessive hand on the small of my back. "Relax. She'll be here."

"I wish you had found out more about this mysterious client. I don't like going into things blind." Blind had nearly gotten Daniel killed just a few days before.

He settled in close to me, his lips against my ear. "Hey, it's not like last time. You're here. There's a whole staff ready to watch your back, and I promise I won't let anything nasty happen to you. Well, not anything I am not directly involved in."

"Could you be serious for two seconds?" He hadn't been there last time. No well-trained staff could have handled the angels.

"Look, you said you wanted a job. I found you a job." Dev let his hands make soothing circles across my back. "You'll have to forgive me if I didn't have her fill out a questionnaire when she called. Next time, I'll know better. Now let's talk about my payment, sweetheart, because I didn't do this out of the kindness of my heart."

He whispered something truly filthy in my ear that made me want to forget about the client and Neil and Chad and everything that was going on and head straight up to the grotto. Since Dev had come into my life, I'd started to rely on mind-blowing sex as a distraction from everyday woes.

"She called you?" I asked, his words finally penetrating through a haze of lust. "Not the other way around? I thought you heard something through the grapevine and made a call to her."

"No, she called me out of the blue." He bent down and laid a proprietary kiss on my neck. "She said she needed a mediator. That was the word she used."

"What was her name, Dev?" I asked, even though I was pretty sure I knew what her name was. She'd told me she would try again. I was just a little shocked at how fast she'd come back.

He thought about it for a moment. "I don't remember. I should remember her name, shouldn't I? I'm sorry, I might not be as cautious as you but I should remember her freaking name. Did I write it down somewhere?"

I turned and reached out, taking his hand. "It's not your fault, Dev. It's what she does. I bet she called you right before you left to come and get me."

He shook his head in confusion. "I remember telling her I couldn't help out until tomorrow. I had a meeting with some vendors tonight. I must have canceled. I don't remember doing it though. Why would I do that? I need to renegotiate my liquor contracts. I wouldn't just cancel."

Angelic influence made vampire persuasion look like child's play.

I looked around the club and, sure enough, there she was. She sat at a table watching Dev and me with a hopeful look on her face. Felicity Day was wearing an approximation of club clothes, but even with a short skirt and flouncy top she looked out of place—like a brilliant shaft of light on an otherwise cloudy day. I had to suspect the effect was for me and Dev alone, as everyone else completely ignored her.

Dev's eyes followed mine. His arms drifted from around me, and he simply stared her way. "Wow, she's beautiful. She is really beautiful."

He couldn't take his eyes off her, and I rolled mine. She was playing those games again, but I wasn't buying it this time. I wasn't sure if it was because I had recently taken Daniel's blood or perhaps it wasn't as strong the second time around, but I could control myself around her more easily this time. Dev seemed to be having some trouble. "You aren't going to be very helpful, are you? Why don't you go and do whatever it is you do. I think I have to take care of this on my own."

I picked up my drink and stalked across the bar to Felicity's table. "I said no."

She gave me a sad smile. "Please sit and talk with me, Zoey."

"I'll talk with you." Dev sank his lanky frame into the chair and stared at Felicity with his head in his hands. He looked like a twelve-year-old with a crush. It was odd to see Dev so open. "Can I get you anything? I own this place. I can get you anything you want. I own a lot of places."

"Dev, it's a glamour." It was at least the angelic equivalent of a glamour.

Dev nodded, a spacey grin on his face. "Yes, she's very glamorous. I'm glad you see that." He looked up at me and there was suddenly a pathetic sympathy in his eyes.

I got a bad feeling about what he was going to say next. "Don't say what you're about to say. You're going to feel stupid about it later, so just keep your mouth shut, babe. This really is a glamour."

Dev wasn't listening to anything but the magic Felicity was working. "I love her, Zoey. I know this is going to hurt you, but we have to break up. I've enjoyed the time we've spent together, but I've found real love now. We're going to get married. I hope you can be happy for us. I really want us to stay friends."

It took everything I had not to burst into laughter. He looked so sweet and earnest that I really wished I could pull my phone out to capture and replay the moment over and over again. Instead, I just nodded. "Yeah sure, Dev. I completely support your new relationship with a woman you barely talked to on the phone. Maybe I can be a bridesmaid."

"That would be great." He sent a swoony look back at his beloved.

Felicity had the grace to look embarrassed. "I forgot about that.

I'm really sorry. I'm afraid it just comes naturally." The light around her dimmed visibly. "That should take care of it."

Dev shook his head as if to clear it. He looked around. "Did I just break up with you?"

I grinned. "Yes, I'm very sad about it. I'm devastated."

"What the hell was that?" Dev's face hardened.

"That was an intense angelic glamour. It's a little more powerful than the stuff you can do." Dev had a plentitude of magical power, but his control was crap. Sometimes the things he tried went haywire.

Dev's eyes found the angel, suspicion plain there. "I was ready to do whatever she wanted. I would have left you and gone wherever she wanted me to go. I would have left you here and anything could have gotten to you. You wouldn't have been protected. I made promises, and I would have just tossed them away to follow her around."

"It's all right, Dev. I knew what was going on. I didn't take you seriously."

"I'm really sorry." Felicity bit her bottom lip, her eyes apologetic. "I did use my influence to get you to bring Zoey to me because this is important and time is running out. But I am sincerely sorry that you were caught in it this time. It wasn't my intention. I can only blame the imbalance."

"I don't care. You can get the hell out of my club," Dev said, nearly snarling. "This is a neutral place and that means no magic. No weapons and no manipulative magic."

Felicity proved that angels could flush and she turned to me, tears in those seemingly innocent eyes. "Please, Zoey. I really need to talk to you."

I shrugged. I didn't like the way she manipulated people either. Dev took the rules of his club very seriously. The only weapons allowed in the club were safely tucked away in his office and in the armory he kept locked away in case of trouble. "You heard the man. You aren't welcome here."

"I'll have a bouncer show you the door." Dev stood, his hand coming out to grip my own as he pulled me with him.

We began to walk away. I hoped she would get the hint and haul her ass back to Heaven. Throbbing dance music beat through the air around us, but I could plainly hear Felicity over the chaos.

"Zoey, I can pay you two million dollars."

She knew how to get a girl's attention. Of course, I probably would have stopped for one million. Who am I kidding? I'd have stopped for way less, but I wasn't about to tell her that. I was wondering if I could bump her up to two point five. I winced but pulled back as Dev tried to propel me forward.

"Zoey, I don't think this is a good idea." Dev looked back, his mouth turning down in a wary grimace as he studied the angel. "If she could trick me into breaking up with you, she could trick you, too."

"I'm willing to risk it. You said it yourself. I should be safe here. If you're worried, go and get Albert. I bet her glamours don't work on him."

His hand tightened on mine. "I don't know."

He was getting to be as bad as Daniel. There was no way I could let two million dollars walk out the door without at least listening to the deal. "This is business. We have a deal, Dev. I'm the boss when it comes to business. I'll be fine. I'll stay where you can see me, but I need to go talk to moneybags."

"Fine," he said with a bite to his voice. He might not like it, but Dev was willing to let me be the boss when it came to this. In the one job we'd run together, he'd been very good, obeying orders and keeping a cool head. In exchange, I let him take the lead in other places. "I'll be at the bar. You tell her if I see her try anything, I swear I will have Albert take her apart."

He stalked away, finding a place at the bar as I walked back to the table. Felicity's face lit up when she realized I was coming back. There was a weird sense of peace that came over me the moment I got close to her, a sense that this was right, that everything would work out.

I ignored it.

"Talk." I sat down and took another sip of my drink. Maybe vodka helped with angelic communications.

"Okay, first of all, I am so sorry about the way things went with Oliver." She spoke quickly, as though she expected me to get up and leave any minute. She didn't know me as well as she thought she did since I wasn't going anywhere until we talked about those digits.

"He won't be around anymore. I'm going to be the one you deal with so you should feel free to bring your vampire around. I promise he won't come to any harm."

I continued to stare because she hadn't said anything yet that required my verbal response. I knew Daniel was going to be safe because I wasn't letting her get anywhere near him again. I glanced over at the bar. Dev had a beer in his hand, and he was watching everything that Felicity did. I noticed he'd called some of his security team over.

Her eyes followed mine. "I didn't mean to upset Devinshea. It really was the last thing I wanted to do. I find this plane very frustrating sometimes."

"Welcome to Earth." I held up a hand to let the waitress know I needed another drink. She hurried off. Sleeping with the owner had its perks.

Felicity stared for a moment at Dev, and then blushed and looked down. "What is it like to sleep with someone?"

"You mean sex?" I had an angel asking me about sex? I might need the waitress to bring me a pitcher.

"Yes," she replied, an eager look in her eyes.

This woman had nearly gotten Daniel killed and pissed Dev off. I wasn't about to become her sex therapist. "What are we, girlfriends? Do you expect me to sit here and swap sex stories with you? You've got like five minutes before I walk out of here, and I will not take another meeting with you, do you understand?"

She nodded, her eyes slipping away from mine. Her hands were threaded together, and she took a deep breath before continuing. "All right. I'm sorry for prying. You just have to understand that one of the reasons we're having problems with control is the loss of Felix. We balance each other. We watch after our charges and nudge them with our own particular talents. I embody love, you see."

"Yeah, I got that." The waitress set another drink in front of me. I lifted it up, giving my hands something to do. It wasn't a good thing to show the potential client how nervous she made me. "So what's Ollie embody? Wait, let me guess. Oliver is the embodiment of an asshole."

"He is judgment. You might call it justice," she replied with just a hint of prude. "But normally he's not so difficult. Everything requires a balance. Love alone can be very destructive without sound judgment. But Felix is the most important of all. He is faith. Without Felix, Oliver and I are adrift, with nothing to anchor us."

I apparently didn't understand how Heaven worked. "So, why don't you just talk to your boss? I hear he's all powerful. Why doesn't he just reach into Hell and pull up your boy?"

Her head shook. "It doesn't work like that. If it were meant to happen that way, it would. Since it did not, I've taken it upon myself to save Felix. It is as it should be."

Her logic was hard to follow, but I pressed on anyway. "So why don't you and your angel friends just charge the Hell plane with swords ablaze and rescue him?"

She smiled, obviously amused at the image. "That's what you would do in my position, isn't it?"

"Damn straight."

"You would have been an archangel," she concluded. "I am not. I do not fight in that manner. Besides, we've been forbidden to enter the Hell plane. It's one of our highest laws. I'm not supposed to even try to influence actions on the Hell plane, but Halfer didn't play by the rules so I shall not either. I won't go there myself. I must find a different way. I must find a paladin. I found you, Zoey Donovan. You are my knight."

"Thief is a better classification for me, lady." I wasn't a knight in shining armor. I didn't tend to throw my own needs out for the greater good. I watched my own back and took care of my people. For the most part, the rest of the world could hang.

Her blonde hair shimmered in the low light as she shook her head. "You don't give yourself enough credit, but I have faith in you. You are a paladin. You'll always make the right choice in the end. You're clever, and when the time comes, you'll use your talents for good."

"How about I use my talents for two million dollars? We are talking about dollars, right? Not some strange Heaven currency, because that does not work here." I didn't care what part of my nature she was attempting to call to. I was concerned about the part of my nature that was excited about doing the job I wanted to do and getting paid a shitload of money for something I would have done for free. "Where the hell does an angel get two million?"

"I merely requested it from one of my charges. He is a very nice man in Seattle," Felicity explained. "He has more money than he could ever spend and doesn't mind helping out good causes. I also got him to throw in a laptop and something called software. It will be delivered to your house tomorrow."

"I'm going to need that in cash." If she was talking about who I thought she was, I did not want a million lawyers jumping on my ass when I cashed that check.

Felicity smiled brightly, lighting up the room. "I'm so excited. It's going to be so good to work together."

"We're not working together." The last thing I needed was to babysit the physical embodiment of love. "I'll give you progress reports, but otherwise you stay on the sidelines."

"Absolutely," she agreed.

"Now, how about handing over that Revelation thing?" The quicker I learned how to use it the better. We would be going to the party in a few weeks, but there was no reason I couldn't start working with my ace in the hole.

"About that," she started, and I knew I wasn't going to like what she said next. "I don't actually have that, but I know where it is."

"How about using those powers of persuasion and getting it? Don't tell me it's on the Hell plane." I planned on spending as little time there as possible, and planning two robberies there was just beyond my talents.

"Not at all. It's in Arkansas."

I rolled my eyes. "Close enough. I take it the current owner doesn't wish to part with it?"

"She's proven very stubborn." Felicity held her hand out and suddenly there was a thumb drive in her palm. "I think you'll find this has all the information you need. My charge taught me how to use a computer."

"Great." I took the drive and shoved it in my pocket. My two million was looking harder all the time, and I hadn't thought it looked that easy in the first place.

She watched as I took a drink. I have to admit I'm not a delicate sipper of a good cocktail. I tend to down them pretty fast. The waitress was already on her way back with another one. "What is that like? It looks pretty. I have never tried alcohol before."

Apparently the Heaven plane didn't boast a hopping nightlife. I slid the fresh glass across the table. I was a little chattier now that I knew I'd have two million at my disposal. "Give it a try."

She shook her head. "Oh, no, I couldn't possibly."

She looked back at the bar, and then seemed to come to some decision. She took a long swallow and came up choking. Perhaps I should have started her on something easier because the bartender knew how I liked my Cosmos and that was heavy on the vodka.

"You should probably take it slower."

"That was strong." She sputtered a little, clearing her throat. "I drank it the way you did."

"Yes, but you didn't start sneaking into your father's liquor cabinet at the age of seventeen." I thought of one really nice night when Danny and I tried making margaritas and ended up giving it up for tequila shots. I still can't make a margarita. My dad had been pissed, and Danny had tried to take all the blame.

"You're thinking of your husband." Felicity leaned forward, her hand almost touching mine.

"Get out of my head." I didn't like anyone poking around in my brain.

She shrugged. "I can't help it. When you love someone the way you love your Daniel, I can't help but feel it. It telegraphs very loudly."

"It isn't really love, you see," I started to explain. "I'm a companion, and he's a vampire."

"And what do you think a companion is, dear?"

I stilled because if I answered that question, I opened a whole new can of worms. Felicity claimed she could tell me what I was. Did I really want to know? Against my better judgment, I heard myself speak. "A companion is something like a slave."

Felicity chuckled a little, but her face softened and I could practically feel the warmth of affection pouring off her. "I'm sorry, dear, I didn't realize that the knowledge was gone from this plane. A companion isn't a slave—far from it. A companion is just as powerful as a vampire."

I rolled my eyes. "Yes, my superpower is—wait for it—tasting good. That's a hell of a superpower. Someone call the Justice League and get me an application."

"They really don't tell you anything, do they? A companion is balance against the vampire. It's why they're attracted to each other. A vampire needs a companion and a companion needs a vampire. They balance each other. It is the way of this world. You realize you saved your husband the night he died? He is as he is because of your blood."

"I don't understand anything," I admitted. An odd sense of vulnerability stole over me.

She gave me a reassuring pat. "Okay, I'll try to make you understand. I probably should start at the beginning. Long before there were humans on the Earth plane, angels and demons used it as a battlefield. As happens on occasion, not all demons are entirely bad as not all angels can maintain their perfect goodness. Some fell from both sides. Some male and some female. Do you understand where I'm going?"

"Yes, some of the demons hooked up with some of the angels and started making babies." I summed up the story as old as time.

Felicity nodded. "Exactly. They could no longer live on their planes and chose to populate the Earth plane. Later, my father created humans and the bloodlines became mixed. It's rare, but sometimes the demon blood shows up in the population, almost always in the male, and a vampire is born. The same is true of the angelic blood in the female. This is what you call a companion."

It was my turn to sputter. "You're telling me I'm descended from an angel?"

Neil was going to get a kick out of that one, but I finally understood why I could use the Revelation and Daniel could not. I suppose it also made sense that faeries were closer to angels, while a werewolf took after the demonic side.

"Yes, you are. It's the balance to the demon. It's why they're attracted to you. They want the balance. Vampires, for the most part, don't wish to be destructive. But the companion's true role was lost over time, and they became very rare indeed. Now, apparently the vampire's possessive nature has taken over and they subjugate their companions, never understanding what that companion can do for them."

"What can I do for him?" As far as I knew, I was just around to feed Daniel.

"You've already done most of the work. A vampire is very impressionable when he turns. The Council chooses to use this to fashion an army. You mentioned the word slave, but it better refers to the way the Council treats vampires. New vampires are forced into blood oaths that make them pliable and eager to serve those who are stronger. They lose much of their own free will."

"Daniel went through the same training." He rarely spoke of it, but when he did, it was with a deep bitterness. Those three years he spent in the Council's care were the worst of his life. I'd learned from Marcus that Daniel had proven difficult to train.

"Daniel was different. The day he rose he took his companion's blood into his body. There is no blood oath strong enough to break the promise you made to him that night. They could feed him ancient blood every day, but it couldn't change who Daniel is. He learned to conform but never to fit in. It's caused him much anxiety because he didn't understand. Your blood was his misery and his salvation. I believe it will be the salvation of all this plane's unique creatures."

A little shiver raced across my skin. "What do you mean?"

Felicity became very serious. "I mean the Council has become corrupt. They seek dominion over the supernatural world. They believe they can use Daniel to force their will on the other creatures. They don't understand the bond between you and Daniel. As you balance your husband, so I believe he will prove to balance the Council's threat. We watch him in Heaven, too." She gave me a moment to soak that in before she leaned over. "I know you worry that your love for Daniel is tainted because of your unique biology. You view this in the wrong fashion. You have fears because you don't understand your own nature, but you won't be afraid forever, Zoey. Rejecting your husband's love is like saying you wouldn't accept love from a man because men are attracted to women. It's foolish."

"You don't understand." That phrase was becoming my mantra.

"There is much on this plane I don't understand, but this I have experience in." She sat back and glanced at the bar. She watched Dev for a long moment. I wondered what he looked like to an angel. "You should go to your lover. He'll need you tonight."

I was a little surprised. I'd gotten the impression she wouldn't approve of my relationship with Dev. "No lectures on fidelity?"

"I've lectured you enough for one night. Heaven is not the place you think. It is you humans who make it a harsh place for only the most worthy. My boss, as you put it, has an entirely different version of worthy than you could imagine." She stood up. "I wish you luck, Zoey. I know you will succeed."

I felt compelled to speak. She'd answered my questions, but I refused the only one she'd asked of me. "It depends, you know, on why you're sleeping with a person."

"I wonder because I know nothing of the physical. I only have experience with the spiritual. I always wondered. You think you don't love Devinshea, yet still you enjoy mating with him."

"I care about Dev," I pointed out, not wanting to admit anything even to myself. "I really do. I enjoy sleeping with him because it feels good. He's a very skilled lover. There's nothing that can take your mind off your troubles like a man who plays your body like a fine instrument, and Dev is good at that. It's good to feel close to someone."

"And what is it like with your Daniel?"

I blinked back the tears that sprang up. I took a deep breath before I answered her as honestly as I could. "I don't know what Heaven's like, but I would bet it feels like that."

Felicity smiled and took my hand briefly. "It's all right to be scared a while longer, Zoey. Things will play out as they are meant to. You'll find your balance, all three of you. Your path is set. Now go and take care of your lover. As I said, he needs you tonight more than he'll admit. My earlier actions have brought back bad memories for Devinshea."

I glanced over at Dev, who frowned as the bartender passed him another beer. When I looked back, Felicity was gone.

Dev walked through the crowd when he realized I was alone again. "What did she say? You look sad. I could have her thrown out if she hadn't vanished into thin air."

I shook my head. "I'm just thinking. The good news is we have a job."

"Tell me about it later," he demanded, taking my hand. "Let's go upstairs."

I let him drag me along, thinking about Felicity's words, when a young woman ran from the dance floor and threw herself at my feet.

She was maybe twenty and Hispanic. Her dark hair was tangled, and she had a cut on her face. Her eyes were wide with desperation.

“Please, help me,” she said, trying to take my hand.

Chapter Nine

I looked down at the woman at my feet and back up at Dev, who shrugged. I had no idea why she'd come to me, especially when there were big strong men all around, and she obviously needed defending. "Is someone coming after you?"

"In my club?" Dev looked through the crowd, his eyes seeking a threat. He found his predators as two big werewolves made their way across the floor. They had their target in their sights.

"My name is Angelina Hernandez, and they are trying to take me from my master," Angelina said quickly, her voice shaking. "I beg of you, mistress, don't let them. They will kill me, and I have no wish to leave Justin."

"Justin, as in the Vampire Justin?" I had only recently met Justin and already he was a pain in my ass. And since when did people start calling me mistress?

She nodded, huddling closer to me. "Yes, ma'am. I called him, but he's not here yet. Please help me. You owe me protection. I was told I would be protected."

"I told you those new vamps were trouble," Dev muttered as the big bad wolves were upon us. I was grateful to see that several members of the security team were already behind us. Dev held out his hand and one of the bouncers pressed a shiny semi into it. Dev checked the clip as he looked up at the wolves. He obviously knew the two men, but they didn't seem friendly. "Hello, Mitchell. Do we have a problem here?"

"Not at all, Quinn," the older of the two wolves spat. He was roughly fifty but powerfully built. He was just the tiniest bit past his prime, silver showing at his temples. "I'll just take my bitch and be out of your way."

"I don't think the girl wants to go with you." Dev understated the situation.

The girl in question cowered behind me. She was obviously a wolf, making her faster and stronger than little old me. I wondered if maybe my reputation had finally exceeded my ability. It had always been a goal of mine to be considered a tough chick, but this might be pushing it. I didn't even have a gun, and she acted like I was solid protection against two werewolves.

"She belongs to the pack." The younger man stepped up. I pegged him at twenty-five, but he looked so familiar. I would have sworn I'd seen that face somewhere. "You have no right butting into pack business, Quinn."

"I have every right when pack business messes with my business. You all know the rules." Dev looked at the two wolves with distaste. "I don't allow young females to be abused in my club."

"I no longer belong to the pack," Angelina insisted from behind me. "I belong to Justin, and he belongs to me."

Justin needed to get his butt down here because I didn't want to deal with a lover's quarrel. My mind made a sudden leap. There was something about the word "belong" that made me think. "Angelina, did you make a blood oath to Justin?"

"Yeah, the stupid bitch sure did." Contempt flavored every syllable Mitchell uttered. "All because she didn't want to mate with the male selected for her. Normally we would cast her out, but she's of breeding age. We'll punish her, and she'll serve the pack."

Yeah, I bet she would serve the pack on her back or however the hell they did it. "Angelina, were you forced into the oath?" I had to ask. It wouldn't be the first time it was forced on a woman.

"Absolutely not," she said vehemently. "I chose Justin. We were matched by the king, but I didn't have to say yes. He told me it was my choice. I love Justin. Please don't let them take me, ma'am."

And that answered the question of why me, and why I was suddenly being called ma'am and mistress. Of course, Daniel decided it was a good idea to start matching up vampires and stray wolves. Nothing bad could ever come out of that. No wonder all the vamps were coming to Dallas. Daniel was busy playing pimp. As was custom, the vampires offered their servants and lovers protection. This protection came from all of Vampire, and not merely the one being served or loved. Angelina had looked around, and I was the closest thing to a representative of Vampire she could find. She'd been smart to find me because I might not be a Good Samaritan, but I would be damned if I let some girl be dragged off and raped. I also knew the rules. "If she took an oath, then she no longer belongs to the pack. She belongs to Vampire, and I will call the Council in if you push me."

I really wouldn't. I hated the Council, but everyone feared them so I would invoke that name whenever I could. I would, however, make Daniel clean up his own damn mess. Hubby and I needed to have a talk.

"Look, you stupid bitch, it isn't any of your concern." The younger wolf was beginning to get on my nerves.

Mitchell stepped toward me, menace in his dark eyes. He was intimidating, his face all hard planes and stark lines, his body built on solid muscle. "Wyatt, don't talk to the pretty lady like that. She doesn't know who she's messing with. I'll explain it to you, sweetheart. Stay out of our business, little human. You might be Quinn's plaything, but he can't be with you twenty-four seven. He'll tire of you sooner rather than later. If you screw with the pack, we'll have to assume you want to be messed with, darling. I don't think you'll like how I mess with you. I won't be as pretty as Quinn there, but you'll know I've had you. I like it rough."

I kind of expected this would be a good time for Dev to roar his indignation or shoot someone, but when I looked over, he was merely rolling his eyes with disdain. "Oh, Mitchell, you're such an ignorant man. Don't keep up with your son's circle of friends, do you?"

Mitchell looked confused and shot a look at the younger wolf. "You talking about Wyatt? What does she have to do with Wyatt?"

"I was talking about your other son, Neil," Dev replied. "You know the one who took a blood oath to protect Daniel Donovan and everything that belongs to him, including his wife, Zoey."

Mitchell had the good sense to go a little pale at the mention of my hubby. "You mean the vampire everyone is talking about. This is his wife?"

I was too stuck on the fact that this asshole was the man who'd put Neil through such hell. He was the one who'd tossed him to the street and allowed him to be abused by the pack. Neil had suffered and sold himself because this man couldn't handle his natural biology. Now I knew where I'd seen Wyatt's face before. I saw it every day on my friend.

Dev was still talking as my rage started to boil. "Yes, she's married to the vampire, who will probably kill you when he finds out you threatened to rape his wife. He's tolerant when it comes to me, but I doubt he'll let you into our little ménage."

"Dev." I didn't dare say anything else because I didn't want to give anyone notice of what I was about to do. I held out my hand, letting him know what I wanted.

He sighed because he knew exactly what I was going to do, and he also knew it would probably cause trouble down the line. "Any way I can talk you out of it?"

"None."

He slapped the gun in my hand and before that no good, backwoods, homophobic, raping son of a bitch had a chance to move, I aimed and fired. A surprisingly high howl cracked through the room. Mitchell fell to the floor, big hands covering his now defunct private parts.

I stood over him even as Albert showed up to hold back Wyatt. "That was for Neil. If you ever come near me again, I won't stop shooting. I swear I'll fill you so full of silver, you'll bleed metal. My only regret is that eventually your dick will grow back. But I bet it hurts." I handed the gun back to Dev and gestured to Angelina, who seemed much surer of herself now. "She belongs to Vampire. We do not give back what is ours. We do not share what is ours"—Dev cleared his throat—"unless we really want to, and we won't share with you. You don't have to worry about my husband, Mr. Roberts. You mess with Angelina and I will hunt you down."

I turned to find Angelina holding on to the long-delayed Justin.

He held his girlfriend close but looked awfully impressed with me. "I would threaten him, but it would probably look silly after what you just did. I think you just cured me forever of companion fascination."

"You want to explain to me what's going on, Justin?" I asked as the Roberts family was being escorted off the premises. There was a very efficient cleaning crew already swabbing up the blood so no one went all blood lusty.

Justin frowned. "Mrs. Donovan, as frightening as I find you I…"

I could finish the sentence for him. "You are way more scared of Daniel. Well, I'll take this up with him and trust me, he should be afraid of me."

Dev was watching me, his foot tapping impatiently. "Are you done? Is there anyone else you would like to maim?"

"Not anyone who's here," I replied honestly.

"I would really like to get to the sexually deviant portion of the evening." Dev took my hand and led me through the crowd and up the stairs.

He blew past several employees who wanted to talk to him and told the bouncer at the bottom of the stairs that he wasn't to be disturbed for the rest of the night. By the time he slammed the door of his office, he was in a state. He pulled me to him, ours chests bumping with the force. He tangled a hand in my hair, his lips moving on mine. I might have been intimidated, but I remembered what Felicity had told me. Something about the way her magic had worked on him brought back bad memories. The way he was devouring me now made me think those memories must be beyond bad.

When he finally let me come up for air, I pulled back just a little. "Dev?"

His breath moved his chest in a steady, deep pace, a sure sign of his arousal, but he let me go and walked around his desk. He threw his body into the chair and ran a frustrated hand through his hair. "If you don't want to be here, there's the door, Zoey. I'll have the driver take you home."

"I didn't say I wanted to leave." He was so testy. Dev was my good-time lover. We laughed and teased and played. I guess if I was honest, that was what he really was to me. He was a playmate. I hadn't seen this side. "I just thought maybe we should talk about what happened."

I thought it was just a funny little episode. We'd all been caught at one time or another in some form of magic, but this was serious to Dev.

His green eyes were dark and that sensual mouth turned down.

"I don't want to talk, Zoey. I want to fuck. I want to bend you any way that pleases me and make you scream when you come. I want you soft and sweet and entirely submissive to me. If you can't do that, then walk away and I'll figure something else out. If you hadn't already unmanned the local werewolf alpha, I might have been able to start a fight."

So much anger and pain. It was right there, etched on his gorgeous face. He'd never shown this much of himself to me. I know there are many women who would have walked out, determined to not be used by another to forget their troubles. But I knew when my lover really needed me. I made my decision. He didn't need to talk tonight. He needed something else. He needed to know I was here for him.

I drew my shirt over my head, tossing it to the side. He sat back in his chair, just a little of his rage dissipating and turning into desire. Slowly, so he couldn't miss the show I put on just for him, I pushed my jeans away, toeing off my shoes and standing in front of him in nothing but my undies and bra.

"Come here, lover." He held a hand out, guiding me down to sit on his lap.

There was only a single lamp lighting the room. Soft light made him look younger, more vulnerable than usual. I leaned forward, kissing his nose and cheeks and his furrowed brow. I wanted to kiss away his troubles.

His hands brushed across my breasts before unhooking the clasps of my bra and tossing it away. I leaned back, giving him the access I knew he wanted, and he fastened that sensual mouth on my nipple, tugging and sucking it with affection. I could feel the hard length of his cock pressing against me.

I wrapped my arms around him, adoring the heat of his skin. While his tongue played on my breasts, I let myself be surrounded by him. His scent, his warmth, the slide of his skin against mine. The world seemed to disappear when I was with Dev.

And I'd lied to Felicity. He meant more to me than a good time.

My fingers found the bottom of his shirt, and I pulled it overhead, exposing the beauty of his chest. He was built on lean lines, every muscle sculpted and perfect. His mouth found mine again, tongues playing as his fingers delved past the waist of my panties. I was already wet and ready. He really only had to look at me to get my motor running. His fingers slid over my clit, every nerve I had lighting up.

"I need you," he whispered against my skin. "I need you so fucking much."

It hadn't been so long ago I had asked something very similar of him, and he had not disappointed me. I wouldn't let him go through this, whatever this was, alone. "You have me. I'm here."

His eyes hardened, rough desire taking over. "Show me. Show me how much you want me." His hand tangled in my hair, pulling on it with a gentle bite. "I want you to suck me, Zoey. I want you on your knees, taking me in your mouth."

It wasn't a request he made often. He tended to please me, taking his own satisfaction only after I'd come several times. Oh, he certainly was in charge when we were in bed together, but he tended to prefer to be the one tasting.

I slid off his lap, more than willing to do what he was asking of me. Desire thrummed through my system as I unbuttoned his slacks.

"Slow, Zoey." He was staring down at me, completely unmoving except for his hand in my hair. "Take your time."

He might think he was in control, but I wanted this. I'd wanted it for a very long time. Sometimes I felt useless in bed. Oh, there was always pleasure there, but I wanted to please him, too. I wanted to mean so much more to him and I couldn't when he always gave and never took.

I let my palm run over the soft material of his boxers, feeling the hard erection under there. Dev's cock was already poking its way out of the top, touching his navel. Big and thick, the head of his cock was bulbous and already creamy with the evidence of his arousal.

The masculine scent of his desire wafted over me. Dev smelled like the soap he'd used and sandalwood and the musky smell of his sexual arousal. His deep groan reverberated across his skin as I swiped at the head of his cock, gathering the little bead of cream I found there. The salty taste of Dev spread across my tongue and I sucked, trying to draw more from him.

"That's it." His hand tightened in my hair, the sensation lighting up my scalp and rushing across my skin. "More, Zoey. Take more of me. Take all of me."

I reached up and drew the full length of him out of his boxers. I couldn't hold him in one hand. I needed two. Green Men didn't do small cocks. He pulsed against my palm and I loved the silky feel of him. My entire body was primed to please him, wanting nothing more than to have my tongue coated with him as I took all his troubles away.

Something had happened to him in the past, something terrible. He wouldn't talk to me about it so this was the only way I had to help him through. I knew how it felt to sit up at night and go over and over one terrible moment. I would have given a lot to have someone with me, making me forget. I could be that for Dev. I could be essential to him.

Sex is important. It binds us to other human beings. I know I'm naïve in thinking that way. There are many people who can just lose themselves to pleasure, but I'm not one of them. I learned that my heart and all those girl parts I had were deeply connected. I couldn't seek pleasure without also getting my heart engaged and Dev was making my every emotion spark even as I drew his cock into my mouth.

"Yes. That's what I need, sweetheart."

It didn't matter how he saw me in that moment. He could have seen me as nothing more than a cheap lay. I knew the truth. He needed me. I was the only one who could take him to a place where he wasn't worried, wasn't back in that place where Felicity's magic had taken him.

I closed my mouth over the head of his cock and drew him in. My hair spread out over his thighs and I drew hard on his dick, sucking as I lowered my mouth on him. His heavy balls felt good against my palm. I rolled them up, loving the weight.

It took forever to work my way down most of him. I couldn't take his full length. My mouth wasn't big enough. I took as much as I could and sucked hard, letting my tongue run around his width. Silky skin played against mine, Dev's cock thickening further even as I drew on him.

He pushed me down gently, forcing me to take another inch. His cock hit the back of my throat and I forced myself to breathe deep.

"Do you know how fucking good you feel?" Dev's voice was hoarse, sexy and low. "Do you know how much I need you?"

It was exactly the right thing to say to keep me going. I drew back almost to his cock head, tonguing around the ridge it formed.

"Zoey?"

I let my eyes drift up and he was staring down at me, both his hands in my hair now. I didn't say a thing, didn't pull my mouth off him. I wouldn't let up, simply let him know that I was listening.

"I'll take care of you. For as long as you'll let me, I'll take care of you."

I had zero intentions of him not taking care of me, but the specter of Daniel sat firmly between us. There was no doubt in my mind that was what he was talking about. Even as I worked on Dev's cock, Daniel was there between us.

I was caught between my rage at my husband and a growing, deepening emotion that defined how I felt about Devinshea.

Desire swamped me, causing me to let go of my every inhibition. Nothing mattered except taking Dev to a place where no one but I could touch him.

My tongue ran up and down his dick. Over and over, I dragged my mouth up and down, working his flesh with my tongue and teeth and mouth. His cock filled my mouth to overflowing, invading me and overtaking me. I let my hand circle the part of his cock I didn't have in my mouth, stroking him in time to each drag of my tongue.

His hips started to move, thrusting up to meet to my mouth as I drove his cock deep inside.

A low moan came out of his mouth and I felt the moment his balls drew up, hugging close to his body. "I'm going to come, sweetheart. If you don't want a mouthful of me, you should lean back and let me finish this."

Oh, but I'd been dying for a mouthful of him. I realized just how careful he'd been with me. He'd denied himself in order to please me. He'd focused on me and we'd missed out on so much because of it. I needed this as much as he did. I needed to know that I could transport him the way he could transport me. Dev could take me to another place when he made love to me. He could make all my troubles and worry drift away, take me to somewhere I didn't have to worry about anything beyond the next dizzying peak, the orgasm that was rolling over me.

His hips rolled up, his dick filling every inch of my mouth and I heard him groan as come spurted over my tongue.

Salty sweetness overtook my senses, his orgasm making me shudder. I lapped up every ounce, swallowing him down. A deep sense of satisfaction floated through me because he was relaxed now, his muscles losing their tension.

I kept licking him, his hand softening in my hair until he was petting me.

And his cock was coming back to life.

When I looked up at him, the dark look in his eyes was gone, replaced by a smile that drew his gorgeous mouth up.

"You have the most amazing mouth, lover. But I think it's time for a little payback. Come up here." He pulled me up and into his lap.

This time when he kissed me it was a long, satisfying exploration. He was certain I would be what he needed me to be, and he was content to take his time.

* * * *

It was almost two in the morning when I finally slid out of bed. I hadn't drifted to sleep the way I normally would have. Too many things were running through my mind. This night had been different. Sex with Dev was fun and playful, but this was a different Dev. He'd been demanding, and I felt, for the first time, he needed me for so much more than an orgasm. We'd made love, and it gave me so much to think about.

I thought Dev had finally fallen asleep, but he turned and propped his head on one hand. I was about to get dressed but sat back down on the bed.

"You can go, Zoey," Dev said quietly. "I'll be fine now."

"I wish you would tell me what was riding you tonight." I reached out to touch his chest, placing my hand right over his heart.

He smiled, a lascivious little grin, and his hand ran itself up my arm. "I don't mind telling you what was riding me tonight. That would be you, and you rode me well, sweetheart." I rolled my eyes and started to get up again but he pulled at my hand, his eyes sobering. "It happened a long time ago. I was just a kid. That fucking manipulative magic just brought back some bad memories. You drove them away with your amazing therapy."

And that was all I was going to get. "Well, I'm glad I could be of service."

He pulled me down and kissed me. "Thank you, my Zoey. I couldn't have asked for more. Now, go and give Daniel hell like you want to."

"I don't have to go." I didn't want to leave him if he needed me, but Danny and I had a few things to iron out. I wanted to talk to him about the job, and I really wanted to kick his ass for letting me walk into that situation with Angelina and Justin unaware. He had to know there would be repercussions. If I was supposed to be queen to his king, I needed to start getting the debriefings.

Dev yawned and looked generally content. "If you stay, you'll have to wait an entire day to yell at him. I don't want to be the one who kept you waiting. Go, woman. I sleep better alone anyway. You snore."

"I do not," I protested, getting off the bed and finding my clothes.

"Do, too," he insisted. "And Zoey, whatever this job is…"

"I know, I know, you want in." Those would be the three words carved into his headstone one day. I was sure of it.

"That's right. And you can be damn sure when you go to the Hell plane to rescue Sarah, that I want in on that, too."

I stood staring at him. I'd been really careful to keep him entirely out of the loop on that one. I'd never mentioned it and been careful to never speak of it in the club.

Dev turned over with a satisfied smirk that had everything to do with one-upping me. "I know everything, Zoey. I'll talk to you tomorrow. And don't kill the vampire. We're going to need him."

* * * *

I shut the door to the limo and listened as it drove back off into the night. Of all the people my move had inconvenienced, I was certain Dev's driver was the worst. The night was quiet, but the light was on in the living room. My heart clenched a little bit at the thought of Neil sitting up. I let myself in and, sure enough, there he was sitting on the couch. He was still in his slacks and polo, though they weren't as crisp as they had been. He looked more nervous than sad.

When he glanced up at me, his eyes went wide, shock replacing that haunted look.

"Zoey." He actually shrank back a bit. "You were supposed to stay with Dev."

"I need to talk to Daniel." At least he was speaking to me and not shutting me out with a flippant wave of his hand. "And I definitely need to talk to you. But before we get into that, I have to tell you something. I don't want you to hear through the grapevine. I kind of shot your dad."

Neil perked up at that. "Really? Is he dead?"

I shook my head. "No, but he probably wishes he was. I sort of shot him in a spot most guys don't want to get shot in."

Neil smiled wistfully. "Thereby fulfilling many a childhood fantasy. I wish I could have been there, Z."

"Hey, it happened at Ether so it was more than likely caught on Dev's security tapes. We can have a watching party."

"Cool," Neil agreed. "You didn't happen to shoot my brother, too?" I responded in the negative. "Next time."

At least he wasn't distraught. I could move on to other painful conversations. "Now, where is Danny?"

Neil is possibly the worst liar on the planet. Most of the time he knew better than to lie and, when faced with a situation that required fabrication, merely kept his mouth shut and allowed those of us with skill to handle it. He was up shit creek when he was left to his own devices, as nothing that came out of his lying mouth sounded believable. He couldn't just stick with a little lie. Once Neil started talking, everything snowballed. I watched as he tried really hard to come up with something, anything, that might make me believe.

"There was a Council thing, and he forgot that he was supposed to go," he spat out finally.

The Council was in Paris. Danny had up and gone to Paris? I just stared at him knowing that the longer I kept him pinned with that look, the worse a hole he would dig. Neil never met a silence he liked. He just had to fill it with something.

"Marcus called and said he was late," Neil continued, unable to stay silent while I stared. "And that there was a big vampire emergency and all the vampires had to go to this meeting because of the emergency. It was a very important meeting but Daniel finished what he was doing, 'cause you know Daniel, he's all 'nobody tells me what to do' and then he decided to go ahead and go anyway because…"

"It was a vampire emergency," I finished, sarcasm dripping. I looked down at my still-lime green carpet. The boxes of flooring hadn't been touched and his tools were right where he'd left them. "Neil, he didn't even start the project. Where is he? Is he out finding more little wolves to feed to his vamps? Is he at least getting a finder's fee?"

Neil's mouth dropped open. "Oh, shit, you know about that. I told him you would find out. Zoey, you don't understand."

No, I didn't and somebody had better start explaining it to me. I stalked through my house, searching for my secretive vampire husband. He was playing some sort of game, and I wanted to know what it was. His truck was still parked outside, so despite Neil's sad efforts, I knew he was here. Neil followed behind me, begging me to wait.

"Daniel is going to explain everything, Z."

It wasn't until I got to the kitchen that I realized just how much explaining Daniel would be doing.

I looked out the window in my back door and saw Daniel talking to Chad in the moonlight. They stood in the yard, and Daniel had one hand on the smaller man's shoulder. It looked like Daniel was giving the other man some advice. I say "looked like" because I was so deeply wrong.

In the next second, Daniel's free hand stabbed a knife straight through Chad's heart.

Chapter Ten

I was out the door and flying across the porch before Chad's dead body could hit the ground. Daniel stood over the corpse, but I was pleased to see a look of pure terror cross his handsome face when he realized I was coming his way. He let the knife drop and actually tried to back away.

"Daniel Donovan," I screamed without thought. It didn't matter. My nearest neighbor was a mile and a half down the road. Of course, that neighbor was Chad, and he wouldn't be calling the police any time soon. "You murdering son of a bitch."

I swung and caught him in the chest, and he had the very good sense to try to look wounded. Neil stood in the background with plenty of distance between himself and whatever violence I was about to visit on my husband.

"Zoey, it's not what you think." Daniel's voice was calm, his breathing steady.

"Not what I think? You stabbed him through the heart! He's dead on my lawn, Daniel. What are you going to tell me, that he committed suicide?"

"Would you believe me if I tried?" he asked, his voice slightly hopeful.

I slapped at his chest again. "No, I will not believe that he ran at the knife you just happened to be holding out at the very exact level his heart was at. I can't believe this. What the hell are we going to do with that body?"

The trouble with human bodies is that unlike most supernaturals, they decompose very slowly. Most vampires will turn to ash if hit by enough ultraviolet light, or they have been known to explode from time to time when staked. If you're going to stake a vampire, don't wear your best clothes because no amount of dry cleaning will ever get that shit out. Werewolves and other shifters decompose very quickly, so if you take one down you really only have to keep prying eyes out of your kill zone for a day or two. Chad would not be going down so easily. Chad would hang around for years just waiting for some snotty CSI wannabe to solve his untimely murder.

"Don't worry about the body," Daniel said with assurance. "I got that covered, baby."

I laughed a little hysterically. "Good, I'm really glad you thought this out. I wouldn't want you to go around murdering our neighbors without a really good plan in place."

Neil tried to interject some reason. "Zoey, if you would just let us explain."

I turned on him, and he shrank back. "You stay out of this. You don't want to be on my radar right now. I already shot one wolf in the balls tonight. Don't think I can't make it two."

Neil gulped. "You're on your own, Daniel."

I rounded on my husband again. "Yes, you are because I am so not taking the fall for this one, Danny. Those guys earlier this year in the hotel room I will concede deserved to die."

They'd tried to kill all of us, but Danny and Neil took them out. Luckily a nice group of fairies took care of those bodies since we'd been too busy to do our own cleanup. I didn't like having to deal with bodies. Bodies were messy.

"I'm glad you approve." Daniel was far too calm for the situation. I knew he'd been forced to do wet work for the Council as part of his parole, but now I wondered just how much it was affecting him.

"I do not approve of this. He didn't do anything, Danny. He tried to kiss me once." I whirled on Neil. "And you! I thought you liked him. He makes one mistake and you let Danny murder him? No one is going to be hot to date you after this makes the rounds."

Daniel laughed outright. "You think I killed the kid because he kissed you? Seriously? I sent you off with Dev, who was obviously horny out of his mind, so I could murder some gay dude who kissed you and then spent the rest of the night salivating over me and Neil?"

Put like that, it did sound stupid. However, there was still a dead lawyer at my feet. I sidestepped the ever-growing pool of blood, praying I didn't track it back into the house. I remembered something Michael had said a couple of days earlier. "I believe the term is righteous kill."

It was the term the Council used for legal executions.

Danny actually bent over laughing. "This is not a righteous kill, Z. Dev, who flagrantly screws my wife at every given opportunity, would be a righteous kill if we hadn't reached an agreement. Chad here is an idiot who didn't know better. The Council doesn't let us run around killing every human who happens to hit on our wives. I know you haven't met any other companions, but as a class of females, you tend to rate high on the hot scale. There would be a lot of male bodies piling up if we did that."

He'd said a lot, but I really only caught one part of it. "Agreement?"

Vampires really can pale when they get scared. "Yeah, I agreed to not kill him."

There was way more to that story. "That was our agreement, Danny. What was your agreement with Dev?" And why the hell hadn't Dev mentioned it?

Daniel crossed his arms and frowned. "You couldn't just expect me not to talk to him. I had to find out what his intentions were."

"If I know Dev, he was ridiculously, vulgarly detailed in describing his intentions to you, Danny." The man had no sense of self-preservation.

"It really wasn't like that, Z," Daniel said defensively. "We both care about you. I love you, and the truth is I can't watch over you during the day."

"Son of a bitch! He hired a PI to follow me, didn't he?" That was how he knew everything.

"I couldn't be sure Halfer wouldn't come back. You hurt him last spring, Zoey. You hurt his pride. He's not going to let that stand. I can make sure he can't get to you during the night, so Dev takes the day shift or he makes sure someone does. You can't expect us to just let you walk around with a big neon sign on your back saying *get your revenge here*, can you?"

"How about discussing the situation with me like adults?"

Daniel rolled his baby blues. "Yeah, 'cause you're so reasonable. It's why I didn't tell you I was gonna kill Chad."

"Fuck me! That was really horrible." A low moan rose from the ground. Chad coughed, sitting up.

I screamed and jumped behind Daniel. Even in my line of work, I don't deal with a whole lot of reanimated corpses. "He came back."

Neil moved from behind me, reaching toward Chad.

"Not yet, Neil. He's not ready." Daniel placed himself between me and Neil and the reanimated corpse.

Chad managed to get to his knees, and he patted the hole in his chest. "You were right. I should have picked strangulation. Anything would be better than that."

Daniel shrugged. "Nobody ever listens to me about strangulation. You think the whole knife thing will be quicker, but I promise I could have cut off that oxygen pretty damn fast."

"Fine, next time I get my pick of method of death, I'll listen to you." Chad caught sight of me. His fangs lengthened for the first time, hunger etched on his face. "I want her. She glows. It's so pretty."

Daniel walked over to Chad and pulled him up roughly by the back of his shirt. Daniel's fangs were fully out, a savage look on his face. Chad struggled in Daniel's grip, but couldn't break the hold.

Daniel turned his eyes to me. "Zoey, I have things I have to do. There are certain rituals that must be performed. You should go inside."

I stood my ground. The importance of what Daniel had done, what he was doing, wasn't lost on me. I wasn't sure how he'd known Chad would survive his bloody murder, but I was damn sure Danny wouldn't call the Council to take Chad for training. This was the dangerous game Alexander had mentioned. "Not on your life, buddy. If I'm in this mess, then I'm in it one hundred percent. I won't let you shut me out. Am I your queen or just your companion?"

"You are always my queen, baby," Daniel said. "But don't say I didn't warn you."

Neil came over and slipped his hand into mine. He took a deep breath as though steeling himself.

Chad flailed, arms and legs thrashing as he strained against Daniel's hold. His face was no longer recognizable, just a blur of fangs and eyes and need. His hands reached out, grabbing for me. Prey. I was prey, and he wanted to drain me. Neil stepped in front of me, not obscuring my view but placing his body in the way should the hungry vampire manage to get free. Instinct told me to flee, to put as much distance between us as possible. Trust kept me rooted in place. Daniel would never let him get close.

Daniel's hold on Chad became brutal. Sharp claws sprung from his right hand, sinking into the flesh of Chad's throat. He spoke in guttural tones. "I know you're hungry. You will not feed until I will it, do you understand? I'm your master and you will obey me."

Chad didn't look like he was big into obedience. He looked like he was going to fight tooth and claw against anything Daniel said. This was a monster that would tear up everything he could get his hands on. He was a ball of hunger, destruction, and violence. It was utterly unlike the way Daniel was on the night of his turn, and I finally understood what Marcus had tried to explain to me. Daniel was different. His strength went far beyond the physical. The turn was violent and twisted, but Daniel had been unaffected. A new vampire always kills, and he doesn't stop killing until he's trained. But Daniel hadn't killed that first night. He'd risen and retained his personality. He'd fed but left that first victim alive. Then he came home to me. He'd taken me gently, and we made love after. There was nothing in Daniel that first night that vaguely resembled Chad.

"He's done this before," I whispered more to myself than anyone else.

"Yes," Neil replied. "But this is only the second time he's tried it on his own. The other times, Marcus was there to help him. Chad seems stronger than Justin."

Long, sharp fangs gleamed in the night as Daniel struck, piercing Chad's throat with a sickening force. His throat worked, draining Chad of what the knife had not taken. The lawyer who'd sat cordially at my table for dinner spasmed, his legs kicking, trying to fight the inevitable. When he finally stilled, was finally calm, Daniel released him, blood dripping from his mouth, tongue working to save each precious drop. Daniel let him slip down, and Chad fell back, no strength left to even hold himself up.

The still of the night was broken with Daniel's low words. "Do you make your oath to me?"

Chad could barely make his lips form the word. "Yes."

"You will protect me and mine?"

"Yes."

"Yes, what?" Daniel demanded.

Chad didn't seem to understand for a moment, but then the words came. "Yes, master."

Daniel judged him ready, and with those magnificent fangs, tore a hunk of flesh from his wrist and spit it to the ground. He held his wrist over Chad's limp form and let the blood, his unique, precious blood, flow from his body into the new vampire's. It didn't take long for Chad's need to overcome his weakness. He pulled himself up through sheer force of will and attached himself to Daniel's wrist, drawing hard on the flesh. After what seemed an eternity, Daniel forcefully detached the fledgling from his arm, and Chad was able to steady himself enough to stand.

I thought about stepping back because Daniel was no longer holding the fledgling. Yet now Chad seemed steadier, more in control. What the Council achieved with months of force-fed ancient blood, Daniel had done with two minutes of himself.

"Welcome to the night, Chad," Daniel said quietly. "I am your master, but I will never force myself on you. In return, if I find you've forced yourself on someone else, I'll be your executioner. I require your loyalty, but offer my protection from all that would harm you. Do you understand?"

"I do." Chad took a long, steadying breath.

"You hungry?" Daniel asked, but it was my Danny's voice again, just a hint of teasing behind his words.

"So fucking hungry," Chad replied, but he made no move to acquire his meal.

Daniel motioned, and Neil dropped my hand, walking forward. Neil winked back and smiled. There was no fear in his eyes, just a hot anticipation.

Daniel placed a hand on Neil's shoulder. "Chad, this is my servant. He has agreed to feed your hungers this night. You need blood and you need sex. If the turn has changed your preferences, tell me now and I'll find you a female."

Chad shook his head, his eyes on Neil. "No. I'm happy with Neil."

"Chad, if my servant is damaged, I'll be angry."

"I understand."

Neil rolled his eyes at Daniel but looked at Chad with a welcoming smile. "I'm hard to damage, honey. You don't listen to him. You do your worst. I promise I'll like it."

Neil took his hand and started back into the house. They walked by and before they managed to open the door, they were kissing, eating each other's mouths, hands finding new places.

Daniel fell to the ground, exhausted by his efforts. His chest heaved as he tried to calm his own emotions and relax. I'd just witnessed the birth of a new vampire. It had been a brutal and powerful experience. It deserved the quiet contemplation Daniel was giving it.

I'm not a contemplative girl. All I knew was the whole ritual thingie was over, and we could fight again because Chad's turn had interrupted a very important ass kicking.

I walked over to my prone husband and straddled his waist, falling to my knees so I was over him. He looked up and his hands went to my waist. A slow, sexy smile crossed his face, telling me he completely misunderstood my intentions. I made them clear by using my thumb and middle finger to thunk him strongly on the forehead.

"You're a dumbass." It was so obvious.

He'd just performed a ritual that was sacred to the Council. If they found out, he would be declared an outlaw and hunted. It was more than Daniel's life on the line. If Daniel was declared an outlaw, I would be sold to the highest bidder, Neil would be without protection and at the mercy of his temporarily castrated father, who probably wasn't in a good mood. And Dev, well, Dev would be righteously killed. Then there was the question of a bunch of baby vamps Daniel had apparently decided to lead into I didn't know what. I had questions, and he was damn sure going to answer them.

"Oww," Daniel said, rubbing his head. He flipped me over and my back was hitting the ground as he loomed over me. "I know, Zoey. You don't have to point it out. I've had a rough night. I need a drink."

He got up but not before hauling me along with him. He stalked off toward the kitchen, leaving me no choice but to follow.

Daniel was opening a bottle he pulled from the refrigerator. He always kept a supply of blood at my place. It wasn't mine since he had gone through his stash a couple of nights ago.

"Neil's?" I asked, wondering who else had been donating. I wasn't jealous or anything. I really wasn't. I sat down, ready to talk.

He laughed as he placed the thermos in the microwave, setting the timer. There's a reason blood should be at the proper temperature. It tends to coagulate otherwise, and that's just gross. Daniel pulled a shot glass out of a cabinet and set it down on the table. He poured a shot from the warm thermos and drank it back like we used to shoot tequila when he was alive.

He sighed and poured another, quickly downing it. "That's the stuff. I have no idea whose blood this is, but they drank a shitload of Scotch before they donated. You can buy it at the club. It's strictly black market. Sorry, Z, but I could use a buzz."

"I'm so glad you've found a way to get a little fucked up since you've managed to fuck up all of our lives. Hey, before the Council cuts off your head, do you think they'll let you have a little O pos with vodka?"

Daniel took another shot. "Just ask your questions, Zoey. I promise I'll answer truthfully."

I felt the smallest amount of sympathy for him. His blue eyes were tired, and though his face hadn't changed in six years, for some reason tonight he looked older. I decided to start with the simplest question. "How did you know Chad was a vamp?"

"You mean beyond the fact that he was obviously gay but couldn't resist you?"

"Yes, beyond that." He would definitely have to do better.

He sighed. "Fine. You know how I can feel when a new vampire rises?"

Somehow Daniel could feel the moment when a human began the transition to vampire. He could sense it and where it was happening. It gave the Council time to intervene before the vampire started destroying everything around it. It was a very rare talent and it had kept Daniel alive according to Marcus. "Yes, but I thought you could feel it at the moment of death, not before."

"When I was hauled back to Paris earlier this year, some of the Council members had certain experiments they wanted to try on me. The last king who rose was able to sense latent vampires. Even though the vampire walks and talks in a human body, there are subtle differences. So they wanted to test me. You see the DNA, like all DNA, runs in families, but it skips around a lot. The Council keeps genealogical records that would make the Mormons look like amateurs. Thousands of years of family records from each vampire and still they can't tell who will rise and who will just rot."

Daniel paused, and I knew we were going to get to the nasty part of his tale. "What did you have to do, Danny?"

Another shot and the talking seemed to get easier. "Fuckers brought in a hundred men from all over the globe. They just took them off the street, away from their families and their lives, all because they had the misfortune of being the direct descendants of vampires. They told me to find a latent vampire, one they could turn while he was vital to swell our ranks, to regain our power. I couldn't. So they killed them all and brought in another hundred. This time there was one guy, a guy from Greece. He had two kids. He cried anytime I got near him, but he was different. I can't put my finger on it, but I knew."

"Did they make you kill him?"

"Oh, yes, Zoey. He's why I strongly advocate strangulation," Danny said with a bitter laugh. "He rose and the Council took him. Obviously they just had me kill him, not take him through the actual turn. He doesn't care about his kids anymore. He was the only one I could find, and they killed the rest. I guess there was press about the missing people, so they stopped. I'm supposed to investigate the names they send me and, if I find one, send him to the Council."

The implications chilled me to the bone. "They're building an army."

"Yes."

I shook my head, more than a little confused. "They let you keep Justin?"

"They don't know about Justin, Z. They don't know about William or James or Jean-Marc or Bryan. Now they don't know about Chad. Luckily I'm the only one left who can feel when a vampire rises. I have Marcus to thank for that." Daniel poured another shot. I wondered how I was going to get a drunken, two hundred twenty pound vampire to bed because he looked like he was shooting for pass-out drunk.

"So you found all these guys and they just let you kill them?"

Danny shrugged a little. "You don't understand what it's like, Z. Chad could explain it better. I never met a vamp when I was alive. Something inside Chad recognized me. The vampire part of me called to the same part of him."

"That sounds a little hot," I joked.

Blue eyes rolled, but he smiled at me. "I don't know if it's because I'm stronger than other vamps, but I don't have much trouble convincing them. That sounds horrible. I'm convincing them to die, but if I don't the Council will figure out something else. I need them, Z."

And those men would likely have lived out their lives and been put down by the Council when they turned during their old age. Daniel had offered them their birthright. I couldn't complain. The way I understood it, persuasion didn't work on latent vampires.

I looked for the problem with the scenario. It didn't take me long. Just because no one else could feel when a new vamp rose didn't make him safe. "They trust you? That doesn't sound like the Council, Danny. They have to have someone watching you."

Danny giggled. There's no other word for the sound. Yep, the liquor was working. "They absolutely have a spy. He sends in a report every week on my activities and has ever since I came home. He's been writing his little reports for almost three years. You wouldn't believe the file he has on me. They think they're so smart. He made his oath to me six months ago. I approve every report he sends out."

There was only one vampire it could be. "Michael."

Daniel nodded. "Yes. And Alexander knows. He doesn't know about all of it, but he knows enough. He's more afraid of me than he is the Council. Michael was willing. He came to me. Marcus came to me."

I caught my breath. Marcus was a Council member, one of the oldest vampires walking the Earth. "Marcus Vorenus made a blood oath to serve you?"

"Yes," Danny said quietly. "He's not as bad as you think, Z. He's been a good mentor. He doesn't want the Council to succeed any more than I do. They've waited centuries for their weapon. They learned their lesson with the last king to rise. They had a plan this time. My training was unique. It was developed to completely break my spirit, to make me a vessel for their will. Most vampires are trained for no more than a year, but they kept me for three. They would have kept me longer if Marcus hadn't taught me how to fool them. He taught me to act the part. I have to appear to be what they need. I'm the weapon they'll use to subjugate the other races, to build our ranks, to make the Earth plane our feeding ground."

The room was silent. I thought about what Felicity had said earlier. If Daniel hadn't come to me that night, their plan might have worked. The Council wanted to upset the balance, and the only thing that stood in their way was Daniel. He took another shot and now his hand was unsteady. I reached out and covered it with my own. He sighed and turned it over, weaving our fingers together. He was so alone.

While the rest of us were living our lives, he was planning a war.

"I'm going to have to sacrifice one of them, Z." His hand tightened around mine. "They're pressing me. It's been months since I started this project, and so far I've delivered nothing. I can't have them getting suspicious. It would out me and Michael and all of us. I'm going to have to send one of them to the Council. I'm not ready to start a war yet. I would lose."

A fierce practicality came over me. "Then you'll pick the strongest, and he'll be our spy."

Daniel nodded. "I believe my blood will hold. I don't think they will be able to turn him if he's strong."

"Promise me something, Danny." Rage and fear curled in my gut, fighting for precedence.

"Anything, baby."

Rage won. "Promise me we're gonna kill them all."

Daniel's smile held not an ounce of humor. "Oh, yeah, baby, we'll kill 'em all."

* * * *

Two hours later, dawn was near. I knew everything now, and I wouldn't sleep a wink knowing what was coming. Daniel, however, didn't have the choice to sit up and worry. I managed to get him to his feet, steering him toward the third bedroom where Daniel stayed when he slept here.

"You don't want to do that, Z." Daniel laughed as if I'd done something hilarious.

There was a whole lot of moaning from behind that door and something that sounded like a howl. He was right. I really didn't want to interrupt that. Unfortunately, Neil and Chad were in the only light-tight room in the house. "Where am I supposed to put you?"

Daniel smiled and raised his eyebrows suggestively. "Baby, I can think of a few places where I would fit just fine."

I rolled my eyes but had to laugh. He always got horny when he was drunk. "There's a body bag in my closet."

It was sad but true. Most girls' closets were full of shoes and sweaters, and I had a body bag.

Daniel protested, but I got him to my room and sat him down on the bed. I pulled out the heavy bag and laid it out on the right side of the bed. It was habit. For years I'd taken the left side and he'd slept on the right. I still slept on the left side. I unzipped the bag and turned back to my husband, who was trying and failing to get out of his shirt. I pulled the soft cotton over his head and kneeled down to work on his jeans. He threaded his hands in my hair and pulled back, forcing my face up. He looked down at me, his face flush with desire. I closed my eyes and let him kiss me, his lips molding mine softly, his tongue seeking entry. It felt like forever since he'd been this close. My skin lit up the minute he touched me.

He groaned as I opened my mouth beneath his and let him fill me. My hands found the hard muscles of his chest, and I couldn't help but remember the last time we'd made love. He pulled me up and pressed me close with one hand as the other started to explore, trailing down my neck toward my breast. Gentle and smooth, Daniel treated me like I was made of glass, precious and fragile. It was so different from the sensations Dev pulled out of me.

I pulled away, pushing against his chest. Daniel dropped his arms and sat back, a hollow look in his eyes.

"I'm sorry. I thought…I don't know why I thought that. I had too much to drink. God, Zoey, I can still smell him on you, but I didn't care."

I sat back against the closet, and didn't even try to stop the tears that came. It was so fucked up. I loved Danny, and I just realized that there was a part of me that was starting to love Dev. Anything I did, any way I went, I hurt someone. Anything I chose would break my heart.

"Don't, baby." Daniel kneeled down and pulled me into a hug, settling me on his lap. "Don't cry. I won't push anything. I won't mention it again. Just don't cry, Zoey." He held me for a while but dawn was coming, and it didn't care that I needed his arms around me. "I have to go to bed, Z. I hate that. I pray every dawn that I'll wake up and I'll turn over and you'll be next to me. I'll tell you about the really crazy-ass dream I had and we'll laugh. I'll get up and go to class, and we'll graduate and get married. We'll have kids and yell at 'em and cry when they leave home. We'll spoil our grandkids, and we'll be happy."

I thought about it all the time. I dreamed the same dreams. My head rested against his chest. "It's a nice thought, Danny."

"It's a comforting lie. I'm never gonna wake up."

He kissed my forehead and lay down in the dark, heavy plastic that would protect him from the sun. I forced myself up.

"That life is dead, Danny. It's gone," I whispered as I started to zip up the bag. "Until we let it go, we can't move on. We have to find a way to move on."

He nodded, but I could see the dawn stealing his strength, his life. His eyes were closing. "I love you, Zoey."

And then he was dead until the night came again. I leaned over and kissed his lips while they were still warm. "I love you, too, Danny," I breathed against his skin.

I zipped him up the rest of the way and prepared for bed. I climbed in next to my husband. I laid my head against the cold bag and let my arms wrap around him. It was the longest time before I managed to sleep.

Chapter Eleven

"OMG," Neil said from the back of the van. "Then we decided to go to the lake, and you won't believe what we did there."

I would. I could take a big old guess. It involved various sexual practices that Neil was going to go into way too much detail about. Apparently in the last week, Neil and Chad had decided to reenact the entire *Kama Sutra*, gay supernatural edition, in various semi-public places. And Neil liked to chat. He'd been chatting for the last five hundred miles.

"Should I tell your gay husband a few tales, sweetheart?" Dev asked from the passenger seat. He didn't actually look at me. He was laid out as languidly as he could stretch his long, lean body in the confinement of the van. He wore jeans in deference to our cover story, his glorious eyes covered by a pair of aviators, and his lips curled into a wry smile.

Since that night when he'd driven his demons out, I saw him differently and it hurt. Loving Dev made him even more beautiful. Maybe I could have handled it if loving him had cut one centimeter of Daniel from my heart, but it hadn't. My heart had an enormous capacity for disaster.

"You should keep your mouth shut around my gay husband if you ever want to do any of those things again." Our little road trip was turning into a game. Who could make the human blush the fastest? So far Neil was leading by a mile, but only because Dev had kept his mouth shut to this point.

Dev turned to me and gave me a look that made more than my heart race. "I haven't had sex in this state. I really want to be able to check that off so I'll hold my tongue, unless you'd like to hold it for me."

"I totally am!" Neil exclaimed. "I'm your gay husband. Does that mean we're involved in a four-way? Or would it be five if we count Chad?"

"We are involved in a no-way." The last thing I needed was more men in my love life.

We'd been on the road since the ungodly hour of seven a.m. Sure, that's when most of the world is heading off to work, but I was nocturnal. My husband was a vampire so no daytime there, and my lover owned a nightclub. Dev wasn't a morning person either. I slanted a curious look at my boyfriend. "Just how many states have you had sex in?"

He thought for a moment, tallying some ungodly number in his head. "Forty-two. But I've done it on all the Hawaiian Islands, and that should count for something."

"Did you and your girlfriend take a tour or something?" It was the first time he'd mentioned any other woman. As the current girlfriend, I was naturally curious about the women who came before me.

Neil erupted in fits of hysterical laughter. I turned briefly to watch him lean back against his dead boyfriend's body bag. We'd bought the van with cash thanks to our lovely two million, which I absolutely rolled around in before putting it in my safe. It was already a good buy. It was perfect for lugging around vampires in body bags. Unfortunately we'd had to take out all the rear seats because we were also carrying our equipment, which included computers, night vision goggles, some really cool motion detectors and, of course, a complete traveling arsenal. I drove five miles below the damn speed limit the entire way because I didn't think highway patrol would appreciate any excuse I came up with for the guns and dead bodies.

Neil continued his laughter, but Dev merely smiled knowingly.

"What?" I was not in on the joke.

"It's the thought of Dev having a girlfriend," Neil said, finally calming down. "You have no idea what his reputation is."

"Was," Dev corrected quickly. "What my reputation was."

"He was a total manwhore." Neil settled against the sleeping body again. Chad was smaller than Daniel, so we managed to spread him out a little. Daniel, we'd had to kind of cram in, and then we needed some place to put the luggage.

"Manwhore?" I kept my eyes on the road. I wasn't familiar with the phrase, but it didn't sound like a good way to refer to one's boyfriend.

Dev sighed. "Yeah, I guess that would work. Forty-two states, forty-two different women, and like I said, six in Hawaii alone. I don't apologize for my past, sweetheart. I'm part fertility god. It goes with the territory."

"Wow." I couldn't compete with his breadth of experience, and he knew it. Dev and I had gone over my sexual history, which before him had included only one other man, and he was currently zipped into his daytime coffin.

"Sorry, Zoey." Dev took off the sunglasses, his emerald eyes fixed on me. "I thought you knew. I wasn't real big into exclusivity. When I left the *sithein*, I enjoyed the human world for a while. I also enjoyed several werewolves, a couple of shifters, and some of the more exotic creatures on this plane. I was just having fun."

"Finding monogamy difficult?" I was more than a little intimidated at that recitation. I knew Dev's little black book was probably bigger than mine, I just hadn't realized it resembled a phone book. The culture he grew up in was different, but maybe I should have put a little more thought into it before I'd jumped into bed. Faeries are very sexual creatures and Dev more so than most given his unique ancestry. It might have been naïve on my part to think one woman, and an inexperienced one at that, could keep him satisfied.

"Not at all," he replied intensely. "I told you a long time ago I would give you what you need. You need commitment. I haven't slept with anyone but you since we met. I have no intentions to."

Neil had fallen silent, probably in the belief that the minute I remembered he was there, I would put the kibosh on the entire discussion. He seriously underestimated my need to keep Dev talking. Besides, he was my gay husband, and I'd end up telling him everything later on anyway.

I stepped on the gas as we entered the rolling foothills of the Ozarks. The trees were a canvas of oranges, reds, and browns. The scenery was beautiful, and I didn't really care about a bit of it.

"What if I didn't need commitment?" I needed to set that

pothole to see if he would fall in.

His eyes became suspicious slits. “Then I would figure out what it is you do need, and I would give it to you. I still would have no intentions of sleeping with other women. I’m content where I sleep now. I don’t need a ton of women, Zoey. I just need the right one.”

My hands tightened on the steering wheel. I was happy neither of the boys had wanted to drive. The fact that I had something to stare at was very helpful. “And you treated all your former girlfriends with such kindness?”

Dev grimaced and his hand played with the five-o’clock shadow on his face. He’d started the day clean shaven, but the hours had pulled that sexy beard out of his skin. I loved it. He hated it because it proved him less a Fae than he would like to be. “See, you keep putting an ‘s’ on the end of the word girlfriend. You are trying to be jealous of women who never existed. I slept with a lot of women, but I didn’t have relationships with them. They were fun and I like to think I pleased them, but I never had any intention of permanence with them. Let me make this plain. In the six years since I left the *sithein*, I’ve had exactly one girlfriend. Her name is Zoey, and right now she is being a pain in my ass.”

I smiled and chose to continue to watch the road. I knew what his expression looked like. It would be that slightly put-out look he got any time I tried to get him to talk about his past. Well, he better get used to it because we were about to spend a lot of time together. I intended to find out a few things. There was a voice in the back of my head sending out a warning. This was why you didn’t sleep with the people you worked with. This was why you tried to keep those relationships on a business level. My father’s best friend had been George Donovan, Daniel’s father, and a master thief. Dad didn’t work with George. I wasn’t following my father’s sound advice.

“You need to take this exit.” Neil looked down at the road atlas. After we bought our trusty new van, Daniel had made sure any identifying marks, including the GPS that came with many new cars, were wiped out. We lived off the grid, and when the grid tried to encroach, we were pretty ruthless about beating it back.

It was another hour until we reached our destination. I pulled the van into the small cemetery we’d found. I spent much of the last week trying to plan a tight heist. I was thwarted by the fact that, while Felicity knew who had the Revelation, she wasn't sure where it was being kept. For someone who, at least according to legend was all-seeing, she really didn't know shit. What we did know was that the Revelation was held by one Mary Jo Renfro. She was the owner and operator of the Hideawhile Bideawhile Bed and Breakfast, situated in a very remote section of the Ozarks. There was next to nothing out here, and that B&B was the only place to stay for thirty miles. They specialized in honeymoons. We came to the conclusion that me, my husband, my lover, my gay husband, and his boyfriend would probably stand out if we decided to ask for a group rate.

It's always easier to have truly excellent intelligence. More likely than not the intelligence a client gathers is crap at best, complete lies at worst. There's a reason the client is paying top dollar for services. If the item was easy to steal, the client would more than likely steal it for themselves and save on my rates. In some cases, there's information the client would prefer to keep to themselves. This usually ends in me having to think on my feet. In my line of work, you have to be flexible and you have to do your due diligence. Daniel, while pressing firmly for all due diligence in our collection of information, was not happy about the flexibility required to do so.

Mary Jo Renfro, owner of above mentioned B&B, also owned a small farm four miles north of her business. It was off the beaten track and therefore a fairly decent place to hide one's valuables. The Revelation had to be in either the B&B or on the farm. It was perfectly logical to split our resources in order to pin down the location of the item. The question then had been who would go where? It made sense that Dev and I would book a room, and Daniel, Neil, and Chad would check out the farm. Reason dictated that Dev and I made the only believable newlywed couple as Daniel couldn't be seen during the day, same thing with Chad, and Neil was hopelessly, helplessly incapable of looking like he wanted to sleep with me.

While all of this was the reasonable conclusion, it didn't make my husband a happy man.

His accommodations for the duration of the job weren't going to put him in a better mood. The cemetery was a small place with no more than fifty headstones, all of them from the turn of the century.

There were two small mausoleums, each etched with the name of what I suspected would be some local family of note. The cemetery had fallen into disuse and disrepair. It was far enough away from everything that I was sure visitations, even for artistic purposes, were rare. It was exactly what we needed. It would provide adequate cover for our vamps during the daylight hours. That didn't mean Daniel would be happy about sleeping in a graveyard, especially while Dev was sleeping in a heart-shaped bed with me.

I parked the car near the larger of the mausoleums, and Dev and Neil immediately got out to stretch. There was a second car parked behind the smaller building, and I silently thanked Daniel's friend Nathan, who had driven the car up here two days earlier. Newlyweds seldom drove minivans. The sedan was just another layer of cover. Dev and I still had to drive a couple of miles north to make it to the B&B, but I wanted to make sure the boys were settled in before we left. We didn't have long to wait as the sun was going down even as I parked the car.

"Zoey!"

I got out of the car and slid the side door open. Daniel was awake, and he really wanted out of that damn bag. Neil saw me and went to the other side of the van to wake Chad.

"I'm flying next time." Daniel growled as he shoved the luggage off his legs and scrambled out of the car. When Danny mentioned flying, he wasn't talking about the type of flight that involved deciding between coach and first class. He could fly all on his own. "Where's your boyfriend?" He snarled the question.

It was right then that I remembered Daniel could listen in on daytime conversations when he wanted to. It was an easy thing to forget because he looked really, really dead during the day. He'd only mentioned it once, and that was a long time ago. My earlier conversation with Dev came back to haunt me.

"We need to get out of here, Danny." I tried to reason with the jealous, pissed-off vampire. "We need to check in and get settled so we can look for the package tomorrow." I mentioned business in the hopes that Daniel's professional side might come out.

"Quinn!" Daniel yelled as he planted his feet solidly on the cemetery ground.

There wasn't even a small part of me that thought Dev would

take that as a smart-man's cue to run. He wasn't that guy. He was the guy who walked straight up to the angry vampire and smiled. "Hey, Dan, nice ride?"

"You motherfucker," Daniel spat, invading as much of Dev's space as he possibly could. "I swear to god, if she gets sick I'll kill you."

Dev dropped the arrogance, his brows coming up in a look of complete confusion. "What the hell are you talking about, Donovan?"

"I'm talking about you being a walking, talking venereal disease," Daniel snapped. "I'm talking about you sticking your dick into anything that moves."

"Whoa, slow down there." Dev always gave as good as he got. His face flushed with anger. "I'm a fucking faery. I might not be full blooded, but I've never so much as had a cold, you idiot."

"I don't like my wife being one of hundreds." Daniel continued to try to back Dev into a corner, which in the cemetery consisted of the mausoleum.

"I don't like my girlfriend needing a fucking blood transfusion every time she has to be in the same room as her vampire husband. Do you like draining her, Daniel? 'Cause you seem to do it on a semi-regular basis."

"Hey!" I yelled, trying to bring some reason to the situation, but Dev was plowing through, apparently thrilled at the chance to get some stuff off his chest.

"While we're talking about it," Dev said with an arrogant smile on his face, "I'll put your mind at ease. I wear a condom when I screw your wife. Not because I'm worried about contracting anything. I know how sweet Zoey is. I would never hurt her, so until we decide to make a baby, I'll wear a condom. You might be shooting blanks, man, but I assure you I am not. When she's ready to get pregnant, I'll fill her right up."

I groaned because Dev really had Danny's number. There wasn't a single more hurtful thing he could have said. It wasn't surprising when Daniel roared, picked up Dev by his shirt, and tossed him across the cemetery. My green-eyed boy flew about a hundred feet before a tree stopped his progress. He landed with a thud but, dipshit that he was, he got right back up, shaking off bits of bark.

"That the worst a vampire king can do?" Dev sneered. "I've been in better bar fights."

Chad moved toward Daniel. I prayed he wasn't going to protect his master by taking out Dev.

Neil stopped him as quickly as he could. "What are you doing?"

"Stopping the fight," Chad replied as though it were a foregone conclusion.

Neil shook his head as though Chad really was naïve. "You want to stop two really hot guys from putting their hands all over each other and maybe getting a little bloody and ripping some clothes off in the confusion?"

Chad stopped and smiled devilishly, proving that even blood-oathed vampires had priorities. "Put like that it seems like a stupid thing to do."

I wasn't getting any help from the gay guy contingent.

Daniel stalked his prey, fangs gleaming in the evening gloom. This had to stop. Danny could kill Dev without even thinking about it. I started to run up behind him, fully ready to plead for my dumbass boyfriend's life, when I was knocked to the ground, my hands grabbing at dirt. I rolled out of the way, instinct taking over. I was surprised to see I'd tripped over some really thick vines that seemed to have a life of their own. The vines moved like snakes, winding this way and that. When I looked up, Dev was on his feet, his hands to the side, fingers spread wide. The thick vines were stalking their prey even as Daniel made his way to Dev. The vines were shiny and green, like new spring plants, but it was almost winter.

"I will kill you if you knock her up," Daniel said. "Fuck any deal we had, Dev. She's not one of your baby mamas, and I'm sure with the life you've led, you have plenty."

"I don't have any children in this world. Like I said, I take care of my lover." Dev was letting Daniel get really close. "I don't put her in the hospital."

Daniel stopped. "This world? How many kids did you leave behind in Faery when you decided to fuck half the Western world?"

I got to my feet because I was interested in that discussion. It was, however, a conversation that should be happening between me and Dev, not aired for all our crew to enjoy. "The two of you need to stop it."

Then Daniel was the one on the ground, his powerful legs tangled in a flurry of vines and shiny weeds. They wound themselves around his body, starting at his legs but were more than happy to envelope every inch of him. They came from everywhere, springing from the dead ground to hold their master's prey tightly to the dirt.

Daniel struggled against the tide, but there were too many of them. This was often the way Dev's magic went, utterly wild. Daniel couldn't have picked a worse place to have it out with his rival. The woods around the cemetery were thick with plants waiting for a part fertility god to bring to life and command.

That burst of spring in the winter started to pull Daniel underground. He punched through the vines but more came to pull him back in. I saw a clawed hand attempt to rip through his bindings, trying to clutch the ground as he began to go under. It was like the earth was dragging him down, and I'd had enough.

"Stop it, Dev. You've made your point." My hands shook. The last thing I needed was a pissing contest.

Dev's hair was wild, and that perfect male-model image he went for had been ruined to the point that he looked brutal. I'd seen Dev fight before and knew he was more than competent, but now I realized he was just as capable as Daniel of loving the kill. Dev just hid it better.

"I'm serious, Dev," I shouted.

Daniel was completely underground, every trace of him erased by creeping vines. It was too much like a grave, and the thought of Daniel in it gave me the chills. Dev finally dropped his hands and walked to me. There was no tenderness in his eyes as he took my hand and started to pull me away.

"Let's go," he growled. "Wouldn't want to miss cocktail hour."

"Daniel." I turned back to where I had seen him last.

"He's a big boy. He'll manage."

The ground quaked as Daniel "managed." He burst from the earth sending dirt and plants flying in all directions. Dev instinctively pulled me close and covered my head with his arms. Daniel flew up and was back on his feet, not caring to brush the dirt from him before he was coming for Dev again.

"You, get in the car," I ordered Dev.

"Sure thing, boss," he replied, sarcasm dripping.

Daniel pointed our way. "Not on your life, Quinn. We finish this."

"Can't," Dev said in a calm tone that would drive Daniel crazy because he wanted a fight. "My girlfriend says I'm not allowed to fight."

"You're gonna listen to her?" Daniel taunted. "You're pathetic."

Dev shrugged as he backed up. "Hey, I might be pussy whipped, but at least I got some pussy. Come to think of it, I got your pussy, buddy."

Dev had the good sense to duck as the several hundred pounds of marble headstone flew at his head. He flipped Daniel the bird as he got into the sedan and started it up.

"Nice, Danny." What a way to start a job. "I swear if the two of you fuck up this job, I'll leave you both. I'll move to a new city, and I'll find a new crew."

"I'm trying to protect you," Daniel argued.

I shook my head, not willing to go into it with him. Protecting me was Daniel's excuse for everything. He stayed away to protect me. He left me behind to protect me. He lied to me to protect me. Now he tried to start World War III with Dev because it would protect me. I didn't want to hear it.

And, to top it all off, Dev hadn't bothered with the luggage. He was far too busy revving the engine to help me out. Chad came over and was kind enough to lift the two suitcases Dev and I had brought. He carried them to the car and tapped the back. Dev was gracious enough to hit the button that released the trunk, and Chad slid the luggage in.

"Don't be too hard on him," Chad said quietly.

"Which one?" I had to ask because I was thinking about throttling them both.

"Daniel," Chad clarified. "I was listening in, too. I think Daniel is figuring out what the rest of us already knew."

"And what's that?"

"Dev isn't some fling. It might have started out that way, but you're not the kind of girl who can be that intimate with a man and not have her heart get involved. Daniel is waiting for you to get Dev out of your system and come back to him. He's starting to realize he could lose you. I don't think he's going to handle that well."

I shook my head. Chad had seen an awful lot in a single week. "I can't deal with that right now. I have to go. We're on a deadline. We have to be in Vegas next week, and if I don't have the Revelation, I can't even try to rescue Sarah. We're never going to get a better shot at this."

"He'll be fine." Chad was along on this endeavor because Daniel wouldn't leave the fledgling alone. He was too young to be trusted, but Chad was proving to be stronger than all expectations. "Just keep him and Dev apart, and we'll get through it. I've been told I get to hunt in something called 'the old ways' tonight. I think that involves some form of cattle. Why I have to drain some poor unsuspecting cow when my little piece of hotness over there tastes so good, I have no idea."

"Zoey, let's go!" Dev yelled out the window.

I rolled my eyes. Chad smiled sympathetically. "You know, I used to envy you with your two superhot guys."

"It's not all it's cracked up to be."

Chapter Twelve

"Welcome, Mr. and Mrs. O'Malley," Mary Jo Renfro greeted as Dev and I entered some form of pastel hell.

The Hideawhile Bideawhile Bed and Breakfast was a rambling Victorian with a large porch and vaulted ceilings. It was also painted pink. The lawn was a meticulously groomed piece of green surrounded by the wild Ozarks. Unfortunately, the lovely lawn was covered in statuary one can only find at the finest of home improvement stores and probably a local Walmart. There were several Venuses, countless cherubs and angels, and I spotted a couple of well-placed garden gnomes. I'd hoped the inside would be better, but I was disappointed.

Our proprietor, and unknowing mark, was a small woman in a long khaki skirt and a fussy button-down shirt. She wore comfortable shoes, and her non-descript brown hair was in a ponytail. I noticed her necklace, a silver angel. It was a theme of the B&B. Little angel statues littered every available space. I especially liked the ones where a giant angel loomed lovingly over a small town. I'm sure the purpose was to show the angel protecting her charges, but I just wanted the angel to start stomping out the little town like a big old heavenly Godzilla.

"We're so happy you made it," Mary Jo was saying. "We were getting a little worried about the two of you. We didn't want you to miss our little cocktail hour."

Dev smiled, a smooth expression guaranteed to melt the heart of any female within a hundred yards of that high-wattage charm. "We're thrilled to be here, Mrs. Renfro."

Mrs. Renfro actually giggled. "Oh my, you're an exceptionally attractive man, Mr. O'Malley. You should make quite the splash in our little community. All the girls will just be swooning."

Dev slung his arm over my shoulder and pulled me close. "Unfortunately, I'm off the market. My lovely wife and I just got married. I'm afraid I only have eyes for her. You know how newlyweds are."

"I do, indeed." Her voice had a girlish affectation to it. "You're a lucky woman, Mrs. O'Malley, to have snagged such a handsome man."

She gave me a once-over, obviously wondering exactly what I had done to deserve him since I wasn't in his league.

Dev was the lucky one because he was still alive. I thought several times about murdering him during our brief car ride. He'd been sullen and silent throughout the trip, refusing to answer my questions. When I'd ask about the possibility of children left behind in his *sithein*, I'd been told to mind my own damn business. I really couldn't wait to get to our room so I could let my boyfriend know exactly what my damn business was.

"I am lucky. It took a lot to get this one pinned down, let me tell you." It hadn't. I'd managed to pin him down the first night we were together, and he'd been happy to do it. I sighed with what I hoped was a look of longing. "I think we'll skip the social hour tonight, Mrs. Renfro. You understand, right?"

We were supposed to be newlyweds after all. It was supposed to be our first night of wedded bliss.

"Now, honey," Dev replied. "We don't want to be antisocial. We've waited this long. We can wait a few more hours."

I quietly brought my entire body weight down on his big toe. I was rewarded with a muffled groan. Dev had never waited for anything in his life. I especially didn't like the fact that our hostess was now looking at me like I was a sex-crazed maniac, and Dev was some poor man at my mercy. Dev was going to find out later tonight that I didn't have any mercy.

An elderly man took our bags while Dev signed us in, and then we were shown into the parlor where cocktails were being served from a small tray. The backwoods version of cocktails was a little different than what Dev and I were used to.

"Where's the vodka?" I whispered as I looked around the room. This was supposed to be a place frequented by honeymooners. Dev and I were easily the youngest people in the room by forty years.

"I don't know," he whispered back.

"Let me introduce you." Mary Jo pressed a tiny glass of something that vaguely resembled wine into my hand. "Sherry. It's your honeymoon. Live a little."

As pissed as I was at Dev, I smiled up at him because this was a story we would tell for a very long time. He graciously took his tiny glass and let his free hand cup my waist. We were introduced to three other couples. The Milmans, the Ruckers, and the Bells. Dev smoothly managed to mingle, putting everyone at ease. It wasn't long before we were seated for dinner, and Dev had all eyes on him. It was where he felt most comfortable. As I watched him converse with the older couples and our host, I was struck by how polished he was. Sometimes it was easy to see that he was the son of a queen. I rarely thought about it, but Dev's upbringing more than likely consisted of a lot of training in courtly practices. I spent enough time with Fae creatures to know a little about their culture. Royalty in the faery world kicked it old school. There was no democracy. The queen's power would be absolute, until someone killed her or she gave her throne to one of her children. I wondered if Dev was the oldest. Had he been promised a throne only to have it taken away when they discovered his mortality?

"How many children are you planning?" the blue-haired woman I thought was the new Mrs. Bell asked. She and Mr. Bell had recently married after her husband of thirty years had kicked the bucket last spring. It hadn't taken me long to realize this place was popular among the geriatric honeymoon set. They might have mentioned that on their website.

"Oh, now, Mrs. Bell," Dev replied, his voice all teasing seduction. I rolled my eyes as several of the women actually sighed. "That's the kind of thing that sorts itself out. My wife and I will be willing to accept any babies we're blessed with."

"But don't you think we should talk about any possible kiddos?" He needed to know this conversation wasn't finished. "It's too important to just leave it up to fate."

Mary Jo Renfro vigorously disagreed with me. "You just have to have faith, Mrs. O'Malley. You have to trust in God. He knows best. I've been blessed with four little ones, each a gift. I'm sure you and your husband will have beautiful babies."

I was still wondering if my "husband" already had beautiful babies. Dev swiftly moved the conversation to a thrilling recitation of Mr. Rucker's passing of a kidney stone. I glared at Dev the rest of the meal.

* * * *

We finally made it to the "Seraphim Suite" a few hours later. It was a monstrosity of love. The bed really was a heart completely decked out in ruffles and more pillows than any two people could ever use. The evening had been a complete bust with the exception of planting a few bugs that I was pretty sure would only catch more of Mr. Rucker's health horror stories. I was tired, having driven all day, so my plan was to get some sleep and start snooping tomorrow.

After I settled one little issue.

Dev stretched out on the frilly bed. He looked out of place in this room. I couldn't help but think of his condo. That was Dev's natural habitat. The mixture of nature and the sleek lines of the city perfectly defined Dev. He looked silly surrounded by ruffles and lace. He turned on one side and rested his head in his hand. He patted the bed beside him and gave me that smile. It was the one he had when he knew he was getting some.

"No." I turned away and started shoving clothes in the ornate dresser.

"What is that supposed to mean?" He asked the question as though no woman in his life had ever said no to him when he was trying to seduce her. It was a viable possibility.

"It means that I'm not sleeping with a man who thinks his children are none of my business." I pulled off my sweater and jeans and exchanged them for sweat pants and a tank top.

"Zoey," came that silky smooth voice as he walked up behind me. His arms surrounded me, and he pulled me back against him, letting me feel every bit of what he was offering. It was a substantial offering. "This is a stupid fight. This is exactly what Daniel wanted to happen. Come to bed and we can play a game. You can be the reluctant virgin bride, and I'll teach you everything you need to know, sweetheart."

It would be so easy to let him pick me up and toss me down and envelop me in his unique magic, but I was falling in love with the man. I couldn't risk my heart on a man who just wanted me in bed and not in any other part of his life. "No, Dev. You can either open up and talk, or we can spend a nice evening sleeping with no touchy touchy."

"I don't take well to ultimatums, darling," Dev replied, his voice harder than I'd ever heard it. "I wish you a good night's sleep." He undressed, sparing me not a moment of his breathtaking body. He slid under the covers and turned away from me. "Now I know why Daniel's pissed off all the time. Being married to you really cramps a person's sex life."

He managed to get to sleep, but I couldn't force myself to get into bed. I knew what would happen. I would end up cuddling with him, and I didn't want that right now. I wanted to keep my righteous indignation fully stoked.

An hour passed and then two, and I decided it was time to get a little work done. It was past midnight. I doubted the other three couples were real big into the nightlife. I got my story straight. If I got caught, I was searching for the kitchen because I needed a glass of water in order to take my medication. Surely this crowd understood the importance of medication. I just intended to get really turned around.

I slipped thick socks on my feet because it was cold, and for the same reason added a sweater. I was careful about not waking Dev as I slipped quietly into the hallway.

There are a couple of necessary skills to perfect when your chosen profession is thievery. The ability to move silently is right up there at the top along with a certain moral flexibility and the patience to put up with wearing a lot of black. While other fathers tossed a baseball with their kids or carted them to dance class, my dad taught me his profession. I learned to walk almost silently a long time ago, and the skill came in handy this night. I shut the door behind me and stuck as close to the wall as I could. Unfortunately, the floors were wood. Carpet or anything with a pad is best at covering sound. When you find yourself dealing with hardwood, your best bet is staying near the wall. This minimizes creaks and groans. I also had stretched carefully before starting out, paying careful attention to the joints.

You would be surprised how loud an elbow can be when it pops, and if you're cold it just might. It's better to stretch out all the kinks before starting.

There were three rooms on the second story. Dev and I were in the largest. All of the rooms were dark now. I passed by the Ruckers and could hear one of them snoring loudly. The paintings on the walls were all of angels. Mary Jo Renfro was really into angels. It begged the question why Felicity hadn't been able to work her charms on the proprietor. It also gave me an in when it came to engaging the woman in conversation. Once I got someone talking about their favorite subject, they tended to give things away without thinking about it.

I made my way down the stairs, again sticking close to the wall.

I had already seen quite a bit of the first floor. There was a frilly foyer that led into the parlor, where I'd learned I really didn't like all liquor. The dining room was large, with a nice-sized table covered in white lace. Mary Jo had cleaned up. Everything was pin perfect neat. There were two bedrooms on this level, and I would have to find a way to search them tomorrow. There had been talk of a backgammon tournament. It would serve Dev right to have to spend an afternoon playing board games.

Then, there it was, right off the kitchen, a little door. It could have been a little laundry room or maybe a pantry, but I seriously doubted it. This one had a brand new shiny lock. I smiled in the darkness. I really liked locks. They were like big neon signs pointing the way to treasure. A shiny lock was one big X marking the spot.

The light in the kitchen came on, and I whirled around. Maybe I wasn't as good as I thought I was since I hadn't heard anyone at all.

"Oh, it's you, Mrs. O'Malley." Mary Jo wore a long robe that probably covered an old-time nightgown. I wondered where Mr. Renfro was and those four blessed children.

I smiled and held up my hand. "So sorry to get you up. I was just trying to find the kitchen. I forgot to take my antacid. Boy, if I miss one pill, my reflux can be ferocious."

"You should pray about that," she said piously as she got me a glass of water. "Your husband seems like a nice man."

"Yes," I agreed because supposedly I had just married him. I should think he was nice.

She nodded, a glazed look coming over her. "He has a glow about him. I noticed that the moment I saw him. He's a special one."

I swallowed the antacid and passed the glass back to her. It really was an antacid. In my line of work, stomach issues can be a hazard. "This is a really nice place."

Mrs. Renfro smiled as she immediately washed the glass, dried it and put it in its place. "It's my labor of love. My husband lives out on our farm. That's what pays the bills, of course."

"And your kids? Are they on the farm?"

She looked confused briefly, but then her face settled into that passive smile. "Yes, my babies. They live with their father. I get out to the farm at least three times a week."

I took a deep breath because she was just full of creepy goodness. There was nothing in her manner that should have had my crazy-ass bitch meter going wild, but it still was. Then there was the fact that Felicity's information pegged her as a witch. She didn't seem like a witch to me, but I would know more after I got into that little room. "Thanks. I should get back to my husband."

"Of course, dear," she said absently. "Men have their needs. We just have to think of pleasant things while we lie there." She shuffled off and the light went out.

I made my way back up the stairs, not bothering to hide my steps. I had what I needed. I would find a way into that little room and hopefully it would yield up my treasure. It had been a while since I used my trusty lock-pick set, but I was itching to give it a try. I closed the door behind me. When I turned, I had to stifle a scream. There was a shadow hovering right outside my window. I almost woke up Dev when I realized who it was.

I parted the filmy curtains, and Daniel gave me a wave. Seeing Daniel flying was magical to me. He looked so carefree floating outside my window. Though Daniel hadn't aged a day since he was twenty-one, the heavy mantle of responsibility often made him look older. Now he had that mischievous gleam I remembered so well. I turned the handle, and the shutter-like window swung open.

"Zoey," Daniel said softly, holding out his hand. "Come out and play. You gotta see this, baby."

"What?"

Daniel shook his head. "Nope. Seeing is believing. Come on."

I stepped up onto the window seat, and Daniel pulled me into his arms. He cradled me to his chest and then we were flying. I held on for dear life because I'd only done this once before, and I was definitely not used to the sensation. Daniel seemed surer of himself this time. He veered past trees and soared over them. The night wind whipped through my hair, and I managed to open my eyes. I looked up at Daniel. He grinned down at me. I was glad to see he finally understood there was an upside to his undead status.

I relaxed in his arms and let myself enjoy the view. It was cold, but Daniel was warm against me. He must have fed well because I could feel his heart beating, and it only felt that strong when he was full of blood. I suspected that certain tabloid publications would be making their way to this part of the world soon to investigate a rash of bovine exsanguinations.

"Look down, baby," Daniel said in my ear.

We were flying above a field, and I looked down to see several large animals running, their big bodies defined by the moonlight. They ran in a pack and seemed to be playing. I strained to see the details. Daniel floated over to a group of trees and settled himself on the high branches of an enormous oak. He set me down once he found his footing. I leaned forward. It was easy because I knew whatever I did, Daniel would be there if I made a mistake. I stared down on the pack and realized what I was looking at.

Razorbacks. They were enormous. The large pigs were, at the very smallest, a hundred and fifty pounds. The largest was likely two fifty. I counted twelve. Some of the pig were chasing each other, nipping and playing with affection. Then three much smaller pigs came into view. These were obviously babies. They jumped over each other, tumbling and snorting as they played.

"Oh my god, Daniel, are those what I think they are?" My breath caught at the thought.

"Werepigs," he replied. "I saw them earlier tonight. It's a full moon. I thought they were going to chase down Neil and eat him. I've never seen that wolf run so fast. One minute he's sniffing the air talking about how good bacon is gonna taste, and the next his tail is between his legs and he's hiding behind Chad. I had some fast talking to do, baby, or our wolf was going to be serious slop."

"You talked to them?"

He nodded. "I'm glad I ran across them. I've been trying to make inroads with the two-natured. If I'm going to take on the Council, I'll need allies. They don't really know it yet, but it's their war, too. I can bring us together, Z. I can make this work."

"Is that why you've been pairing up stray wolves with your baby vamps?"

Daniel grinned. "Justin told me you found out about that. You scared the hell out him, by the way. When you think about, it makes sense. Neil and I made sense. We're stronger together than we are apart. Angelina's happy. Justin's happy. I don't see the problem."

"I think Neil's dad sees the problem." Daniel was messing with some very long held traditions. Some of the members of the supernatural world would not let go of those customs so easily.

"Yeah, I've been having problems getting the local pack to recognize me. I don't think they'll be coming around anytime soon since you castrated their alpha."

I made no apologies for that. "He's an ass."

"Yes, he is, but if you happen to get pissed off at the local werepanthers, try to contain yourself. I've managed to work out an alliance with their alpha. If you shoot his balls off, it might kill my deal."

"I'll try," I said with a smile. "But I can't promise anything. I have a taste for it now."

Daniel laughed, pulling me close and looking into my eyes. "You are the cherry on top of my crazy cake, you know that, right? I love every crazy-ass inch of you."

"Chad talked to you, didn't he?" I figured the new vamp might be giving his boss advice on the romance front. I was just surprised Daniel listened.

"Chad is a smart guy. He was right. I was stupid to think you were just using Dev to get back at me. And I'll admit I was pretty sure Dev was using you because he likes the adrenaline rush of sleeping with someone forbidden. That wasn't the way he sounded when he talked to you earlier today. He sounded serious. I'm not willing to give you up without a fight, Z. I love you. You're my world. Dev might not be a complete asshole. He might care about you, but Dev will never love you the way I do. I'm going to fight him every inch of the way. I'd say it's working because your little honeymoon suite reeked of sexual frustration tonight, baby."

"That's not something to be proud of, Danny. I have feelings for him. I don't know that it's going to go anywhere. I don't know that I'm anything to him but a good time."

"I stand ready to kill him at your earliest request," Daniel offered with a grin that told me he was happy to hear that news.

I laughed. "Don't you dare."

"Fine," he conceded. "I'm gonna win, Z. We're meant to be together. In the end, I'll win. So heavy relationship discussion over. Do you want to run with the pigs?"

I looked down at the field. They were free and happy. Daniel knew there was nothing I loved more than a crazy experience I could hold in my heart. "Hell, yeah!"

Daniel pulled me back in his arms and flew us down to the field. He let us float to the center and landed gently. I ended up slightly behind him. I stayed where I was because this was where Neil always stood during formalities. I wasn't sure how formal this would get, but I knew Daniel was going to be negotiating with this pack and there were rituals involved. Daniel looked back at me curiously, then pulled me to his side. "You stand beside me. Always."

The pack stopped their run. They all turned toward the interlopers. The largest of the razorbacks came forward and a smaller pig followed behind him. The rest sat back on their haunches, content to watch the action play out. The two pigs that had come forward changed, their forms slipping back into human so smoothly I knew they were unquestionably the alphas.

"Your Highness," the male said. He was naked but I expected that. I was getting used to the two-natureds' liberal views on nudity.

Daniel nodded. "Jasper, this is Zoey Donovan."

"Your mate?" The alpha's eyes slid over me in an assessing manner that had nothing to do with sexual interest and everything to do with politics.

"My queen," Daniel corrected.

Jasper nodded and his female came forth. "This is Hillary, my mate."

Hillary was a larger woman. Her face was set like she expected me to reject someone like her. It wasn't a surprising attitude. Those in the vampire world tended to be arrogant and disdainful of those not. I was going to have to change those attitudes. It was the first time I realized I actually could help Daniel in a capacity that didn't involve blood or sex. I smiled my brightest smile and walked forward with my hand out. "Hello, Hillary. I'm so pleased to meet you. Please call me Zoey."

Hillary's lips curled up, and when she smiled she was quite lovely. "Pleased to meet you, Zoey."

I looked at the little pigs whose tails were shaking with excitement. "Are they yours?"

She looked back, her face glowing with pride. "Two of them. My sons, Bobby and Chris."

"They're adorable," I said, smiling down at the piglets.

Jasper held his arms out. "Your Highness, we can talk about alliances tomorrow. Tonight the moon is full and we run. Your wolf might not be welcome, but your queen is."

I looked back at Daniel, who watched me with a quiet satisfaction. Jasper and Hillary took their forms once more and we ran. I frolicked with the babies, loving the way they licked my face and rolled in the grass. I played in the moonlight with the pack until the sun was almost up. Daniel was content to watch.

When the pack began to move on, Daniel picked me up, and with a nod to the alpha, took off. I leaned my heavy head against his chest, perfectly content with my evening.

I stepped back through the window and felt the air rush away as Daniel left to find his daytime resting place. I tried to move quietly, but Dev was sitting up in bed looking at me. I was surprised he didn't look angry. There was just a weary sadness to his face. It was not an expression I had ever seen on Dev before.

"Can you come to bed now?" he asked softly.

I thought we should talk. I thought I should explain. He looked at me like he'd lost something, and there was nothing I could say to that. How did I explain that I loved two men? How did it ease him to know I didn't want to give up either one?

My expression must have given away my inner turmoil because Dev pulled back the covers. "No talking, Zoey. No explanations are needed. Just come to bed, unless you no longer want to even share a bed to sleep with me."

I tossed the sweater on the dresser and stripped down to the tank and underwear. Dev gave off an enormous amount of heat, and I knew no matter how cold the room was, I would be warm under the covers. I slid into bed even as dawn was breaking. Dev started to turn away from me but I wedged myself close to him. Though he was upset, his strong arms wound their way around me and hugged me to his chest. Despite his earlier protestations of sleeping better alone, Dev always ended up draped around me whenever we slept together. He preferred to sleep in a tangle of arms and legs.

"Was he good to you tonight?" Dev asked quietly.

"Yes."

"All right, then," he said and then his breathing took on the steady slow beat of sleep.

I let his warmth surround me and sank into sleep myself.

Chapter Thirteen

I wasn't used to quiet, contemplative Dev. I watched him across the luncheon table. I wanted to say anything, do anything to bring back the outrageous, reckless man I'd fallen in love with. His high-wattage grin was muted, his charm strictly business.

We'd slept in, skipping breakfast. When he woke me up at eleven, we politely discussed what we needed to accomplish today. He'd been showered and dressed when he got me up, and I knew the minute I saw his jeans and sweater that I was in trouble. I expected teasing and seduction. I expected him to try to tempt me into sex because that was just what Dev did. Before I had fallen asleep, I'd just known that Dev would wake me with his morning friend and try to put last night behind us.

Now I realized this was a real fight, and I wasn't sure I could win.

"We sure missed you at breakfast this morning, Mr. O'Malley." Mary Jo placed a steaming bowl of vegetable beef stew in front of Dev. She held court at these meals like a queen on a very fussy throne. "It was French toast and bacon."

This is when Dev would usually make some comment about how much he would have loved the French toast, but his wife greatly preferred a nice big sausage. He would have grinned at me to let me know he would be happy to provide it for me whenever I wanted. Today he smiled blandly and made an excuse about sleeping in. He talked pleasantly with everyone present, including Mr. Renfro, who had made a surprise appearance for lunch. Renfro was a hard-looking man in overalls and a John Deere cap. He hadn't taken his eyes off Dev the whole time we were eating.

I moved my chair a little closer to Dev in an attempt to ward off

Mr. Renfro's obvious jealousy. I suspected his wife had spent too much time going on about her handsome new guest. It was only to be expected because even in a big city, Dev stood out. I was sure they hadn't seen anything like him here in…well, possibly ever. Apparently Mr. Renfro had come to make sure his woman wasn't doing anything she shouldn't with the city slicker.

I laced our fingers together, and Dev looked down at them. I hoped he didn't brush me off, but Dev really was good at this. He pulled our joined hands to his lips, brushing them over my knuckles. It sent a little spark of heat through my body, but he just gave me a tight-lipped smile and started to eat his lunch.

As Daniel and the vamp crew had been sidelined with politics the night before, I still didn't have any intelligence on the farm. They were going to try again tonight. Daniel also planned to talk to Jasper. I hoped the alpha might be able to give us some sort of information on the Renfros since the pack more than likely lived in the rural communities that dotted the area. The B&B was fairly isolated, but there was a small town ten miles to the north, and someone had to know something.

I stared down at my lunch, not hungry at all. Things seemed to be changing so fast. Dev was mad. Daniel was playing a shockingly dangerous game. And I just wanted to get the job done. We had a few days left, but I needed time to figure out how to use the object. We were due in Vegas in five days. Two days after that was the ball. Time was running out. I was getting desperate, and I always make mistakes when I get desperate.

Lunch broke up in favor of games. Two of the older couples set up backgammon boards, while the Ruckers took up Mary Jo on her offer to show them around the grounds. Apparently there was a lovely garden up the road. We were invited, but Dev complained about his slipped disc and everyone nodded sagely and agreed he should rest. Mary Jo had sent me a dirty look like my lust had damaged him. I was glad her husband decided to escort his wife and the Ruckers around.

I'd slipped my trusty kit into the pocket of my cardigan before we came downstairs. It was a basic lock-picking kit, but that's really all I needed. The lock looked to be a simple pin tumbler, probably bought at a hardware store. It was standard, and I was good with standard. My father provided me an array of locks to practice on when I was in my teens. He considered it my real homework. I spent hours at the kitchen table using a torque wrench and a half-diamond pick.

I glanced at Dev, who nodded slightly to signal he knew what to do. We'd gone over the plan this morning. If we could find a time when everyone was accounted for and away from the kitchen, I would go for it. Normally I would wait until dark, but Mrs. Renfro had proven to be a very light sleeper last night, and I wanted to get this job done. Dev argued for waiting until dinnertime, but I thought the room was too close to the kitchen. All it would take was a forgotten salt shaker for us to get our butts kicked out of the establishment and possibly shoved into the local jail.

Dev leaned back in his chair and looked up at me as I stood. I affectionately ran my fingers through his hair, wondering if this might be the last time I got to do it. His dark hair was thick and silky in my hands, and I let myself linger for a fleeting moment. Dev's emerald green eyes were curious before he pulled me in for a light kiss. There was no force behind it, no teasing hint of tongue. It was a kiss between partners, not lovers, and I took that as my cue to get the job done.

"Hey, baby," I said with a smile I was sure didn't come anywhere near my eyes. "I'm going to run back to the room for a minute."

"Don't be too long," he murmured.

"I won't." I wouldn't. I would be fast because I was good. I might be a crappy girlfriend, but I was a good thief. As I walked out of the parlor, my hands were already pulling out my kit. I walked quietly to the back of the house. Out the back window, I watched as Mary Jo and her husband led the older couple up a wooded path, and when they were safely out of sight, I got to work.

The door was small, but the minute I stood in front of it, I knew there would be no reason for Daniel to cut short his meeting with Jasper tonight. It was here. I could feel it behind the door almost calling to me. It was like Felicity had said. This was an item of angelic origin. It wanted to be with its own kind. I was the closest thing to it, so it had decided I would do. I put my hand to the door and felt it vibrate gently beneath my fingers. If every job was as easy as this, I would be rich. It would be so much simpler if every item I decided to steal just called out and said "hey, I'm right here."

I slid the torque wrench in first and then the pick. I raked the pins quietly, holding them in place with the wrench when it slid into the right place. It wasn't long before I felt the lock pop gently into its correct position, turning in my hand like a soft caress. I loved that sound, the simple click of a lock opening just for me. It was intimate and always felt like a victory.

The others might be able to yank a door off the hinges with a single pull. They were able to yank a safe from a wall and gut it to take its contents. I was just a little human with female strength, but they couldn't do what I could do. They couldn't seduce a little lock into sweetly offering up its treasures.

I slipped into the dark room, closing the door quickly before anyone could fumble into the hall. Darkness swallowed me, and I had to take a deep breath before starting to feel around for a light switch. My hands ran up the wall, though if that slight stench was what I thought it was, I might be better off not seeing. The switch was next to the door on the right side. I was glad it was daytime so I didn't have to worry about light spilling under the doorframe and giving away my position.

The light blinked on, coating the room in yellow harshness. I did a double take because it was hard to believe what I was seeing. Looking around that little room, I realized that my crazy-ass bitch meter was functioning just fine.

It was an altar room, and Mary Jo was definitely a witch, and not the white kind.

There was black magic all over that room. The rest of the house was a distraction. This little room was Mary Jo's soul. It was where she did her real work. Small and devoid of any of the fussy trappings of the rest of the house, the altar room reeked of darkness. Hex bags sat on a small work table. A small clump of red hair was waiting to go into one of those bags. Mine, I would bet. For the thousandth time, I considered cutting my long hair. I might just shave it all off and wear a wig because I really hated hexes, and they worked better when a piece of the person being hexed could be included. Hair was the easiest way to go. I picked up the hair and shoved it in my pocket because I wasn't leaving a piece of myself behind for her to play with.

An open book sat on the altar surrounded by black and red candles. I assumed it was Mary Jo's grimoire, her personal book of spells. From the look of the leather, it was old and probably passed from crazy-bitch witch to crazy-bitch witch for generations. The pages were yellowed with age, frayed around the corners. The grimoire was opened to a page, a spell laid out in red ink. Ick. Blood. "*Dico Angelus*" was spelled out in ornate letters across the top of the page. I wasn't great with Latin, though I'd been brushing up since I lost my witch. I was pretty sure it was a spell to call angels.

The rest of the altar was decorated with photographs. There were at least twenty taped to the side, the interior, and down the front. Some were old Polaroid pictures, but there were several new photos that could have been printed off any home printer. It was good to know that even a witch as obviously disturbed as Mary Jo kept up with technology. It was not good that there were several photos of one Felicity Day. She could have mentioned that she was being stalked by Mary Jo Renfro, but no, the ever-perky angel merely described her as difficult.

My heart half stopped when I saw the latest photos. They were of Dev. One was through a window as we had eaten dinner last night. That answered one question. She had help since she'd been with us during dinner. The second one was the most terrifying. It was of Dev asleep, alone in the big heart-shaped bed. I remembered Mary Jo talking about the glow Dev had. The witch thought Dev was an angel or something close to one. It was not a good sign because from the feel of this room, she wasn't going to be asking him for advice or protection.

We needed to get out of here, and we needed to do it now.

I turned to a little bookcase. It was full of all the crap one would expect a black magic practitioner to keep hanging around the office. There were various jars filled with part of things that used to be alive. It was formaldehyde that I'd smelled when I first entered the room. Formaldehyde scared me worse than the smell of decomp because there was always the possibility that the decomp had happened naturally. No one naturally shoves fingers into a jar and covers them with formaldehyde.

I tried to ignore the ick factor as I looked for the Revelation. I found it in a small box on the third shelf. As I opened the box, the amulet was glowing and pulsing softly. I sighed with satisfaction because I had what we came for, and now I could get Dev out of here.

"I thought it was just the man," a voice said from the doorway, which was swung open.

I turned and wished I had been smart enough to carry a freaking gun, but no, I hadn't wanted to hurt the civvies. If Felicity had been more open with her info, I wouldn't have come into this house without an arsenal. John Renfro moved quickly, and there was no room for me to run. His hands tightened around my neck before I could scream, and then there was a stinging sensation in my shoulder.

"Our master is going to love you," Renfro said as the world went wobbly and dark.

* * * *

I woke up with a dry mouth and a sense of déjà vu.

"Yeah, sweetheart, this is how all our big dates seem to end," Dev said wryly.

I tried to hold my head because it was throbbing like it was going to attempt to separate itself from my body and run away, but my hands were tied firmly behind my back. Handcuffs, and not the sweet cushioned versions Dev used when he played cop and call girl. My legs had been bound as well, our captors proving themselves very thorough. "What the hell happened?"

Dev, who was tied up similarly beside me, sighed. "I got roofied. I don't know what happened to you, but I bet it was the same thing they used on me, only the injectable version. Our hostess is completely insane."

"Yeah, I got that." I flipped from my side to my back. My bound hands helped me roll onto my butt where I could look around. My eyes adjusted to the low light, but I wasn't surprised to find myself in a shed that could have been used as a *Texas Chainsaw Massacre* set. There were carcasses of woodland creatures hanging everywhere. "I take it this is the farm?"

"Yes, and maybe if your husband had been concerned about the job last night instead of getting into your pants, we would have been more cautious." Bitterness dripped from every word. I'd been thrown on the floor, but Dev was tied to a post. His shirt was gone and someone had used his chest as a demonic art project. Arcane symbols covered his chest, painted in a dull, metallic red. More blood. I was sure if I could read whatever dead language it was written in, the symbols would form an invitation for demons to come and take a bite.

"We weren't off somewhere doing the nasty, Dev," I shot back at him. "He met a pack of werepigs. It was a meeting. I'm his queen, so it makes sense for me to help out. Daniel needs allies if he's going to take down the Council."

"Daniel needs his head examined if he's going to take down the Council. You're seriously telling me Daniel is trying to join the packs to form some sort of army so he can take power?"

"The Council is the one planning a war, Dev." I knew where Dev stood, firmly in a neutral position. He was the supernatural equivalent of Switzerland. "They want to take over the supernaturals, and then I think they're going after the humans."

"Well, it won't matter now, sweetheart, because we're going to be sacrificed after dark. You can stop worrying about potential slavery and start worrying about just which demon is going to show up for dinner. Did I mention we're on the menu?"

"Daniel will come for us."

Dev laughed. "No, he won't. If he tries he'll be the fried food portion of the evening. While the crazy twins were painting me up, they were discussing all the anti-vampire stuff they were finally going to get to use. You wouldn't believe it. They have motion detectors that shoot UV light. Apparently Mr. Renfro is paranoid about vampires, and he's spent a ton of cash on defense which he can now proudly use."

That was bad news. "How the hell does he know about Danny and Chad?"

He growled a little, a sure sign of his complete frustration. "Well, what do you expect when Danny boy spends the evening introducing himself to the locals? He's being an idiot about this. He has to start using some discretion or he's going to bring the Council down on all our heads, Zoey. There are ways to handle these things with more diplomacy."

"He's doing the best he can." I was defending myself as much as Danny. We weren't raised to play these games. Dev had been raised in a royal court. Plots and subterfuge and coups might be second nature to him, but Danny and I were fumbling.

Dev rolled his eyes. "It doesn't matter. It's all a huge clusterfuck. The witches don't even realize we have anything to do with the vamps. They're just paranoid. That stupid amulet thing we came to steal glows around me, so she thinks I'm an angel. It glows around you, but she thinks it's because we had sex. She's sure you're some evil human who's trying to make me fall."

Frustration welled up. "Why does everyone think I'm the one leading you into sin? Have they met you? Since I started sleeping with you I have done things I would never have thought to do. That thing with my feet, who would think to do that? You have the single dirtiest mind I've ever met."

"A lot of good it did me." His eyes moved away from mine.

"What is that supposed to mean?" Why wouldn't he just come out and tell me?

Dev seemed to think about it for a moment, and I worried he would shut me out again. "It means I always knew we had an expiration date, Zoey. I just didn't realize it would be so fucking soon. I knew you would probably go back to him. I just thought I could keep you for longer than seven months. I overestimated my skills, it seems."

"I wasn't trying to leave you." I scooted on my butt to get closer to him. "I was just pissed because you wouldn't talk to me. You never talk to me about anything important. Come to think of it, you never do anything with me except have sex and run jobs. It makes a girl think."

He frowned. "We hang out at the club."

"Great, let me add drinking to our list of activities," I replied, tears threatening. "You won't even tell me if you have a kid. I don't know anything about your life, Dev. I'm in love with you, and I don't know if you left a family behind when you fled the mound."

"What did you say?" Dev didn't have a problem looking at me now. His body was tense, every bit of his focus pointed at me.

I shrank back because I hadn't meant to say it. I hadn't meant to ever let him know how I felt. It made me too vulnerable. Whatever had been in that sedative was screwing with me. I decided to be obtuse. "You won't tell me if you have a kid."

He smiled and looked distinctly wolfish. "Oh, no, darling, you're not getting off the hook that easily. You love me. You said it."

"Don't get excited." I had to make something very clear. "It doesn't mean I don't love Daniel, too. It just means I'm screwed whichever way I go."

"But you love me," he said as though the statement satisfied him deeply. "I made you love me."

"Well, it doesn't matter now. Unless you have the keys to get us out of these cuffs, it doesn't matter."

"Oh, it matters, sweetheart," Dev replied. "We have maybe an hour before the sun goes down and the coven comes for us. I can still check this state off. All you have to do is use your teeth to get my zipper down. I don't care what anyone says. It counts as sex."

I laughed because that was my Dev, always thinking with his dick. We were going to be human sacrifices, and he was trying to get a hummer before we went out.

Dev moved his feet so they touched mine. "I thought you didn't want to sleep with me anymore."

"No, I just wanted to mean more to you than a warm version of a blow-up doll."

Dev laughed. "You are so much more trouble than a blow-up doll, sweetheart. You make me crazy with your hazel eyes and those luscious tits of yours, but I have to admit it's the violence I'm really attracted to. Now shut up and I'll give you what you want before they slice us up. Don't waste time trying to get out. They have three guys with shotguns on the door, and I watched them remove everything we could possibly use as a weapon from this room before they left to get ready for the ceremony. Mary Jo is going to the hair salon."

"Good to know she's taking it seriously." I got as close as I could and was able to lean against him. If we only had a little time left, I wanted to hear the story. "Now, are you a daddy or not?"

He smiled sadly. "I don't know. It's possible. When my grandfather died back in World War One, he took the tribe's fertility with him. He got too involved in human affairs. Even a full-blooded Fae will die if you put enough bullets in him and he's far from a *sithein.* My mother became queen, but she couldn't bear children, and trust me, she tried with every full-blooded Fae she could. It became clear she should try something else. She came to the Earth plane, met my father, and immediately became pregnant with me and my brother, Declan."

"You have a twin?" One Dev was almost too much for the world to handle. The fact that there was another who looked just like him made me think things I probably shouldn't if I wanted to be considered a good girl.

He grinned, likely guessing what was going through my head. "I do, but he's very different from me. He's older by a couple of minutes so he's the heir. He's much more serious. His training was different than mine."

"Your grandfather was a Green Man." A Green Man facilitated fertility rites and oversaw the harvest.

"Yes, and it quickly became evident that I had received his talents," Dev continued. "Even as a small child I can recall playing with plants. The tribe was thrilled. My brother would be trained to rule, and I would be the new Green Man bringing fertility and sexual vitality back to the tribe."

I knew where this story was going. "Then they discovered you were mortal."

"It was a shock since my twin is fully Fae. I was trained to be a priest. You have to understand it doesn't have the same connotations in the Fae world as a Catholic priest. Pretty much the exact opposite. In the Fae world, sex is a part of the divine. It's a part of our rituals. There's no shame attached to it. I was trained to please sexually and to transmit that pleasure to others through magic."

He'd been trained well. I finally understood why he wrapped up his worth in his sexuality. When I refused him, he thought I was bored with him because he'd never been valued for anything else. Now that I looked at it, Dev tried to work himself into my world the only ways he'd known how. He became my lover, and he worked his way onto my crew. He tried to give me what he thought I needed. He tried to make himself valuable.

"The fact that I was mortal was a flaw they would not accept in a priest," Dev explained quietly. "So my mother decided that I should attempt to pass my grandfather's genes on to a more suitable candidate. I was barely twenty-one when she decided it was time for me to procreate. Don't get me wrong. I didn't have a problem with the sex. It wasn't like I hadn't screwed every pretty Fae girl in the mound. I was a priest. It was a part of my training. My brother and I were a little wild to say the least. We left the *sithein* once and ended up in a Tijuana prison. God, I miss Declan sometimes."

"Skip the good time." I didn't need to hear that story. "I take it she had someone in mind."

"She believed that if I mated with a full-blooded Fae of excellent bloodline, that I had a good chance of producing another full-blooded Fae. I didn't like being told what to do, much less who to fuck. Gilliana was a horrible woman. When it was proven I was mortal, she advised my mother to leave me outside the mound to die."

"Why would your mom want you to sleep with her?"

"Because she was fertile and of a royal line. I refused. I told her I would rather leave the mound and make my way in the human world. My father had left years before when he realized his use was done. He tried to take me with him, but my mother forbade it. I thought I could go to my father. The night before I was to leave, my mother used some very powerful magic on me."

"She forced you?" No wonder he'd had a bad reaction to Felicity's magic. It brought back his mother's betrayal. It also explained why he preferred me submissive during sex. Dev liked to take control. He seemed to need it. He tried to hide his darker impulses in the form of play, but I'd seen his face when he'd tied me up and dominated me. He craved it.

"The worst part is I remember everything," Dev explained in a far-off voice. "I tried to make myself stop, but I couldn't. The next day I left without a word to my mother."

"Did you find your father?" I didn't ask for further details. He didn't need to think about the fact his mother had facilitated his rape, because that was what she'd done. There had been no violence involved, but he'd been unwilling and that was rape in my book.

Dev moved on. "Time moves differently in the *sithein*. It's like that on other planes as well. It can be unpredictable. My father was very old when I found him. I was twenty-one, but he'd aged fifty years. I spent six months with him, caring for him until he died. He hadn't had any other children, so he left me his fortune and I started Ether."

"Fortune?"

Dev grinned. "You can't think I make that much money off the clubs, Zoey. Turns out I'm quite good with investments. My father left me fifty million and a multi-national company. I hired a CEO and now I just cash the checks."

I shook my head. "And yet you spend your time chasing chump change with me?"

"I don't do it for the money, lover. I do it all for the nookie."

"Be serious."

He leaned over, and his lips brushed my forehead. "I have never wanted a woman the way I want you, Zoey. I knew it on our first date. I knew it the first time I saw you. Why do you think I made such an idiot of myself the first time I met you? You make me feel alive. I can't believe you've spent our time together thinking I was only interested in sex with you. How hard up do you think I am? Sex with you meant having every vampire in the world wanting to kill me."

"I rather thought that was part of the allure," I muttered.

Dev chuckled, a self-deprecating little laugh. "Well, at least you know me. I might get off on the danger a little, but I assure you, knowing that you'll eventually leave me for your husband doesn't do anything for me. Since we're mentioning your spouse amid my confessions, let me warn you. If Gilliana did bear a child from that night, my mother would likely declare us to be married. My absence at the ceremony wouldn't mean a thing. The queen wouldn't want her new Green Man to be illegitimate. I should have told you, but we had enough roadblocks. Besides, it's not like she's going to show up and demand her wifely rights. The woman hates me. She has everything of me she will ever get. Everything else I have is yours."

"Do you wonder?" I asked because I sure did.

"If she got pregnant and the baby was like me, my brother would have done his duty," Dev said solemnly. "My brother cut off ties with me when I left, but not before making a promise. If Gilliana's child was a Halfling, he was to smuggle the baby out. If the child was a full Fae, then it doesn't need anything from me."

I could have argued mightily with him, but it wouldn't do any good. Dev was probably right. The Fae world was harsh, and the child would have been raised to despise weakness. I promised myself if I ever met Dev's mother, she would get the same treatment as Neil's dad. My father might not have been the most conventional father, but he'd always loved and protected me. I'd been lucky to have him. A thought occurred to me.

"If we survive this, Albert and I are having a major discussion about your wife." I was greatly looking forward to the conversation. The half demon had spent much of the last seven months scowling at me disapprovingly for tempting his master into adultery. It would be nice to see those judgmental eyes turn to Dev.

"I might not be married," Dev pointed out.

"That probably won't come up in the discussion," I admitted.

"You're such a bitch." His eyes became very serious. "I love you, Zoey. I've never said those words before this moment. I love you, and if you leave me for that blood sucker, I'll lose the best part of me. I promise you, if by some miracle we survive this, I'll be a better boyfriend. Up to this point, I've concentrated on the lover part because it was easy for me and I really like that part. But I can do the other part, too."

"I love you, Devinshea." The truth settled around my heart. Daniel might be my first love, but Dev held a chunk of my soul in his hands. Daniel protected me, but Dev let me fly.

The door above us opened, and the Renfros walked down the stairs. Mary Jo was dressed to impress in black robes and a really well-done bouffant. Even Mr. Renfro had dressed for the occasion.

I covered my complete terror with sarcasm. Maybe if I was really bratty, no one would notice the pounding of my heart. "What's up? Is this not a family affair? Where are the rug rats?"

Mary Jo smiled, showing her even white teeth. "Like I told you, you slut, they're with their father. In Hell."

John Renfro pulled me to my feet while three other coven members undid Dev's cuffs. He struggled, but they were too much and had his hands back in the cuffs before he could fight his way out. He looked at me as they began to drag him up the stairs. "Stay alive, Zoey. Daniel will find a way. Just stay alive, do you hear me?

I love you, Zoey."

I let my body go limp because I would be damned if I walked to my own execution.

Chapter Fourteen

I forced the fuckers to drag me all the way out of the barn and to the clearing they had designated for the ceremony. Night had fallen, and the forest around us looked foreboding and ominous, shadows clinging everywhere. The full moon had passed the night before, so the werepigs wouldn't be running. They would be meeting with Daniel. It could be hours before he thought to come to my window and find out how my day had gone.

I'd rather thought the coven would wait until midnight or three a.m., the preferred times for calling a demon. I started to panic. Daniel would wait, thinking Dev and I were on some errand. The upshot being that Dev and I would be cooling corpses by the time Danny thought to look for us.

They dragged me out into the open field. Orange light sparked off several torches held by coven members. Two altars dominated the field, one for me and one for Dev. As they pulled my limp body along, they were already chaining him to the first one. Two of the black-robed members fought to hold Dev down, and then two more came over to help. As he struggled, one of the coven members shoved a needle into his arm. Fear sparked through me. What the hell had they just given him?

"Stay still or you'll get the same and I know our demon lord would rather have a screaming victim than one who just laughs when he eats them," the man dragging me along said.

I relaxed a little because they wanted us alive. Whatever they had given Dev shouldn't kill him.

After a moment, Dev went limp, and I vowed I wouldn't struggle because I needed every faculty if there was any way to get us out of this. If this coven was for real, there would be a demon coming. Demons liked to make deals. I had a couple of things to offer. I would invoke Daniel's name. I would bring up Marcus Vorenus. Hell, I'd call the fucking Council in if it meant that Dev was alive at the end of the night. It wouldn't be the first deal I made with a demon. I seriously doubted it would be the last.

The altars were circular and man-sized, or regular man-sized. Dev kind of hung off it. The good news was I would fit just fine. They shoved me down on the pentagram. It was upside down and perverted, just the way black magicians like them. The pentagram is a sacred symbol to witches. In the white witch world, it's a symbol of man in spiritual harmony with the natural world around him. The inverted pentagram says screw the natural world, I'd like demons to come and fuck everything up.

I was placed on the pentagram, my arms and legs reaching out from my torso. I was passive, allowing the witches to do their work. I needed to keep the one with the needle at bay. They did their job, making sure I couldn't move, and then they stepped back.

"Zoey," Dev yelled, his head coming off the altar, trying to find me.

"Yes, baby." I could see him if I really stretched. He was smiling, his eyes a little bit glassy.

His laughter filled my world. "I'm really high, sweetie. That's some good shit they have. You should try it."

He would have been a blast in Vegas if we'd made it there. Mary Jo came into view, her pinched face looming over me. "You should be ashamed of yourself, trying to force an angel to fall."

"That's rich, lady, considering you're about to sacrifice him to a demon."

That brown bouffant shook. "Do you think crops just grow themselves? I don't particularly like having to do this, but if the okra doesn't come in, what is our community going to do? The demon is just going to eat the angel. I'm sure he'll float back up to Heaven. If you had your way, he would fall."

"This isn't going to go the way you want it to. I'm not who you think I am, and trust me, there isn't a demon around who wants to mess with me." I didn't mention that it was my husband they didn't want to mess with. It tends to take a little of the "badass factor" out of the speech. "Whatever demon you're about to call, once I tell him my name, he'll kill you."

I hoped that was true. Demon kind wasn't allowed to write contracts with anyone considered the property of Vampire. It really only made sense that they weren't allowed to eat us either. I thought I was fairly safe, but I had some fast talking to do if I wanted to save my supremely stoned lover. He was giggling as a couple of coven members made sure the symbols on his chest were properly drawn.

"Stop it. That tickles," he said.

"You aren't an angel." Mary Jo stared at me like I was a piece of trash.

"Neither is he," I told her. "You have no idea what you've gotten in the middle of."

Mary Jo laughed. "The truth is I'm saving him. He was going to fall if he stayed around your kind. This way his soul will go to Heaven, and my master will be happy. Your soul, if you even have one, will go with my master."

I lifted my head as far as it would go. "I'm a companion. Do you understand what that means?"

Mary Jo's eyes widened. "A companion? Like a vampire's companion?"

It wasn't shocking she was surprised. She could be surrounded by witches and demons and werepigs and it would never have occurred to her that I could be a companion. We're extremely rare, and as such, very few companions live outside of vampire society.

"Yes, I am."

"You're lying."

"Then why were there vampires in your woods last night?"

"It's a coincidence." But she looked around as if wondering what was hidden beyond the light of the torches.

I made one last try at reason. "Do you understand the nature of a vampire, you crazy witch? Do you think you can take me from him and he'll let that pass? Do you have any idea what he'll do to you?"

She stared down at me, her face lit with pride. "I am protected. I have given four innocent souls to the lord Nemcox. He won't let some nightcrawler harm me. I'm important."

I laid my head back down because there was no point in talking to the clinically insane. "Then bring him on because I bet he's more rational than you are."

The witches gathered in their circle, and after settling some coven business like nailing down the date for the next potluck, they finally got around to the business of chanting. Chanting is very important to witches. They take it seriously. They also take their damn time doing it.

"Zoey." Dev called to me as I was trying to see if I could tell anything from the Latin they were chanting. "Zoey, I had a thought. I've never done it on a black altar right before a coven calls a demon. We could check it off."

I groaned because Dev's sexual bucket list was getting longer by the minute. I knew we were getting closer to the grand finale when the name "Nemcox" was chanted over and over again. I hoped this was the real thing and not some group of deluded asylum escapees. I might have a shot dealing with an actual demon. If they were all just taking a little of what they gave Dev and spilling some blood and calling it a ritual, then we were screwed.

The thought also occurred to me that I might be overestimating my celebrity. What if this Nemcox hadn't been reading the demonic version of *People* and had no idea who I was? I was certain it wouldn't be the first time some poor sacrifice had tried to talk him out of his dinner by claiming they were too important to eat.

The chanting reached a crest, and Mary Jo held her hands up as she finished the incantations from the black leather book.

The minute I smelled the brimstone, I knew I was in luck. I forced my head off the wooden altar, and sure enough, there was a medium-sized, red-skinned demon looking around. When I say medium-sized, I mean for a demon. They can run to the extra-large, so I was less intimidated by this one than I had been by Lucas Halfer. Of course, I was really intimidated by Halfer, so it's all relative.

The demon roared, greatly impressing the coven. They were effusive in their praise for their master. There was a lot of butt kissing inherent in this ceremony. Mary Jo was particularly good at telling the demon how much she worshipped him and how devoted she was. Apparently, she and Mr. Renfro were trying for innocent sacrifice number five. I was really going to have to kill her if I got the chance.

"Great Nemcox, we have not one but two souls for your

pleasure this evening," Mary Jo stated grandly, her hands gesturing toward the altars. "I've used my special divining necklace to bring an angel to feed your hunger."

The demon turned his head toward the altars, suddenly very interested in what was on the menu. I strained to try to see him. His dark eyes looked at Dev, and then he took a deep inhale, scenting the air. I expected him to leap onto the altar and begin the bloodletting, but that great horned head was thrown back, and a menacing laugh filled the air.

"You really are a stupid bitch," the demon said in a very familiar British accent. My heart sank. He was walking my way. "There are absolutely no angels here. You managed to bring me something even better." The demon smiled down at me, his fangs shining brightly. "Zoey Wharton, what a surprise. Long time no see."

Of all the demons in all the planes, Mary Jo had to sacrifice me to Stewart. He was the one demon who had a personal beef with me, well, besides Halfer. He'd tried to ruin a job I ran earlier this year, and Daniel had broken his neck and then shot him and then Dev had killed him, too.

"Hey, Stewart." I tried a bright smile. "Nice to see you survived. I knew you would pull through."

"No thanks to you, love. I don't suppose you brought along your sweet little puppy, did you?" Stewart had been very impressed with Neil. Not that it helped us since Stewart had then sicced a weretiger on him. "And where is that nasty vampire you married? Felicitations on your wedding, dear. So sorry I haven't sent a gift yet. I'll have to remedy that. Let's see who you did bring with you."

The demon jumped from my altar to the one holding Dev.

Dev looked up at him and laughed. "I don't think that's Stewart, Zoey. He looks weird."

Dev had never seen Stewart in his demonic form. Unlike Halfer, Stewart couldn't change forms at will. If he wanted to look human, he had to possess some poor sap. He liked to call it his meat suit. It usually ended poorly because Stewart didn't take great care of his clothes.

Stewart grinned as much as someone with enormous fangs can grin. "Maybe I should have a little of what he's having. Hello, Fae creature. Your mind is so open right now. You're a dirty, dirty boy. He's about to die and would you like to know what he's thinking about?"

I could guess. Stewart was an empath. He picked up on emotions and could magnify them for his own use. It was important to remain calm around Stewart or he could learn things you didn't want him to learn.

I needed to bring his attention back to me and away from the never-ending porno that likely played in Dev's brain. "Leave him alone, Stewart. You deal with me."

One of the witches slapped me hard across the mouth. My head snapped back and hit wood. Pain ripped through me. I managed to maintain consciousness, but I could feel he'd drawn blood.

"You do not talk to the Dark Lord, bitch," he snarled.

Stewart looked at the witch, his face darkening. "Don't you touch her." Stewart hopped off the altar, stalking the witch who struck me. His cloven hoofs stirred up dirt. He hauled the witch up with one hand, and I could see the witch start to choke, his legs twitching. "She's worth a hundred of you. She's a companion. Do you know how rare a creature she is, you mundane idiots? Even the ridiculous Fae creature is worth more than all of you put together. Her value is immense, and if one of you harms her again, I will kill the lot of you."

Stewart let the witch drop to the ground, but I didn't think he would get up again.

"Thank you." I was polite because I needed him. I didn't do defiance when courtesy would work just as well.

"Don't thank me, love," he replied shortly. "If anybody is going to hurt you, I want it to be me."

"Great Lord." There was a tinge of hysteria to Mary Jo's voice, as though she was just figuring out I had told her the truth. "How can you choose some human slut over your devoted followers?"

The demon rolled his dark eyes. "Yokels," he muttered. He waved his hand. "Witches, silent."

The witches found themselves robbed of the power of speech. They touched their throats trying to speak but nothing would come out.

He looked back down at me. "So, I was looking forward to

seeing you at the ball, love. What were you going to wear? I was thinking Brad Pitt. I don't know though, he's getting a bit long in the tooth. If I wanted to be terribly ironic, I could wear that boy from the *Twilight* films. Note, dear, I am using the past tense since you won't be going to the ball anymore."

"You aren't going to kill me, Stewart," I said with a surety I wasn't feeling.

Stewart smiled and walked slowly around Dev's prone form. "He thinks I am. It's just now penetrating his drug-addled brain. He's very upset." Stewart ran a finger over Dev's sculpted chest. "He really is lovely, dear. You have excellent taste in men. You are fucking him? These images I get from him aren't just his fantasies? You must tell me what you're doing to these men to keep them in line. This one could screw anything he wanted. He's descended from an actual sex god, but he follows you around like a pathetic lapdog, and then there's the vampire. He should have killed this one the instant he looked at you with those covetous eyes of his. Yet the Green Man lives and shares your bed. Seriously, companion, what's in those pants of yours because I need some of that."

"Cut the crap, Stewart," I said flatly, not willing to engage him. "Do you really want to deal with the Council? It didn't go so well for Halfer."

"It wasn't the Council that tripped up old Brix, love. That was you." Stewart was still running his hands over Dev's body, caressing him like a lover. Stewart did love a hot boy. "I should have sent you a thank you note. Sometimes I forget my manners. You really did set Brix back, and that helped me immensely. He's making a bit of a comeback, though. I really would like to know how he's doing it. But I digress."

Suddenly one the witches decided this game had gone far enough. The witch came at the demon, a ceremonial knife held above her head. She probably thought that little piece of engraved silver was defense against a Lord of Hell. I had no doubt that whoever had sold it to her had promised a demonic killing machine. Unfortunately, you can't get something like that off the Internet or at a little shop that sells incense and herbs.

This is the problem with calling demons that almost no one is willing to accept. Demons are evil. They might help you out to start with, but sooner or later they will turn on you. Being able to call a force of nature to your hand might seem like a powerful thing to do, but after a while, you forget who has the real power. Stewart showed her. With a flick of his hand, her throat came open and sprayed across the field.

"Son of a bitch," I screamed as I got a nice coating of witch blood.

The rest of the witches were running, but it didn't do any good. Their throats split, heads falling back like broken dolls. Blood ran and the demon licked his chops. He breathed in the death, loving the feel of all those souls rushing to Hell.

"I really was getting tired of coming here anyway," Stewart said, brushing off the deaths of people who had worshipped him. "Now that's over and we won't be interrupted. I've thought about what you said, and the truth is you make a point. Ripping your heart out and gobbling it down while you watch really will cause me more trouble than pleasure. I suppose your vampire would be very upset. I doubt he would let the matter drop. So you're off the hook, so to say."

I sighed, thankful that demons really were easier to deal with than backwoods witches. "Let me up, Stewart, and I think you'll find that my husband will be grateful."

Stewart ran a finger across Dev's now blood-soaked chest and brought it to his lips. "Yes, he will be grateful, won't he? Your boy has ambitions. Anyone can see that. The Council is arrogant if they think they can control that one. I, for one, think he can do it. I've played around in his head, and I think he's capable of far more than you could dream of. You think he's doing this for the greater good, companion, but you're underestimating the lure of power. It calls to him. He's caught between his love for you and the need to see if he can be a god. Which need do you think is going to win? I have a suspicion. I think your boy is going to give this world hell. I think this plane will run red with blood before he's done. That is a man whose gratitude I would find useful. He might be thankful if I let you go, but how much more would he value me if I did the one thing he cannot do?"

Suddenly that knife was in his hands, and he was tracing a light line across Dev's very vulnerable throat. That dumbass knife had meant nothing to the demon, but it would nicely spill my lover's lifeblood. Terror engulfed me. I strained against the ties that held me down because all it would take was a little flick of the demon's wrist to end Dev's life.

"Please, don't." I would do anything, say anything to keep that knife at bay. I couldn't just lie there and watch it happen.

Stewart's eyes lit with triumph. "There, now, that's what I was waiting for. You're awfully good at keeping me out, but there's that terror I love. This is excellent, dear. You love him. That can't make your vampire happy. Poor little Zoey, caught between two men. They're going to chew you up and spit you out. I would be doing you a favor, too. This one is going to get you in trouble. Take my advice. Serve your master, companion. Give him the blood he craves and warm his bed. That's your job. It's what you were born to do. This one might bring you pleasure, but he'll bring you all down in the long run. Trust me on this. In the end, you'll thank me."

He took the knife in both hands and held it over his head.

"I know what Brix is doing," I shouted, giving up the last card in my hand. If this didn't work, Dev was dead, and I would spend the rest of my probably short life trying to kill one demon.

Stewart let the knife fall harmlessly to the side. "Now, see, you really do know how to get a gentleman's attention. I'm listening."

This was desperation but I didn't know what else to do. I couldn't let Dev go, and there was no way to lie to Stewart. He would know immediately if I wasn't truthful. He was smart to bring out my emotions because I had nothing to hide behind now. "He has an angel."

Stewart thought about it for a moment. "Are you serious?"

I opened my mind as wide as I could, letting my every emotion spill across the demon. He actually took a step back as he took it all in. "You tell me if I'm serious."

"Fine. So Brix is juicing an angel. That explains his resurgence. How is this supposed to help me? I'm not in a position to steal from him, and snitching tends to get you in hot water on the Hell plane."

"I'm going to handle it." I was grateful for the damn ropes now because my hands were shaking.

He looked at me like I was insane, which I probably was. Then a light of recognition lit those black eyes. "The witch's divining amulet. Of course, that's why you're here. It really works? I thought she was just bat-shit crazy."

"It works. I'm going to use it and free the angel. Halfer will lose his advantage on the very night he needs it."

There was a triumphant smile on his really scary face. It was nice to know my plan was demon approved. "You're an interesting woman. You plan to sneak out of the ball with your little divining rod, find the angel, unbind him because the only way Brix could keep him is to bind his magic, and then return him to his plane. You're going to die, you know."

I had him in my trap. I just had to close the door behind and make sure he was in. "Probably. But what if I don't?"

"I think it will be immensely entertaining either way." Stewart waved his hand and my limbs were free.

Though my every muscle was shaky and weak, I forced myself up and made my way to Dev. I climbed on his altar, taking his face in my hands, reassuring myself that he was alive. Tears clouded my eyes as I stared down at him. So close. That damn knife had been so close to his throat. With aching hands, I started to work on his bindings.

"Allow me." Stewart didn't need hands to undo Dev's binding. They simply fell away.

I pulled Dev's head into my lap, my hand smoothing back his hair. He opened his eyes, obviously fighting the drugs that were coursing through his system. "Zoey, you need to run, sweetheart."

And leave him here? I knew it was the most expedient thing to do, but I simply couldn't. "Not on your life, lover. You go back to sleep. I'll take care of everything. It's going to be all right now."

"Touching," Stewart said with disdain.

In the distance, a siren began to wail. I turned toward the sound and down the mountain I saw red and blue lights turning in the darkness.

Stewart sighed as he watched the police cars move ever closer. "Apparently your husband realized it was time to call in the cavalry. These idiots might have been fairly useless, but they set up a good defensive perimeter. Well, my time here is at an end. I look forward to the ball, dear. See that you don't disappoint me. I might not be able to contract with you, but I still think it might be a good idea to get in your husband's good graces. I can do that any number of ways. It's your choice. If you want your lover alive, you'll do the job." He reached down and picked something off Mary Jo Renfro's dead body. He tossed it to me. "Don't forget this."

The Revelation. In all the horror of the evening, I'd almost forgotten about it. I put it around my neck, a sense of peace coming over me.

With a blast of brimstone, Stewart was gone, and I was left with thirteen dead witches, one stoned faery, and very few explanations anyone would believe. I should have run. It was standard. *Don't get caught by the cops.* It was rule number one in the thieves' handbook. I was supposed to run and deal with getting Dev out later. But I sat there, kissing his forehead and feeling the reassuring beat of his heart against my hand. I just sat there and waited to be taken into custody.

It occurred to me that Stewart was right. My love was going to take us all down.

Chapter Fifteen

"Hey, sweetheart, I just thought of something," Dev laughed, looking up at me. "I haven't done it in a jail cell. Well, not in the U.S."

Faeries can handle their alcohol. They can handle a substantial amount of it. Don't try drinking a faery under the table because he's still going to be sitting there long after you fall out of your seat. Hard-core drugs, on the other hand, are a completely different story. It had been three hours since the police found us huddled together surrounded by corpses, and if Dev had sobered up any, I couldn't tell.

The Bristol County Jail was so small it only had one holding cell, so Dev and I had been placed in the cell together. It was better that way because Dev was very difficult to handle. This was a police force that was built to take care of the occasional drunk and perhaps citizens who refused to acknowledge the annual burn ban. It was not ready for mass murder. The entire police force had answered the call. One sheriff and two deputies had shown up, guns drawn, and the two deputies promptly began throwing up. At least the sheriff had been able to hold it together.

I ran my fingers through Dev's thick hair, the softness soothing me. "We don't have time to check anything off your list, baby. Daniel will be here soon."

He sure as hell better be. It had already been far longer than I expected to wait. Daniel should have been here busting open the freaking bars and getting us the hell out of here. I'd already been booked on suspicion of multiple homicides. The fact that I was covered in blood didn't help my case. It also didn't help that the police knew all the victims, but I was an outsider.

I wore an overly large jumper because the police had taken my clothes. Evidence. I wasn't supposed to leave behind evidence. The sheriff was on the phone calling larger cities in an attempt to get an actual crime scene unit to the farm. From what I understood, the local vet served as the county coroner, and he was on a fishing trip.

I'd given an alias for my name, and Dev was incapable of giving them anything. I'd been through processing and had everything taken from me. Knowing the Revelation was in some evidence room was just one more problem I didn't need. I was going to have to pay a visit to that little room before I left. To top off my trouble, I heard the sheriff calling for someone to take the male to the hospital. I really didn't want that to happen, hence my wanting Daniel to hurry the hell up. It was time to blow this backwoods town before the feds showed up, and they were going to show up.

"I am looking for Sheriff Jones." A familiar voice was speaking quietly.

I checked the clock. Three a.m. I was going to kick Daniel's ass for making me cool my heels this long. Even as it was he hadn't come in person. He'd sent Chad. I scooted out from under Dev's now sleeping form and walked to the bars. I had to strain, but I could see Chad looking very professional in a suit. His face was flat, and he looked pissed to be pulled out of bed to have to deal with this shit. There was a man beside him, but he was in sweat pants and a T-shirt. I pegged his age as close to fifty. He yawned as he stood beside Chad.

"I'm the sheriff," a gruff voice replied.

Chad held up a handful of papers. "Sheriff, these are the three lawsuits I am prepared to file. One is against the county, one against the police department, and the last one names you personally for the wrongful arrest of my clients, Katie Johnson and Devon Finn. They're the victims of an awful cult, and yet they're sitting in your jail cell not getting the medical attention they deserve. They were victimized first by your citizens and then again by a corrupt police force."

"Corrupt?" The sheriff stared at Chad and then looked away. He shook his head as though trying to clear it.

"I've already spoken to Judge Laurence who instructed the district attorney's office to look into the matter." Chad kept talking but that wasn't all he was doing.

I could feel the power he was pushing around the room. To the inexperienced, it would feel like the room was getting overheated. It was like a small voice in the back of their head imploring them to do the right thing. It was the very persuasive power of a vampire. It could be used for anything from getting a little blood and a little sex, to persuading a victim to sign over their life savings. Chad was just a baby, but he was already incredibly impressive. He might never be the strongest or the fastest vampire, but he wouldn't need to be. He could talk people out of what others would take by force. In the vampire world, it was a talent to be highly valued.

"Howard, is this true?" The sheriff looked at the papers, appearing to read them briefly, but even from my vantage point I could see they were blank. They wouldn't appear that way to the sheriff. He was seeing what Chad wanted him to see.

"I have no idea what you were thinking, Sheriff." The dude in pajamas seemed to be the district attorney. "It's obvious those two are the victims. Do you want to make us look like a bunch of small-town idiots? This is going to be a big case. This is going to make the national news, and we're all going to look like bumpkins."

Chad nodded. "I've already contacted the national news networks. Several major reporters are on their way here even as we speak. This is big news, Sheriff. Two tourists almost become the victims of a local cult. Trust me. Every media outlet in the country is going to cover this story. The question is do you want to be the officer who helped the victims or the one who tossed them in jail?"

The sheriff straightened up, smoothing down his wrinkled shirt. "Really? You mean like CNN?"

Chad nodded. "If you let my clients go now, we'll do the show from the station with you looking like the hero who rescued them. Otherwise, I'll be standing outside the station with a protest group talking about the largest lawsuit this county has ever seen. I can make your career, Sheriff, and I promise you I can break it. It's your choice."

Dev and I were processed out within fifteen minutes. We were in the van and on our way before anyone thought to ask for credentials.

"You are damn good, Chad," I said as he steered the car onto the road that would take us to the cemetery.

Chad smiled at me in the rearview mirror, obviously satisfied with a job well done. "You think that was a tough crowd? You should have met my law professors."

I sat in the back of the van with Dev draped across me. He sighed happily in his sleep. Chad turned into the cemetery. I hated to break it to him, but the job wasn't over yet. "We have to go back."

"Not going to happen, Zoey. I have orders. We stay here until Daniel and Neil get back." Chad got out of the van. He opened the back door so we could talk face to face.

"You don't understand. I had the item in my hand. It's in the evidence locker at the jail. I can sneak in and get it. I just need you to pull some vampy mojo on the desk clerk."

Before Chad could give the multitude of reasons why that was a bad idea, Daniel landed at the edge of the cemetery. He wore all black, from his denims to the duster that billowed around him as he landed with a thud. The ground shook as he hit it. Normally Daniel floated gently, so I knew that sound was meant to get my attention. He looked straight at me as he landed, his mouth a flat line with just the tiniest hint of fangs to let me know he was pissed off. His boots thudded across the dirt, stirring dust in his wake.

His hand came up, a glint of metal shining in the moonlight as he tossed the Revelation my way. I reached up and caught it. The little piece of jewelry hummed in my hand.

"See, Zoey," Daniel all but snarled at me as he advanced. "I still know how to steal."

I placed the Revelation around my neck as I eased out from under Dev. This was obviously a conversation that required me to stand toe to toe with my husband. I scrambled out of the van before he could force me to stay inside and lose the chance to stand up to him. "What the hell is that supposed to mean, Daniel?"

Neil ran up the road in wolf form. He took his place next to Chad, who absently stroked his lover's fur. He was busy watching Daniel and shaking his head in surprise.

"What it means, baby, is it's time for you to hang it up." Daniel loomed over me. The trouble with going toe to toe with Danny was the crick I got in my neck from staring up at him. "Let's talk about how you fucked up tonight. First, you went into a situation with no intelligence whatsoever."

I felt my face start to flush with anger. How dare he? I'd been through hell and he wanted to lecture me? "I didn't have any intelligence because you were too busy playing politician to do your job, Danny. You had one job to do—check out that farm. But no, you got too caught up in your own plans to consider the job you were hired to do."

"Hired? You want to treat me like a hired hand, baby, you better pony up some more cash because you pay shit for all the crap I have to do to save your ass." Daniel looked over my shoulder toward the van. "Hey, Quinn, get out here because I have a few things to say to you."

"Leave him alone, Danny."

"Is he asleep? He fell asleep after getting you arrested?"

"Don't you blame him. He fought like hell. They drugged him. We were both drugged and carried out of the B&B. We were taken to the farm after I found the Revelation. I found it, Danny, not you. I had it in my hands when those witches came for me. I might have been a little more on my guard if you had done the reconnaissance. If I'd known I was walking into a killing field, I might have taken that bitch a little more seriously."

Daniel held me by the shoulders. "Maybe if you hadn't been so hot to take your boyfriend on a job, you would have had adequate backup. You need to make a choice, baby. Do you want to be a pro or do you want to get a cozy house in the suburbs and start spitting out Dev's illegitimate children?"

"Jesus," I heard Chad sigh under his breath.

"How dare you?" I screamed because just saying it didn't express my rage. It was welling up inside me, all the pressure and terror of the night forcing its way up like a champagne bottle begging to be uncorked. I could handle it one of two ways. I could let him hold me while I cried or I could vent that rage at him. He'd chosen path number two, and I didn't even feel a hint of guilt for following him.

"I dare because I'm the idiot who had to watch you fuck everything up, Zoey," he yelled right back. "Did you think I wasn't watching? Do you think I didn't try to get to you? I tried to fly to you and got hit with some ultraviolet light laser shit. Damn near took my head off. I tried everything I could. I couldn't get to you, but I saw every mistake you made, babe. You were just asking to get killed, and it was because you were going to do anything you could to save that idiot. You had a chance to run. You had a chance to get away, but you sat there with him. You let them take you."

"I couldn't leave him." I knew what I should have done. Danny didn't need to tell me.

He shook me lightly. "Yes, you could. You could have done your job, which was to get the item and get out. We could have gotten him later. You were reckless and stupid."

He forgot so easily. "Like I was when I didn't leave Oliver to fry you?"

"That was me, Zoey. It was different."

"No, it wasn't," I said very clearly. I wasn't thinking. He pushed my buttons and I reacted. "It wasn't different at all."

Daniel stopped, and if he'd taken any blood that night, it didn't show in his face as he went stark white. "What are you trying to say, Zoey?"

I threw my hands up. I shouldn't have gone there. I tried to backtrack. "This is why my father never worked with the same crew twice, Danny. Neither did your dad. The rules don't apply when you care about the people you work with."

Daniel wasn't buying it. "That's not what you meant, Z. I can see it in your face. I saw it when you went to him after that demon let you go. Why did he let you go, Zoey? What the hell did you promise him? Screw that. Just tell me why you didn't run. Just say it. Say it!"

"Because I love him." I shook a little as I said it, but he left me no choice.

Daniel's fangs popped out, his claws lengthening. For a split second I was afraid of him, but he took his anger out on a large tree, shoving his fist clean through it. He stood there shaking with emotion, and I started to come down from my volcanic rage. It was like this between me and Danny sometimes. We pushed and pushed until something broke, and we had to put us back together. I just didn't know how to fix it this time.

"It doesn't change how I feel about you, Danny." It was a stupid thing to say, but it was all I had.

He laughed, a nasty, bitter sound. "It changes everything, Zoey. I love you and only you. My whole life it's only been you. I've never even slept with anyone else. Even while you fucked him mindless, I was faithful because I knew you would come back to me. No, there weren't any hookers, baby. I spent that money protecting the new vamps. I spent it building something to protect you. I was willing to wait for you because he might have your body, but I had your heart. Now you tell me you love him? Maybe your love isn't worth what I thought it was."

It no longer mattered that there were other people watching because I couldn't stop the tears. All I could see was years of my life, years of my love, being tossed away. "Guess that whole 'I'll fight for you' thing didn't last very long, did it? After everything you did, Danny, all the lies, all the times you pushed me away and told me to move on because you didn't love me anymore, and you want to end it this way? By telling me I wasn't worth it? Fine. That's what you want, fine." I took a second to breathe through the pain, but there was something else I needed him to understand. "I wouldn't take back a minute of it, Daniel. Not a minute. Not even this one. Now we do this one last job and then we can be done. I'll even leave the city after we get Sarah back. I wouldn't want to contaminate your power base."

Daniel was finally calming down. His claws retracted, his shoulders slumped, and he sighed as he looked at me. "Zoey, I'm not doing this job with you. I'm sorry for what I said before. You took me by surprise, but I shouldn't have said what I did. That being said, I won't take you with me to Vegas. If I learned anything tonight it's that you're not up to this. You can't be unemotional or professional. You're going to get yourself killed, and I won't be a part of that."

"You owe me this," I stammered, shocked that he would threaten to torpedo my operation. He knew how important this was to me.

"No," he said implacably. "I need to keep you alive. That's what I owe you."

"I'll find another way, then." I felt like he'd punched me in the gut. How could he take away my best option to save Sarah? It didn't matter what she'd done. She was a part of our crew. We didn't leave our crew behind.

He shook his head, his jaw a stubborn line. “You need an invitation to that ball, Zoey. I assure you, you won’t find another vampire willing to escort you.”

A dumbass, stupid, likely to get me killed plan went through my head. “Who said I was going to ask a vampire, Danny? I believe the demons will be looking for dates, too.”

Daniel stopped cold. “You wouldn’t dare.”

“If you can say that and mean it, then you don’t know me at all.” I stared at my husband, my first love, and let him feel my will. I’d never let him tell me what I could or couldn’t do. I hadn’t done it when we were together, and I would be damned if I let him do it after we broke up.

Daniel’s blue eyes widened. “Who the hell was that in the field, Zoey? What did you do? What did you promise that demon in order to save Dev?”

Because I was no longer interested in answering his questions, I turned away and started to go back to the van. I was already thinking of all the things I would need to do when I got back to the city. I was going to have to call Stewart to me in order to arrange an invitation to the ball. It would be hard because my witch was in Hell, but Christine would help me. The good news was with Danny out of the picture, I could leave my lover out of it as well. I could protect Dev by running the job alone. He wouldn’t like it, but he wouldn’t have a choice. I had the Revelation. I could get Sarah out myself.

Daniel pulled me around. He wasn’t taking the silent treatment well. “Tell me, Zoey.”

“It was Stewart,” I told him because he would probably find out anyway.

“Shit.” Daniel slapped at the van, his hand denting the metal.

I pushed at his chest because he was crowding me, but it didn’t do any good. Until Danny wanted to move, I was trapped. The only weapons I had were words. “I would think you would be thrilled. According to Stewart, the demons are all rooting for you. You have a real cheerleader in our old friend. He wants to get in your good graces, Your Highness. Would you like to know how he thought he could really please you?”

Daniel’s eyes strayed to Dev’s sleeping form. “I have never…”

I hit his chest because I could see in his eyes that he had thought it. He'd thought about someone doing that job for him so he could get the benefit and not pay for the crime. He would never say the words out loud, but it had clearly crossed his mind. "How long, Danny? How long until one of your minions decides to move up the ladder by killing Dev?"

I could see Daniel was upset by the thought. He shook me lightly by my shoulders. "I have done everything I can to protect your lover. I could have killed him many times over, but I allowed myself to look like a pathetic chump while you worked out your angst. Don't you blame me for this. You're the one who brought him in. And don't you dare blame me for wanting him out of the picture. You know how I feel about you. Do you think it's been easy watching you with him? I want to rip his heart out every time he touches you. You're mine, Zoey. You've always been mine."

"Then you should have taken me with you to Paris."

The night after Daniel and I performed the ritual that made us man and wife, he'd been carted off to answer to the Council for his actions concerning Lucas Halfer. I was his companion and I was told there was a seat on that plane for me, but Daniel had forbidden it. He took Neil and left me behind to wonder about his fate. I would have followed him anywhere in that moment. I would have faced anything. I would have accepted our marriage and never thought to even speak to Dev again. I would have been his faithful wife and done the job Stewart said I was born to do. It was Daniel's rejection that caused me to seek Dev out, but I couldn't go back now. I realized now that moment when he looked up at me and said "I forbid it" had broken something in me. I was no longer sure it could be fixed.

Daniel's face fell, his eyes nearly pleading. "I wonder if you're ever going to stop punishing me for that. I was protecting you."

Weariness threatened to take over my system. This was an argument that never seemed to end for us. "You do an awful lot of that, Danny. Maybe I didn't want to be protected. Maybe I wanted to be your partner not your possession. You don't trust me. Now that I'm standing here, I realize that you've never trusted me. The whole time we've been working together you've been indulging me. You've just been waiting for me to make a mistake so you could shut it down."

"I trust you, Z."

I sniffled a little, finally coming down from my anger. Only a stark sadness was left. "No, you don't. When you came back and we decided to try the whole friendship thing out, you promised me no more secrets. That was a lie. You didn't tell me about the little army you're gathering until I forced you to. You're always going to do it because you need to protect me. Because you don't trust me to be able to handle your world. What you need from me, what you want from me, is sex and blood and the joy of ownership. You want a queen by your side, but you want her to be a pretty plaything."

Daniel shook his head and tried to pull me into his arms, but I shoved a hand between us to keep my distance. "That's not true, Zoey. I don't see you that way. You're my whole world. Everything I do is for you. Everything I've done since I was eight freaking years old has been with you in mind."

My heart ached as he brought up our past. "You think I don't remember? You think I don't remember when we were so much more than this? I was your best friend. I was your lover. You wouldn't have thought to keep secrets from me. We were partners. When we built something, we did it together."

Daniel ignored the distance I placed between us and pulled me to him. I stood in his embrace wanting to return it, but if I gave in now, I would become what he wanted. I would be his sweet companion to be coddled and protected. Maybe I could have been that at one point in time, but I was a different person now.

Daniel held me as if he was afraid to let go, but I just stood there. "This is stupid, Zoey. I was angry and scared out of my mind. I was watching the whole time. I watched those witches die, and I just knew you were next. Then I watched them arrest you. We're both tired and angry. Neither one of us means a damn thing we're saying. We'll pick up the conversation when we get back to Dallas."

He took a step back, but I couldn't look at him. I heard him walk over to the boys who'd sat silently while Danny and I had blown up eighteen years of our lives. I suppose it would have been politer for them to have walked away, but it wouldn't have mattered. They still would have heard everything.

"Come on, Chad. We're going to fly home," Daniel ordered quietly. "It'll be faster anyway."

I finally looked over at them. Chad was shaking his head and Neil remained in his wolf form, a gorgeous arctic wolf at Chad's side.

Chad's eyes widened. "I'd rather drive. I don't really like heights."

Daniel straightened his duster, buttoning it up. "You're strong, but you've only been a vampire for a week. You can't be trusted around her."

"I'm not the one with control issues around your wife, tonight, Master," Chad said solemnly. He knew that there was no arguing though, and he knelt down to hug Neil. The wolf thumped his tail and licked his lover's face. "See you soon."

Daniel turned and our eyes met again. "I'll call you tomorrow, and we'll go somewhere and talk. I meant what I said about Vegas, but we can talk about finding alternatives. This isn't over, Z."

But it was, at least for tonight, as Daniel put an arm under Chad's shoulders and they were gone. I slumped to the ground, my back to the van. Neil came to sit beside me and nuzzled my neck. He licked my face until I put my arms around him and let him comfort me.

"You can change back, Neil. I'm not going to yell anymore." Sometimes Neil stayed in his wolf form to avoid arguments, but I wasn't angry with him.

Neil thumped his tail twice for no.

I looked down at him and realized what was wrong. "You can't find your pants, can you?"

One thump confirmed it. I sighed. "Come on, then. We have a long drive ahead of us."

Chapter Sixteen

I looked down at the amulet in my hand. It felt good to hold the Revelation. In the two days since I'd driven back from the Ozarks, I spent a lot of time with the item. I held it and inspected it often. When I wasn't using it, I wore it around my neck and found my fingers playing with it even as I thought and did other things. It was mine, and it liked being mine.

It was, as Felicity had said, an odd little piece of jewelry. It was fashioned from gold, although knowing it had been made by an alchemist's hand, I wondered what that gold had started out as. The amulet itself was teardrop shaped, the center a large, near-perfect diamond. If I looked closely I could see a golden strand of hair trapped in the diamond. It was oddly beautiful. It stopped glowing around me the second day I wore it. According to Felicity's information, this was because now the amulet was used to me. It was primed to its owner.

All around me, music throbbed and club goers danced and drank and generally partied. Ether was packed. The moon was new, and when the wolves weren't running, they liked to get their drink on. I ignored everything around me, watching the amulet as it started to gently pulse. Every time I managed to get the sucker to work, a little thrill went through me.

West. He wasn't making this easy on me. The dance floor was between me and my target. Using the amulet was like a game of hot or cold. I had to pay very close attention or I would get off track and have to figure out where I'd gone wrong. If I tried to go around the gyrating werewolves, I could lose the signal. It was odd. I could get fairly close to some wolves, but the minute the bouncer named Kevin walked into the room, the Revelation went dead. I had to make sure Kevin was working the line outside the club if I wanted to practice with it. I'd decided it had to have something to do with how strong the wolf or vampire was. It immediately went dead when Neil walked in the room, even faster than it did with Kevin.

Dev had made sure he was off tonight, and Neil had a date with Chad, so I could practice with relative ease. The pulse became stronger, and through the crowd I caught a glimpse of what I sought.

Dev leaned against the wall, one foot propped up behind him. He'd been patiently allowing himself to be experimented on for the last couple of days. The Revelation recognized him, though I suspected the effect would be stronger when I went looking for Felix Day. Dev and I had been playing hide and seek all night.

"That was fast," he said over the noise as I joined him. "You're getting better with that thing."

I placed the amulet back around my neck, a sense of satisfaction flowing through me. "I think I'm ready."

His face went grim. He wasn't exactly on board with my new plan to call up Stewart and ask him to the prom. Dev was already upset that I was in debt to the demon for his sake. He didn't want me in any further, but there was no other way around it since Daniel wouldn't take me. I also suspected Dev wasn't happy about my request for new living arrangements after the job. I was serious about leaving the city. I couldn't move on when Daniel was everywhere I looked. I asked Dev to consider coming with me to Miami. He owned a club there. Albert told me he had a condo right on the beach.

I was waiting for his answer. The idea that I could lose both Daniel and Dev was a heavy weight on my heart.

Dev looked up, his eyes on the dance floor. He frowned. I turned to see what had caught his attention. My husband stood across the illuminated dance floor, looking incongruous among the throng of party people. No happy dance time for Daniel Donovan. No, he was like a big-ass bird of prey looking for a mouse to swallow. His eyes latched on to me and he headed my direction. I had to bump my way through the dancing crowd, but they moved for Daniel. He was like Moses parting the Red Sea. People just got out of his way.

"I told you to call him back," Dev said with a shake of his head.

He had. He'd told me to call Daniel several times, but I was stubborn. I hadn't even gone home because I wanted to avoid this confrontation. We said all we needed to say in Arkansas. He'd left me high and dry, and I needed to concentrate on the job at hand. Daniel had been the one to accuse me of paying too much attention to my personal life. He'd been the one to point out that I was letting the job suffer. Well, I'd paid my love life almost zero attention in the last couple of days. I ignored Daniel's every attempt to contact me. As far as I was concerned, I would see him at the ball.

Dev put an arm around me and leaned down to whisper in my ear. "Please try to remember everyone is watching. Keep it civil."

"Zoey," Daniel shouted. So much for civil. "What the hell do you think you're doing? You ignore my calls. You don't even bother to go home. Did you think I wouldn't come looking for you?"

Dev smiled broadly and held out his hand. Daniel just looked at it like it was diseased. "Shake my hand, Daniel, or I'll have you thrown out of this club."

Daniel huffed out an amused laugh. "I'd like to see you try."

"Every wolf in town is here tonight." Dev spoke slowly as if he was talking to a child. "You know, the same wolves you're trying to negotiate with. They're all here, and they're all watching you right now. You can take my hand and act like we're friends, or you can throwdown with your wayward wife and her lover in front of the world. Trust me. You don't want those wolves thinking you can't handle your bitch."

"Hey," I protested.

"It's a technical term only, sweetheart," Dev said, his lips quirking up with humor.

Daniel looked around and confirmed that he was, in fact, the center of attention. They were far enough away that they probably couldn't hear over the loud music, but they were definitely interested in us. Daniel took Dev's outstretched hand and shook it.

"Now, kiss your wife," Dev commanded quietly. "Like you mean it." I shot Dev a surprised look, but his face was bland, like this was an ordinary situation. "Don't get stubborn on me, Zoey. It's only a kiss, and it will spare us all so much trouble later."

Daniel looked apprehensive, but I walked into his arms and let his lips find mine. It wasn't our most passionate kiss, but I still felt his warmth. Then it was over, and Dev looked down at me. He smiled a slow, seductive smile. He kissed me, snaking his hand through my hair, leaving no one confused about his intentions.

"I had to watch that, why?" Daniel nearly growled the question.

"Because we're creating an illusion, Daniel. Now we all go upstairs." Dev gestured toward his second floor office.

"Why are we going upstairs?" Daniel asked, very confused since this scenario wasn't playing out as he'd obviously planned.

Dev's green eyes rolled, his frustration evident. "Keep your voice down. We're going upstairs because I don't want to do this in front of everyone, you imbecile."

"Look man, if we go upstairs now people are going to think…" Daniel started.

"Yes, that's what they're going to think, and in one swift move, you go from cuckolded husband to a man of some exotic tastes. One is pathetic. The other is infinitely more interesting. It's your choice, Daniel. Now, Zoey, take your husband's hand and try to look like you're leading him to the Promised Land." Dev took my hand and started toward the stairs that led to his office. Daniel slipped his hand into my free one, and the three of us made our way through the very interested crowd.

"Boss." The bouncer at the stairs acknowledged Dev. He smiled at me, but his eyebrows rose at the sight of Daniel.

"Mike," Dev replied as the bouncer let us up the stairs. "I think we're going to require a few hours of privacy. Wouldn't you say, Dan?"

"At least," Daniel stammered.

Dev led us the rest of the way and used his card to open the door. I took one last glance at the crowd. Sure enough, there were very few people who weren't watching us disappear into the office. Dev dropped my hand as he shut the door behind us. He took a deep breath and proceeded to take a seat behind his desk. He held out his hand, indicating the two seats in front of him. Daniel and I sat down because I don't think either of us was sure of what else to do. I personally felt like I'd been called to the principal's office.

"What the hell was that?" Daniel asked.

"That was me saving your ass because you were about to make a huge mistake," Dev explained flatly. "I've watched you screw up long enough. I'm done. If you don't start playing this thing smart, you're going to get us all killed. I personally couldn't care less if you choose to commit suicide, but it affects Zoey, and that is my business."

Daniel's face flushed. I knew he didn't like me being Dev's business. "I didn't come here to talk to you, Quinn. I came here to talk to my wife."

Dev slapped a hand on his desk. "You came here to have a knockdown, dragout with your wife in a public forum. Rule number one in a royal court is this: Keep your problems behind closed doors."

Daniel looked at me like I knew what the hell Dev was talking about, but I was in the dark, too. He'd been very pensive since we returned from our trip. He hadn't been distant. To the contrary, he lathered affection on me at every given opportunity. He seemed happy I was staying at his place. He took time from his business to have dinner with me each night and to sit and watch whatever I wanted on television. He was trying to keep that boyfriend promise he made to me. It was nice, but the whole time I could see he was thinking. I had a suspicion I was about to find out where his mind had been.

"I am going to make you an offer, Daniel." Dev sat back, and I wondered if this was the way he dealt with vendors and business contacts and employees. There was nothing teasing or reckless about him now. He was all business. "I'm only going to make the offer once. If you refuse, I'll take Zoey where she wants to go and you can do this on your own."

Daniel waved his hand, a gesture for Dev to continue. Condescension was plain in his every move. "Please, let me hear this plan of yours."

Dev's long fingers made a thoughtful steeple as he spoke. "It's not a plan. You already have a plan. It's just obvious to me you don't have the training to carry it to a successful conclusion. What I'm offering are my services as an advisor."

Daniel threw his head back and laughed. "What the hell am I supposed to learn from you, Dev? I'm not going into the nightclub business. I suppose you could teach me how to dress like a metro douchebag."

"You have no idea who I am, do you, Daniel?" Dev asked, and I was surprised because there was no small amount of sympathy in his voice. "God, this is worse than I thought. Everyone keeps assuring me you're a highly intelligent man, but if you don't even have a file on me, I'll have to disagree."

"Why would I have a file on you?"

Dev got up and took out a key. He walked to a large filing cabinet. Dev pulled out a fat file folder and tossed it to Daniel. I heard his shocked intake as he realized what it was.

"Know your enemies, Dan," Dev said, settling back into his chair.

I'd seen that file before. It was just about anything anyone ever wanted to know about Daniel Donovan. I was sure there were things in that file that Daniel had forgotten about himself. He flipped through the folder quickly. I saw the minute Daniel decided this was a serious discussion. His face lost the arrogance, and he settled down, staring at the folder. "And just who are you, Dev?"

"I am Devinshea Conlan Quinn, second son of Miria, Queen of Faery. I am second in line to the throne behind my brother, though I doubt I would last long if I took a crown. I come from a royal line that is so long, no one remembers where it began. I was raised in a royal court and acted as my mother's envoy to almost every type of supernatural creature you can imagine. If you want to know what I can teach you, besides how to dress like a douchebag, I will tell you. I can teach you how to be a king."

My heart nearly stopped in my chest. What the hell was happening? They couldn't be in the same room for more than a few minutes without insulting each other. "Dev, why are you doing this?"

Dev leaned toward me. He slipped into the more formal speech pattern he took when he was serious. I guessed it was from his training when he was young. Court was probably a very formal place. When Dev stopped using contractions, I always knew he meant business. "I know one of the reasons you are content with me is the fact that I support your freedom in this relationship. I rarely question your decisions, and I tend to do anything you ask of me. This is not entirely contrary to my nature. I prefer to please you. I am finding it difficult to do that now. You will not be happy if we move to Miami. I doubt that you will ever be happy so far from your home and the people you love. You see my quandary? I can do what you ask of me, but it will not make you happy. I have the additional problem of being able to see that your husband is going to get himself executed by the Council. Has either of you thought about where that leaves Zoey?"

"She would be sold." Daniel confirmed our worst fears. "You could try to defend her. You could try to hide her, but eventually they would kill you and take her into custody. Marcus would attempt to buy her, but I can't promise that he would succeed. Companions are very rare, and she's exquisite."

"If Marcus is even alive at the end of it," Dev murmured. "Tell me if I am wrong, but you had to have a powerful ally in the vampire world to be able to get as far as you have without detection. Vorenus seems the most likely as he's your patron and on the Council. He could provide a certain amount of protection."

Daniel's jaw clenched, and I could see him thinking. He didn't want to see the wisdom in Dev's offer. He wanted to laugh and call him an idiot and walk out of the office with his full pride intact. He didn't want to see Dev as someone who could help him. I watched Daniel very carefully. Stewart's words played through my head. There was a part of me that wanted Daniel to get up and walk out of that room. It would prove that he didn't care about power. It would prove beyond a shadow of a doubt that Stewart was wrong.

"What am I doing wrong with the local wolves?" Daniel asked, and I knew his path was set.

Just like that my lover became my husband's chief advisor.

"Oh, so many things," Dev replied. "The first is the fact that you bothered with the local pack at all. Mitchell Roberts is an idiot. You're never going to get anywhere with him. He owes fealty to the alpha in Colorado. Get that alpha on your side, and Mitchell will fall in line. If he doesn't and he breaks rank, we can take him out with no repercussions."

Daniel was nodding, and I suddenly felt invisible. I was no longer needed as the men in my life talked about negotiations and political ramifications and potentially advantageous assassinations. They talked forever as I sat there and wondered when the hell I had lost the upper hand.

I wasn't mad at Dev per se. He was trying to please me. He

believed I would be unhappy if Daniel and I were completely estranged. He knew I would be devastated if Daniel were killed, so he placed himself in a position to stop that from happening. I just didn't see how having the two men I loved working together would be anything but a disaster.

After a long discussion, Dev turned to me. "Zoey, are you listening?"

I wasn't, but it was easier to lie. "Of course."

Dev looked suspicious. "This is about you, too."

"I don't want to be queen." It hadn't seemed real until now. Daniel's war had seemed so far off, and I wasn't really a queen anyway. But now it was right in front of my face. In that moment, I just wanted to go upstairs and go to sleep, and in the morning everything would be back to normal or something close to it. Dev might have been right about my eventual dissatisfaction with Florida, but in that moment I wished he'd just packed up and left with me.

"Zoey," Dev said, but now he sounded more like my Dev. He was cajoling softly. "You're his greatest asset, sweetheart. It won't work without you. The other tribes or packs are going to be suspicious of a vampire. You soften him. Listen, we can all talk about this when we get to Vegas. I'll take care of the plans."

"I don't think that's a good idea." Daniel frowned, looking anywhere but my way.

"If you leave her behind, she'll just do it on her own. You can take her with you and let me help, or she and Christine are going to use me as a magical battery to call up old Stewart tonight. I assure you he'll be happy to be of service."

"Shit," Daniel cursed under his breath.

"You don't have to have anything to do with it, Danny." Even to my own ears I sounded petulant.

Dev walked from around his desk and pulled my hand to his lips. "She wouldn't be Zoey if she weren't so stubborn. Again, it's your choice, Daniel. You can go with us and we can run the job as planned, or she takes it in an entirely new and insanely dangerous direction. I will be going with Zoey. We can all go together or you can go alone. I think you'll find me immensely useful in Vegas, but I have to think of Zoey first."

I knew there was a litany of curses running through Daniel's brain, but he took a deep breath and sat back. "Fine. We need to be in Vegas at least two days before the ball. I have meetings to attend. I have a room at the Flamingo."

Dev actually shuddered. "Not anymore, you don't. We'll stay at my place. I have a penthouse at the Palms. My club is located there. The Council has already contacted me about hosting some of the events, so it won't be such a surprise for me to be there. The penthouse has enough room for all of us, including Neil."

Daniel's jaw firmed, his eyes lowering as if he was attempting to contain some well of emotion. "You can't expect me to share a room with you and Zoey."

Dev looked him straight in the face, not flinching a bit. "I don't expect it, Daniel. I require it. How exactly did you intend to explain my presence at this ball? I can be in Vegas for business, but that won't get me into the ball."

Daniel ran a frustrated hand through his hair. "Everyone brings their crew."

"Their retinue, Daniel. Stop talking like a kid off the streets," Dev corrected. "Does everyone's retinue include their wife's lover? Think for a moment and you'll realize what we all have to do."

Daniel got up and started pacing. "You want me to take you to the ball as my lover? Dev, no one is going to believe that."

Dev waved a hand toward the club outside his door. "They already do. Every cell phone in the supernatural world has been ringing tonight with the news that Daniel Donovan enjoyed a threesome with his wife and her lover. They're shaking their heads because now it all makes sense. Why would you kill me when you could enjoy me? How do you think a vampire makes his fortune? He doesn't work on Wall Street. He takes wealthy lovers. Hide in plain sight, Daniel. That is the only way this works."

Daniel let out a long, deep breath. He looked over at me, and his expression was one of naked pain. "How the hell did we get here, Z?"

The enormity of everything that had happened, that would happen, was crashing in on me. I didn't want this. I didn't want to be a queen. I didn't want to fight the Council. I didn't want to mix my lover up in Daniel's seemingly unavoidable destiny. My fears must have shown on my face because Dev hugged me tightly.

"It's going to be all right, sweetheart," Dev said, stroking my hair. "I know you're used to being in control, and you still are. If you still want to leave, I'll fuel the jet. We can be on the beach by dawn. It's your choice."

I looked at Daniel, who averted his eyes, choosing not to watch. It would be so much easier to leave. I could laugh and play and love Dev. And Daniel would probably die, and everyone I knew and loved would be in danger. Why couldn't I break with him? Even after everything that had happened, I knew in that moment that I would never have gone through with it. I would never have left Daniel. Even the limbo we were in was better than nothing at all. "No. I'll go to Vegas. I'll be what he needs."

Dev nodded. "I'll handle everything. Now you, my love, need to go on up to the grotto and horribly disappoint your father's girlfriend. Daniel and I are going to go back to the club and try to look like two men who just made one woman very happy. I believe the Mavs are playing. Shall we?"

Daniel looked at me for a long time before getting up and joining Dev. When they were gone, I sat back in my chair and wondered if I wouldn't have been better off with Stewart.

Chapter Seventeen

"What is this?" I stared down at the sheet of paper Dev handed me as the limo pulled away from the airport. I glanced back at the small jet we'd flown to Vegas in. It was a private plane, one he'd borrowed from the corporation he owned. My boyfriend really did know how to live.

"It's your itinerary." Dev passed out a schedule to both Daniel and Neil. "There are several things you need to do while we're here."

I scanned the list, grimacing a little. Since Dev took over as Daniel's advisor, I'd discovered he was damn serious about schedules. "I have three fittings? What am I trying to fit into?"

"He has me down for fittings, too." Daniel frowned.

"Did you think I was going to let you wear a *Hellboy* T-shirt to the ball? And don't try to tell me you brought a suit. You need a tux, and I don't trust you to not buy something in powder blue with ruffles," Dev explained. He turned to me. "As for you, your dress was custom made, and it needs to be fitted."

Daniel was still staring at the itinerary. "And what the hell does this mean? This asshole has me brooding every day from seven to nine."

A little smile curled Dev's lips up. "That would be your free time. If you can think of something to do besides brood, feel free. Would you like me to try to fit in some scowling time? Perhaps time to rail against fate?"

Daniel shook his head, but I could see the slightest hint of smile. Danny always had a good sense of humor. It was good to see it making a small comeback.

Neil practically hyperventilated. "I have spa time!"

"I thought you would like that," Dev acknowledged. "It's one way to make up for spending most of your time babysitting."

"I don't need a babysitter." I didn't fool myself that he was talking about someone else. Daniel and Dev had spent endless hours discussing how to best protect me. It was obnoxious.

This time when Daniel laughed, Dev laughed with him. Dev was smart enough to cover his smile with a cautious hand. "Consider Neil an escort."

"Consider Neil an order, Z," Daniel said, crossing his arms defensively. "This place is going to be full of vampires. You don't walk out of that room without one of us. Most of the time, it's got to be Neil."

Dev's eyes widened, and he shot Daniel a look that plainly said "Shut the hell up and let me handle her." Daniel's mouth quirked in an obvious "Good luck handling that, dude."

The men in my life had started having entire conversations about me with looks and gestures. Neil and I made up the dialogue in our heads and compared notes. Strangely we came up with different takes on the same conversation. Neil's mostly consisted of both of them realizing they really loved each other and throwing down on the floor for some homoerotic bliss. I glanced at Neil and he grinned. I knew my babysitter had a new fantasy about a limo.

"Sweetheart, I would feel so much better about this whole enterprise if I knew you were protected." Dev slid a hand over mine. Dev was never content to just hold my hand. His thumb made sensual promises against my wrist. "We're very close to an actual physical entrance to the Hell plane. It makes sense to have a bodyguard."

"And a shopping buddy," Neil pointed out. "Hey, Zoey, let's get those big margaritas you can wear around your neck and then we can storm Prada." Neil turned to Dev, his mouth turning down. "With the money Zoey and I have, we can probably buy a whole key chain."

Dev was good-natured about being milked for cash. He pulled his wallet out of a pocket in his sport coat and extracted a jet black card. I thought for a moment Neil was going to cry. His hand whipped out, but Dev held back. "Neil, do you know what this is?"

"The key to my heart," Neil replied with an adoring smile.

"This has no spending limit. When you flash this card, every salesperson within a two mile radius will come running. They will offer you champagne, caviar, hell, they'll give you a foot massage in the middle of the store. They will do anything to get you to use this little piece of plastic." Dev squeezed my hand. "So, what do you say, sweetheart? Should I give your bodyguard the keys to the kingdom?"

I rolled my eyes because I was so perfectly caught there wasn't even a way to yell at him about it. "Bastard," I managed to mutter, but it came out as an affectionate grumble. "I'll shop."

Neil kissed the card as Dev passed it to him. "I'm going to protect you with my life," he whispered to the card lovingly. "You too, Z."

Dev shot Daniel a look that said "See that's how you handle a woman. You go through her gay husband." And Daniel wordlessly replied with "Well played, dude with endless cash." Neil was watching the two of them, and I had a suspicion in his version they were already kissing. I caught Neil's attention, and he wagged his eyebrows lasciviously to let me know I was right. I couldn't help but dissolve into laughter.

The boys shifted their eyes between me and Neil and then looked back at each other, trying to figure what we were laughing at. They seemed deeply confused, and it just made me laugh more.

The limo pulled up to the Palms, and Daniel got out, followed by Neil. I waited for Dev. He always got out of the car first and then opened the door for me. He even got pissed when a valet tried to help me out. It was something he enjoyed doing, so I didn't scramble out of the limo after Neil, preferring to wait for Dev. Instead of getting out, he stopped Neil, tugging on his coat. Daniel was halfway in the building when he noticed no one was following him.

"Neil," Dev began, completely losing the counselor's smooth tones and sounding reckless again. "Spend whatever you want, and I mean whatever. Go crazy, buddy, but you have to do me two favors."

"Anything."

"One, lingerie," Dev said. "I don't mean that pretty Victoria's Secret shit. I want slutty. I want to be able to eat it off her body, man. If it requires double A batteries, consider that a plus. Two, buy her shoes. She wears a seven and a half. Manolos, Jimmy Choos, good, high-end stuff. She's going to try to talk you into a kitten heel.

Screw that. I want a full-blown cat. Nothing under a four-and-a-half-inch stiletto. I look particularly good in jewel tones. Understood?"

Neil gave Dev a quick salute. "She'll look like your wet dream by the time I'm done with her."

Dev let him go and sat back. "You can't imagine my wet dreams, little boy. Now, go tell your master I'll have his queen back in plenty of time for the party. I have to debrief her, you understand."

The limo door slammed shut. When he turned to me, I had to catch my breath. The last two days Dev had been very much in a professional mode. He'd been affectionate but circumspect out of respect for working closely with my husband. That cool, respectful man was gone, and in his place was one hungry boy.

"Drive until I tell you to stop," Dev commanded over the intercom, and the limo pulled away.

"Jewel tones?" My heart rate tripled as he turned those gorgeous green eyes on me.

"I don't know if you've noticed, sweetheart, but they complement my skin tone. Since those gorgeous shoes end up around my neck, I thought I should get something that looks good on me," he drawled as he shrugged out of his coat. "I'll tell you something else that looks good on me—your very naked body." He reached across the limo and pulled me into his lap. "I need to make a few things clear to you, lover."

"I'm listening." I sighed, leaning my head back against his shoulder.

I'd felt very neglected over the last two days. Dev spent much more time with Daniel than me, and I wasn't secure enough to not be a little jealous. I wondered if I was going to lose both of the men I loved to power and politics. He'd come to bed late, and though he had pulled me into his arms, he'd kissed me and promptly fallen asleep. I wasn't used to a Dev who didn't try to get into my pants twice a night.

Now he was making up for lost time. He slipped his hand between my legs and up my skirt. With unerring accuracy, his long fingers started teasing their way inside my underwear.

I'd felt so alone the last few days. I worked with the Revelation and planned out my heist, but mostly I sat by myself and worried. I needed a few minutes where I didn't think about worst-case scenarios.

"I would give anything to not send you into that welcoming party tonight," he whispered. His tongue lightly traced the shell of my ear, sending shivers up and down my spine. His fingers played in my pussy, spreading my labia wide. I was already slick with desire. "It's killing me that I can't go with you."

He was talking about the first party of the conference, one that was being hosted in his club. I'd expected that we all would go. I didn't like the thought of being separated. There were too many things that could go wrong. It was getting hard to think though. He was teasing me, making me antsy and edgy. I wanted to force that finger inside me where it would do some good, but Dev held me tightly, unwilling to give up his game. "But it's your club."

"Not tonight it isn't," he explained. I caught my breath as one clever finger caressed that bundle of nerves that made me scream. Dev toyed with my clitoris, sliding his fingers along either side and twisting lightly. "Tonight it belongs to the vampires, and I'm not welcome. Vampires and companions only, with the exception of staff. I can go to the ball as part of Daniel's retinue, but it's still dangerous. I have to be prudent around you while we're here. I don't think you're going to like that. I need you to understand that I hate this situation. I want to be somewhere fucking you, teasing you, pleasing you. The last thing I wanted was to get involved in a coup attempt."

Dev's hand pulled away. Before I could protest, I was flat on my back. Dev's weight settled on top of me. I hated the clothes between us. Skin to skin. That was what I needed. His body nestled against mine like puzzle pieces that fit perfectly. "Then why are you doing this?"

His hair fell across his forehead, and he was so beautiful, my heart skipped a beat. His green eyes were intense and filled with something far beyond simple lust. He leaned over, his nose nuzzling mine. Since he'd given up being strictly my lover, he'd become more and more affectionate, his sweetness growing daily. "Blame yourself, Zoey. I might have been happy with a nice long affair until you climbed on that altar. I know I was high, but don't think I can't remember that moment. I'll remember it as long as I live. I was going to enjoy you, lover, for as long as I could. Then I was going to respectfully allow you to go back to your husband because I thought that was what you would want in the end. Fuck that, Zoey. You blew that plan all to hell, and I'll do anything to stay in your life. You should have run."

I brought my hands up, cupping his face. We hadn't really talked about that night. "I couldn't leave you."

"All of my life I have been the expendable one." He lowered his forehead to mine, cuddling up against me. "I was the spare, and after I proved too human, I wasn't even that. Do you know how many people have told me they love me? I can get an 'I love you' out of a woman by looking at her. It's meaningless. It's a phrase designed to get me to do something. Even when you said it to me in the barn, I didn't really believe it. I thought you wanted to keep your lover for a while longer. I was pleased that it wasn't over, but I didn't believe. You proved me wrong. You would have done anything to save me."

I brought my hands up to hold his head to mine. "I love you."

"You would have sacrificed yourself."

"I love you," I repeated because he needed to hear it. He needed to believe it. Despite his good looks and wealth, he was just a man with all a man's insecurities. I loved him. I meant to be his safe harbor, as I once had been Daniel's.

"You love me," he whispered, wonder in his voice. "Know this, Zoey, I will do my best to advise your husband. I will do everything I can to see you on a proper throne with all due rights as his queen. I will stand in the shadows. I will concede my place at your side. I will never concede my place in your bed, and I will not concede your heart. Love Daniel all you like as long as there is a place for me."

When he kissed me, it was with everything he had. He didn't bother to undress me, simply shifted a bit and pulled up my skirt before tugging my undies down. The situation was far too urgent. He fumbled, a word that almost never described Dev. He was smooth and silky but tonight he faltered.

I took charge for the first time. I unzipped his pants, reaching for his cock, stroking him until he groaned. I guided him to me and wrapped my legs around him, offering him everything I had. He kissed me as he strained to work his way inside me, slowly, inch by inch, teasing his way in, letting me get wet around him.

Dev groaned and pulled himself out.

"Condom," he muttered with a grimace. He pulled one out and rolled the hated piece of latex over his cock, and then came back to me.

"I love you, Zoey," he whispered as he started to glide his cock over that sweet spot he always found so quickly. "Remember that. No matter what you see tonight, no matter what you have to do, I love you."

An hour later, the limo rolled back in front of the casino. Dev set down his drink and tried to smooth his clothes into something that resembled a presentable state. After the things we'd done in that limo, there was no way his clothes stayed perfectly pressed. My comfortable clothes had held up better, but it was time for me to get ready for the party.

The driver opened the car, and the first thing I saw was Daniel. He leaned against the side of the building, a hollow look on his face. When he glanced up and saw me, his face went blank and he made his way to the limo.

"It's time, Zoey," Dev said, picking up his drink again. He took a long swallow of vodka. "Go with your husband. I'm going to find a poker table and hope no one tries to righteously kill me."

I leaned over to kiss him good-bye, but he put a hand between us. "No, Zoey. No more affection where anyone could see us. I told you you wouldn't like it, sweetheart. Unless we are with Daniel and playing out our happy ménage, I will treat you with the courtesy of a servant. This game has started."

Daniel held out his hand to help me out of the limo. His eyes were dark, but he swallowed his anger. "I would appreciate it if you wouldn't do that again, Dev."

Dev inclined his head slightly to show his agreement. He looked at me and his face was blank. I was staring at the face of a politician, not my lover. "Zoey, you do not dare enter that gathering without his mark on you. Do you understand?"

I understood. Tonight Daniel would be drinking straight from the tap.

"How long?" I demanded. "How long do we have to play this stupid game?"

Dev reached for the vodka bottle. "We play until we win or we die."

I let Daniel help me out of the car. He shut the door and the limo took off.

"Zoey, people are watching." Daniel pulled me close, and I let my arm go around him.

I was grateful for his strong arm around me because I didn't like being the center of this attention. When Daniel said people, he meant vampires. I suddenly felt very ill equipped to do this part of the job. I was ready to slip into Hell and rescue my friend, but I wanted to hide at the thought of having to fit into vampire society.

"Mr. Donovan, Mrs. Donovan." A well-dressed man approached us. He was a middle-aged man with a solid build.

"Roman." Daniel shook the man's hand. "Zoey, this is Roman. He runs Dev's club here in Vegas. He's been assigned to make sure we're comfortable."

"It is a great pleasure to meet you, Mrs. Donovan." Roman bowed my way, a gallant gesture. "Know I stand ready to meet your every need. My employer was quite adamant about making sure you were comfortable. Please understand that credit has been guaranteed at any store you would like to shop at or any restaurant you care to dine at. There is a driver at your disposal twenty-four hours a day."

"We get it," Daniel said irritably. "He wants her taken care of."

Roman stopped, his eyes slightly confused. "You do understand that he's done the same for you, Mr. Donovan? My employer was quite adamant that you both be taken care of."

That stopped Daniel for a moment. "Thank you. I appreciate it. Could you please show us to our room? We don't have as much time as I thought we would."

Roman led the way into the casino. Daniel and I walked behind him. I'm sure I looked like a gawky tourist, but I didn't care. Vegas was completely new to me, and I was kind of awed by the decadence of it.

Daniel leaned over and whispered in my ear. "This place is full of vampires, baby. Be very careful. That one over there is a Council member named Niko. He knew Socrates on a personal level. He's looking forward to meeting you, Z. Everyone is very curious about us."

I started toward the elevators but Roman diverted us.

"Your rooms have a private elevator, Mrs. Donovan." He indicated a lovely glass elevator off to the side of the lobby. He punched in a code and the elevator began to slide down toward us. "They're going to be curious, Mr. Donovan, because it has been a very long time since the Council designated a *Nex Apparatus*. It scares the hell out of everyone. As for you, Mrs. Donovan, they're likely wondering what kind of woman shares a bed with such a man. A companion is used to a certain hardness in the vampire she serves. Mr. Donovan is believed to be on a whole new level. The other companions, they pity you."

The elevator opened and Roman entered, but I grabbed Daniel's hand. His eyes were downcast, his mouth a tight line. I looked around and, sure enough, there were at least ten pairs of eyes looking at us. Three women looked at me with great sympathy.

I could be angry with Daniel, but I wasn't letting anyone pity me for being married to him. I smiled and with great tenderness, lifted my lips to his. There was no mad lust in my intent. This was affection and caring, and Daniel responded in kind. His lips touched mine, sweetly saying so much more than passion could. I laid my head on his shoulder, and he wrapped me in a protective circle. We stayed there for a moment and then entered the elevator. I watched as they gawked at us. Daniel leaned down and set his chin on the top of my head, watching the lobby as well.

"Thank you, Z," he said quietly.

"They don't know you, Danny." If they did, they would think I was lucky. At that moment, I was thinking I was insane. I'd just left the arms of one man I loved and promptly found myself wrapped up in another. And my heart was just as content here.

"Maybe you don't know me," he said, pulling away.

I rolled my eyes. "Is this your 'rail against fate' time or are you brooding? And what the hell is a *Nex Apparatus*?"

Roman piped up. "It means Death Machine. Daniel Donovan is the Council's Death Machine."

Daniel looked down again with a sort of shame that made my heart ache.

Still, I snorted. I couldn't help it. "That is the worst super villain name I ever heard. No one knows what *Nex Apparatus* means. What's up with all the Latin? When you show up to kill someone and give them your name, they're supposed to quake in fear, baby, not ask you for a translation."

Daniel laughed, and I was happy to get that look off his face. I didn't blame him for anything he'd done while working for the Council. He'd done it to survive. "I'll try to come up with something more suitable for you, Z."

"Good." I looked back down at that lobby. I would have to face those people soon enough. "And I'll try to find you some spandex."

"Neil will be thrilled," Daniel admitted, and he squeezed my hand. I got the feeling we'd be doing a lot of hand holding in the next couple of hours.

Whether I was ready or not, Dev was right. This game was on.

Chapter Eighteen

When I stepped out of the shower, Daniel was sitting on the bed, slacks on, shirt off. I stopped, my feet planted to the ground. Intimacy. Even at home, we'd been careful of not catching each other in moments like this. Moments that felt like before, when it would have been perfectly normal for him to see me wrapped in a fluffy robe.

We were stuck in this suite together, pretending to be lovers for days. What would it feel like when Dev was here, too? When we were all thrown together, forced into a fake intimacy?

"Zoey, I'm sorry." His hands were shaking slightly, evidence of his need. "We should get this over with."

"All right," I said, loosening the belt of my robe. "Where do you want me?"

It was awkward. I was thinking about the fight we'd had and all the horrible things we'd said to each other. And I was thinking about the good times, too. I was thinking that we'd always talked about getting married in Vegas and avoiding a big wedding because it seemed silly when my father was our only family.

Of course, our little elopement wouldn't have included an entourage and a fabulous suite, and those fangs in Daniel's mouth.

They gleamed, primitive and ferocious in the low light. I'd never been afraid of them because they were a part of Daniel, but the minute he noticed me looking, he closed his lips, hiding that part of himself.

"Sit in my lap, Z. It's the easiest way."

I settled onto his lap, his arm curving around my waist and pulling me close. I could smell the soap from his shower and feel the smoothness of his skin as I wrapped my arm around his waist. I looked up and his eyes had bled to a gorgeous, surreal blue, the white disappearing.

"Zoey, please let me pull you in. I don't want to hurt you." Pulling me in was his code for using his powers of persuasion to make the bite orgasmic. I'd had it both ways and firmly came down on the side of pleasure. "I won't take advantage."

I nodded, not trusting myself to speak. He wouldn't take advantage. Daniel had proven to have excellent control when it came to denying himself. It had cost us years. I sat on his lap, the world narrowing to him. There was no worry in this place. There was no king or queen or Council. There was only pleasure and joy.

"I can hear your heartbeat, baby," Daniel said, his voice a deep, rich seduction. His free hand stroked my throat, tracing the veins he found there. "I can hear the blood rushing through every vein. It's like music, and when I listen close enough, my whole body responds until we're in harmony. I never feel my heartbeat unless I'm with you."

My head fell back and I shivered as the warmth of Daniel's mouth enveloped me. He kissed my neck, his tongue laving affection, getting me to the perfect place where I wanted one thing. I wanted his bite more than my next breath. Every part of my body responded. My nipples peaked. My skin sang. I would swear I could feel every inch of my body opening wide to welcome him.

And my pussy was the greediest bit of all. Warm and wet. It didn't matter that Dev was out there somewhere. In that moment, with Danny's magic riding me, I just wanted him. An image played through my head. Daniel's fangs. Dev's hands. Together.

I was caught, trapped in those eyes and perfectly content to be there. My arms tightened around him, my heart thudding when his fangs penetrated. Bite doesn't cover it. It was penetration, his body in mine, my blood in his. The orgasm bloomed across me, rolling in wave after wave of joy and pleasure until I simply let it be and gave over to him entirely.

I don't remember when my robe came open, but when Daniel was through, it was hanging off me.

I probably looked extremely wanton, laying there in his lap, my naked body relaxed from a surfeit of pleasure. He'd pulled me close so my nipples rubbed against his chest.

"You okay, Z?" He moved me on the bed because I couldn't quite move my limbs yet.

Nodding, I looked up at him. I knew what he wanted. He wanted to nick a vein and hold me to him as I sucked, his blood an exchange, strengthening the bond between vampire and companion. He wanted that exchange and the sex that inevitably followed, but Daniel merely laid me down and brushed the hair from my face. He was not enough of a gentleman to close my robe. He stared for a moment as he licked his fangs, getting every last drop. For just a second, he forgot to hide himself from me. He was a gorgeous beast.

"God, you're beautiful, Zoey." He shook his head and laughed. "I took off my shirt in case I spilled. I should have taken off my freaking pants. I have to change."

But he stood there, looking at me as I giggled like a drunken schoolgirl because it wasn't blood he'd spilled. His face cleared and his fangs disappeared. He sat on the bed, a rueful smile on his face. "Thanks for coming with me tonight. I want you to know I'll keep you safe."

I reached out, my limbs beginning to come back to life. "I wouldn't be anywhere else."

He reached for my hand, and we sat there for the longest time.

* * * *

"This is what the inside of Dev's head looks like." Daniel said an hour later as we stared at the scene in front of us with no small amount of shock and awe.

This particular club was called Descent. It was everything a Las Vegas club should be—decadent, rich, plush, and more than a little vulgar. Ether was a nightclub. Descent was something slightly different. It was a strip club, which I would have appreciated knowing in advance. There was one large stage complete with a shiny pole that even now a lovely woman was contorting herself around. No one can work a stripper pole like a shapeshifter. There were two smaller stages with dancers and patrons sitting around watching.

The room was full of vampires. By the looks of it, there were roughly two hundred in the club. It was a good portion of the vampire population. These were the movers and shakers, the old ones. Daniel was the youngest vampire in the room by hundreds of years. If it hadn't been for his unique talents, he would never have been invited to these proceedings. He would have been a fledgling and beneath most vampires' notice. They all noticed Daniel Donovan as we walked into the room. Every head turned, and I saw fear and suspicion in their eyes.

"Wow, you know how to make an entrance," I said under my breath.

"They're all afraid of me," Daniel explained. "They know that if they step out of line, I'm the one the Council would send. I'm the one vampire they never want on their doorstep because if I'm there, I've come for one reason only. I'm their executioner."

"See, The Executioner would work," I pointed out. "It's kind of humdrum, but it's better than the *Nex* thingie."

Daniel's lips turned up in a half smile. He put his arm around my waist, his hand settling on my hip. He was staring down the room. I suddenly realized there were maybe thirty women in the room who could possibly be companions. Thirty scrumptious snacks and two hundred hungry vampires.

"They know you're mine. You'll be safe. These are well-trained vampires. If one of them steps out of line, well, they know I can take care of it. Zoey, if one of them even looks at you the wrong way, you let me know." He was staring at my neck, and I knew he was looking at the mark he'd left. I couldn't help but think about it, too.

A deep voice pulled me from my thoughts. "Daniel, it's good to see you."

I looked over to see it was the man Daniel had pointed out earlier. Niko, the Greek Council member, shook Daniel's hand. He was shorter than my husband but looked strong, his hair a tawny blonde and his eyes almost golden.

He turned toward me, zeroing in on my neck before meeting my eyes. "Mrs. Donovan, I presume."

I did not merit a handshake but received a polite half bow, a gesture from another era.

Daniel's hand tangled in mine as though he wanted to be able to pull me back at any moment. "This is my wife, Zoey Donovan. Zoey, please meet Niko Rallis, honored member of our Council."

I wasn't sure if I was supposed to curtsy or something. Daniel had never had me presented to society, so I was ignorant. It didn't seem to bother Niko, who took my hand and flipped it over to lay a very short kiss on my wrist. Marcus had done the same thing once, and now I figured it was the vampire equivalent of kissing a lady's hand.

"She is stunning." He looked at me but his words were for Daniel. I felt like a piece of art. I was there to be admired, but no one would take me seriously. "No wonder you chose to keep her to yourself until your reputation was secure. You would have fought many a duel over rights to one such as this. I might have been willing to give up my Lauren for her. I don't suppose you would consider a trade?"

Daniel's fangs were suddenly very large, and I was yanked back into his arms. "I would not consider it."

Niko smiled and took a step back. He treated Daniel like a tiger whose tail he'd inadvertently tugged on. "Understood. I apologize. You understand that sometimes deals are made at events such as this."

Daniel stared the older vampire down. "I understand that some vampires will allow themselves to be bullied into giving up what is theirs. I'm not that man, Niko. If I was, I wouldn't be any good to the Council, would I? She is mine and will remain mine."

There was a deep laugh from behind me, and I turned to see Daniel's patron, Marcus Vorenus, walking up with a smirk on his face. The Italian was impeccably dressed in a sport coat, slacks, and silk shirt. "Niko has fallen into your trap, *bellissimo ragazza*. I warn you now, Niko, Daniel does not take well to such offers. I should know."

"Did he just try to buy me?" I asked, finally catching up. I was getting really tired of people trying to buy me. Earlier this year, Daniel had sold me to Dev for two million, though Daniel had eventually given the money back. Marcus's lips curved in a secretive smile. "Yes, Zoey, he did indeed, and you should hope his companion never finds out for she will be very jealous. She is not known for her kindness. Now, Daniel, I believe Niko would like to speak with you about your presentation. Please allow me to escort your companion around while you take care of business."

I wasn't particularly happy about being separated from Daniel, but he indicated that it was fine. Marcus wasted no time hauling me away. He offered me his arm and I had no choice but to take it.

"You are lovely tonight, Zoey," Marcus stated as he led me through the crowd.

If I looked nice it was probably because I hadn't picked out my own clothes or done my own hair or makeup. After Roman had led us to our ridiculous suite, I had spent several minutes just gawking. It had three bedrooms, two bathrooms and a hot tub that overlooked the entire strip. The bathroom in the master had a huge garden tub and a ridiculously decadent mirror covered the ceiling in the bedroom. I didn't have to ask if Nevada wasn't already crossed off my boyfriend's bucket list.

After I'd managed to close my mouth, I was introduced to someone named Kelly, who lamented the roundness of my curves and hoped she'd brought something to make me look taller. Kelly was a stylist. She'd dressed me in a turquoise cocktail dress that showed more of my chest than I normally would, but the girls looked good. As I glanced around the room, I realized I stood out in the crowd for an entirely different reason. These people seriously liked black.

"I think I might have gone with a darker color," I muttered as people turned to stare at me.

"Not at all," Marcus argued. "You're different, Zoey. Even among the companions, you're rare."

"And why is that?" I really wanted to know. The women all around me were stunning. They were model-quality beautiful. Like Kelly said, I was short and probably too curvy. I couldn't really see the attraction when compared to the others.

"How do I describe it to you? You can't see it yourself, of course. A companion has a certain glow to a vampire. It's how we identify them. Most of the time this glow is subtle. Sometimes it is quite lively."

"So I'm lively?"

Marcus stopped, his eyes taking on a serious look. "You are like the sun, Zoey. Everyone else here is a pale reflection of the way you shine. Every vampire here knows that if he could taste you, your blood would be the sweetest he had ever known. If your Daniel had not been the man he is now, he would have been forced to fight for you or make a deal to sell you. Daniel chose not to present you to our society because he didn't want to put you through that particular ritual. It was a good choice. Now they're too afraid of him to make a real play for you. So relax. They will look, but I assure you they will not touch."

"Good to know." I wished I was back up in my nice big suite ordering room service and watching pay-per-view with Neil. "So where's the buffet?" I asked because Dev had taken up the time I would have spent eating dinner with his sexy debrief.

Marcus raised his eyebrows. "In vampire society, there is no buffet, Zoey. Companions do not eat food around their masters. *Mi scusi*, you prefer the term husband. It's not the same for all, of course, but for most vampires, human dining practices are considered vile and something to be hidden. Most of the vampires in this room would be classified as warriors. This is a class that is not known for its tolerance. Companions eat, of course, but they try to make sure their husbands do not notice."

No wonder they all looked vaguely underfed. I was starting to realize what Daniel had been telling me all along. We were weird. We didn't work the way other marriages worked. Daniel still took his ass to the takeout line when I wanted Mongolian beef. He still sat beside me while we watched TV or played games and passed me the ketchup for my fries. He might not be able to eat, but he wasn't about to deny me the pleasure. For my birthday he'd gotten me a gorgeous red velvet cake.

"Class?" I'd never heard the term before.

Marcus nodded. "I always forget you were not taught as you should have been. Yes, there are classes of vampires. Most are known as warriors. They're physically the strongest, but tend to be very rigid in dealing with humans, even companions."

"And you?" Somehow I couldn't see Marcus as a warrior. He was too urbane, too smooth.

He smiled. When he smiled, he really could light up a room. "I'm not a warrior, Zoey. I'm something else. I would feed you and coddle you and enjoy every moment. I would make sure you had the finest cuisine and cuddle you as I fed you from my hand. My companions have always been precious to me." He shook his head, sighing a bit. “But that would be frowned upon here.”

“Fine, so no mini corndogs,” I lamented. “Please tell me companions are allowed to drink.”

“Of course,” Marcus replied. “We aren’t barbarians.”

“Good to know.”

He led me to the very decadent-looking bar.

“You, servant,” Marcus said flatly, and the bartender turned. He was obviously a were of some type, and he really didn’t like the duty he had pulled. He was biting his tongue as he looked at the vampire. “Give the lady what she desires.”

I smiled brightly at the bartender, trying to soften his very understandable attitude toward me. I looked down at his name tag. He was a handsome young man, probably twenty-two or so. “Hello, Zack. What are you really good at making?”

I got a smile out of young Zack. “I make a mean martini.”

I clutched my heart. “Zack, I love you. Two olives, please. Hit me, man.”

Zack chuckled and grabbed a bottle of Ciroc and a shaker.

“He does make a mean martini,” a soft voice to my left said.

I looked to the side and saw a beautiful woman with brown hair and luminous dark eyes. She was wearing a female approximation of a tux, sans jacket. It fit her tall figure perfectly. She tipped her cocktail glass in salute to the bartender, who seemed much more at ease now.

“Kimberly,” Marcus addressed the woman.

“Marcus,” she replied. “Please tell me this is Mrs. Donovan. I’ve been so excited to meet the woman who can handle that hunk of vampire. He is absolutely the scariest, hottest piece of vampire ass I have ever seen.”

If I’d had a drink, I would have spit it out in surprise. This was not the way I expected these beautiful women to act. Instead, I simply stated the obvious. “You think he’s hot now, you should see him naked.”

Kimberly smiled. “If only it worked that way. Hi, I’m Kim Jacobs. You must be Zoey Donovan.”

She held out her hand. I shook it, grateful someone looked at me like I wasn’t a cupcake.

Marcus leaned against the bar, looking at the two of us

indulgently. "Would it do any good to point out Mrs. Jacobs is a horrible influence? What am I saying? I should be telling Kimberly that you will be the wretched influence. Tell me, Zoey, how many weapons are you wearing under that lovely confection tonight?"

Kimberly's eyes widened, and I took the hint that most companions didn't come fully equipped with an armory.

I took my martini from Zack, who was definitely interested in me now, and widened my eyes to their most innocent, innocuous gaze. "Marcus, this is a place of peace. Why would I bring a weapon here?"

"Because you are Zoey Donovan," he replied with a grin. "The last time I saw you, I recall the promise to stake me if I got out of line."

I would never wear a weapon into Ether. Dev would kick my ass, and I trusted the staff to take care of me. This staff had no idea who I was, and I was surrounded by vamps. I was merely wearing a small pistol and a nice long silver knife. The knife had been at Daniel's insistence. He'd handed it to me earlier in the evening, treating it with almost reverence. It was the traditional weapon of the *Nex Apparatus*. It ran almost the full length of my upper leg, so one could also call it a sword. Both weapons were in thigh straps that my stylist had bemoaned the use of.

"I promise I am stake free." I would never bother to carry a stake. They were far too easy to find in the field.

Kim stared at me, a surprised look in her eyes. "You threatened to stake Marcus?"

"He pissed me off. So did some dude named Ivan and like five other fangs. It was a rough night."

"Sounds like it. I've heard a couple of rumors about you. I hope you don't think me impolite, but I have to ask. Is it true you're a criminal?" Kim leaned in, waiting for my answer.

"I prefer to think of myself as a liberator of enslaved objects. If I make a profit off of it, then everybody wins." Except the mark, of course, but that went without saying.

"That is so cool." Kim asked Zack for another drink. "I wish I could do something like that. I was a fourth grade teacher when I was kidnapped and sold to the highest bidder. Did that come off as bitter? I meant it that way."

"Now, Kimberly, someone would think you are not content," Marcus commented.

Kim smiled mysteriously. "Well, I was lucky. Henri's not so bad. But the other companions are boring sheep, so don't be surprised I'm excited by the possibility of having someone cool to talk to."

"So what are we supposed to do at something like this?" From what I could see, the men were either talking business or staring at strippers, and the women were busy viewing each other with a sort of controlled hostility.

"I believe you are supposed to look beautiful and remain silent, but you aren't going to do that, are you?" Marcus seemed excited at the prospect of me behaving badly. It made me wonder what type of women Marcus usually hung out with.

I opened my clutch and pulled out one of the ten hundred dollar bills Dev had made sure I had. I flashed it at Zack. "Hey, can you break that into fives for me?"

"Normally no, but I will certainly do it for you," Zack replied and was handing over a bundle of fresh cash.

I looked at Kim with a gleam in my eye. "Want to go stuff fives in a stripper's G-string?"

"Do you think we could get a lap dance?" She started looking around the room.

"I bet Marcus here could arrange that for us," I said in my most flirtatious voice.

Marcus took a deep breath and held a hand out to let us lead the way. "Ladies, I assure you, if I was capable of having a heart attack, I would."

As almost all female patrons are in a strip club, Kim and I were a big hit with the strippers. I also think it helped that we were the only non-vampires offering up cash. Kim and I were halfway through our first round of fives when the music was turned off suddenly, and all eyes turned toward the stage. Roman walked out, a microphone in his hand.

"Gentlemen, welcome to Descent," Roman said, his voice a flat monotone. "I have been instructed that there will be an offering this evening, followed by a formal presentation."

I heard Kim's sharp intake of breath. Her skin drained of color as a fine tremble began.

"Ladies, let's find your husbands." Marcus drew me from my seat, his hand cupping my elbow, pulling me away from the stage.

All around me there was a sudden buzz in the air.

"What does that mean?" I'd never heard the terms before. Niko had mentioned he wanted to talk about Daniel's presentation. Was something happening with Danny?

Marcus didn't have to lead me far. Daniel was at my side very quickly, grabbing my hand.

"It means that a new companion has been discovered, and she'll be offered for auction tonight," Daniel explained, his face scanning the crowd as if looking for something to go wrong. "It's time for you to head back up to the suite. I'll have Neil meet you at the elevator. I have to stay in case there's trouble."

Marcus laid a hand on Daniel's arm. "She should see, Daniel. This is her world now. The position you wish her to have is not one for the weak or faint of heart. She is neither." Marcus turned to me. "Zoey, the girl will be brought in and auctioned to the highest bidder. There will be a formal presentation. It is a public showing. There is nothing you can do to help this woman. The only thing you can do is cause a great deal of trouble for your husband. Can you watch and not act?"

I nodded, my heart in my throat. I did need to see it. I needed to understand why we were going to fight. I looked at Kim. Her fun was done for the night. "Did you go through this?"

"Yes." Her eyes trailed toward the stage.

Suddenly there was a blond-haired vampire pulling at Kim's hand. He was only as tall as Kim and while attractive, it was in a bland sort of way. There was no mistaking his anxiety for his wife.

"Let's go, Kim," he said as he tugged her out of her chair. His accent was German or Dutch, perhaps.

He looked around and realized who he was standing next to. He took a huge step back from Daniel but placed himself squarely in front of his wife. "Mr. Donovan, if she has done something to displease you, I would appreciate it if you dealt with me."

Daniel looked down at the smaller man with an annoyed expression. "What the hell are you talking about, Henri?"

"He isn't upset with Kim," Marcus said. "I told you he isn't someone to be afraid of."

"I was making friends with his wife, Henri." Kim's eyes kept straying to the stage.

Henri stared at me for a moment, but then he shook his head at his wife. "Jesus, Kim, when you look for trouble you find it. No offense, sir."

Daniel flashed the vampire a genuine smile, and it seemed to startle Henri. "None taken, Henri. She is trouble. But I would appreciate it if you would allow your wife to visit mine. Zoey doesn't know anyone here. She could use a friend."

Henri looked to Marcus, who nodded, and the blond vampire seemed to relax a bit. "Of course. Perhaps they could have lunch, but I'll take her to our room now. She doesn't need to see this."

Henri and Kim were gone in a second, disappearing into the crowd. All around us other guests moved in to get close to the stage.

Daniel leaned toward his patron. "Are you going to bid? You could use a companion. You need to be as strong as possible."

Marcus didn't take his eyes off the stage. "No. We need to reserve our cash for later. This will get very expensive. It's been a while since a new companion was discovered."

"It won't touch your wealth. You're not the strongest vampire in the first place. Companion blood would make you strong for the fight."

"I said no, Daniel," Marcus returned sharply. "Trust me, this is the right course."

"Fine." Daniel glared at his patron. "We'll do as you wish, but make sure that is your reason, Marcus, and not because you're pining over something you can't have."

I would have asked Daniel what that meant, but a vampire in formal wear took the stage. The auction was about to begin.

Chapter Nineteen

Roman and the staff disappeared, moving like smoke through the room until only the vampires and companions were left. This was a private ritual and no one outside the vampire world was welcome.

We weren't bidding, so we ended up toward the back of the crowd. Daniel slipped his arm around my waist, pulling me against him. Marcus took up a position on the other side, and we were given a wide berth even as the crowd began to move toward the stage. The women stayed in the background, though very few of them were left. Most of the companions who stayed behind took up seats near the bar, continuing their drinking and soft talk. I was the single female in a sea of eager males, but I was forgotten in the rush to get a look at the fresh meat.

A tall vampire took the stage, his body lean, an elegant predator. A deep voice came over the microphone. "Good evening, gentlemen. I welcome you to the presentation of a new companion. It is an event to be grateful for."

"His name is Sebastian," Marcus whispered, indicating the vampire on stage. "He facilitates all of the Council's public rituals."

Dressed in a form-fitting tuxedo, Sebastian's long limbs gestured around the stage in a dramatic fashion. "This companion is offered for auction by Trent Walker. The proceeds will be divided between Mr. Walker and the Council."

It seemed an odd thing to say. I intended to take advantage of this learning opportunity. "Does this Trent person already have a companion?"

"No. He's single." Daniel didn't look at me, his eyes steady on the stage.

"Why would this Trent person give up rights to her? I thought it was a finders, keepers thing."

It had been that way between Daniel and me. Daniel was the first vamp to get his fangs in me, and the Council honored his rights. At the time, we had no idea what we were doing. Daniel was hungry, and I was his lover. I'd been lucky Dallas wasn't a vampire haven. It was just coincidence that I'd never run into a vampire or what had happened to Kim, what was about to happen to this woman, would have been my fate.

"Trent Walker is very young," Marcus explained. "He serves one of the Council members, which is why he's here. It's very likely he found the companion while he was trying to kill time. He couldn't hold her on his own. A stronger vampire would challenge him, and these challenges are to the death. It's better that he sells her and takes the finder's fee. In a couple of hundred years, perhaps he will be strong enough."

Daniel hugged me tightly to him, and I felt him lay a kiss on my hair. We were thinking the same thing. We might bitch and moan and complain about the cards fate had dealt us, but those aces saved us from so much heartache. Daniel would never have been pragmatic enough to sell me. He would have defended me. He would have died in a duel had he not risen as he had.

"Without further ado," Sebastian was saying, holding his hand to the stage entrance, "allow me to present the lovely Meredith."

Two vampires led a woman dressed only in a robe out onto the stage. She seemed dazed and very bewildered, her eyes turning from the bright lights. She didn't fight, merely allowed them to lead her out, her bare feet shuffling along.

I wondered where she'd been when Trent Walker plucked her from her life. Had she been playing the slots or dancing the night away? I wondered who would be looking for her, missing her.

Sebastian looked down at the woman and smiled. It was the way a snake would smile, if a snake could. He touched her cheek, turning her eyes up to look into his. "Sweet Meredith, welcome to your family."

Meredith beamed suddenly. "Hello," she said, and though her voice was shaky, it held no real fear. Sebastian was working some of that good old vampire persuasion on her.

"She's so young." Her face held the flush of youth, her skin perfectly smooth.

"I assure you she is of age," Marcus replied. "If she wasn't, she would have been flown to Paris and all of this would have taken place in the catacombs. She would have been held at the Council stronghold until she turned eighteen. The Council is careful. The last thing they wish is to involve the human authorities. If anyone finds this woman while she's here, it will be assumed she has taken a new lover. There will be nothing criminal about her abduction when Sebastian is through. He is very thorough."

I bet he was. He softly spoke to his victim, a hand on her shoulder, as though she was a beloved daughter. She looked up at him with adoring eyes, agreeing with everything he said. The two vampires who had delivered her were able to retreat. Meredith now took center stage.

"The men at the front are unattached. They'll be the ones bidding on this companion." Marcus turned slightly to nod at Daniel. "You should be ready. There will more than likely be trouble. There have been rumblings about the lack of companions. The men, they are hungry."

Daniel pulled a pair of thick leather gloves out of his pocket. He tugged them over his hands. "If I ask for the sword, Z, please don't hesitate."

I nodded. We had decided I should carry the silver sword the Council had gifted him with when he'd become their officially sanctioned assassin. It was some important ancient weapon that only the *Nex Apparatus* could carry. Kelly convinced him it ruined the line of his jacket.

My heart started to thump inside my chest. Vampires surrounded us on every side. If it all went crazy, Daniel would be the one wading into a sea of ancient killers.

The crowd swelled toward the front of the stage as Meredith moved forward. I wondered what Sebastian had her seeing. I wondered if she would remember any of this tomorrow or if she would wake up in some vampire's bed and wonder how the hell she'd become a blood bank. After Kim's reaction, I thought not. She would remember everything. Her compliance in the humiliation would make the reality of her situation so much worse.

"Come forward, companion," Sebastian intoned smoothly.

"Come forward and present yourself to your masters. Can you feel their excitement? They want so much to see your sweet flesh, Meredith. Are you going to deny them?"

Meredith shook her head as though such a thing was unthinkable. She shrugged out of her robe and wore nothing beneath it. Her naked body was presented for the debate and discussion of the men who decided just how much she was worth. I felt her degradation like it was my own. Indignation sparked through me, and I felt my face heating up.

"Don't." Marcus bit the word at me. "Don't you dare weep, Zoey."

"Marcus," Daniel warned.

Marcus ignored him, leaning in and speaking directly in my ear. "Don't you dare cry. Do not give them a second of your emotion, *mio regina*. Swallow the sorrow and let it burn in your belly until it fuels your rage. Do not weep for her. Avenge her when the time is right. Be her warrior."

"Don't be so hard on her," Daniel said under his breath, but there was no doubt this was an order.

"Leave it, Danny."

Marcus was right. For the first time, I felt myself softening toward the Italian. He didn't treat me like a lovely piece of glass. Daniel would have held my hand and led me away, but I needed this. I needed to see the way they treated her. This was the way they wanted to treat the world. We were their playthings.

Meredith presented herself to the company, holding her body out with pride. I had gotten used to many forms of nudity. I had no problem running around the grotto without a stitch of clothes on while Dev chased after me. I hadn't minded earlier when Danny had seen me naked. He'd looked at me with lust and love, and there had been no shame in it. Often Neil walked in when I was dressing, and I no longer dove for the nearest available cover. These were my intimate companions and being with them had changed my views of nudity.

This reminded me why we guard our bodies against prying eyes.

Our bodies tell a story. There was a small, healing cut on her leg she'd probably gotten from shaving. Though it was winter, she still had tan lines. It spoke of modesty. Even in a tanning bed or a spray salon, she wore her bathing suit. She had a small butterfly tattooed on her right hip. It was in a place where even a bikini bottom would hide it. It was meant for a lover's eyes, but now it was commented on. That small, likely meaningful tattoo, would drive her price up or down.

Soon there would be another mark on her body. It would be like the one on mine, twin holes that marked her as a possession.

The silver sword pressed against my leg, and there was nothing I wanted more than to draw it and start slicing my way through the crowd. But I could do nothing to stop this crime against Meredith's person. I let the anger wash over me, adding Meredith to a growing list of offenses the Council was going to answer for.

"I begin the bidding at ten million," Sebastian intoned.

The next several minutes were a flurry of activity that I wasn't capable of keeping up with. Voices yelled, the vampires speaking over one another in a cacophony of sound. Sebastian didn't seem to have the problem I did. He simply nodded and occasionally announced another ridiculously high offer as the bidding continued. The room seemed to swell with tension as the price tag went higher. Daniel's face was completely calm, but his eyes shifted around the room, constantly looking for trouble.

Before long it was down to two men. They spat figures at each other as the room went silent with the exception of their voices. All eyes had turned to the two vampires. Sebastian stood beside the still naked Meredith, who simply smiled and swayed a little as though listening to some pleasant music only she could hear.

"Who is it?" Daniel asked Marcus, trying to see around the crowd.

Marcus turned to him, a grim look on his hawk-like face. "Paul and Adam."

Those names seemed to mean something to Daniel. "Damn it."

"They don't like each other," I surmised. The last thing we needed was a little vamp feud.

"Not at all," Marcus confirmed.

"Seventy-five million," the one Marcus indicated was Adam pronounced.

I watched as Paul's jaw clenched. He didn't want to stop, but he fell silent.

"Do you have anything further?" Sebastian asked Paul. When he didn't answer, Sebastian held Meredith's hand up. "Come and meet your master, companion."

Eager Adam was up on that stage faster than I could think "rat bastard," and I thought that pretty damn fast. He had his hands on Meredith, his fangs long and sharp. I expected him to whisk her away, but they stayed on the stage, his eyes burning into hers as he obviously took over the persuasion reins from Sebastian.

"They're going to do that here?" This was the most intimate act Daniel and I had ever performed together. This was the act that married us, the giving and taking of blood. I might be bitter about the circumstances, but that sharing was a beautiful thing between two lovers. It was not meant to be watched like a porn film.

Daniel's hands tightened on me. "That's why they call it a public presentation, baby. This is why I couldn't take you to Paris. I could never do this to you. Please forgive me."

There had been so many other reasons and I knew he was grasping at straws because we had already been married at the time. There would have been no need for a public presentation, but my heart softened toward him anyway. He always had me in mind. He always wanted to protect me. He simply didn't understand that if he kept me in a protective cage, our marriage could never work.

Before I had a chance to say anything to him, a loud roar filled the air. The crowd moved as Paul vented his fury. I tried to see, but I was far too short. The vampires around me started to shift as though giving Paul space. I caught the action in small glimpses even as Daniel moved in front of me.

Paul's face went savage, his fangs gleaming in the spotlight.

A shout went up as I saw a spray of blood. Paul struck out at anyone left around him, claws sinking into flesh.

He leapt onto the stage, reaching out, and in a single move, he picked up Adam and tossed him back into the crowd. A low growl reverberated through the air as he began to stalk Meredith.

Sebastian had moved to the front of the stage, his hand over his brow as he fought the bright lights to look into the crowd. There was no doubt in my mind who he wanted to see.

"Marcus?" Daniel didn't move, simply asked the question.

"You have the Council's permission." Marcus shook his head,

watching the situation like a father disappointed with his unruly toddlers.

"Zoey, I'll need that sword now." Daniel leapt onto one of the tables, giving himself a better view of the room.

I lifted my skirt slightly and unsnapped the sheath. The sword fell into my hand and, in one motion, I pulled it out and tossed it up to my husband. Daniel caught it without ever taking his eyes off his prey. The minute the sword was in his gloved hands, he pushed off the table.

To my eyes it looked like he was running above the crowd. He leapt from tabletop to tabletop, landing only briefly on one leg to push off again as he avoided the crowd and moved toward the stage.

Everything stopped as Daniel danced his way toward his target. He pushed off the final table, and the sword sang through the air, moving like an extension of Daniel's arm. He wielded the weapon with flawless precision. He seemed to hang in the air for a moment. No one breathed or moved a muscle, even Daniel's victim, who seemed to be a deer caught in the headlights.

With no hesitation, he brought the sword down on Paul's neck, neatly separating his head from his body. The other vampire had no chance to run, no chance to fight. The moment Daniel had decided to kill him, his long life had been over.

I caught my breath because while it had been brutal, there was a beautiful grace to it.

"He is magnificent," Marcus swore. "I have lived almost two thousand years and not seen his like."

Daniel landed in a crouch but was up quickly enough to catch the head before it hit the floor. He tossed it at Adam, who had managed to get back up on the stage. "You are satisfied with the judgment of the Council?"

Adam was shaking as he held the head of his rival. He took a step back but managed to agree that he was, indeed, satisfied. Even as he held it, the head turned to ash in his hands, covering the stage with dust.

"The Council is satisfied with their *Nex Apparatus*?" The words sounded deeply formal coming out of Daniel's mouth, holding the weight of long years of custom.

"As always, Mr. Donovan," Niko said, speaking for the Council.

Daniel surveyed the crowd, his sword still in hand. "If the Council is satisfied, then I beg permission to take my companion and quit these proceedings." Daniel looked at the men in the crowd. "I assume the rest of you will behave."

I could practically hear the collective gulp go through the room.

"You have leave, Mr. Donovan," Niko offered. "Take the rest of the evening off. Enjoy your companion."

Daniel leapt from the stage and was given a very wide berth by the vampires on the floor. They moved away from him as though his very touch could bring them death. Daniel walked to me and tossed the sword my way. I caught it and placed it back in its sheath. At that moment, all eyes were on me, and I saw the minute they started to think of me as something more than Daniel's plaything.

"She's seen enough," Daniel said to Marcus as he picked me up and started to carry me out of the club.

As we left, I watched over Daniel's shoulder as Adam pulled his new purchase into his arms and bit down for that first taste.

* * * *

When we arrived in the room ten minutes later, Daniel sank onto the couch, and I fell down beside him. We didn't speak, just let the events of the evening sink in. We sat there in the cool quiet of the suite for the longest time with that strange sword between us. We watched the lights of the strip as the clock turned ever closer to morning. Finally the door to the suite opened, and Dev walked in. His clothes were wrinkled, and he smelled like cigarettes and vodka.

"You two look like I feel," he muttered as he sank down beside me. I have to admit, I liked the fact that I was between them. I could almost pretend it was normal. "Nice sword. What the hell happened to you, Daniel? You have blood on your coat."

"Execution," Daniel answered.

"I had to witness a young girl get sold and raped in front of an adoring crowd." I put my two crappy cents in.

"I lost a hundred grand," Dev admitted.

So it had been a shitty night all around. "This town sucks."

Both men looked at me, not amused by my pun.

"Well, it does," I grumbled because at least tonight it really did.

Chapter Twenty

"So what happens to her now?" I asked Kimberly the next day.

We were sitting in one of the hotel's restaurants. Kim had been patiently answering my questions for the last thirty minutes as we enjoyed lunch. Our version of lunch occurred as most people were enjoying dinner. We were a nocturnal lot.

"They call it the honeymoon period." Kim seemed to be treating this conversation as an intellectual lecture. There was very little emotion in her voice. "For the next month, she'll be held in her rooms, first here until the meetings are completed, and then in London where Adam lives. She'll be under his persuasion and will feed him daily. She'll take his blood and do all the other things that go along with it."

Sex. It was a part of the bonding process. For Daniel and me, it had been an extension of our previous relationship. We'd made love when we were both human, and he certainly hadn't needed persuasion to get me into bed. What must it have been like for Kim, who'd never met Henri before she'd been forcibly married to him? "I know this is painful, and I apologize. I just don't understand the process."

Kim's brown eyes slid away from me. "I can't imagine what it was like for you. I'm sure the Council's *Nex Apparatus* was brutal to say the least. I joke about how hot he is, but he scares every one of us. I heard he killed Paul last night."

Damn straight he had. "Paul was an ass. Paul deserved killing. Daniel isn't brutal."

"I think Paul would disagree. You haven't been in society. Do you know what he's done? He killed twelve vampires on his own with his bare hands in the arena. They kept sending them in, and he kept killing them. The Council was finally forced to concede the battle to a fledgling. It was the most horrific thing I've ever seen."

"Should he have let them kill him?" I asked, getting a little annoyed. "Whatever Danny has done it was to survive. He might be brutal in a fight, but he has to be to survive and protect the ones he loves. He has never hurt me. He would never lock me up to train me or force me to comply."

Kim sat back and looked at me seriously. "I'm sorry if I offended you, but you have to understand the way the majority of vampire society feels about your husband. If you want me to explain how things work, you have to be willing to hear things that won't make you happy."

That was fair. I had to respect her for stating it in plain terms I could understand. "I love Daniel. It's hard to hear how people view him. Please continue."

I looked over at the bar where Neil sat with some fruity drink. He was talking to the bartender, who was naturally a hottie, but I knew all I had to do was whisper and he would be at my side. Neil had been a very good bodyguard/shopping buddy. He'd even kept his promise to Dev, forcing me to buy some of the filthiest lingerie I'd ever seen. I just wondered if I was ever going to get a chance to use it.

"It's been almost a thousand years since anyone saw that sword Daniel carries," Kim explained. "Henri practically shakes when he sees it. It's the official weapon of the Council's Death Machine. Henri wasn't around for the last *Nex Apparatus*, but the way he talks about it, it's a little like the vampire version of the boogeyman."

That gibed with what I saw around the group. Everyone, even the oldest of the vampires, looked on Daniel with a deep suspicion.

Kim looked around as though trying to figure out who might be listening in. She leaned over. "Before they presented the sword to Daniel, there was talk about changing the Council. Some vampires had formed the opinion that the Council is corrupt and dangerous. The more modern of the men wanted a say in the way the Council is run. That all shut down with the arrival of your husband."

Daniel explained this during one of his conversations with Dev—one of the conversations I'd managed to stay awake during.

There was discontent among the vampires at the way the Council controlled every aspect of their lives. Before they could organize, Daniel was designated as the official executioner. He was scary enough to have quelled that probably destined to fail rebellion.

"It must be strange for everyone to be so afraid of a fledgling." I kept my mouth shut about Daniel's plans. Like I said before, I tended to sleep during the lecture portions of my time with Daniel, so I wasn't about to play politics.

Kim laughed at that. "He isn't considered a fledgling anymore. The arena test put that term out of everyone's mind. Daniel is a king. It's the term they use for a vampire whose talents exceed what a vampire should have. As far as I know, Daniel is the first king in a thousand years, since the last time that sword was seen. Of course, the last king actually took power and the crown. Daniel seems content to use his gifts in other ways."

"What happened to the last king?"

"Ask Marcus Vorenus," Kim said mysteriously. "From what I understand, he is the one who dealt that king the killing blow."

Marcus and I were going to have to have a long talk.

Kim shook off her serious face and smiled a little. "It's my turn for questions. Please tell me if I'm being far too personal. Henri says I have no discretion, but then I don't remember Victorian England. The rumor is Daniel brought a lover. Is that true? He seemed so into you last night."

I smiled slowly because this was the part of our ruse I was going to have the most fun with. "His name is Devinshea Quinn. He owns Descent, the club we were in last night. He also owns a club where we all live. He's half Fae."

Kim looked flummoxed. "I just wouldn't have guessed. My gaydar was perfectly silent around Daniel. God, that just kills a whole bunch of my fantasies."

I laughed long and hard. "Let me give you new fantasies, Kim. Daniel isn't gay. Daniel likes to watch."

Kim's mouth just about hit the table. "He shares you?"

I shrugged, and then grinned because, speak of the devil, Dev walked into the dining room. He was dressed to kill in a designer suit that I was sure had never seen a rack. It was custom fit to his body and showed off his lean grace to its best advantage. He was even wearing a tie. I'd never seen Dev in a tie. He always was the picture of decadence, but now he was professional and it looked good on him. Even his hair was under ruthless control. It should have lessened his sex appeal, but it just made me anxious to mess up that perfection. I watched as Kim's eyes widened when she caught sight of him.

"Wow," she sighed. "That's just wrong. I think I've just seen god's actual gift to women."

"He thinks so," I replied as he spoke briefly to Neil and then zeroed in on me. "Kim, you're about to meet Dev."

"Daniel shares you with him?" Kim's voice probably got louder than she had intended, and I watched Dev's lips quirk briefly.

"Mrs. Donovan." Dev acknowledged me formally with a slight bow. "Mrs. Jacobs. I can see Mrs. Donovan has already informed you of who I am. It's a pleasure to meet you."

"And you, Mr. Quinn." Kim managed to breathe, but only barely.

Dev glanced around the room, his voice going low. "Mr. Donovan was actually hoping to speak to your husband. He will look for him at tomorrow night's ball. Please let Henri know Daniel would appreciate a few moments of his time."

Kim went a little pale. "Did Henri do something wrong?"

Dev gave her a smooth smile. "Not at all. Daniel has some business he would like to discuss, and he would greatly appreciate Henri's input. Your husband is renowned for his business sense. I believe Daniel is going to suggest that the two of you might enjoy visiting us in Dallas in the near future. We were thinking of having a few friends out. I believe you will find that Hugo Wells and Brendan Ford have already accepted invitations."

Kim stilled. Those names meant something to her. "Yes, I think that would be something we are very interested in, Mr. Quinn. It seems Mr. Donovan has more layers than any of us thought."

"Excellent. I look forward to speaking with you further. Now, I am afraid Mrs. Donovan is needed. Daniel is awake and craves his wife's attention. I've settled the bill, but if you need anything else, Mrs. Jacobs, please feel free. The maître d' will charge it to our account." Dev held out his hand and helped me from my seat.

I said good-bye to my new friend and waved at Neil, who told me he was off to enjoy the strip now that his babysitting shift was over. Dev picked up a package at the bar and then hustled me out.

"Why did she know those names?" I asked when we were safely in the private elevator.

Dev pulled a bottle of Scotch out of the package and inspected it as the elevator shot up. "Brendan and Hugo were part of an earlier group that had discussed the possibility of overthrowing the Council. Nothing could be proven, and after Daniel ascended to his current post, the group quickly disbanded. It isn't surprising they never got past the talking stage since they didn't have a strong leader."

Dev pushed the button for the elevator, and we began to rise toward the penthouse. I couldn't help but think about how lonely I'd been the last couple of days. "I suppose you and Daniel are going out this evening after we're done. I guess I'll watch TV or something."

"Zoey, I hate this, too." Dev stared out the glass, looking down.

Dev had slept in one of the smaller bedrooms the night before, completely surprising me.

"I just thought we could be normal when we're alone." I'd been left to sleep with Neil, who I loved, but didn't bring me the comfort Dev did. Both my loves were behind closed doors, unavailable to me.

Dev stood across from me in the elevator, the distance between us clear. "We're never alone here, Zoey. If I get into that bed with you, how long will it be before my hands are on you? How long until you moan and wail because you are anything but quiet, lover. Do you want Daniel to lie in his bed knowing what we do? Do you want to hurt him in this fashion? If you do, we might as well just fuck on the couch where he can see us."

"That's not fair, Dev." I didn't like the guilt the image brought up. I also didn't like his sudden prudishness. "You haven't cared about Daniel's feelings up to this point."

"It's not about Daniel," Dev admitted, and he looked so tired. "I didn't love you before, Zoey. It was fun, and there is this big part of me that liked the fact I was sending the entire vampire world a big old fuck you. It's serious now. Our relationship, it deserves respect. I would want Daniel to do the same for me. If this thing is going to work, Daniel and I can't be at each other's throats twenty-four seven."

"I don't like this, Dev." I went with emotion because I couldn't argue with his logic. I wasn't used to using logic and Dev in the same sentence.

Dev rolled his eyes. "You think I like the fact that I have spent the last few days of my life delving into vampire politics when I promised myself I was leaving that life behind? Do you think I liked watching you walk away with him last night after promising I would behave myself? I don't like to behave, Zoey. I want to take you on the strip and spend fuckloads of cash and drink and get stupid. I want to bring you back here and just blow your mind. But we can't do that anymore even if you wanted to because I have learned something over the last few days. Daniel is right. His cause is more than just. It's imperative. It might have been fine before to just laugh with you and fuck you and send you on your way later. I can't do that anymore. If they get their way, you get hurt. Everything we love comes under their mercy if they succeed."

The door to the elevator opened, and I nodded because I understood but I didn't have to like it. Dev groaned, pulling me out of the elevator. He moved us out of sight of the lobby.

"Zoey, don't make me feel like I'm failing you when I'm trying so damn hard to avoid that," he pleaded, holding my face in his hands.

I softened immediately. "I'm sorry. It's just been a long night, and I was looking forward to being with you."

He leaned down and kissed me, a gentle touch of his lips against mine. "I know, sweetheart. I love you. It will be better when we get home. We have much more freedom there. People are used to seeing us together. As long as we include Daniel in some of our public outings, we can protect his reputation. Just hang on a few more days."

I didn't have much choice. Hopefully we would all still be alive in a few days. I forced myself out of that mode of thinking.

"Who is the Scotch for?" I asked because Dev was a vodka boy. It was one of the reasons I loved him.

He shook his head as he led me down the hallway. It was quiet on this floor. "The Scotch is for me. Well, not really for me, but I have to drink it. If I have to drink it, I think you should, too. Daniel is ready for us, and I thought we could prepare for the evening together."

I grinned, totally letting go of my previous sorrow. Tonight was the night both Daniel and Dev had been dreading since we decided on this course of action. Our explanation for bringing Dev along was that he shared a bed with Daniel and me. You don't share a bed with a vampire without baring his mark. Companions might get away with it, but Dev couldn't. Tonight, Dev got to feed Daniel.

I, for one, was looking forward to some very awkward fun. It had already been agreed that I had to be there to bring some much needed femininity to what Daniel called a horrible "sausage fest".

Dev slid his card into the door that led to our suite. He held it open for me, and there was Danny, nervously pacing the floor. I couldn't help giggling. "Are you nervous about your date?"

"Zoey!" both men said in a perfect symmetry that should have scared me, but I was still laughing.

"Look." I pointed at Dev. "Dev got all dressed up and everything."

Daniel groaned and shook his head. Dev popped the top off the Scotch bottle and took a long swig. He passed the bottle to me, and I obediently took a shot.

"She's never going to let us live this down." Daniel frowned.

"I could leave the two of you alone," I offered as Dev took a swig that lasted a really long time. "I could find Neil, and we could just use our imaginations."

"Neil already offered to tape the whole thing." Dev shuddered. "This stuff tastes like shit."

Daniel grabbed the bottle, studying it. "I disagree. You got a twelve-year, right?"

"Yes, I got pubescent Scotch, just like you ordered. I'm sure it's just as confused about its sexuality as the rest of us are going to be after this," Dev replied, loosening his tie. "Where are we going to do this?"

"The big bed," I said. Dev and Daniel looked at me like I was insane. "It's the only one that will fit all three of us."

It could fit an army regiment. I figured it would work for us. It shouldn't take too long, but we would all be comfy on the big bed.

Dev laid his tie aside. "We don't need to bring a bed into this."

"I don't want you to fall on the floor. When I feed Danny, I tend to sit in his lap so he can hold me when I would normally fall to the floor because my muscles stop working. I don't think you'll fit on his lap." Though I was amused at the picture in my brain.

Dev stopped drinking long enough to snort. "My muscles won't stop working."

"I'm not pulling him in, Z," Daniel said, sounding shocked that I thought he would.

I was so glad I was here because they obviously needed someone to keep them on the right path. "Oh, yes you are. It hurts otherwise. It really fucking hurts, Danny. You will pull him in. He's not into pain."

Dev was a baby when it came to pain. He complained bitterly when he got so much as a stubbed toe.

"He can't pull me in." Dev laid his suit jacket over a chair, and his hands went to work on the buttons of his shirt. "It doesn't work on me, sweetheart. Do you really think I've never been bitten before? I told you, Zoey, I've slept with just about everything with breasts on this plane."

Daniel looked surprised and slightly scared. It made me very curious about what a female vampire was like. "Dude, there are exactly two female vampires in the entire world, and you're telling me you slept with one of them?"

"I did indeed and I'll be honest, I don't get it. It hurt, and the sex wasn't that great. You vamps are supposed to be sex on a stick, but it was highly forgettable with the exception of how fucking much it hurt. I know Zoey tells you it's good, but she's faking it."

Daniel's eyebrows shot up in one of those deeply offended masculine looks. I grinned at him to let him know Dev was crazy, but I wasn't going to defend his reputation. He could manage that all on his own. "Faking it? We'll see about that. Let's get this over with. Zoey's right. We should go to the big bed. I don't want to have to catch you when you fall."

Dev shrugged out of his shirt as he entered the largest of the bedrooms. "Fine, but you're going to be disappointed. It doesn't work on me."

"We'll see about that." Daniel pulled his T-shirt over his head, and I was surrounded by really lovely chests. Dev was taller than Daniel, and his body was all lean muscle. Daniel was more solidly built, with big biceps and strong shoulders. I kind of sighed as I looked at the two of them. They were so different, but each so hot in their own way.

It made me wonder what it would be like to be in between those hard bodies. I wasn't a tiny, thin thing, but Danny and Dev made me feel petite. Ever since Dev and Danny made their little bargain, I couldn't help but wonder what it would be like if our fake ménage was true.

Dev started toward the big bed. "You, too, Zoey. If we're bare-chested you should be, too. I don't want you to ruin that blouse. It's Mark Jacobs, from the spring collection. I can't replace it. The color complements your eyes."

"It's only fair." Daniel watched me, his eyes narrowing. He could tell I was getting very interested in the proceedings in more than an amused way. Daniel's senses didn't lie. He could hear my heartbeat, and it was anything but steady.

I unbuttoned my shirt. There was a practical reason for bare skin. Skin is a hell of a lot easier to get blood off of than fabric. I tried to get the dirty thoughts out of my head but, god, it was hard. Hard. My mind just kept going there.

"And the bra." Dev held out his hand. "I need a distraction."

"Seriously?" Being half naked was not going to make this easier. I looked back to Danny. He would probably be deeply uncomfortable.

He was standing back, his eyes on me.

"It's nothing he hasn't seen before," Dev said reasonably. "If you want me to do this, give me something to distract me from the fact that your husband is about to sink his fangs into me."

"Danny?"

Finally his lips turned up. "He's right. It's nothing I haven't seen before. I'll take what I can. And we could both use a distraction. Give up the bra."

I unclasped my bra and tossed it to Dev. Cool air hit my skin, making my nipples pucker. The fact that their eyes were focused on me didn't help it at all. Daniel's fangs came out. Dev sighed. It was enough to make a girl feel confident.

I realized beyond a shadow of a doubt why the boys wanted me here. Dev might not understand it, but Daniel knew this process was deeply sexual. If I was there, the boys could concentrate on what they loved—female flesh. It would make everything easier—until the feeding was over and we all had to go back to our lonely rooms because Dev had put in the no-sex rule. I was probably going to eat an enormous amount of ice cream in an attempt to forget how much I wanted sex.

And I was definitely going to fantasize about what could have happened.

In the end, I knew Dev was right. I couldn't hurt Danny that way. I didn't want to. I wanted something else entirely, but I wasn't going to get it. I had to be satisfied that my men were willing to not kill each other. Just getting them in the same room, working together, was a miracle.

An awkward moment passed and then another. Silence hung in the air and I wasn't sure any of us was ready for what we were about to do. Working with Daniel was one thing, but this was intimate and suddenly I realized just how serious our situation was. We were going into something dangerous. We might not get out. Like it or not, the men in this room had to rely on each other. We were all we had.

Daniel cleared his throat and kicked off his shoes. I couldn't help but notice he'd left his boots and sneakers behind. He was wearing shiny Italian loafers, the leather rich and expensive looking. He hadn't bought those himself. Dev's influence was already showing up in Daniel's clothes. "We should get this done. I don't want to take up too much time."

Dev nodded, looking back toward me. He slipped out of his loafers, too, and climbed on that decadent-looking bed. He held his hand out to help me up. "Come on, Zoey. This will be easier if you're here."

Daniel gave me a tight smile that let me know he agreed and I followed Dev. The curtains were drawn though it was full dark. The room was huge, but now it felt intimate and close. The whole world felt like it had narrowed down to the three of us.

Dev's big hands immediately went around my waist, cupping my hips. The rest of the room was chilled, but his hands were hot and restless on my skin. "Hold on to me, Zoey."

I put my hands on his chest, his anxiety an almost palpable

thing. He really thought this was going to be unpleasant. His heart beat against my hand and his breath was unsteady. I smoothed a hand across his skin, trying to calm him. "It's going to be okay."

One of Daniel's hands came around Dev's body to rest on my back, pulling all three of us together. Daniel was at Dev's back, trapping him in between our bodies. "I promise it's not going to hurt. Just relax, man."

An unsteady laugh rumbled from Dev's chest. "It occurs to me that this could be a good way to get rid of me."

Danny's eyes rolled. "If I haven't killed you by now, I'm probably not going to. I'll make it short but sweet. And you have to promise to respect me in the morning."

It was my turn to laugh because if Daniel was joking, then everything really would be all right.

A grin quirked up Dev's lips, and he relaxed a little. "I promise nothing. I hope the Scotch works. It tasted like shit to me."

Daniel's free hand found Dev's hair, sinking in. A soft pulse of his persuasion started to slide over me. "Well, you finished the whole bottle in record time. I'm looking forward to a little buzz. Maybe we can stay in, all three of us, and watch some movies or something."

"Sure." Dev gasped a little as Danny ran his nose along his throat.

He was using his senses to find that perfect vein he loved to pull from, but it was having an effect on Dev I didn't think he'd planned on. He bit his bottom lip, his eyes sliding closed, and became very still. I couldn't tell if he was forcing himself not to run away or if he was scared he might lean into Daniel, offering him more.

Yeah, that got my motor running.

Daniel's eyes found mine, and I sent him a smile. It wasn't a happy little thing. It was a seductive look, and Danny's fangs seemed to lengthen. The hand he'd placed on my skin seemed to tighten as though in invitation. Or command. I didn't really care. I was getting drugged by the closeness of them, by the picture they were making across my suddenly lust-addled brain.

I couldn't help it. The fact that the two men I loved more than anything both had their hands on me aroused the hell out of me.

"Let yourself go, Dev." Daniel's voice was deep, his irises

starting to bleed blue. "This won't hurt. You want this."

"What the hell is that?" Dev asked. I could feel the magic starting to work on him. The evidence was suddenly poking me in the belly. His erection popped up, straining at the fly of his slacks, and his heart was thumping against my palm for a different reason now.

"Heaven, baby," I replied because there was nothing Dev loved more than pleasure and this was exquisite.

Looking up at Dev's confused face, I found myself filled with more than simple lust. It was the only time in my relationship with Dev where I had more experience. He was the innocent one now, and I got to lead him through an encounter that would blow his mind. I didn't know what was wrong with his previous vampire, but there was nothing painful about Daniel when he was on his game. I knew my Dev. He was going to enjoy this and more than likely feel absolutely no shame afterward.

Daniel growled a little, the vampire inside him taking over. I caught a flash of gleaming white fangs when Daniel struck. Dev's whole body tensed as Daniel drew hard against Dev's neck. The whole while, Daniel's eyes were up, focused on me, drawing me into their intimacy.

"Fuck, that's amazing." Dev tried so hard not to moan, but it came out of his chest, a low, sexy sound. His hands finally found my breasts, fingers tugging in time to the beat of Daniel's mouth. He pinched at my nipples before cupping my breasts and groaning again.

I let my hands run up the sides of his torso, glorying in the muscles I skimmed over. My hips seemed to move of their own accord. They nestled against his erection and I could feel it lengthening further, getting ready to go off and ruin those expensive slacks of his.

Daniel stared at me while his throat worked. I brought a hand to touch his sandy blond hair, holding him to Dev's throat.

"Oh, god. That feels so fucking good." Dev rubbed his erection against me. "Zoey, sweetheart, you know how my magic goes a little crazy sometimes?"

His magic went wild at times, which was precisely why he almost never used it. "Yes. Just hold on, Dev. He's almost done."

"Too late. It's already here. It feels so fucking good. Yes." His head rolled back, touching Daniel's, fitting against him. "This is going to be wild."

The room was filled with Daniel's will, but suddenly there was something else. It was much stronger, and it crowded out that soft passion of Danny's. It pulsed from Dev's body, and it was lust. There was no other way to describe it. It was lust and need and love all rolled into one pulse that screamed across my skin, making my every nerve ending roar with wanting.

Every cell in my body seemed to come alive. Blood pounding. Heart racing. Pure grade A lust.

Daniel released Dev and, sure enough, my faery promptly fell over, a ridiculously happy smile on his face.

Daniel's chest worked, trying to get enough oxygen into his body. He'd already forgotten Dev. His eyes were focused on me, and I was pretty sure I might not need that ice cream. Desire pulsed through the room. His fangs were still out, his eyes a glorious blue, and his cock was pressed hard to the front of his slacks. "I hate to fucking admit this, but he tasted really good. Almost as good as you, but nothing, nothing compares, baby."

It was wrong. It had to be. I was in the same room with Dev, but I couldn't take my eyes off Danny. I wanted him so much it was an ache in my body. The idea of having to walk away didn't even make sense, but I couldn't make love with Danny while Dev watched.

Could I?

"God, can you feel that?" Dev pushed himself up, looking from me to Daniel and back again, his green eyes darker than I had ever seen them. "Can you feel it?"

I could. It was Daniel's need, and it rolled off his body, a wave of desire that crashed against me.

"Tell me no, Z," Daniel commanded because he never merely took what he wanted. His hands twitched, but he didn't move toward me. "Tell me no, and I think I can leave."

"Don't tell him no, Zoey." Dev hopped off the bed and then got behind me, his chest pressed to my back. His hands wound around, finding my hard nipples and playing with them, rolling them between his thumbs and fingers. I could feel the insistent twitch of his cock against my backside. I couldn't help rubbing back against it.

He whispered into my ear. "I can feel how much he needs you. It's like a drug in my system. This could be so fucking good. Don't deny him. Don't deny us. Just stop thinking and feel, Zoey. You too, Dan. This can be good if you two just let it."

All I had to do was move the slightest bit toward my husband, and he was on me. He pulled me to him, slamming our bodies together. His mouth came down on my mine, overwhelming me with his dominance.

This wasn't a soft tease. It was a full-on assault and I let him in.

He kissed me, our tongues playing around his fangs while his hands found my ass and pulled me up against his straining cock. He rubbed himself against my belly, letting me feel everything he was offering me. I shoved my hands between us to unbutton his jeans and ease the zipper down. Need filled my world. I needed to touch him, needed him inside me. It had been so long since I felt him moving over me, connecting us and making us one.

He rewarded me with a groan as he fell into my hand. Big and thick, his dick filled my palm and I could barely close my fingers around it.

"Fuck, yes, Z. Touch me. Stroke me." His hands wound in my hair, dragging me close so he could kiss me again.

While our tongues tangled, I stroked along his cock, from the plum-shaped head all the way to the base. He was big and hard in my hand, and I loved the soft feel of the skin that covered all that steel. He was already coated with cream, and it made my hand glide easily back and forth.

Dev moved on the bed, putting a hand on me.

Daniel growled his way.

"Don't you fucking pull that shit with me, Dan." Dev didn't move an inch, didn't back down despite the fact that Daniel was fully in beast mode. He didn't take his hands off me. "I'm sharing with you, not the other way around."

Just for a moment I thought Daniel would attack, but then his hips moved, thrusting up into my hand, and I knew we'd moved past the violence point. He finally put his lips on mine again, devouring me with luscious kisses.

A million erotic images skimmed the surface of my mind. I wanted to taste him, to take that hard cock in my mouth and swallow him whole. I wanted Daniel in my pussy, my mouth, anywhere I could take him. I wanted to be his.

And Dev. Oh, I wanted everything that half fertility god could give me. I wanted to kneel in utter submission before him and let him have his way, pounding into me from behind.

But most of all, I wanted to be between them.

I wanted to never have to choose.

"Time for this to come off, sweetheart," Dev was saying behind me as he slid my skirt over my hips, his fingers taking the opportunity to glide across my core, causing me to cry out. His fingers made soft circles over my clitoris, enough to make me shake, but not to push me over the edge. And I was close, so close.

Daniel pulled back, taking the moment to get out of his jeans and boxers. He stood back, his cock hard against his belly. "Fuck, she's gorgeous."

Dev cupped my breasts, holding them up like an offering to Daniel. "She's the most beautiful thing I've ever seen."

"I should kill you for touching her." But Daniel's words were soft, non-threatening. His hand stroked his cock, running the full length over and over again. I couldn't get my eyes off the sight even as Dev's fingers tugged on my nipples.

"You like watching," Dev said, his voice as sultry as the air around us. Dev's magic was thick, catching us all in its spell.

"Get rid of those panties." Daniel didn't bother to give Dev a yes or no answer, but his actions spoke plainly. "Spread her legs. Show me her pussy."

"I can do that." Dev's tongue traced the shell of my ear before he dispensed with the rest of my clothes, eager to do Daniel's bidding. All the while, lust thickened in the air, filling my lungs and brain until I couldn't think of anything but them.

When I was naked, Dev eased me back into his arms, his back against the headboard. He hooked his ankles around mine and spread my legs, showing off my pussy for Daniel's view. When he'd had the chance to undress, I had no idea, but I pressed myself against his heat, loving the way he felt against me.

The magic heightened the effect, and I didn't even try to fight it. I could have left the room. It wasn't the kind of magic that robbed you of your will. It was like a long, slow intoxication. I could walk away, but I was with two men I loved and trusted. I wasn't about to walk away.

"She's wet, Dan. But you know that because you can smell her. Fuck, I can smell her and I don't have your senses." His fingers slid through the petals of my pussy, showing my husband how aroused I was. I tried to wiggle, to get him to fuck me with his fingers, but he held me tight.

Daniel looked down at the picture Dev and I made and stilled, his hand falling away from his cock. His blue eyes were heavy with desire, but he didn't move to join us. "What the hell is this?"

Dev kissed my hair as he played with my pussy. "It's a sort of magic. It comes naturally to me, though I haven't felt it so strongly before. It's attached to the three of us, but it's going to spread through the hotel."

"Sex magic?" Daniel asked, his whole focus on that place where my legs had parted for him.

Dev's hand had found my clitoris and was rubbing gently, taking my breath away. "Yes, it's a part of who I am, but this is a breakthrough for me. It's so fucking strong. It feels so good. I would use it to start a ceremony; you would call it an orgy. I didn't mean for it to come out, but if you really don't want this, Daniel, you should leave. I'd put at least four or five floors between us to be safe."

He did want this. He wanted it so bad I could feel the need pouring off him, but still he hesitated.

"Do you love her, man?" Dev asked flatly.

"Yes." There was no hesitation, no pondering of his answer.

"I love her, too," Dev stated. "So what the hell's wrong with loving her together? This would be perfectly normal in my birthland. It would be good and right to bring her as much pleasure as we can."

Daniel still seemed reluctant. "It's not normal here."

"Fuck normal, man. Normal will make us all miserable. We make our own normal." Dev kissed my ear. "Zoey, your husband wants permission to join us tonight. I don't think he's going to take anything but a vocal invitation from you."

"Daniel, please." I would do just about anything to get him to join us. The last thing I wanted was for him to walk away. Tomorrow would be another problem entirely, but I wanted tonight.

That was all he needed. Daniel crawled across the bed, his big body covering mine, and I was finally where I wanted to be, surrounded by them. Dev was at my back and Daniel spread out on top of me. My legs wound their way around that powerful body, hooking around his waist so I was spread as wide for him as I could be.

"I love you, Z." His cock was poised right at the entrance to my pussy, teasing me with his width.

"I love you, Danny." He'd been my everything for most of my life. It felt natural and right to be there with him.

He didn't have to get me ready. I was so wet he just slid in with a groan, stretching my pussy until I was so full of him our breaths were in synch and his heart beat in time with mine. His chest rubbed against mine as he brought our foreheads together. He held himself inside, tight against my body as he kissed me, his tongue penetrating while his cock made a place for itself deep inside me.

Slowly, so slowly I thought I would go mad, he started to move. Dev's magic was pulsing from his body, feeding our passion and making us both groan. There was no more arguments from my husband as he pressed his face into my neck. I felt the tips of his fangs graze my skin, and I prayed he would bite down.

"Hold her still for me, man." Daniel's voice was guttural, almost drugged with lust.

"She's ours tonight. Do you understand, Zoey?" Dev's lips were against my ear, his words hot on my skin as Daniel started to thrust. "We're going to make you scream for us. We're going to hold you down and make you come until you don't remember a time when one of us wasn't inside you. We'll pass you back and forth until we're satisfied, until we don't have an ounce of come left in our bodies."

Daniel's lower body worked hard, pumping into me, pounding his flesh into mine, seeking the connection we'd been missing for months. "You'll take everything we give you, Z. And I intend to give it to you all night long. I'm going to fuck you until I can't anymore. Until the sun comes up and I can't move and even then, I might sleep with my dick inside you. I missed you, baby. I missed you so fucking much."

His fangs grazed my neck and his magic was working in tandem with Dev's. I would have done anything they wanted me to, anything to keep them close to me. I was willing to be their plaything, their sweet little sex toy.

All the while, Dev was whispering to me. He told me how much he loved me, how much he wanted me, how beautiful I was. I pushed back up against Danny, finding that special spot and working it as hard as I could.

Then my eyes were rolling into the back of my head, and I screamed when Daniel's fangs pierced and he began to feed. I dug my nails into Daniel's back and clutched Dev's hair with my other hand. My orgasm washed over me, a wave that threatened to drown the world and I wouldn't care. Pleasure still hummed through me when Daniel released the vein.

Daniel pushed up on his arms as his pace picked up, and he drove himself into me as hard and fast as he could manage. He threw his head back and cursed as he held me still, pumping his release into me. He fell forward, landing on my chest, his adoring lips finding my breasts.

"Love you, Z." Daniel sighed as he rolled off me.

Dev took immediate action, twisting me around until he was on top. He kissed me, his hands wandering everywhere. When he came up for air, there was a happy decadence in his eyes, and I knew Dev was in a place he'd missed for a very long time.

"Let's have some fun, lover."

They proceeded to show me just how much fun three people could have.

Chapter Twenty-One

I woke up with a sigh because I really didn't want this particular dream to come to an end. It was the craziest, most erotic dream I'd ever had. It came from nights of sexual frustration. In the dream, I was between Dev and Daniel, passed between them like some plaything they really wanted to please. They were tireless in their quest to see how many times they could make me come. I didn't have to choose between them. I just had to wait to see whose turn it was. I smiled because that decadent thought made me happy. It was a good dream.

So why was I so sore?

My eyes flew open, and I realized I'd taken this whole crazy Vegas thing to its limits. There was no way to deny it because there was a mirror over the bed. I heard my shocked breath as I took in the picture.

Dev was asleep on his side to my right, his hand reaching toward me as though I'd turned away from him in my sleep. Daniel was on the other side, asleep on his stomach. He'd kicked the covers off so his perfectly muscled backside was in glorious view. I could see all of this because, despite the fact that the heavy curtains were closed, we left the lights on. Apparently boys really like to watch.

I sat up like a shot, and the night came back in a rush. I might have thought about it further if Neil hadn't been standing at the end of the bed, Starbucks in hand. His mouth was open wide, and he stood perfectly still.

"How long have you been standing there?" I hoped the answer was not very long because apparently we might not have noticed extra people.

"I think the coffee's cold now," Neil managed. "And it was like four hundred degrees when I got here. I thought you might like some. I spent the night out. I see you spent the night in."

I struggled to find anything to say. "Would you believe we were all just really tired?"

Neil took a deep inhale and looked at me with an amused light in his eyes. "Nope. The nose doesn't lie. Then there are all the condom wrappers. It's an impressive collection. Zoey's been a very bad girl."

Dev growled as he stretched. He didn't seem to care that he was completely naked and not alone. He sat up and kissed me briefly. "Zoey was an awfully sweet girl last night in my book. I'm going to go take a shower. We have a big day ahead of us."

"A big day to go with a big night," Neil said.

Dev ignored that statement and stood up, nodding at Neil, who didn't even try to hide the fact that he was looking. Dev lifted the coffee out of his hand and tasted it. "This is cold. Call down and have them send up, oh, everything. I'm so hungry. And mimosas. I can still taste that Scotch. We have to do something about Daniel's taste in alcohol."

Dev walked into the bathroom, and Neil turned to me. "Zoey, holy shit. Did you see how big that thing was? Why isn't he gay? It's just wrong."

I threw a pillow at him. "Just give me that shirt."

Twenty minutes later I was still in shock as Neil passed me a cup of hot coffee this time. We'd gone into the living room of the suite which was now covered in a lovely breakfast spread, though it was almost three in the afternoon. I was still in Dev's dress shirt. The buttons were askew because I hadn't really been paying attention to them. I kept going over last night in my head, trying to figure out how I felt about it.

"You're going to be troublesome, aren't you, sweetheart?" Dev held a champagne glass in his hand. He looked delicious in a masculine robe that showed off that chest of his to great advantage. I could also see the marks on his neck. He could see the one on my neck, but there was another fresher set on the inside of my thigh. Daniel needed a late-night pick me up. He'd expended a lot of energy. Hours and hours of sex will do that to you.

"She grew up human." Neil was already on his second plate.

"They have very different ideas about sex."

"Please explain to me the problem you have with what we did last night. I know it had nothing to do with the pleasure because I got the feeling you were satisfied. It has to have something to do with odd human ideas about sin and guilt," Dev said, sounding deeply annoyed. "Let's get through this so we can get to the part where I get to cuddle you and tell you how much I enjoyed last night and what an amazing sex goddess you look like in my shirt. It really gets me hot."

I had to smile because he really did know exactly what to say. "I'm worried it will change the way you and Daniel feel about me."

He looked at Neil. "What the hell is that supposed to mean?"

Neil translated. "She thinks you'll think she's a slut."

Dev's eyebrows climbed up his forehead as he shook his head. "Why would I think that? You've slept with two men in your life. Last night did not elevate your numbers. I wouldn't care if you fucked a thousand. If you're worried I'll view you as a sex object now, let me put your mind at ease, sweetheart. I always viewed you as a sex object. From the minute I saw you, I viewed you as something I really wanted to put my dick in and last night didn't change that. I would like very much to put my dick in you right now. I love you. As long as we both want something, I can't conceive of how it's wrong."

"It wasn't normal," I whispered.

"I thought I went over this last night with your husband. Darling, you slept with a faery prince and a vampire," Dev pointed out. "You passed the exit for normal a couple hundred miles back. You're going to have to explain to me how wanting to watch isn't a perfectly normal impulse."

I pointed an accusatory finger at my lover. "You didn't just watch, Dev. When I was doing that thing that Daniel really wanted me to do…"

"It's called a blow job, sweetheart." He had no discretion at all.

"When I was doing that you didn't watch, Dev. You just joined right in."

A slow, satisfied smile spread across his face and he sighed. "Well, lover, that soft, sweet part of you looked very lonely and neglected. I couldn't stand to see it looking needy, not when I was so capable of filling it up."

I laid my head in my hands to hide the embarrassment. I just couldn't talk about this the way Dev could. I looked up at Neil, who was playing with his cell. "Oh my god, are you tweeting?"

Neil shoved the phone behind his back. "No," he said in a way that meant yes.

Dev's eyes widened as though he had a sudden revelation. "Has this event made you think of me differently? Perhaps you no longer love me because I shared you with your husband. I hadn't considered that. I was so happy to be using that magic again that it never occurred to me you would be upset I was willing to share you sexually."

"Dev, I didn't say that." He didn't understand me at all, but then I didn't understand me either. I'd been given everything I wanted and I kept poking at it, trying to find holes in it.

"I shared you with him because you love him. I place value on your love, not my singular possession of your body. I thought last night was something all three of us would enjoy. I didn't realize it would make you think less of me." He looked like he was trying to think of what else he could say. He was looking for some way out of the trap he thought he'd fallen into.

"Stop it." I tossed my embarrassment away like a tissue I no longer needed. I sat in his lap and brushed the hair back from his face. "I don't think any less of you. I always knew you were a horny, dirty, filthy man, and I love you. You're right. I'm being ridiculous."

"We aren't normal, Zoey," he said quietly, and there was a certain sadness in that admission.

"I know," I replied and kissed him. I was still worried about Daniel and what would happen when he wasn't under the influence of Dev's magic, but I needed to reassure my lover. "Can we get to the part where you cuddle me now?"

There was a knock on the door. Neil got up muttering something about how lunch had taken its damn good time getting here. He hadn't wanted breakfast. Apparently there wasn't enough meat on the buffet for him so he'd order a couple of cheeseburgers. I hadn't even eaten breakfast yet, but I was suddenly busy as Dev kissed me and let his hands wander across my legs. He flipped me over so he was on top of me with my back pressed in the couch.

It was a flirty thing with no real intent. He smiled down at me. "Now you can tell me how good I was. I've taken your silence after our times together as human silliness, but now that I love you, I feel I should be able to ask for the things I need. I need praise."

It was a selfish thing for me to have forgotten. I'd grown up around a Fae couple, and they complimented each other constantly. I let Dev praise me but never thought to return the favor. "Which part of you do you need compliments on? They're all worthy."

Dev smiled, happily winding his arms around me and settling in. "Let's start with my cock. I think that's a good place."

I laughed. "A most worthy place to start. I love your cock, Devinshea. It is simply sublime."

I was going to say something more, but one minute Dev was in my arms and the next he was gone. His body was lifted straight into the air. I sat up as Dev was hauled up by a hand around his throat.

"Zoey, Marcus is here," Neil explained uselessly since I could already see that Marcus was here and pissed off.

I certainly hadn't expected any vampiric visitors, but Marcus was a daywalker. It was his specific talent to be able to move about during the daylight hours. Apparently, today he decided to come calling. He had to be looking for me since Daniel would be asleep for hours.

"Marcus, put him down." I scrambled to my feet, not an easy task given the fact that Dev's shirt was huge but still didn't cover enough of me.

"You think to touch a companion?" Marcus ignored me. He growled his question at Dev. I was really glad he didn't have Daniel's claws or my lover's throat would have been a mottled mess.

"I do more than think about touching her, you son of a bitch," Dev choked out. Even with hands tightening on his throat, he was going to spit out some vulgar defiance. "I fuck her on a regular basis. She won't be grateful if you kill me."

Marcus growled and shoved Dev against the wall, the force making the floor beneath my feet shake. I dove for my purse where I had a revolver loaded with some specific rounds.

Neil did have claws, and he changed his right hand. "Let him go, Marcus."

"Stay out of this, wolf," the vampire replied. "I will handle it."

"Can't do it, Marcus." Neil grabbed the vampire and tossed both men across the room. Marcus let go of Dev in midair. Marcus landed against the window, which managed to take his weight and bounced him back onto the carpet. Dev landed in a heap on the sofa.

I ran to Dev and stood over him, waiting for the vampire to recover because I knew he would. Dev caught his breath and started to get up. "Stay down or get behind me," I ordered as I aimed over him. "I mean it, Dev."

He held a hand up to let me know he would behave. He slid off the sofa and got up behind me.

Marcus sprang up, showing no effects from his encounter with the werewolf. If anything, he looked even more pissed. He pointed at Neil. "You, wolf, you will pay for your interference. You are tasked with protecting your master's possessions and you let her whore for that *pezzo di merda*? I will see your head on my mantle, wolf. You have failed your master."

Neil changed quickly, his clothes tearing around him, and then that big white wolf was at my side growling threateningly. He thumped his tail to let me know he was ready to go when I gave the word.

"I'd like to try to talk some sense into him," I said to Neil because the ramifications of this whole scene were just starting to hit me.

We needed Marcus on our side or we could all be declared outlaws. Marcus held an enormous amount of power over us. It would also be hard to explain why I'd had to kill a member of the Council. It suddenly scared me just how much control Marcus could exert over us if he chose to.

"You won't be able to reason with him, sweetheart," Dev said quietly. "He wants you, and he's pissed I've had you. He isn't being rational or he'd think to ask certain questions."

"I do not have to ask questions, *fottuto.*" Marcus spat out a litany of Italian I didn't understand, but I was pretty sure there was a lot of cussing going on. "I can see plainly that Mrs. Donovan has committed adultery. I could kill you, Zoey, and no one would question it."

"Daniel would," I muttered, but Marcus wasn't listening.

"Daniel will have to wake up to your faithlessness. He has

indulged you, but that time is done. I will have you brought to my villa. Daniel can take his time training you there. You will be properly trained and submissive before you are allowed to see the light of day again. I hope you have enjoyed your Lancelot, *piccolo puttana*, because he might have cost us everything," Marcus snarled as he stalked toward me. "If you wanted another man in your bed, I would have been more than willing. You did not have to go slumming."

I might not know Italian, but I know when someone calls me a whore. "These rounds are silver, Marcus. I will shoot you. When I get done filling you up with silver, I'll let Neil finish you off."

"It should be interesting to see how many shots you can get off before I take your lover's head," Marcus offered.

"As amusing a situation as this is, I have to ask you not to shoot him, Z," Daniel said as he walked out of the bedroom. He'd put his jeans on but that was all. He rubbed his forehead with his palm. "I actually think I have a fucking hangover. The sound of gunfire might crack my skull. Dude, how can you drink that much and still stand up?"

"It's a gift, and I did more than stand. I performed quite heroically." Dev relaxed behind me. He seemed comfortable that Daniel would handle the situation.

I just stared at Danny, my eyes wide with wonder.

Daniel yawned and scratched his chest. "Got into trouble, Z? I'm sure it was Dev's mouth. He's gotta learn to tone it down."

"I have authority issues," Dev admitted. "Marcus there has some issues of his own. He plans to kill me and wolfie here and set his place up as your pleasure palace. He thinks our girl needs some training."

Daniel looked around as I lowered my weapon, and Neil sat back on his haunches. Marcus looked from Daniel to Dev, a confused expression on his face.

"I get Dev, man. There have been plenty of times I wanted to kill him, but why Neil?" Daniel asked.

I just stood there with my mouth open, waiting for someone to figure out what was wrong with this picture. Why were we talking about Marcus when there was a much more pressing issue?

"I caught your wife and her lover." Marcus looked at me long and hard, his eyes traveling the length of my body. "The wolf tried to protect her lover. He is obviously involved in their deception. He should have killed the interloper. I am sorry you must discover the truth about her in this fashion."

Daniel stared at Marcus. "Neil is supposed to protect my property. My wolf does his job. He stopped you from damaging that which belongs to me. Or do you claim rights to all I own?"

Dev piped up and pulled the collar of his robe back, showing off the fang marks on his neck. "Just one of the questions you should have asked, asshole."

"You have taken the faery as your lover?" For the first time since I'd met him, Marcus seemed genuinely shocked.

Daniel faltered, uncertain how to answer that question, but Dev didn't have a problem with it. "Zoey has certain fantasies Daniel likes to indulge. I come in handy from time to time. I assure you Daniel and I observed all the rules of a devil's three-way. There was no eye contact. We managed to communicate through a series of hand gestures. Put your mind at ease, Marcus. We were all about the girl."

"Is anyone going to comment on the fact that Danny is awake at three in the afternoon?" I asked quietly.

Everyone stopped. Neil was suddenly a very naked human male standing next to me.

Dev came to my other side, a satisfied look on his face. He crossed his arms across his chest. "I'm a badass."

"Zoey, this is what we've been waiting for." Marcus's prior rage morphed into something like excitement. "This has been his weakness. Daniel, I told you she could make you strong. I told you her blood and her sex would make you strong. Whatever you did to him last night, companion, keep it up."

I thought about that strange magic of Dev's that filled the room to bursting last night. Vampires can use sexual energy to strengthen themselves. Dev's magic was all about sex. "I don't think it was me."

Daniel and Marcus turned their heads to Dev, who had gotten himself a new drink and was smirking as he relaxed on the sofa. "Oh, it was definitely me. There's no question of that."

"How?" Marcus asked.

"I'm a priest. You know about Fae priests, I assume. Apparently all Daniel needed was some extraordinarily powerful sex magic." Dev crossed his legs, looking very proud of himself.

"You are Miria's son, the wild one?" Marcus asked. "I knew your grandfather. He was extremely powerful. He used to be able to simply walk by a group of men and women and they would be overcome with lust."

"That was Granddad," Dev acknowledged. "He was always a good time. I really hope everyone used protection in this hotel last night, otherwise there's a lot of stuff that happened in Vegas that won't be staying in Vegas."

"It was a fertility ritual? That is very powerful." Marcus looked at Daniel with thoughtful eyes. "You have chosen your friends carefully, Daniel. If this one is who I think he is, he can be useful. You can make inroads to Faery with him. His brother will take the throne one day. It's said his brother would do anything to mend the rift between them. He's a powerful pawn."

"He's more than a pawn, Marcus," Daniel said. "He knows the rest of the supernatural world. He can advise me in a way that you cannot. He can get me meetings with people who wouldn't talk to you."

Marcus nodded, but hadn't taken his eyes off me. I was aware that I was half naked and standing around with a pistol.

"I can accept all of that, Daniel," Marcus continued. "I am finding it difficult to accept that you would whore out your queen to bring him into the fold. Surely some other arrangements could have been made. If you needed a third, I would have been more than willing to indulge her perversions."

Suddenly the pistol was a welcome weight in my hands because I'd had just about enough of Marcus. I stepped over the couch not caring what I revealed because I needed to make that vampire understand something. I shoved the muzzle of the gun under his chin and he stilled. "Look here, Vorenus. Daniel didn't choose Dev. I did. I'll put this in terms you can understand. He is mine. If you even look at him the wrong way again I will kill you. I know you seem to think that a companion is a submissive piece of ass to be dealt with as you please. I can't change thousands of years of history, so you need to stop thinking of me as a companion and start referring to me as your queen. I will not submit to your will, Marcus. Is that understood? And if you call me a whore again, I won't be responsible for my actions. I'll get that silver sword my husband, who I also choose to sleep with, carries and I will separate your head from your body. Do I make myself clear?"

"As crystal, *mio regina*," Marcus replied with a savage smile.

Daniel took me by the arm and looked at his patron. "I would like to speak with my wife now. Can I trust you not to kill my advisor?"

Marcus straightened his tie. "Yes, I did not understand the relationship. My instincts took over my good sense. I can certainly work with the prince. Please go and speak with your queen while I smooth over this situation."

Daniel stopped, his eyes finding Dev's and a moment passing between them. "Dev?"

My boyfriend's lips curved up in a soft smile, his eyes on me even as he spoke to Daniel. "I'll take care of things, Dan. I don't think you need any more disturbances this afternoon. Enjoy the sunlight."

"Thank you. I will. And Neil, go put on some freaking pants. What's with you and pants?" Daniel pulled me back in the bedroom. He turned me around and looked at me seriously. "That was a mistake, Z. He'll want you even more now. Your forceful personality is the reason Marcus is interested in you. That was practically foreplay in his mind."

"That's not my fault. Am I supposed to let him walk all over me? He tried to kill Dev. I'm not going to sit back and let that happen because defending my lover might get him off."

"I just think you should be careful around Marcus," Daniel explained. "Just know what he wants from you and be careful. He's not a bad man, but he is a product of his time. Can I kiss you now?"

I looked at him, surprised at the turn of his thoughts. "I thought you would be upset about last night."

"I don't have time for that, Z. Unless you've decided to forget this whole insane plan to save Sarah, I can't waste time worrying about the fact that we had a threesome last night, and we aren't in college anymore so we can't call it experimentation. All I know is you came back to me last night. We have to work things out, but we have to do it later. Have you changed your mind?"

"No, I have to do this."

"Then let me kiss you and, god, go over to the window and let me see the sun hit your hair again." Daniel pulled me close. I let my hands feel the warm skin of his chest, and it was all right because Dev was fine with this. Last night had changed something, and it didn't feel wrong to show Daniel I cared. "I can see the sun, Zoey."

I kissed him, and he held me for the longest time. After a while I walked to the heavy drapes and pulled them open. Daniel stepped back out of habit, but we were facing the east so there was no direct light this late in the afternoon. I opened the balcony door.

"Come on, baby," I said, asking him to come outside with me.

His shielded his eyes from even the indirect light but after a moment he was used to it. He stood behind me and rested his chin on my head, his arms going around me. "It's so beautiful. I never thought I would see this again."

I squeezed his hands in mine and thought about the fact that this might be the last time I saw this. I was so glad I got to spend this time in the warmth with Daniel. I was grateful for every moment with Danny and Dev and Neil, and if I was successful, Sarah would have a chance at this again. There was a part of me that wished I could walk away from her and just enjoy my men and my friend but I couldn't. I would feel her loss the rest of my life. I would spend it knowing that she suffered while I sat back.

"Shh, Zoey," Daniel said, brushing my tears away. "We'll get her back. It will be all right."

We stood there together until the sun finally left the sky, and it was time to get ready for the night. Daniel was right. We would get her back or we would die trying.

Chapter Twenty-Two

The thing about having a really good plan is realizing, no matter how carefully you have constructed the design, no matter how you have planned for every contingency, something will always happen to fuck up your previously perfect plan. It's even worse when that perfect plan you should have come up with is actually a half-ass plan that requires an enormous amount of improvisation. Improv might work well for a comedy routine, but it sucks when planning a theft.

As I looked at myself in the mirror just hours before the heist, I realized how much I couldn't control about tonight's operation. The best heists run something like a play. All the actors know their lines and when to enter and exit. There is only one plot and it follows through. Tonight there were enough plots to confuse even the most avid follower of the theater, and I wasn't even aware some of them had been written into my play.

As Kelly dressed me and instructed the hairdresser how to fix my hair, I considered all the things that could go wrong. The list was close to endless. The first pitfall I thought about was how I was going to leave the party and enter the Hell plane. I doubted there would be a neon sign blinking "exit" so I was going to have to figure that out on my feet. Once I got onto the actual plane, I had no idea how big it was. What if I had to walk for miles? There were so many variables I couldn't account for that I had to admit there was a high probability of this plan falling on its over-bloated ass. I was going to have to be prepared to call the whole thing off.

"Or you could just have a little faith," a soft voice said behind me.

I looked up at the hairdresser who I had previously paid no

attention to. Felicity Day's face smiled down at me. "Hey, don't move, you're going to ruin my curls." She directed my head to face forward. "Demons aren't the only ones who can sense doubt, Zoey."

"It's an insane plan," I said, looking at her reflection in the mirror.

"Yes, but some of the best plans are born of desperation. You don't have to save her, you know. Most people would leave her to rot after what she did. You could walk away, and no one would really care except you and Neil. Daniel and Devinshea are only going along with the plan because they know you would do it on your own if they didn't."

"I should have found a way to save her before she got dragged to Hell. She was on my crew. She was my responsibility."

Felicity wrapped another lock around the curling iron. "No, she wasn't. Her path was set before her birth. It only changed when she met you. She's not your responsibility. She made her own choices. Have you considered what you are risking to save this one person, Zoey? You risk many more people for the justice of one."

"Are you trying to talk me out of this?" I sort of needed Heaven on my side here.

"No, I am trying to make you see that this is who you are. This is your nature. Your vampire thinks of the greater good. With a singular exception, he can sacrifice much for what he believes is just. You, on the other hand, tend to think in terms of personal justice. You're concerned with individuals. When dealing with your husband, know that your concerns are just as well. They provide balance."

"Am I going to succeed?" I asked, knowing she probably wouldn't answer.

She smiled. "I believe so, but it will cost you. You will possibly pay for the events of this night for years to come."

"Want to give me an example?" I really hate the way angels and demons like to talk about all the crap they know is going to happen in the future, but then they never go into the specifics. They always say something like "If you pursue your present course there will be many consequences." Like I don't know that. Just once I would like for one of these warning to include something like "Hey, don't take a left at Brown Street because a car's going to hit you."

"Just know that you control the outcome, Zoey. Your will is the strongest weapon you have. And know that forgiveness is the greatest gift you can give yourself."

I turned to complain about her deeply nonspecific warnings, but she was gone and another woman was curling my hair. She pronounced me finished when I heard the yelling from the living room area.

"This is bullshit!"

"Calm down."

I rushed out. Neil was shouting. He was on one side of the room and Daniel and Dev were on the other. Everyone was dressed for the evening. Daniel was in a classic tux, Neil in an expensive suit and Dev just looked like sin. He was in a black three-piece suit without the jacket. The suit fit perfectly, and he'd eschewed a tie in favor of leaving the shirt open to show off his throat and the beginning of his sculpted chest. It was a conscious display of skin. At this type of event, servants dressed conservatively and lovers showed why they were lovers.

Daniel's jaw was a straight, harsh line. "You knew this would happen, Neil. I have to present the Council with proof that their plan can work tonight. If I don't, I risk exposing all of us."

"It doesn't have to be him," Neil shot back.

"Oh, god." I realized who we were talking about. The men all turned to look at me.

Neil rushed over, a glint of hope in his eyes. "Zoey, tell him no. Tell him to use someone else. Don't let him send Chad to the Council. Justin can go. Justin is older. Just go over there and change his mind. Please."

I looked at my friend, who was panicked at the thought of his lover being sacrificed to the Council. I was horrified, too, but I wasn't sure there was anything I could do about it. I'd been kept in the dark about all but the vaguest of plans. Now I realized why. I would have said no. I would have tried to change their minds. I looked at Dev, who would be the easier of the two to persuade. "It should be someone else."

He shook his head. "It's too late. It's already in motion."

Daniel looked at us with sympathy. "Chad is the only choice. He is stronger by far than the rest of them. He can do the job. I am sorry this upsets you, Neil, but sacrifices must be made."

Neil rounded on him. "You would never make this sacrifice, Daniel. You told me once you would never ask anything of me that you wouldn't do yourself. Tell me, Your Highness, would you sacrifice Zoey to protect your secrets? The answer to that question is hell no."

Daniel's face hardened. "This was Chad's choice. I didn't order him to do it. He volunteered."

"How can I know you're not lying about that? You won't let me see him. You kept this hidden from me," Neil pointed out. "How do I know you didn't convince him to do this? You could have threatened him."

"I didn't," Daniel shot back, his face flushing with emotion. "I didn't threaten anyone. And I didn't hide a damn thing from you. Chad asked me to keep it quiet. He knew how you would react."

Neil ignored that line of reasoning. "How about you Dev? Are you going to sacrifice your girl for the greater good?"

"I would never have made that promise to you, Neil," Dev replied, his arms crossed. "It was a naïve promise made by an inexperienced royal. Of course he will ask things of you he won't do himself."

"It's not the same thing, Neil," Daniel tried to explain. "He'll be back. I'm not sending him off to his death or anything. It's one year of training that every vampire goes through. I've prepared him for this."

"You're sending him to the same Council that turned you into an emotionless automaton for years. You're sending him to spy for you, and if he gets found out they will kill him, Daniel." Neil faced Daniel, caught between tears and rage. "I've been your faithful servant for years. I've protected the woman you love with my life. I'm asking, begging you to protect the man I love. When I made my oath, you promised me protection. Chad made that same oath. Please keep the promises that were made to us."

"Daniel, we can't send Chad." I knew Chad. I liked Chad. It couldn't be Chad.

"Then who, Zoey? Who is it going to be?" Daniel exploded. "You tell me because you obviously know what you're doing. You have absolutely no interest in what I have to do on a daily basis until you disagree with me. I can't do this with you. I can't fight them and fight you whenever the whim takes you. I like Chad. Do you really think I want to send him into a dangerous place? I don't. Do you think I want to disappoint you, Neil? I don't. I don't want to do any of this, but if I don't no one will and then all of us will suffer. You think I don't make sacrifices, Neil? My whole fucking life is a sacrifice."

"Then understand how I feel," Neil pleaded.

"I can't afford that, Neil," Daniel replied, his voice tired. "I can't afford to protect your feelings. Chad and I made this decision. It's already in motion. It can't be stopped at this point. It's the right decision. It stands. I'll take you with me to Paris when I have to go. You'll be able to see him. I'll make arrangements. He'll be allowed to return in a year or so. You have to be satisfied with that."

"Then I'll see you in a year, Daniel," Neil said bitterly. He turned away to move toward the door.

I actually felt the room swell with Daniel's rage. I took a step back and suddenly Dev was at my side pulling me close, and I knew there was a real chance that this was going to get violent.

"You think to break your oath to me, wolf?" Daniel's voice took on the tone of that beast that slept inside him.

Neil turned on his heels, his hands shifting back and forth from claws to fingers, not quite deciding which one would be of use. "You've already broken it. This is what everyone warned me about. You just use the people around you. You don't really care about any of us. You aren't capable of caring about anything except your own ambitions. I owe you nothing."

"I'll decide what is owed to me, and never doubt that I will claim my due." There was such will behind Daniel's words that I didn't doubt it was a threat.

"Daniel, what are you doing?" I tried to pull away from Dev. I needed to stop this fight before someone got seriously hurt. The idea of my husband and best friend going after each other made my heart hurt. "Let me go."

Dev trapped me in his arms and whispered in my ear. "You've done enough damage, Zoey. Be quiet now. He's doing what he has to do. Neil is being unreasonable. Don't make this worse."

Neil looked back at Dev and me. His eyes took on his beast.

They were a winter, glacial blue, but there was no mistaking the rage in them. "Hold her, Dev, while you can. You made a mistake last night. You let him in. Do you really think he'll share her with you for any length of time? He's using you to get back into her bed. I assure you, some handy accident will be coming for you. Zoey's grief will only make her vulnerable. She'll turn to him. Can't you see that? He'll never share his precious blood with you."

"Enough," Daniel roared. He held his hand out, and Neil's body jerked, limbs twitching in an odd, ungainly manner. "My blood is in your veins, and it will run true. You will obey me in this. You will protect your queen and guard your mouth tonight. Is that understood, my servant?"

I watched as Neil tried, really tried, to form his own words, but what came out of his mouth was, "Yes, master."

"Now go and stand guard at the door," Daniel commanded.

Neil walked away to do as he was ordered. His movements weren't graceful, as though he was fighting the compulsion.

When he was out of the room, Daniel looked at me, obviously anticipating a fight. His hands were shaking slightly with the force of his anger, but he stuffed them in his pockets. "Get her dressed. It's time to go."

"What the hell was that, Danny?" I dug my heels in the carpet, unwilling to ignore what had just happened. Had Daniel really taken control of Neil?

Daniel stalked toward me, gesturing to the door Neil had walked through. "That was necessary. What am I supposed to do, Z? Am I supposed to let him go? Am I supposed to leave you unprotected? He knows everything. All he has to do is open his mouth and this evening becomes an execution. Do you want to watch as your husband and your lover are decapitated? Don't expect Marcus to save you. His head will be right beside ours. They'll leave you alive, baby. Remember that ceremony you witnessed? If Neil opens his mouth, you'll be sold tonight. I have no doubt your price will make Meredith look like a value meal from McDonald's."

"He would never do that." Neil might be angry, but I knew him. He might run off, but he wouldn't betray us.

"I can't risk it. There's far too much on the line." Daniel looked at Dev, his eyes bitter. "You have no idea how I envy you. She'll blame all of this on me."

Dev looked down at me. "Zoey, you should know I agree with everything Daniel has done tonight. He is right. We can't risk exposure at this juncture. Neil isn't thinking straight. All it would take is one bitter word from him and we could all be dead, including Chad."

"You said it yourself, Z," Daniel reminded me. "You told me we should pick the strongest of our vampires and make him our spy. Did you forget your own advice?"

I shook my head because I remembered it all too well. I just hadn't expected to care about the person we sent off. Daniel was right, but I didn't have to like it. "How are you controlling Neil? You said it was your blood. I've taken your blood. Can you do the same thing to me?"

Daniel walked up to me. I could see how much he wanted to touch me, but he held back. "The relationship is different."

"Neil is Daniel's animal. It's a specific power," Dev explained. "Although up until tonight, I believe the power has been nominal. He could call Neil but not bend his will. I suspect it's another effect of the particular energy you drew from me last night. It's a supercharged sexual energy you seemed to be able to feed on. Can you hold him?"

"Oh, yes," Daniel said with a wicked certainty. "I can hold him. The way I feel now I could hold a whole pack of wolves. I've never felt anything like it. I could make an army of them."

"Let's not get ahead of ourselves," Dev murmured. "I'll make some calls because you'll need to replace Neil. I believe Roman can make a deal with some of the werewolves we have working in the club. The pack here is extremely weak. Money and the promise of power could sway a few. We'll need bodyguards."

I was horrified. "Do you hear yourselves? You're acting like Neil is expendable."

Daniel started to speak, but Dev stopped him. "He's not expendable. He just needs time to adjust. He's had a shock, but it doesn't change the fact that we need muscle. You can see that. We just need to get through tonight and when we're back in Dallas, we can figure this all out."

Daniel's eyes wandered back toward the door. "I hate this, too,

Z. But I meant everything I said to him. This was Chad's choice. He and the others made the decision and I promised to honor it."

"Daniel must honor his soldiers' wishes, Zoey. You have to know that. And we'll deal with Neil when we're back home and away from prying eyes," Dev concluded.

There was nothing to be gained from having it out here. I knew Neil and unless Chad was given back to him, he wouldn't back down. They were making sense. I tried not to think about the look that passed between the men. They were taking positions, bulwarking each other's weaknesses. I couldn't think about it now. It was time to get ready to do my job. Politics would have to take a back seat. "I'll get dressed."

I allowed Kelly to pull and push me around as she fitted me into the dress Dev had chosen. It was more modest than I envisioned. The soft gold color wasn't what I would have chosen, but even I could see how it made my skin glow. Because of security, I also wasn't able to carry any weapons. Daniel would be leaving his sword behind. I was completely on my own.

The Revelation hummed softly in my hand, and I let it drop until it hung between my breasts. I looked at myself in the mirror. The dress was vaguely Grecian or maybe Roman. The bodice was low but not vulgar. There was an emerald green ribbon that wrapped and defined my waist. The golden fabric flowed in soft folds to the floor. At least the footwear was reasonable. Knowing Dev, I expected a stiletto, but this was a soft slipper. I could run in it.

"You look beautiful." Dev dismissed the stylist and the hairdresser.

"I look soft and submissive," I pointed out when we were alone.

"Appearances can be deceiving. Would you prefer to walk in looking like someone about to commit theft? No one will suspect you, Zoey. When the time comes, we'll be able to sneak away with no one the wiser. There are rooms for privacy at this party, do you understand?"

"For sex." I'd been told that pretty much anything went at this party, but when it came to sex, vampires tended to be modest about their companions. First time public presentation aside, a vampire's companion was carefully guarded. Hence the privacy rooms. I was given to understand the demons were not necessarily so circumspect.

"Yes, for sex. The way we look tonight, no one will wonder why the *Nex Apparatus* has disappeared with his lovers. I'm sin. You're innocence. Both are very tempting to this lot." Dev slid his hands up my arms. "I would prefer to just spend that time using the room for what it was built for."

I shook my head and grinned at him. "Haven't done it on the Hell plane, have you?"

He kissed my ear softly. "No, I have not, my mistress. I would love to check it off. If I recall, you denied me the ability to check off Arkansas."

"Let's get Sarah back, and then I'll see if I can help you out," I replied. He'd started to call me mistress as often as sweetheart or lover. It was the title of a servant to his vampire's companion, but when Dev said it he meant something different. He added the "my," and it always let me know what he was thinking. Dev took my hand, and we walked to meet Daniel.

"Wow." Daniel stared at me for a moment.

"It meets your approval?" There was a satisfied smile on Dev's face as though pleasing Daniel in some way pleased him as well.

"She looks stunning. It's everything you said it would be," Daniel stammered.

"Better than prom?" I asked with a genuine smile.

"And I remember that night fondly," he replied, our history there in his eyes.

I crossed the room and slid my hand into his. I couldn't stand him looking so alone. He was right about a few things. I did only get involved when I was telling him he was wrong. I only used my power when it suited me. I owed him some measure of trust. "We'll take care of Neil?"

He breathed a sigh of relief. "Yes, of course we will."

"After this is over, I'll take him on a trip, and we'll shop and party and he'll be okay," I said as much to reassure myself as anyone else. I went on tiptoe and kissed my husband briefly.

He looked down at me, squeezing my hand. Dev took my other hand.

It was time to go.

* * * *

"Seriously?" I asked an hour later as the limo pulled up to the building that housed the physical entrance to Hell.

Daniel shrugged. "They have a sense of humor. You have to admit that."

The driver walked around and opened the door to the limo. Daniel got out and held his hand for me. Dev followed but at a respectful distance. He wouldn't join us until after we'd been announced at the event.

"Is this a sign that marriage is hell?" I asked as the lights of the tackiest wedding chapel I'd ever seen blinked away. They even had a drive-through lane.

"Well, it hasn't exactly been easy, has it?" Daniel grumbled. "Is that thing still not working?"

I shook my head. The Revelation had gone silent the minute I got in the room with Daniel. The reminder that he was part demon wasn't helping his mood.

"Welcome," Elvis said as we walked in.

I shook my head because that was just tacky. We were led to the back and an elevator opened. Dev and Neil entered and then Daniel led me in. I hated the way Neil looked. His face was blank and bland. There was nothing of my happy, sarcastic playmate in those eyes now. Then the doors opened, and I had other worries.

"Mr. Donovan, we have been waiting for your arrival." The elevator opened to a large foyer. It was elegantly appointed, and I could hear music coming from behind twin doors. There was a greeting area with several well-dressed demons doing busy work. "Sebastian has asked me to inform you that your presentation is ready. I heard it's quite impressive. Please check to make sure I have the names of your retinue correct. You will be announced and enter through the double doors."

I caught my breath as the doors opened. This was what a London ball must have looked like during the Victorian era, if said ball was full of demons and lots of people with fangs.

There was a demon at the top of the stairs announcing the guests as they entered. "The Council's *Nex Apparatus*, Mr. Daniel Donovan, his companion, Mrs. Zoey Donovan, and his Royal Highness, Devinshea Quinn, Prince of Faery and High Priest of the

Old Ways." Neil was strictly a servant. No one needed his name.

It was the first time I'd heard Dev's complete title. I was impressed, but Daniel rolled his eyes. "That is the most pretentious thing I've ever heard. You just have to have a longer title than anyone else."

Dev smiled. "I require a long title to go with my very long..."

"Shhh," I warned as we made our way down the long stairs. Every eye watched as the Council's assassin entered the ball. We were greeted at the steps by Niko and two other vampires I hadn't been introduced to. They stepped forward and shook Daniel's hand before giving Dev and me long looks.

"You surround yourself with beautiful blood, Daniel," the largest of the men commented, not bothering to hide his open appraisal. He was extremely tall, with long brown hair and an accent that sounded Swedish or Norwegian.

"What's the point of walking the night if it's devoid of precious blood?" Daniel put special emphasis on the word precious. It was a term of endearment meaning the vampire held those who carried the blood to be very dear. "Elof, Niles, may I present my companion Zoey Donovan, and our very good friend Devinshea Quinn. Elof and Niles are Council members."

Elof nodded to Dev. "Your Highness, I've had the pleasure of meeting your mother, the queen. It was before Faery closed the mounds to our kind. It is very rare to see a Fae such as yourself in the world now, much less a prince. Your brother is the heir?"

"Yes. I am the spare. I let my brother handle the politics. I prefer to pursue pleasure. With the mounds closed, I was forced to enter the Earth plane to discover new diversions." Dev said the last with a sexy drawl that left no doubt he'd found his diversion.

Dev was supposed to act the part of the pretty, insignificant lover. He relished his status as himbo far more than I liked playing the bimbo. I also had to admit, he was really good at it. Tonight he was allowed slightly off the leash as this was a party, and the rules were a little different. With Dev firmly established as part of our threesome, he had some rights to my person as long as it didn't go too far.

"Marcus was right." Niles spoke in a very upper-crust British accent. He stared at me. "She's bloody amazing. She's almost too bright to look at."

"Do I need to say the words, Niles?" Daniel asked, his voice quiet but forceful.

"Of course not." Niles turned away from me, seemingly disconcerted by his lapse. "Everyone knows she's yours, and you won't be at all reasonable about making a deal. That's not what I came over to talk about. Is he ready?"

"I assure you all of vampire kind will be satisfied with my presentation. Sebastian is preparing the exhibition now. It won't be long." Daniel took my hand and set a lingering kiss on my wrist. "My love, go with our lover and enjoy the night. I'll be with you shortly. Dev, I trust you can keep her out of trouble."

Dev took my hand from Daniel's and nodded, his green eyes deep and seductive. "I'll do my utmost to entertain her. We both look forward to the time when you can join us."

Dev led me away quickly. I looked back at the two men I'd been introduced to. "Hey, I didn't even get to say anything."

"Yes, it was a successful introduction." Dev led me straight to the dance floor. "Let's dance, my mistress." He saw my hesitation because this was not the kind of dancing we'd done at Ether. All around us couples moved together in the formal movements of what looked like a waltz. "Just follow my lead."

He put a firm hand in the small of my back and directed me where he wanted me to go. "So your job is to make sure I don't speak with anyone?"

He led me into a turn. "I wouldn't say that. I just think it best you be kept far away from high-ranking members of the vampire world. You aren't known for your discretion."

"I can be discreet."

"Yes, you discreetly threatened a Council member with decapitation already today." Dev looked down and let me know he enjoyed the view. "Did I mention how fucking hot you were defending me today? Please promise me the next time you get in a fight you'll go completely commando again because I found it very distracting. I think the enemy trying to get a glimpse of your hootchie could turn the tide of battle in our favor."

I threw back my head and laughed because with Dev, I'd moved past embarrassment. Dev twirled me around, and I just enjoyed the moment. It didn't last long. The song was over, and I realized everyone was looking at us. Apparently there wasn't a whole lot of uninhibited laughter at these things.

"Don't get self-conscious," Dev said as he bowed at the waist. "They're watching us because we're beautiful and full of life, and they would love to know how one as dark as Daniel managed to get two creatures of light in his bed. Trust me, next year threesomes will be all the rage." Suddenly Dev's handsome face lit with something close to terror. "Zoey, my love, remember when I told you I slept with many of this plane's exotic creatures? Here comes one now. Please save me."

I turned around and was surprised to see a tall woman walking toward us. I use the term walking because anything with two legs technically can't slither. But she came close. Her eyes were strange, and she didn't try to hide her fangs. If you took her apart, her separate features might be attractive, but together they were damn scary.

"Holy shit. You let that bite you?"

"My brother bet me I wouldn't do it," he said in my ear, holding my shoulders like I was his shield. "I was a dumb kid, and I needed to check vampire off the list."

"Devinshea," the icy blonde vampire sort of hissed. I think she meant it to be sexy. "I was shocked when I heard them announce you. Shocked but pleased because I always knew you would seek me out. Once you got over your fear, I knew we could be together again."

"I'm not here for you, Cecilia," Dev managed, not sounding at all like a man who was over his fear. "I'm involved with her."

Cecilia seemed confused as she looked down her thin nose at me. "She is a companion. You're not sleeping with her."

"Oh, yes, I am, as often as her master allows it," Dev admitted. "I also share a bed with her master. Yep, I'm all taken. I'm hers and his."

I laughed because any minute now he was going to declare his love for Daniel in an attempt to get away from his creepy ex-lover. While I would love to hear him declare his mad, gay love, I had to stand my ground. "Please go away. He's still very scared of you."

"Companion, did I give you leave to speak? I see you there with your glow, but it moves me not. I don't like girls so don't try to sway me with your sweet blood. I'll have this one. His blood is the closest I've found to companion blood in a male."

"How about I sway you with the end of a stake, bitch?" I asked, ready to do my best impression of a Jerry Springer guest. Before I got the whole threat out, Marcus took me into his arms and swung me back onto the dance floor.

"You won't mind if I take Mrs. Donovan for a dance?" Marcus asked as Dev's face went shock white. "I see you and Cecilia have much to discuss."

"That was so mean." I looked up at the Italian and saw he took great pleasure from abandoning Dev to Cecilia's mercies. "Is he going to be all right?"

"I assure you, if Cecilia misbehaves, we'll hear it. I think your Lancelot would not choose to suffer in silence. I believe he'll loudly object to any violation of his person. Besides, after what he has done, I feel perfectly justified in leaving him to deal with someone as forceful as Cecilia."

I tried to catch a glimpse of Dev as we moved on the dance floor. "And what has he done, Marcus?"

"You understand why they dressed you as they have, do you not?" Marcus asked. "This is a carefully chosen ensemble. I assume your faery prince selected it as Daniel would have bought something from a shopping mall. The color of that gown magnifies the shine we vampires can see in a companion. You practically have a halo tonight, *bellissimo angelo*. You're merely missing the wings. You glow more brightly than anything in the room. You were dressed to catch the eye of every vampire and every demon in attendance."

"Why would Daniel knowingly want that?" Daniel tended to threaten any vamp who looked at me twice. He didn't like demons looking at all. Daniel had to have planned this with Dev because Dev couldn't see this mystical glow I supposedly had.

"Because no one will pay him any attention when they can look at you and your prince. The two of you are the most vital creatures in the room. There is a reason Devinshea's mother has forbidden vampire kind from the mounds. Faery blood is sweet. The very light of a faery is attractive to a vampire. Even now, Daniel is speaking to certain vampires he might not be able to if the rest weren't distracted by your beauty."

I looked down, unwilling to let Marcus see how upset I was to be left out of this plan of theirs. Daniel and Dev apparently left me out of a lot of their plans.

Marcus wasn't fooled. "I'm sorry to disappoint you. I spoke with the prince at length, and I've decided he is infinitely more dangerous than he looks. When he's not thinking with his cock, he's quite intelligent. He's ambitious, your lover. I'm sure he says he's doing this for you. Perhaps he believes it, but he enjoys the game, *cara*. He's good at it. He'll do whatever it takes to win. This is good for Daniel. It's good for me. It is not so good for you."

"Why are you telling me this, Marcus?" I was tired of playing games.

"Because I figured out several things today. You're not a normal companion and shouldn't be treated as such. You brought Devinshea into your marriage, did you not? It wasn't Daniel's consent that was necessary."

I nodded, not bothering to mention that it was Daniel who had been allowed into my bed with Dev.

"I confess I've had it easy. I've purchased the women I wanted in one way or another. I shall have to take a different tack with you. I find myself excited by the thought of the chase." The Italian's hand tightened on my waist.

"I'm not sleeping with you, Marcus. Daniel would be offended at the thought." I wished there was some way to leave the floor without causing a huge scene.

"Daniel knows how I feel about you, Zoey." We twirled around, and I saw poor Dev being manhandled on the dance floor by creepy Cecilia. "I was warned to not force you. I was told to not try to buy you. He never said anything about seducing you, *cara*. He will laugh at the thought, but I think you will tire of your lovers' games and deceptions, especially when they begin to hurt the ones around you. Know this, Zoey, you're always welcome in Venice."

"Yeah, I'm sure I am." I could just bet how he would welcome me.

"No, *cara*, no strings," Marcus said seriously. "I apologize for my earlier actions. I was overly emotional. It's my only excuse. If you need a place to run, my home is yours, and there will be no payment demanded. I'll attempt to seduce you, of course, but I respect you, Zoey. I'll honor your decision. I merely wanted to make my offer and perhaps cause your Lancelot several moments of pure horror."

"May I cut in?" a very proper British voice asked.

Marcus nodded and smiled at me way too intimately before handing me over to Hollywood's hottest vampire. "Decided to go for irony did you, Stewart?"

Stewart smiled a high-voltage smile. "I look damn good in this one, Zoey. He's terrified, by the way. He keeps wondering if he's had one too many pints."

I hoped the unfortunate actor didn't have an early call time tomorrow. "What happens to the poor boy when you're done with him?"

"Oh, probably a little time in rehab, I suppose. They tend to call it exhaustion. I really like wearing famous people. It's fun. I try to pop into Paula Abdul at least once a week."

"That explains a lot." I tried not to look as disgusted on the outside as I felt on the inside. "What do you want tonight, Stewart?"

"I want to help. You can't do this without me. You need someone to show you a door. There's no way you can find one on your own," Stewart answered. "I've reserved a room for you and your boys later this evening. Way to give it up, girl. There's nothing a hetero male loves more than a nice gangbang. I'll be waiting, and I'll show you the door."

"Why should I trust you? Why am I asking that question? Here's a better one. What's in it for you?"

"Besides costing Brix his angelic Red Bull? I want ten minutes to talk to your husband," Stewart admitted. "I swear on all that is dark and unholy that I merely want to talk to him. I told you I suspect he's going places, and I might be able to help him."

"He's not going to want help from a demon."

"Then he can turn me down, and no one's lost anything," Stewart said oh so reasonably. "It won't cost you a thing, and it will make your little plan go so much more smoothly. You can come to the room in thirty minutes or not. Now that business is out of the way, answer me a question, companion. What's wrong with my puppy?"

I followed Stewart's eyes to Neil. He was watching me carefully. His face held no expression. He didn't look like Neil at all.

"He's just working," I lied.

Stewart's eyes, or the ones he was borrowing, widened. I hated the way he could get into my head. "Poor puppy. Did the nasty vampire put the whammy on him? That's what happens when you take those blood oaths. It never works like you think it would. I wonder what those boys are going to do when you step out of line? I suspect a good spanking, but then you would probably enjoy that, love, wouldn't you?"

I stopped in the middle of the floor and gave Stewart my best "go to hell" stare. "What's the room number?"

"Oh, I suspect you'll figure it out. Looks like your dance card just keeps filling up, though you might want to make sure this one doesn't try any dirty dancing on you." Stewart winked outrageously and practically skipped away.

I turned around just as Lucas Halfer bore down on me.

Chapter Twenty-Three

"Hello, Halfer or should I call you Brix?" I stood my ground with what I hoped was a reckless grin. Inside I was screaming and running as far and fast as I could. My lack of weaponry made my hands twitch for a nice, happy gun. Out of the corner of my eye, I could see Neil starting to make his way through the crowd on the dance floor.

Lucas Halfer was a large, imposing man. His features were dark and looked as though they'd been cut from granite. Unlike many of the demons here, Halfer preferred a human appearance to his demonic state. I'd seen his demonic state a couple of times, and I admit I preferred his human body, as well.

"Oh, that's a good question, Mrs. Donovan." Halfer let his eyes go black as they swept down me. "I think we'll go with Lucas until I get a chance to kill you. Then you can call me Brix. You look delicious tonight, Mrs. Donovan. Someone is offering you up on a lovely platter."

"Stand back, Halfer," Neil said flatly, putting himself between me and the demon.

"I'm just talking to her, wolf. Back down." Halfer held his hands up as though showing us all that he didn't mean any harm.

I sure as hell didn't buy it.

"You were warned to stay away from her, Lucas." Marcus walked around and placed himself at my side. I already felt better.

"I didn't realize there was a restraining order." The demon looked around, pleased at the scene he was creating. "Aren't you just America's sweetheart, Zoey? Oh, look, you didn't get rid of the faery. Well, I called that."

Dev sort of slid in behind me, putting his hands around my

shoulders. He was out of breath. I wondered if he'd had to fight Cecilia to get to me.

"And what the hell do you think you can do, faery?" Halfer waited as if amused that Dev thought he could do anything about it if Halfer chose to attack.

"Well, everybody else came. I'm just following the crowd." Dev's arms tightened as he looked around. He was looking for Daniel.

"Where's that vampire of yours? Or has he already gotten tired of you and made a profit selling you to Marcus here? Well, it was probably a good move on his part. I didn't come to cause trouble. I just had a message from your little witch friend. She sends her best." Halfer laughed. "Hell, I can't lie. She really just cries a lot and begs, but I'm sure she would send her best if I didn't rip her throat out on a daily basis. I would have brought her as my date, but she was in two pieces after I got through with her earlier tonight. I'm sure she's back together by now."

"I'm going to make you pay, Halfer," I swore, all my thoughts of running gone as blind rage pretty much took over. Dev's arms were now a cage.

"Marcus, I believe your bitch is threatening me," Halfer laughed, his voice a silky evil.

Marcus growled, and I knew if I could see him, his fangs would be long in his mouth.

"I love it when there's trouble in paradise." Halfer bowed formally to me. "I believe I'll pass on our dance, Mrs. Donovan. When I dance with you, I'll need a little more privacy than we have here."

Halfer turned, and before I could sigh there was a sudden hush that fell over the ballroom. My gaze moved from Halfer striding away to Daniel walking in with Sebastian at his side.

Dev leaned his head in close and whispered. "This is the presentation we were talking about. Zoey, keep your face free of emotion. Do you understand?"

I nodded, and his arms came from around my shoulders to settle on my waist.

Everyone forgot the excitement of my throwdown with a demon and watched Sebastian. Daniel took a place beside him, both men above the crowd though Daniel seemed to be the authority figure of the two. With the exception of members of the Council, every vampire in the room and many of the demons cast their eyes down rather than meet his gaze. If this had been a wolf pack, there would be no question who the alpha was.

Two demons pulled a heavy cart behind the vampires. It was covered and on wheels. It shook mightily from time to time. It seemed to be a cage of some kind, like the ones they kept circus animals in. I steeled myself because I knew the animal in that cage. I tried to reach out to grab Neil's hand, but he merely stood there and stared at the proceedings, his whole being blank.

"Demon kind, vampire kind, I welcome you," Sebastian greeted the crowd. "It is my greatest pleasure to introduce Mr. Daniel Donovan, the Council's *Nex Apparatus*. He has a special presentation for the Council on this evening. If the Council would come forward?"

Marcus looked back at me. "I have to go, *cara*. Try not to cause too much trouble." He stopped before Neil. "You, wolf, do not leave her side."

Marcus took his place beside Niko, Niles, and Elof. They were joined by the fifth and final Council member. From what I understood from several long, boring lectures Dev had given me, his name was Louis Marini. He was a dark, stunning Frenchman who was born long before Christ. He was the head of the Council. The full Council stood before the cart and waited for the presentation to begin.

Sebastian continued to speak. "I have been asked to explain the nature of tonight's exhibition. As you all know, our numbers fade with each passing decade. We were once an army of blood seekers, feared and worshipped as gods. We now must hide in the shadows as humanity has ravaged the Earth like a plague. Every vampire is precious, yet many choose to meet the dawn rather than walk the night in an aged body. We can no longer wait idly by for our brothers to rise. We must find them. We must turn them when they are strong. We must build our army once more. This is the task set by the Council for the *Nex Apparatus*. Tonight he has brought our first solider, discovered in the prime of his life and brought over successfully to walk the night."

There was a gasp that went through the crowd as Chad was revealed. He looked much as he had that first night. He was disheveled and savage looking. He screamed and howled his rage as he tried to break out of his cage.

"He hasn't fed for almost four days," Dev whispered in my ear. "It was necessary to emulate his recent turn. This way they believe Daniel killed him, but did not feed Chad his blood. The Council will feed him their own ancient blood and treat him as a normal vampire."

"What if their blood turns him?" I asked quietly.

"It won't," Dev said with a surety I certainly didn't have.

Louis came forward, his large body moving with elegant authority. "You have exceeded our expectations, Daniel. He is a prime specimen. Can you do this again?"

Daniel bowed slightly, showing deference to the head of the Council. "I seek them nightly, sir. You'll have your army. I'll see to it."

Louis waved his hand, and Chad was rolled out screaming and beating at the bars of his cage. I watched in complete horror, wondering what made Daniel think this could work. Chad was so far gone I doubted he even had a speck of Daniel's blood left in him. He was wheeled straight by Dev, Neil, and me. I almost looked away, but I forced myself to memorize Chad's face. He was just one more mistake we'd made.

Then amid his howling rage at the world that denied him blood, he looked down briefly and winked at me.

In an instant, he was all scary fangs and creepy eyes again, and I knew Daniel was right. Chad would be everything we needed him to be. He would fool them all.

As Chad was carried away, the head of the Council praised his assassin. "Mr. Donovan, all of vampire kind is in your debt. I would offer you gifts, but what I had planned to give you, I see you no longer need." Louis glanced at Dev and me, smiling knowingly. "If I offered you your choice of the human lovers we brought with us tonight, you would turn me down, would you not?"

"I am content with the blood in my bed, sir," Daniel admitted.

"As would we all be, Mr. Donovan," Louis continued. "We will have to be content with congratulating you on a job well done and perhaps you will find a satisfactory sum in your accounts in the morning. For the rest of the night, we celebrate. Mr. Donovan, you have leave to enjoy your lovers. Please feel free to use the rooms. Anything the three of you require will be provided."

Louis motioned once more and the band began playing again. The Council members moved forward and congratulated Daniel. Louis Marini started to walk my way, his destination plain.

Dev tensed behind me. He whispered directly in my ear. "I was hoping to avoid this. Zoey, he is probably going to bite you on the wrist. Just take it. He has the right. Please don't fight it."

Marini's dark eyes seemed vaguely reptilian to me. "Mrs. Donovan, Your Highness," he held out his hand, and I realized I was supposed to put mine in it.

I forced myself to move my arm, offering my wrist. Unlike the other high-ranking vampires I'd met who bent over and lightly kissed my wrist, Marini pulled it to his mouth. He let me see his fangs, and I felt a tiny sting as he penetrated the vein lightly, his tongue sweeping across my wrist to lick up the blood he'd drawn.

I looked up and saw that Marcus detained Daniel, making sure he didn't note the exchange between myself and the head of the Council.

"You are exquisite, Mrs. Donovan," Marini said with a sigh. "I have rarely tasted your like. My own companion pales in comparison." He stared at Dev with a dark look in his eyes. "Your Highness, if you become bored with our assassin, please consider giving me a call. I find you quite stunning. I would offer the same to you, Mrs. Donovan, if it didn't go against our laws. Perhaps someday it will not. I must admit, I find it rather distasteful that a six-year fledgling has the sweetest blood here, no matter what he can do."

Marini walked away and it took everything I had not to pick a fight with that asshole.

Dev was right there in my ear, playing the savvy politician. "It won't do Daniel any good. It would only get him killed, and we would probably be put in the vampire equivalent of a brothel, and I don't want to go to a brothel. Well, not like that. If you're interested, I could arrange a tour."

"Stop it, Dev. We're not going to a brothel." I watched as

Daniel made his way to us. I put the encounter with Marini out of my mind because I had a job to do. "It's time to get serious."

Taking my hand, Daniel placed a lingering kiss on my lips, and I enjoyed the brief, strong feel of him. For the longest time, Daniel had been the rock I clung to, and it was nice for a moment to be able to hang onto him again.

"Are you ready?" he asked.

I nodded and turned my lips up to Dev's. He played his part and only slipped me the briefest of tongues. It was very subdued for him. Daniel led the way this time as we formed a little train making our way to the back of the ballroom. I could feel Lucas Halfer's eyes on me the whole time.

The hallway that led to the privacy rooms was dark, and I wondered what was going on in those rooms. It was so quiet, I commented on it.

"The rooms have noise inhibiting magic on them," Daniel answered. "Otherwise it could get quite loud."

Demons aren't known for being the tenderest of lovers. I realized there were also a lot of unattached vampires who brought their human lovers with them. The term lover, it should be noted, is one I use loosely. While some vampires might enjoy a human and treat them well, the truth is, most are used for sex and blood. When the vampire gets tired of the human, they're passed around or simply vanish, never to be heard from again. I was certain whatever was going on in those rooms was probably loud, and I was grateful for whoever put the wards on the doors.

Daniel headed for the first available room, but I held him back. He turned and gave me a questioning look.

"I have to find the right room." I wondered why Stewart had thought I would magically know which room he was in. I looked around, hoping he'd left a note or something. At the third door, I knew where that cheeky bastard was.

I stopped in front of the door numbered sixty-nine.

"Excellent," Dev said as he opened the door and entered. "My lucky number."

Stewart was sitting in a chair beside an enormous bed. "I thought you would like it, you naughty faery."

After Neil was in, Daniel closed the door. "What the hell is he doing here?"

"He's here to help." The explanation sounded ridiculous to my own ears.

Dev threw his big body in the middle of the plush bed. He exhaled and looked at me with an invitation in his green eyes.

"Seriously?" I asked him. How could he think about that now?

"Help, Z? He's here to fuck everything up." Daniel pointed to Stewart, his head shaking in disapproval.

Dev gestured to some writing on the walls. The walls of the room were decorated with wards and spells, each drawn with what I seriously hoped wasn't blood. Paint. Maybe demons liked paint. "Those are lust spells, sweetheart. Lust wards. I have no control over it. Can't you feel it?"

Stewart was putting his two cents in. "I saved her when we were in Arkansas, Your Highness," Stewart said to Daniel. "Ooops, are you undercover? Do you have a code name?"

"You didn't save her. You were the reason she was in danger in the first place," Daniel replied.

"Come on, Zoey, I don't think I'll be able to go through with this mission unless I give in to those spells. It's really quite overwhelming." Dev laid back, patting the bed beside him. "I'm so hard right now I can't breathe."

"Dude, we're trying to deal with a demon," Daniel pointed out, ignoring Stewart to complain at Dev. "How horny can you be?"

"Tell me you haven't thought of what we could do to her? This is a big bed, man, and I bet those drawers over there are just full of toys we probably can't get on the Earth plane. How many times can we make her come?" Dev asked. "You can't feel that? Really? Listen, if you're not interested, why don't you deal with the demon, and I'll do what I do best. I'll handle Zoey."

Stewart nearly bent over with laughter. "Those are very weak lust spells. They're really only there for decorative purposes. His magic is all sex, isn't it? Funny."

Stewart stopped, and I could tell he was thinking. I didn't like it when Stewart thought.

"Daniel, he's the only one who can get us through the right door." I hoped Stewart would follow me and leave Dev alone. Once I got him out of this room, he would go back to normal, which for

Dev was still sex obsessed but not spell struck. "He's helping us because it hurts Halfer."

"He really is a sex god," Stewart said thoughtfully, looking at Dev who had grabbed my hand and was starting to suck on my fingers. "You would think an actual sex god would be interested in the very beautiful bodies in the room. I mean, this meat I'm in gets paid millions for his body. The king over there is terribly hot in a dark, violent way, and don't forget my poor little zombie puppy. God, just looking at him makes my mouth water. Yet our Green Man only has eyes for the girl."

Daniel exhaled a frustrated breath as Dev started to tell me all the things we still hadn't done. He jumped up and put a quick fist through the charm on the wall that controlled the lust level.

Dev stopped and shook off his previous haze. "Thanks. Umm, I guess the underworld has found my weakness. I tried so hard to hide it."

Stewart just kept talking. "Even the girl here has thoughts about her own sex. Yes, I can pull out that little fantasy about Angelina Jolie. I can make that happen, Zoey. My point is one as dedicated to sexual pleasure as the faery should be into all kinds of things, not just boring heterosexuality."

"I'm a fertility god," Dev responded, his tone flatly stating he wanted out of this conversation. He hopped off the bed and straightened his clothes. "You aren't fertile, so I'm not interested."

Stewart's face spread into that Cheshire cat grin he got when he wriggled something out of your mind you didn't want him to. "Poor little mortal. That must have really hurt to so set you off men, as deviant as you are."

Dev turned on the demon. "Stay the fuck out of my head."

"Leave him alone," I told Stewart.

Stewart shrugged. "All right, but I warn you it might come up later." Stewart turned happily back to Daniel. "Now, Your Highness, I have a few suggestions. I'm more than willing to help your queen and her…what should we call him? Assistant? Social secretary? Official royal fuck buddy? Never mind, we can come up with some suitable title later. The point is, I'm willing to give her everything she needs to make her way through the plane. I'm giving her the key to the bloody city here. I promise she'll get there, do her job, and come back in one piece. All I ask is a few minutes of your time."

Daniel rolled his eyes and looked at me. "You're really going to leave me here with him?"

"I've done everything you asked of me tonight," I said quietly. "I kept my mouth shut as you and Dev played me like your little pawn. Yeah, I'm going to leave you here with him."

Daniel put his hands up in defeat.

Stewart clapped and opened a bag that had been sitting on the dresser. "All right, companion, I have a few exciting items to make your stay on our plane a little more survivable. This is a little charm that will keep demons from seeing you though you shouldn't really worry about it until you get to Brix's. Hell is vast and we don't really mull about in it, you know. You should be able to use your little prize quite easily until you find the palace." He passed the items to Dev and me and handed me a small key and a glass ball. "This will get you into Brix's little pleasure palace, and when you open the door, smash the globe so any assistants he has in there will sleep for a while. It only works on demons, so your friend will be fine."

Daniel crossed his arms over his chest. "Why don't you just lead the way, Stewart? If you led the way, I could go with her and she wouldn't have to rely on that amulet."

Stewart shook his head. "Oh, no, I can't get caught with my hands in the cookie jar. They actually cut them off if they catch you. The horrible part is the itching when they grow back. It's really terrible. Don't worry about it, Zoey. If they cut your hands off, you'll just bleed out and die."

"I feel so much better," I said sarcastically. "Could you please get the door? We can't be gone forever."

Stewart held a hand up to the wall and a door appeared. He looked at me and the smile was gone. "You've been here, companion. You know how personal this can get. You know that it isn't a land as you would know it. It's something more, something personal. Don't get lost in memory. Follow the amulet. Ignore what goes on around you." Dev stepped toward the door, ready to go in behind me. Stewart turned to my lover. "Whatever you do, try not to think about it, Green Man. Think about something other than what they did to you. Otherwise, you might walk straight into it all over again. I wonder how she'll feel about her paragon of masculine sexuality when she sees you like that. Don't you?"

Dev's face clenched as he tried to ignore the demon.

I took his hand. "Devinshea, there is nothing I could see that would make me turn from you."

"That might be the most naïve thing I've ever heard you say, lover," Dev said bitterly. He opened the door. "Let's get this over with."

I held his hand and walked into his nightmare.

Chapter Twenty-Four

The door closed behind us, but I could see its outline even in the soft light of day we stepped into. Everything in this place was gauzy and beautiful. The very air seemed soft and sweet. A warm wind blew through, brushing against my skin and I heard the sound of crickets chirping in the distance. It was the opposite of what I expected to find on the Hell plane. We were in a field of flowers with the sun warming our faces. I sighed at the feel, but Dev dropped my hand, and when I looked at him I knew this was not a place of beauty for him.

Whatever Stewart had talked about before was still playing through his brain. Or worse, perhaps we were there. The Hell plane was a place to relive all the bad events of your life. I should know. Stewart was right. I'd been here before. It seemed we were about to take a tour inside Dev's crappy memories.

"Where are we?" My hand felt empty without his, but I let him keep his distance for the time being.

"We were told not to get lost in memory, Zoey." Dev ignored my question with a cold practicality. He looked down at my chest where the amulet was still covered by the bodice of my dress. "Is that thing working? We should really get started."

I pulled on the chain and, sure enough, the amulet pulsed in my hand. There was a hearty glow to it, nothing like the weak light it put out around Dev and me. Felix Day was here.

I wasn't sure how it did it but the Revelation pulled me to the north. It pointed the way as though desperate to get to the angel. "This way."

"Well, naturally it's that way," he said with acid under his breath. He ran a frustrated hand through his hair and made a decision. "If this is the way it's going to be, then I can lead us. We'll be going past those caves. Come along, Zoey. I assure you it will be informative."

He started off in the direction of the caves without waiting for me.

"Just tell me where we are, Dev." I raced to keep up with his long-legged pace. My skirts floated around me. I used my hands to hold them up so I could run. I wished I had dressed myself for this mission.

"It's a *sithein* in Scotland, inasmuch as a *sithein* can be considered in a country," Dev explained in an academic fashion. What he meant was the entrance was a mound in Scotland, but the actual land of the *sithein* was a piece of Faery and not of the Earth plane. Though it seemed to be underground, a *sithein* was its own land with its own sun and moon and time.

"But you're Irish." His branch of faery was known as Daoine Sidhe. They were left behind when the Tuatha de Dannan left Ireland. At some point in the last couple of centuries, they immigrated to the States and then formed their own *sithein*.

"Yes, my ancestors inhabited Ireland, but my mother believed it was important to have her sons experience all the various forms the Fae can take. This is an Unseelie *sithein*," Dev continued his lecture. "Do you know the difference between the Seelie and Unseelie courts?"

I did. One was considered blessed and the other contained all the monsters Faery could offer. Dev would be considered one of the shining ones, the Seelie. "She wanted you to understand the Unseelie?"

Dev turned, his eyes practically glacial. "She wanted us to be tortured by the Unseelie, to see if we were strong enough to rule. Or rather she wanted Declan to be tested, and I was fool enough to go with him. He was my brother. I couldn't let him go alone."

I tried to take his hand again, but he pushed me away. I wanted to rail against a mother who would send her sons to be tortured for some ritual, but I held my tongue on that topic. "Dev, we don't have to do this. We can go back. I'll find another way."

"You think me so shallow I would leave your friend here to spare myself this pain? What am I to you, Zoey? Am I your plaything? Do I mean anything to you outside the bedroom? You seem to think I am soft, but you are about to learn the truth of me." Without waiting for me to speak, he turned and continued to his destination.

I had no choice but to follow as the amulet in my hand was insistent he took the right path. I wished I could have left him behind, spared him this pain. I'd taken my own trip to the Hell plane earlier in the year. I knew how it could break your spirit to see all the terrible things inside your own soul. Hell isn't so simple as a place of fire and brimstone. The real torture in Hell always resides within.

A guttural sound broke through the gauzy quiet of the day. We walked through a copse of trees that seemed to reach up, climbing into the sky. There was another shout, though I couldn't tell what the person was saying from this distance. More yelling followed and I picked up the pace, coming out of the trees and onto a grassy field.

From my vantage point, I saw a group of creatures circling like a pack of wolves, though these were no canines. They were goblins, squat but built on muscular lines. I also counted a couple of large, dirty looking trolls and what looked to be a gnome, though his eyes were red even in the sunlight. They circled their prey, keeping them close as they taunted. I glimpsed two human-looking men in the circle.

I realized with a shock they were both a younger version of Dev with long dark hair. This was Dev and his twin, Declan, a carbon copy of his younger self. They were being roughly handled by the goblins. It looked as though they'd been dragged a decent way to get to this place. Both young men sported cuts and bruises and long tears in their clothing.

I started to move toward them, wanting more than anything to stop what was about to happen. I had an idea now, given what Stewart had said, and I couldn't stand the thought of it.

Dev stopped me, his hand on my elbow. "There's nothing you can do. It isn't real, Zoey. It's a memory, and it will play out as it will."

He stared out at the scene in front of him, his eyes focused.

"I like Seelie flesh," the largest goblin announced. "The only thing better is Seelie sex."

There was much laughter and a general consensus that pretty

Seelies were the best lovers, even when they were unwilling.

"Aye, we'll have to thank Miria for sending us these sweet meats," another said. This one ran a hand down the front of one of the boys, rudely cupping his genitals. The boy looked ready to throw up, and I didn't blame him. "They look delicious."

"They're so pretty," a smallish troll said, his eyes lit with anticipation.

Both boys tried to get away, one pulling at the other's shirt as though he wouldn't let them be separated.

"How old are you?" I kept my voice calm, so he wouldn't know how emotional I was already getting. I knew beyond a shadow of a doubt that this couldn't end well for Dev and his brother.

"I am seventeen." He seemed outwardly unmoved, but I knew there was a war going on inside him. He was now in this moment, as he was then, helpless to do anything but survive.

"Which one should we start with?" one of the goblins asked, his large hands twitching like he couldn't wait to get his fingers on that flesh.

One of the boys flinched, and I could see he was ready to run at the first given opportunity. He shrank from every creature, panic in his green eyes.

The other boy stood his ground and an arrogant laugh rang through the meadow. "You start with me, you idiot." It was obvious he'd decided on a path. His shoulders straightened as he began stripping off his clothes. He pulled away from his captors but only to show them his amazing body. It was thinner than it was now, the body of a young man who had not quite fulfilled his full potential, but it was beautiful all the same. His hair was long and shone in the sunlight, a midnight black waterfall down his back. He was proud and every inch the young fertility god. It was no surprise every lustful eye was on him. "You start with me and you finish with me. You'll just break him, and then you'll get in trouble."

"You sound like you want it, little sidhe," the large goblin challenged him through his tusked fangs.

I knew that reckless grin and my heart practically stopped as I realized what he was doing. "I do, you big bastard," young Dev replied with a sneer. "Do you know what I am? I'm a sex god. I always want it. You look like a cock who can give me a run for my money. I bet you give out before I do."

I turned as the goblin laughed and proceeded to take my lover up on his bet.

"Can you guess which one is me?" Dev asked, daring me to say it.

I looked up and this time I didn't let him push me away. "Yes, you're the one saving your brother."

His eyes widened, obviously startled. "Zoey, I took them all that day. I let them do things to me you can't imagine. You know that magic I have? I turned it on, and it was an orgy. I turned that pain to pleasure and, god help me, I managed to enjoy some of it."

And the pleasure had turned to guilt and self-loathing later. I could see that plainly. "And Declan?"

"Declan got away because they were all concentrating on me," Dev admitted. "Why go after him when I was so willing to please?"

Which had obviously been his plan all along. I wasn't shocked at Dev's actions. He'd sacrificed for his brother, but damn I wasn't happy about the way his twin had acted. "He left you?"

"Yes, Zoey, he left me. He ran and shortly after this day, we left this *sithein* and returned home."

I tried to focus on him and not the sounds in the background. It was a perverse version of what Dev and Daniel and I had done. Dev had used his magic for protection instead of pleasure. "At least tell me he was grateful to you for saving him."

Dev laughed, but there was no humor in it. "I wish I could, sweetheart. When I managed to get my very sore, bloody body back to our *brugh* that night, he asked if I even wanted to go home since I enjoyed the perversions of the Unseelie so much."

"Bastard." I looked at him through the tears clouding my eyes. "He was a bastard, Dev."

"No." Dev used his thumb to gently wipe my tears away. "He was a king, and I was his deviant, mortal brother. I was an embarrassment to him. Don't cry for me, Zoey. I'm pleased to see you do not think less of me, but I would rather not have your pity."

"Idiot," I said with all the passion I felt for him that moment. "I'm not feeling sorry for you. I'm proud of you. I'm so proud to be your lover. You were brave. You were unselfish. He's the one who should be ashamed."

Dev pulled me to him and kissed me for all he was worth. He held me and sighed into my hair. "I would like it if you could meet my brother."

I hugged him tightly, willing him to feel my love for him. "He wouldn't. I'm going to kick his ass if I ever meet him."

"That would be one reason I would love for you to meet him." He became serious again. "Zoey, I would prefer to keep this experience between the two of us."

"Of course." It wasn't something I would ever gossip about.

"I would rather Daniel not know about this part of my life."

Stroking his face, I considered his request. I would never tell Daniel, but Dev should know that he could if he wanted to. "Daniel wouldn't care. It wouldn't make him think less of you."

"Daniel already believes me to be a man of no discretion. Let him believe my perversities are contained within the fairer sex." Dev looked out in the distance. "I think we can leave now."

He pointed to a spot behind me. I turned, and a dark mansion had popped up in the middle of all that light. There was a menace to its elegant lines. The amulet lit up like a lantern.

"Come on." There was excitement back in his eyes because with this over, he was all about the adventure again. "I would like to leave this place once and for all."

We hurried off, the amulet leading us up the path to the mansion. I pulled out the globe Stewart had given us. So far we hadn't seen anyone except Dev's ghosts. The charms Stewart gave us seemed to be working. I could only hope that the key and the globe worked as well. I passed Dev the globe. He took a deep breath, obviously feeling the same trepidation I was.

The amulet practically screamed in my hand. It shone with a bright light and pulled me toward the mansion. Felix Day was somewhere in that house, and I had to hope Sarah was with him.

We were silent as we approached the big porch, moving carefully over the stairs that led up to the heavy doors. I slipped the key in and it turned. It took strength to open the door. I struggled with it, but it glided open once Dev put his weight against it.

Dev and I stepped through and were immediately confronted with a very surprised demon. Her small mouth made a startled *O*, but before she could set off an alarm, Dev smashed the globe. It crashed against the floor, a pulse of red energy scattering everywhere. The female demon went down without a sound, her body slipping to the floor.

The house was utterly silent.

"Is it still working?" Dev asked.

I looked down and the Revelation had gone dead. Frustration welled. I moved further into the house, hoping that putting some distance between me and the sleeping demon would help. Dev followed and after I got a wall in between us, the amulet flared to life again. "Got it."

"Good. Let's get moving." Dev took my hand.

"Down there," I said as the amulet started to pull me toward a steep set of stairs.

The top floor of the house was richly decorated. It looked like a lushly appointed mansion, but now as we made our way into the lower section of the house, it started to look like I expected. It was dark on the stairs, the light of the Revelation guiding us. I almost tripped on a sleeping demon but managed to keep my balance. When we reached the bottom, I saw another heavy wooden door. I hesitated.

What was waiting for me? Even if Sarah was behind that door, how much damage had been done?

"Zoey, she'll be all right." Dev was right behind me. "Whatever has happened to her, we'll deal with it. I can get her an awful lot of help. Psychiatrists, therapists, you wouldn't believe what some witches can do with memory. She doesn't have to remember that she was ever here."

I doubted anything could ever completely erase the time Sarah had spent in Hell, but standing out here because I was scared wouldn't change anything.

I pushed the door open and walked into Lucas Halfer's torture chamber. It was lit with a series of torches because track lighting just doesn't scream dungeon. I would have gone with fluorescents, but nobody asked me. Dev and I entered a circular chamber. There was an altar in the center and off to one side I saw a rack. Both devices were currently occupied.

The Revelation had no doubt as to who was held on the rack.

"Please hurt her, not me," Felix Day begged from his place on the rack. He was tied down, all of his limbs roped and bloodied. His head seemed to be the only part of him that moved. It came off the surface of the rack, his eyes imploring me, glowing in the near gloom. "She's a horrible person. I'm good. I'm an angel. You shouldn't hurt me. You should hurt her. Stay away from me. I'm from Heaven."

I ignored him, seeking my friend, and my heart sank when I found her. Sarah lay on the wooden altar, bound by ropes that dug into her flesh. Her body, always graceful and slender, was now far too thin. Her eyes seemed to sink into her face. Her hair was a mousy brown, and that seemed the worst insult of all. Sarah's hair was always vibrant, an outward reflection of her inner personality.

I ignored that asshole angel, who I was pretty sure at this point I was leaving behind, and knelt down by the altar. Tears blurred my sight as I touched her cheek and willed her to wake. There was blood everywhere but her skin was smooth. It was a torturer's paradise. You could hurt someone as much as you wanted in a room like this, and they were always ready for more just hours later.

Felix continued his admonitions that I pick Sarah as my victim as she managed to open her eyes and focus on me. It took her a moment, but then she held her head up and turned to me.

"Zoey? Did Halfer get you?" Her voice was raspy as though she'd been denied water for a very long time. She asked the question and sounded so sad to see me here.

"No, sweetie." I tried to muster a smile. "I'm here to spring you. This is a jail break."

Fat tears rolled down her cheeks. "I can't believe you're here. This is a dream, isn't it?"

I tried to work on her bindings, but they held tight. "Nope. This is a heist. You're my booty this time, Sarah, and you know I never leave my booty behind."

"No, don't take her. You want to take me," Felix said, his voice high and whiny.

Sarah tried to turn toward him. "Felix, you can stop. This is my friend. Did you bring Daniel? Where's Neil? Zoey, this is stupid. You can't get us out of here."

"Daniel and Neil are waiting eagerly to see you. They couldn't come with us," I explained as I finally worked the knot free and undid her hands. Dev moved to the end of the altar and started on the rope that held her feet. "I brought Dev. You remember Dev?"

Sarah laughed, a weak sound that ended on a rusty cough. "I remember Dev was pretty bad at magic. Hello, Dev. It's good to see you. I'm glad to see Zoey followed my advice to jump into bed with you. Sorry you're going to end up spending eternity here with me and Felix. Seriously, you come to bust me out of Hell and the only person you bring is Dev?"

"Oh, ye of little faith. I'm getting you out of here, but that asshole angel over there can rot as far as I'm concerned. He told me to torture you. What the hell kind of angel are you?" I rounded on Felix Day and got my first look at him. He looked an awful lot like his siblings, but the half-starved version. He didn't have their glow. His skin was ashen. "You should protect her, but no, you're trying to save your own ass."

Felix smiled. It was brilliant even in the gloom of the chamber. "She's exactly as I pictured her. Felicity sent you, didn't she, little cousin?"

"Yes, she did, but she didn't mention that you were just like Oliver, who I can't stand," I shot back. "I bet he'd be down here trying to pawn off his torture on someone else, too."

"Zoey, he's trying to get you to torture him instead of me." Sarah struggled to sit up as Dev finished untying her feet. "If he whines he's a better target. They want you to cry. Brix started to torture me when he realized it hurt Felix more to see me torn up than to be harmed himself."

Dev moved to the rack and started on Felix. "Zoey, we can catch up later. I have no idea how long those demons will stay asleep. We need to get out of here." He looked down at Felix. "Can you get us off the Hell plane quickly or do we have to take the scenic route?"

"I can get us out of here," Felix stated without dropping his high-voltage smile. Unlike Sarah, he seemed to think everything was looking up. "Unbind my magic and I promise you it won't matter if they all wake up."

"Felix, you need something of angelic origin to unbind you," Sarah said in a patient tone. It sounded like she had explained it more than once. "Unless Zoey brought along some of your sister's tears, we're out of luck. It's why she needs to run."

Felix's wrists were undone, but still he couldn't move them. There was a large, circular piece of gold on his chest. I looked at it more closely and was disgusted to see someone had sewn it directly onto his flesh, each stitch a mottled, bloody welt.

The angel managed to get one of his hands to work. He held it out toward me. "Zoey didn't need to bring anything but her own sweet person with her. My little cousin will work just fine. Felicity explained what you are, right?"

"Yes, though it's still a little hard to believe." Now it made complete sense that I was the only one in the world who could do this job. Felicity needed my very unique DNA. She might have been able to use another companion, but I was pretty sure I was the only companion with the skills and backbone to pull this off.

Felix quickly explained our situation to Sarah, who looked as surprised as everyone else had to find out I had an angelic connection.

"If you say one thing about my purity, we're going to have a smackdown when we get out of here," I warned her.

Sarah grinned, and I saw some small bit of the girl I'd known before. "I wouldn't want that, Z. Our last fight was a doozy. I'd like to avoid pissing you off in the future. I just suspected Dev there would have done something about your purity. He doesn't seem like the type to just sit back and hold your hand."

"Oh, I've dirtied her up," Dev said with a lascivious grin. It was nice to know that even in the presence of angels, Dev let his libido loose. "I'd like to get dirty with her tonight, but we have to get out of here first. We should hurry because sex after I've had this much adrenaline running through my system has got to be good."

"Poor Felicity," Felix said sadly, but did not explain himself. He cast his eyes at me. "Those tears still clinging to your cheeks will work, cousin. Let your faery prince handle it, though. I don't think the spell will harm you, but I can't be sure. Devinshea, please spread her tears on the gold, and then I'd step back if I were you."

Dev strode to me and looked down, cupping my face in his hands. He brushed my cheeks with his thumbs and kissed me lightly on the nose before turning back to Felix. Touching the gold circlet on his chest, Dev spread the fluid across the metal as it started to glow. It broke down the center with an audible crack, and Dev jumped back, pulling me into his arms and covering my head with his hands. I twisted slightly because I wanted to see.

Felix groaned as he pulled the broken gold amulet from his chest and tossed it aside. The flesh healed before my eyes, turning from a pale, washed out color to a healthy golden tone.

He threw his head back and roared. There's no other word for it, but it was a happy sound. The room filled with light, but this was a soft, joyous light, nothing like the insistent, overwhelming glare of Oliver. This was a vibrant shine that filled the sad chamber with energy.

I caught my breath as Felix Day unfolded his wings and stretched his arm out to the woman on the altar. He glowed, nothing like the creature on the rack a moment ago. He was a glorious light. His halo gleamed above his resplendent face. He was very masculine, but almost too beautiful to look at. Sarah didn't have any problem looking at him. She managed to prop herself up on her elbows, and she watched as Felix made his transformation, her face filled with adoration. I wondered what sort of connections these two had formed during the months they'd spent down here at Halfer's mercy.

"Felix, I am so happy for you," Sarah said, tears shining in her eyes. "You're so beautiful."

Felix folded his wings and knelt beside her. "You're the beautiful one, my love."

And I now knew what sort of connection they'd formed. Love happened in the weirdest places.

Sarah put a hand out, holding him off. "Don't, Felix. I won't be able to stand it. I love you. I can't stand the thought of being without you. I'd almost rather stay here if it means I don't have to lose you. Almost."

Felix chuckled softly. "You've never been without me, Sarah Tucker. Not one moment of your life." Sarah looked up at him, shocked. He pulled her into his arms. "I've been with you from the beginning. I watched you grow and steered you here or there. Do you remember the night you met Neil?"

"Of course." She wasn't struggling against him. Now that she was in his arms, she cuddled against him, making an odd contrast.

Felix was the picture of vibrant life and Sarah looked so close to death.

Felix smoothed back her hair, staring down at her as he spoke. "You decided not to go out that night, but there was a voice in your head telling you to go out and have fun. It was very insistent, and you got dressed and danced the night away with a werewolf who led you to a vampire and his companion, who walked through Hell to save her friend. I was always there, Sarah."

"Then you know all the things I've done." Her voice choked with emotion.

Felix was having none of that. He hugged her closer. "Yes, I know everything about you. I know the things you've done and why you did them. I also know that somewhere along the way you became more precious than the rest of those assigned to me to watch, as Devinshea became to Felicity."

Dev and I looked at each other. I felt a surprising surge of jealousy, but I put it aside as Felix continued.

"Why do you think I allowed the demon to capture me?" Felix asked softly.

"You did what?" Sarah practically screeched the question.

"I couldn't watch you here, so I made myself a very easy target," the angel explained. "I knew that I wouldn't go back to the Heaven plane without you. It's my time to fall. It's my time to experience something new, and I'm so excited at the prospect. I want to share this with you. I want you to teach me, Sarah."

Sarah's smile was every bit as radiant as Felix's halo. "If you're sure, then I will guide you as you have guided me."

"We're talking about sex, right?" Felix finally sounded halfway human, his voice going low as though he didn't really want Dev and I to hear. And I would have sworn his cheeks flushed a gentle pink. "I would really like to have sex, but not until after we're married. The good news is we're close to Vegas, so we don't have to wait long. But Sarah, be sure you love me. I also want to try the whole eating thing, and I don't know how much I'll like exercise. You might want to take a picture because this is probably the last time I'll look this good."

Laughing, Sarah threw her arms around her angel and kissed him for the first time, their mouths forming promises of love and devotion. When Felix pulled back he was solemn. He placed his hand on her forehead and whispered, "You are redeemed, Sarah Tucker. You are redeemed."

His hand glowed, a brightness shining, bringing Sarah love and life and a future. The contract was done, Hell's petty documents and laws broken by Heaven's light.

When he was done, the angel turned to me, inclining his head my direction. "I thank you, my cousin."

"You're welcome." My entire body filled with a happy satisfaction that I'd done the right thing. The glow of a job well done didn't last long as I had a few questions for my "cousin." "So Felicity has a thing for Dev?"

I could actually feel Dev's deep satisfaction at my jealousy. He was going to be insufferable.

"Yes," Felix answered. "Though it's easy to see that Felicity's story won't end as mine. He glows with love for you, and Felicity would never come between lovers. She knew if you came on this journey together, it would cement the bond between you. She is a creature of sacrifice."

I couldn't blame Felicity for loving Dev. He was entirely lovable. I had a thought though. "So if you're Sarah's guardian angel and Felicity is Dev's, which one of us pulled the short straw and got saddled with Oliver?"

Felix threw his golden head back and laughed. "Oh, poor Oliver. He has always gotten the hard task of guarding the true warriors of this world. He watches the most difficult of charges, the ones with a great destiny who stubbornly struggle against it."

"Oh my god, he's Daniel's angel?"

Dev chuckled behind me and patted my back. "He's talking about you, sweetheart. You'll have to forgive her. Self-awareness isn't her strong point."

"I got Oliver? He sucks." I pointed at Felix. "I want to know where I can make a few very specific complaints because he's been laying down on the job. Where the hell was he when I got gut shot with a freaking arrow?"

"He was the one who made sure the arrow didn't hit any vital organs," Felix pointed out, amused at my outburst. "He was also the one who whispered in your vampire's ear, making him so very sure of where you were. He's the one who held the veil closed so you were waiting when your vampire came."

That was all good and well, but I was still pissed about that arrow. "Fine, but tell him next time someone tries to gut me, and let's face facts there will probably be a next time, how about giving me a shove out of the way? Wait. He's not in love with me, is he? You're in love with Sarah and Felicity has a thing for Dev. I don't have to worry about Oliver jumping my bones, do I?"

That really caused Felix to bust a gut. "No, little cousin, you don't have to worry. Oliver can't stand you. He once told me of all the millions he's watched over, you're undoubtedly the most difficult. Now let us be quit of this place." Felix unfolded his wings and motioned for us all to move into their protection. When we had gathered, he folded those wings around us. "You wish to return to your vampire?"

I nodded. I thought about asking him who Daniel's angel was, but the question got trapped in my throat. If Felix told me Daniel didn't have one, I wasn't sure how I would handle it. So I let the question go. Daniel would be worried, and I needed to set his mind at ease that Stewart hadn't led us into a trap.

"All right, I will see you there, but Sarah and I will continue to the Earth plane." Felix regarded me seriously. "Is there anyone you would like me to pick up on the way? I can take him away and see that he is cared for. He's hurting, Zoey. He needs time to heal. I ask your permission because you're the one with the most to lose if he leaves."

He was talking about Neil. Though I knew it was going to get me into trouble, I nodded my consent. I heard Dev curse beside me, but Felix was speaking again. "Put your hand on the Revelation. It will make our connection stronger. It's yours for now. Guard it wisely. Now look at me, little cousin. Think about where you want to go."

In the blink of an eye, we were there.

Chapter Twenty-Five

I knew Stewart had been fucking everything up the minute I saw Daniel's face. Dev and I appeared in the room, and he was sitting on the bed with a hard look in his eyes. There was no thrill that we'd made it back. There was no surprise or joy. There was just a bitter hardness, and I wondered what the hell Stewart had done.

"What happened? What did he say to you?"

Stewart shrugged at me. "I really didn't mean to, Zoey. I was having a perfectly fine conversation with the king here about, perhaps, becoming his familiar when it just sort of popped out. You can't really blame me. I am evil."

"What did you say?" I asked as Daniel turned his blue eyes on me. He looked through Dev as if he wasn't there.

"He pointed out certain facts to me, Zoey," Daniel explained in a cold voice. "It was just things if I had been thinking with my head instead of my dick I probably would have seen myself. God, I can't think straight when I'm around you. I was just so happy to get back into bed with you, I didn't think to ask why."

I looked back at Dev, who seemed just as confused as I was. "Daniel, I don't know what you're talking about, baby. Last night just happened. I'm not sorry about it, either. I love you, Danny."

"Yeah, you love me," he spat back and turned his accusatory eyes at Dev. "You love me so much you're willing to fuck me to save him. It solves a lot of your problems, doesn't it? No one will come after your lover if they think I'm fucking him, too. You two can walk around in public, and no one will think less of you because I'm the idiot husband who lets it all happen under his nose."

I kneeled in front of Daniel and tried to get him to understand. "It's not like that. I didn't sleep with you to save Dev. I love you. I was happy to be with you, too."

Daniel stopped, his eyes dark, and I was sure that whatever came out of his mouth next would be awful. "Then leave with me. You're my wife. Choose me. Prove you love me by walking out of here and being my wife, mine alone."

My heart hurt as I looked back at Dev. He stared at the floor, and I knew what was going through his head. He was waiting for me to do it. He was waiting for me to choose Daniel as he always believed I would. "Please don't ask me to do this."

"What do you want me to do, Zoey? Do you want me to be satisfied when you and Dev there decide you need a third? Am I supposed to wait outside the bedroom door to see if you're feeling up to a threesome?"

"It doesn't have to be like that," Dev said quietly.

The men in my life squared off. "You shut up, Dev. You're the reason for all of this. She's my wife. You couldn't respect that? She belongs to me."

"She didn't say 'I do,' Daniel. As far as I'm concerned, she isn't married at all."

I got between them, putting a hand on both their chests. "Stop it. Let's just go back to the hotel and we can talk this out."

"So Dev can work his mojo again and we'll both fuck you mindless, and maybe I'll be so satisfied with that sweet pussy of yours I'll forget why you're doing it?" Daniel bit off a curse and his hands fisted.

"I should go." Stewart sounded almost apologetic. "I fear my presence is magnifying his anger. I really didn't mean to do this, Zoey. Do you have any idea how hard it is to have these impulses of mine? I have plans, good plans, and I screw them up because I just can't help poking at that open wound I see."

Daniel looked around. "Where's Neil? I'm going to kick his ass for leaving."

That had seemed like such a good idea at the time. "He's gone, Danny."

Daniel turned slowly and enunciated each word. "Where did he go, Zoey? What did you do with my wolf?" He placed a careful emphasis on the "my."

I forced myself to look him in the eyes. "He went with Felix

Day. I had to let him go, Danny. I had to. He was in pain. He was hurting. He needed to go."

Daniel exploded. "What about what I need, Zoey? You think of everyone before you get down to me, don't you? That list of yours is long, and I'm at the bottom. Tell me something, Zoey, did you ever love me? Or was I just that chump who would do anything and everything you wanted?" He looked back again at Dev. "Guess you took over that role. She doesn't need me anymore. Good luck with her, Dev."

Daniel kicked the door open and strode out, leaving me to round on my little demonic visitor. "I really hope you're happy, Stewart."

He sighed. "I told you, I'm not happy about it. He was in complete agreement with almost everything I wanted and I had to go screw it up. If it helps at all, he is being influenced by these rooms. They magnify all sorts of emotions. That rage he's feeling should already be easing by now. We should all leave these rooms because even I'm feeling it. You're terrified at the thought of losing Daniel, the faery there is feeling most insecure because if Daniel hates him, how will you love him? And I'm actually contemplating how my beloved evil nature complicates my bloody life. I don't like being contemplative."

Stewart stood and walked out of the room.

I held my hand out to Dev. "We have to find Daniel. We have to make him understand."

"He isn't going to want to talk to me, Zoey."

"If this is going to work, he'll have to." I dragged him out with me.

Stewart was right. The minute I left that room, a weight lifted off my chest. I strode down the hall, hoping to catch up with Daniel before he could take out his tension on some unsuspecting piece of furniture. My slippered feet made no sound as I chased after my husband. I needed to make him understand that I loved him. I loved Daniel. I loved Dev. We were going to have to figure out how to make it work because I wasn't willing to give either of them up.

I reached the edge of the ballroom in time to see Daniel striding up the steps two at a time. He was heading toward the elevators, and I wondered if he actually intended to leave us here. I almost called out but something happened to make me stop. Just as Daniel disappeared behind the doors to the ballroom, Lucas Halfer stepped off the dance floor and something told me he knew what I'd been doing. Maybe it was the unholy gleam of rage in his eyes or perhaps the fact that there was a long knife in his hand, but I knew my game was up. Halfer knew what I'd done.

Apparently not everyone had respected the "no weapons" rule.

I caught my breath and took a step back, but Dev was already in motion as Halfer bore down on us.

The sad fact about being truly terrified is how it affects your ability to protect yourself. When really looking death in the face, sometimes you completely lose that scream that should come naturally. I felt it in my chest, stuck there like some impotent, useless tool. If I could just get that scream out, I might be able to survive. Marcus would come, hell Danny might hear me if I screamed as loud as I wanted to. But it sat there, my mouth working but no sound coming out as Halfer ran toward me, knife raised. Dev pulled me backward, throwing his tall body in front of mine.

When the knife met Dev's body, that was when the scream came.

My scream filled the room. I watched as that body I loved so much, that had given and taken such pleasure, fell forward and jerked twice as Halfer shoved the silver in and out of his belly.

I fell back, watching it in almost slow motion, praying this was some horrible dream, but then Dev fell forward and the blood started pooling around his body.

I thought about it later and realized how unlike me the next moment was. I should have felt rage. I should have been on my feet ready to avenge my lover. I didn't feel the volcanic anger that should have come. I practically forgot about Halfer in my rush to get to him. Rage wasn't on my mind. Overwhelming grief crowded out everything else. I needed to get my hands on his body as though I could physically stop his soul from leaving me.

"Dev." I screamed his name over and over as I tried to get to his body. I vaguely noted other people were beginning to crowd around to watch.

I almost reached his still body when Halfer pulled me up by the hair and held me a good foot off the ground. My scalp burned, but nothing could hurt as much as the fact that Dev didn't move.

"You think I'd let you get away with that, bitch?" Halfer snarled in my ear. "You think I wouldn't find out?"

I kicked my feet, but they met with nothing but useless air.

Halfer laughed as I struggled. "Don't worry about your boy there. He's already on his way to that great *sithein* in the sky. I wonder where you're going to go?" Halfer held the knife up to let me see Dev's blood still clinging to it. Halfer pulled the blade back. "Let's see if I can hit your heart."

I felt the knife slide slowly into my chest because Halfer didn't want me to go quickly. He slid the knife between my ribs and above my heart. Breath fled. I tried to take in air, but it wasn't working.

"Ooops, I missed," Halfer laughed. "Just took out a lung. Don't worry, Mrs. Donovan. I'll try again."

This time the knife went into my stomach, and I wondered if I was going to see Oliver Day soon. I actually wanted to see the bastard, but I knew with great certainty he wasn't coming for me. He couldn't whisper to me or gently push me this way or that because I was on the Hell plane, and I'd given up or driven off every bit of protection I had.

I felt the knife slide in a third time and could only manage a weak groan. I tried to see Dev laying there so still. Danny was gone and though we'd parted poorly, I knew this would kill him. He would never forgive himself for walking out of the ballroom.

I realized through that horrible pain that I had ruined three lives. I brought this on all of us.

I fell to the floor in a graceless heap as Halfer dropped me. I heard a roar, but it seemed a vague distant thing. There was a rush of air over me, but my vision was fading. I tried to move so I could crawl to Dev. If there was any way I could go wherever he had gone, I would try. I reached my hand out and suddenly Marcus was there pulling me to the side.

"Don't, *cara*. Don't try to move." His dark eyes looked down at me, fear plain in them.

"Dev." I pushed his name through my lips.

He looked at me with great sympathy. "I am very sorry, Zoey. I fear he is already gone."

"Try." Tears or blood ran down my face. I couldn't be sure.

Marcus rolled up the sleeves of his crisp, white dress shirt. His jacket was already gone. "No, *cara*, I have to take care of you. Daniel is busy with the business of killing the demon. It has to be me."

"I think not, Marcus," a heavily accented voice said from above. Louis Marini stood over us, looking down his patrician nose with a faint hint of satisfaction. "Donovan is all about the rules when it comes to his companion. You are not to share blood with her. You may try to save the prince, but I forbid you to give her blood. It is our law."

"Louis, she is dying," Marcus said with something akin to desperation.

"And her master can save her or not," Marini stated flatly. "I'm sure if he survives the battle with the demon, he will try to heal her. I, for one, am interested to see if he can take out the demon with his bare hands. Leave her. Do I have to remind you who your master is, Marcus?"

"Dev," I insisted because time was marching on and he was getting farther away from me.

Marcus cursed in Italian. "I should let him die, *cara*. It would solve many problems. I'm far too old to fall into this trap, yet I am going to try to save that idiot because I cannot bear to see you cry."

He gently lowered my head down to the floor. I turned though it took every bit of energy I had left. I watched as Marcus turned my lover's body over and saw his face fall at the damage he saw there. He felt for a pulse, and it didn't look like he found one.

Marcus tore Dev's shirt open to expose the wounds. He held his wrist to his mouth and spat out a hunk of flesh. He let the blood drip directly over Dev's wounds. He had to open his wrist several times because he healed so quickly. Kimberly's husband, Henri Jacobs, joined Marcus. He, too, offered his own blood. Henri put his open wrist to Dev's mouth and after the longest time Henri jerked slightly as Dev began to drink that precious, healing blood. Marcus looked at me and nodded.

"Thank you." I mouthed the words because no sound would come out.

I let my head fall back and started to float above my body.

I could see Daniel shoving his clawed fists into Halfer's chest. He seemed to be trying to pull out his heart. He was so savage, and yet I only saw my first love. The boy I learned about life with. I saw him at eight, already so handsome I dreamed about marrying him. I saw him at thirteen, filled with the loss of his father and clinging to my hand. I saw him at seventeen, teaching me how to love. God, I didn't want to leave him, but I didn't seem to have much of a choice.

I was above my body watching Daniel fight Halfer and Dev fight for life. I feared my fight was over.

Then I was in a large chamber. It was slightly cold and dimly lit. There was a man sitting on a throne. He was of medium build and nothing extraordinary to look at. Then I saw his eyes, and they were the oldest things I've ever seen. I stepped back from those eyes and realized that I was not alone.

Lucas Halfer stood beside me, and he looked pissed to be in this place. We were both back to our former complete bodies. I could breathe again, and it looked like Halfer had the majority of his chest back. Halfer took a deep breath and made an impossibly low bow.

"My Lord, Lucifer, please tell me how I have offended you," he said in a big old kiss-ass voice.

My eyes widened because it wasn't every day I got called to this particular principal's office. My reaction was the very same as in grade school, though. I pointed straight at the bastard demon who killed me and announced my position loudly.

"He did it!"

Chapter Twenty-Six

"Very mature, Zoey," Halfer huffed under his breath.

He was likely right, but I'd just gotten gutted and wasn't in the mood to be overly mature. "It's true."

"I left you alone," Halfer spat. "I was a very good boy, but no, you just had to push it. You fucked everything up. How can I let that go unanswered?"

"How am I supposed to let you torture my friend for the rest of eternity?" I answered his dumb question with a question of my own. "And you cheated. We weren't allowed to carry weapons. If I'd had my guns, you would never have been able to kill me."

He loomed over me, invading my space. "Oh, I'd have killed you, bitch."

"Shut up, both of you," the Dark Lord of Hell said. Though his voice was quiet, it seemed to reverberate along the floors and across my skin, creeping like an army of insects. "You're acting like five-year-olds fighting over a toy. Brixalnax, it has been brought to my attention that you had an angel captured and tortured on this plane. Is this true?"

Halfer straightened up and got his pride on. "Yes, My Lord Lucifer. It's true. I captured the angel myself. I brought him to my palace and had him on the rack. He's been screaming for me, My Lord. I bound his magic and have taken sustenance from his blood."

"Ewww," I muttered under my breath.

"This one thought to steal the angel from our plane," Halfer accused. "She thought to take what belongs to Hell."

"I didn't 'think it,' Halfer. Do you see your angel?" I asked sarcastically, looking around. "I don't think so. Angel boy has left the building, and I held the door open for him." I laid it on thick because if I was spending the rest of eternity in this place, I wanted to get my bile and vitriol out before I was too tortured to be me anymore.

"Mrs. Donovan," Lucifer said through clenched fangs. "You are exceedingly annoying."

I shrugged because it wasn't the first time I'd heard that.

Halfer bowed again. "She is that, My Lord. I shall handle her. Allow me to take her back to my palace, and I assure you she'll pay for her crimes on this plane."

I was about to say something really brave with my trademark sarcastic zing when Lucifer turned those ancient eyes on the demon. "And who is going to make you pay for your crimes, Lord Brixalnax?"

And my mouth closed because there are some things that do not require comment.

Halfer stopped, his body primed with tension. "My crimes?"

Lucifer regarded him with obvious distaste. "Yes, Brixalnax. Do you really think you were able to capture an angel? Only one demon has ever captured an angel before. It was long before your petty existence began. Would you like to know how that turned out?"

I raised my hand. "I totally would."

Lucifer Morningstar utterly ignored me. "The angel allowed himself to be captured, and he created havoc down here. Your angel was almost surely a spy. Do you think I have no plans I would like kept from the enemy? Do you think I plot and commit atrocity after atrocity so you can fall into an angel's trap and screw everything up?"

I decided to hold my tongue and attempt to look very non-threatening, but inside I was totally pointing and laughing. Oh, I was probably still going to be tortured for eternity, but it looked like old Brix would be there beside me. I certainly wasn't about to point out that Felix allowed himself to be captured for love rather than tactical reasons.

"I was very clever in my capture," Halfer argued, trying to find a way out of this situation. "I came upon him unawares."

"He is never unaware." Lucifer scowled. He was really good at scowling.

Halfer's eyes narrowed to black slits. "How can you know that,

My Lord? You were not there."

"I know that because I was an angel, you idiot." Lucifer's eyes brimmed with red fire. They were endless, those eyes. They seemed to get bigger with every word he said. "We're only safe from their awareness on this plane, yet you offer one room and board. Then when the angel escapes, you choose to break our contracts with the vampires by killing a companion. You killed a companion, a soft, fuzzy little blood bucket. How is that supposed to help anything?"

"You don't know her, My Lord," Halfer explained hurriedly. "She looks like a bimbo, but she's actually quite formidable in an obnoxiously lucky way."

I could have argued that luck had nothing to do with it. I could have proclaimed that I was a badass who killed when I needed to and had beaten back not one, but two of this plane's bad boys. I could have said all those things, but I was far too busy making my hazel eyes really wide and doe-like. I gave Hell's leader my best "I'm not quite following this conversation" look.

Lucifer waved off that line of thinking. "Bah, her only value is to the vampire master she feeds. The vampires are serious about their precious blood, and even a weak vampire could cause trouble between demon kind and vampire kind, but you had to kill the bloody *Nex Apparatus*'s companion. Do you have any idea what he was about to do to you? He is pivotal to everything that's about to happen on the Earth plane, and you turn him against us?"

"I did not know of your plans, My Lord." Halfer got to his knees, his head bowed.

"And I did not realize you required a daily update in order to follow my rules." There was a certain finality to his words as though judgment had already been passed. "I'm not going to kill you, Brixalnax. I'm going to let Mr. Donovan handle it. Perhaps if he's busy hunting you down, he won't turn his rage on my smaller soldiers. I cast you from Hell, Brixalnax."

Halfer's head came up. "My Lord, I have served you for centuries."

"And you failed me today," Lucifer replied with no mercy. "You'll wake up on the Earth plane and your powers will be diminished. You may keep your strength and your present form, but I suggest you run because I have no doubt there will be an angry vampire on your heels. If I were you, I would hope Mrs. Donovan survives."

"I'm alive?" I asked, finally piping up because I was pretty damn sure I was dead. I'd felt the enormous loss of blood, and I knew I had stopped breathing. I'd done the whole "watching my body from above" thing.

"Even now your husband is attempting to revive you. I can't promise you it's going to work, but shoving your soul back into your body may be the jolt of energy you need." The Lord of Hell, Lucifer Morningstar, rolled his eyes and waved his hand. "Now be gone, you annoying children. I've spent enough time on your foolishness."

Lucas Halfer looked at me with hate in his soon-to-be mortal eyes. I knew without a doubt he would be coming for me. "I'm going to kill you, bitch."

"Not if I kill you first," I replied, and then I was shoved back into my broken body.

I came to myself in a roar of pain, but I barely managed a whimper. I went from feeling perfectly fine to horrific agony all in an instant, and the forceful change caused my body to jerk. I struggled to open my eyes as I tasted blood on my lips. It was that rich, velvet of Daniel's. I forced my tongue to lap it up.

"That's right, baby," Daniel said, his voice past desperation. He held his wrist to my mouth, and I felt his tears hit my forehead.

I was lying with my head in his lap, and I could feel the blood running down my cheeks. Later, I understood that Daniel had been trying to get me to take the blood for several minutes with no luck. It ran out of my mouth, and Marcus had tried to get him to give up. Daniel simply opened his wrist over and over, refusing to admit that I was gone.

"Drink, Zoey," he whispered, getting his head as close to mine as possible. "Come back to me. Don't you dare leave me." His free hand caressed my face as though to reassure himself that I was still warm and alive. "I'm so sorry I left you. Please forgive me."

I heard Marcus sigh over me. His skin was pale. He seemed to have given Dev a fair amount of his blood. "Your faery prince lives, *cara*. He'll be tired for a few days, but he lives. We were not so sure about you. You seemed very dead when the demon disappeared and Daniel was finally able to look after you."

"Welcome back, Mrs. Donovan." Louis Marini looked down on me with dispassionate eyes. I was sure every vampire at the ball was watching as the dreaded Death Machine wept over his wife's body. I feared we had made a terrible mistake. "You are stronger than I expected. It's been a most revealing evening. It's good to know that the Council's greatest weapon has at least one weakness. I bid you good night."

He walked away, and I realized that we'd just handed him a mighty weapon.

* * * *

Two hours later, Daniel eased into the suite's large Roman-style bath with me in his arms. My body still felt all limp and noodley, but I didn't care because I was with him and Dev was alive. Daniel had been forced to hold me all the way from the ballroom to the hotel while Marcus carried Dev because he was in and out of consciousness. Dev was asleep on the bed, but Daniel had decided my skin was still chilly and needed warming up.

He sank into the heat of the water, and I groaned with pleasure.

"Is that better, baby?" He eased me onto his lap. The hot water reached his chest and covered me almost all the way to my neck. I rested my weary head on his broad shoulder.

"Warm." I sighed. Daniel's blood was working in my body. The weariness I felt was almost pleasant. In this case, the very cessation of pain was pleasurable.

Marcus knelt beside the tub. I was too tired to protest the fact that I was naked. "The prince is recovering. He's awake and can walk, but he's weak. He needs rest but he will heal. You're going to have to feed her more blood. Are you sure you can handle it by yourself?"

I smiled up at the Italian who I was very happy with at the time. Dev was alive because Marcus saved him. "Oh, Marcus, are you offering to join us and feed me yourself? That is very self-sacrificing of you."

Marcus returned my smile. "*Cara*, this is a sacrifice I would willingly make."

Daniel hugged me. "No, I can do it. I feel perfectly fine. I'll take care of my wife. I hear Marini refused you when you could have saved her." Daniel had assumed Marcus would take care of me while he fought Halfer. It never occurred to him the head of the Council would refuse to save a companion.

"Yes, Daniel. He's dangerous, and she's on his radar now." Marcus stood up, straightening his clothes. "I will leave you to seek my own bed, but I'll call later to see how our troublesome queen fares."

Marcus left, and we were alone. Daniel rubbed my back with his hands and rocked me. I might have been the one who technically died, but Daniel was the one in shock. He was still shaking, and I wondered if maybe we should have taken Marcus up on his offer.

"Are you all right?" I asked after a long silence.

"You died, Zoey," he said, his voice unsteady. "I felt it. You were fucking gone. You died because I was so pissed off I left you there. I left you all alone with no one but Dev."

We had to get one thing straight. I wasn't going to let him take this out on Dev. "You can't blame Dev."

His head shook. "I'm not blaming Dev, Z. Dev did what he had to do. From what Marcus said, Dev died, too. I'm blaming myself because none of this would have happened if I hadn't lost my temper. I got both of you killed."

I had played my part in this fiasco. I had to own up to it. "I let Felix take Neil. He even warned me I would pay for it, and I still did it. You were right, Danny. I did what I wanted to do. I didn't think about anything else. That one mistake could have cost Dev his life."

"Why didn't Dev freaking stop you?" Danny asked.

"Have you tried to stop her?" Dev stood in the doorway, his skin pale.

I looked up and was rewarded with Dev's very much alive face. He was past tired and disheveled, but he'd never looked better to me. He'd shed his bloody clothes and stood there in a pair of jeans. His torso was smooth once more, with no hint of the massive damage that had almost taken him from me forever. I told myself I would have to send Henri Jacobs and Marcus big old thank you gifts if I could figure out the vampire equivalent of a cookie bouquet.

"It happened very quickly, Daniel," Dev explained in a somber voice. "It wasn't like she looked to me for guidance."

"I'm sorry." I wished he would come closer. I wanted to put my hands on his skin.

"It wasn't your fault, Dev," Daniel said firmly. "I wouldn't have been able to stop her, either. She's impulsive, but she thought she was doing the right thing."

"I'm sorry." I didn't like the look on Dev's face. It was altogether too sober for a person who had just cheated death.

"I'll have to disagree with you, Dan. It was my fault. I couldn't protect her." Dev leaned against the door. "I managed to make myself a piece of cannon fodder. That bought her roughly twenty seconds while he gutted me."

"He's a demon," Daniel pointed out. "He's going to be stronger and faster than you. That's why we hire muscle."

I held a hand out to him. "Dev, please just come here and kiss me."

"I don't think that's such a great idea, Zoey," Dev admitted, finally getting to what I'd been afraid of since he walked in the room with bleak eyes. "Look, I'll find your muscle, Dan. I think we can assume Halfer will be back. She needs you a hell of a lot more than she needs me. You can protect her. I can't. I'm going to stay here in Vegas for a while. The two of you should stay at Ether when you get back to Dallas. It's better protected than either of your places, and she'll be more comfortable. The staff knows how to keep an eye out for her. I think you should go with two bodyguards, at least, when you're not with her. Weres are best."

"What do you mean you're staying here?" I forced myself to sit up.

Dev ignored me, preferring to speak to Daniel. "I'll put every investigator I know on tracking down Halfer. You'll get daily updates. If you need anything from me, just call."

"Why are you leaving me?" I hated the way my voice caught. "Is it because I got you killed?"

"No, Z," Daniel corrected with a frown. "He thinks he got you killed, and he's being a self-sacrificing idiot. He blames himself for the fight we had before I stalked off. He thinks if he hadn't come between us in the first place, we wouldn't have had that fight and I wouldn't have left you. What he's not counting on is the fact that we fought before he came around, and if he leaves, we'll still fight. It's our nature. Dev, she still would have let Neil go even if you hadn't been here. I still would have stormed out, and then she wouldn't have had those twenty seconds."

"I still think it's best if I took myself out of the equation," Dev said softly.

"Can we not make any decisions tonight?" Daniel sounded as tired as the rest of us. "I don't want to fight anymore. Look, if all the shit at the ball made you want to pull out, then fine. Stay here in Vegas, and Z and I will manage on our own. I won't blame you. This probably won't be the last time someone tries to rip your guts out if you stay around us. But if you're doing this because you think I won't protect her if you're here, then get the fuck over it, man. Don't break her heart like that. Just get in the tub and help me keep her warm, and we can make decisions when we get home."

Dev looked torn, and I held my breath. I knew this was a moment between the men, and I would only confuse things. "Are you sure?"

"Yes. It'll be dawn soon. I hoped the magic would last longer than one day, but I can feel myself getting tired already. I don't want her cold because I'm too stubborn to share."

He still hesitated, and I knew it was my turn to sway him. "If you don't get in this tub with me, Devinshea Quinn, I won't tell you the story of how I met Lucifer Morningstar."

Dev's eyes went wide, and I felt Daniel tense beside me. "Seriously?"

"Get in the tub and find out," I dared him.

His jeans hit the floor, and he was in my arms as I told my tale.

Later, just before dawn, Daniel carried me out to the big bed. He laid me down in the center and crawled in beside me. Dev was on the other side, wrapping his arms around my waist and tangling our legs together.

When Daniel died with the dawn, I was still warm and happy.

Chapter Twenty-Seven

"Will Felicity and Oliver be all right?" I looked at Sarah and Felix who sat across the table from me.

We were sitting together enjoying a glass of wine after a perfectly delightful meal. Felix was certainly making good on his promise to try the whole eating thing. He'd had a full three course meal and sampled what Sarah and I ordered. The good news for Sarah was Felix had also tried the gym and found it satisfying.

"Another of my kind will be assigned to assist them." Felix's hand brushed his wife's. His left hand was sporting a gold band that matched Sarah's. "It will be difficult, but they'll find their balance. It's not the first time this has happened. It won't be the last."

It had been difficult for me to find my balance since we'd returned from Nevada. The four days since Daniel, Dev, and I boarded the plane without Neil had been trying, to say the least. Daniel and Dev had explained to me that they wanted time to think about how best to handle our situation. I couldn't exactly argue with them. I was the one who screwed everything up, and it still weighed heavily on me.

I was living at Ether as Dev had discussed, but he wasn't staying with me. He slept in his office, and Daniel stayed at his apartment during the day. I spent my nights in the grotto or in the club. When I left the confines of Ether, it was with at least one of my two new bodyguards. Zack, the bartender from Descent, had offered his services and already made his oath to Daniel. Dev was right about the cash and power. Zack was constantly excited about the new strength he had gained in taking the vampire blood. Lee was Zack's brother. He had yet to make an oath, but Zack was working on him.

"Still no movement on the love front?" Sarah asked, looking at me sympathetically. She had been my go-to girl for whining about how much I'd screwed up my love life. Even though she and Felix were deeply involved in their honeymoon period, she took time out to listen to me cry.

"Nope. Dev and Danny have been working every night on whatever the hell it is they work on. They have some big meeting coming up with a couple of vampires, and it requires a whole lot of talking apparently." And left no time to deal with our situation, which was becoming unlivable for me. I would rather we all just fought it out. It would almost be easier to deal with two breakups than to live constantly wondering when they were going to break my heart.

"Are you not feeding Daniel?" Sarah asked.

"Of course I am. I sit in his lap and he feeds, and I get my mind blown and he very politely thanks me and then he leaves me alone."

"Damn," Sarah breathed. "That's cold."

She was right. It was very cold. The minute he walked out of the room, I felt used. I know he thought he was being polite, but I was ready to bring that damn nurse back because it hurt too much for him to walk away when I needed him so badly.

"He just needs time, cousin." Felix took a sip of his wine. "They both need time."

"They're going to make me choose." I had absolutely no idea what I was going to do.

Sarah patted my hand. "Of course they are, sweetie. You can't expect them to go on like this. Daniel is possessive. It goes against his nature to share you. The problem is Daniel needs you more than Dev. As much as you enjoy Dev, you've always loved Daniel. Don't get me wrong, I like Dev. I think you would be better off with Dev, but I know you. You won't be able to leave Daniel."

"I love Dev, too." I didn't want to admit she was right. Just because I'd loved Danny longer didn't mean I wouldn't feel Dev's loss. In some ways, Dev was mine. I had to share Daniel with his freaking destiny, but Dev was mine alone. I just didn't see how I could keep him. I would never be able to leave Daniel. I was tied to him far too tightly, but my heart ached at the thought of never touching Dev again.

"Don't cry, little cousin," Felix said, reaching over to brush my tears away. "It will work out. You have to have faith."

"Easy for you say." He'd been the embodiment of faith for millennia. It didn't come so easily to me.

He smiled brightly. "Yes, it is. It is also true."

I shook my head and banished my misery. We'd talked enough about my men. I had other people to worry about. "Were you able to locate Neil?"

Her bright blue pixie bob shaking, Sarah leaned toward me. "Not a sign of him. I've been trying every night, but he's either too far away or he's staying in wolf form. It's hard to track a werewolf when they stay in wolf form all the time."

"That doesn't surprise me. He changes when he's upset. I just wish he would come home." I missed Neil so much I ached with it.

The loss of Neil added to my misery. Daniel refused to let me so much as speak his name around him. I'd tried to get Dev to put some of his investigators on finding Neil, but he'd flatly turned me down. They considered Neil's defection an unforgivable betrayal.

"Your new wolf seems very professional." Sarah glanced back at Zack.

The young wolf stood a comfortable distance away but was well within hearing range. He could get to me in a single flash of speed. Zack took his new responsibilities seriously. He was dressed in a suit and sported a snazzy communications device in his left ear. He and Lee coordinated their movement through the earpieces.

"Yes, it's all very efficient." I found the bottom of my wine glass but refused when Felix offered to refill it. I'd been drinking far too much since I got back. I needed to stop wallowing. "Everything is running really well since Dev took over. I get a daily schedule. I'm sure at some point I'll have my own secretary so neither of them has to actually talk to me. Speaking of schedules, I have to meet a freaking personal shopper. Dev claims I need a new wardrobe for all the events I have to attend."

I knew what my role was—to look pretty and not cause trouble.

I watched as Zack touched his earpiece and talked quietly. I was probably the only person in the restaurant who was forced to cart around not one but two bodyguards. Lee patrolled the entrances and exits. Since we'd returned, we'd all been waiting for Lucas Halfer to make his move. It was just a matter of time.

"Hey, Zoey, before you leave, Felix and I wanted to ask you to do us a favor," Sarah said a little too brightly.

"Anything." I meant it, but the tight look in her eyes told me this wouldn't be pleasant.

"Don't worry, you're going to like it," Felix reassured. "It's just a little problem of mine that Sarah is being completely irrational about."

"He wants me to chop off his wings," Sarah blurted out.

My eyes got wide. "Seriously? You want me to cut off your wings? Where the hell are they now?"

"I'm holding them in. But it gets more and more difficult with each passing day. The longer I go the harder it is. I need someone to help me get rid of them. I assure you it won't be painful for me. Sarah doesn't believe me. I thought my little cousin would find it an amusing way to pass an afternoon."

I grinned because he was totally right. "Cool. Do I use a sword?"

"I'll leave it up to you," Felix offered. "Tomorrow afternoon?"

Zack was walking up behind me as I agreed. I thought about buying a brand new shiny chainsaw. I should invest in some goggles, too, because it was probably going to be messy.

"It's a date."

Sarah's pale face let me know that it was probably going to be just me and Felix for this bit of amputation.

"Mrs. Donovan, I have orders to deliver you to Ether." Zack offered his hand to help me up.

"I thought I was going to Neiman's." I wasn't often allowed to go off schedule. Zack wasn't like Neil, who I could have swayed with a good bottle of champagne and the promise of hot-guy watching.

"Mr. Quinn and Mr. Donovan request your presence in the grotto," Zack informed me, and my heart just about sank out of my chest.

I hugged Sarah and Felix good-bye.

"I know it's hard, but you know what you have to do," Sarah whispered.

Zack led me to the car Lee brought around, and I walked mindlessly, unable to think about anything but the choice I was going to have to make.

* * * *

"Zack, you and Lee have the rest of the evening off," Dev informed my bodyguard quietly. Zack nodded, and once he disappeared in the elevator, Dev locked us in. He was in his now familiar suit. He'd probably been meeting with someone important. He loosened his tie and turned his beautiful face to me. "Come on, sweetheart, Daniel is waiting."

I was happy for the endearment, but he still didn't touch me. I followed him into the grotto where Daniel waited.

Like Dev, he was in a suit that fit his spectacular body to perfection. His tie was already gone, and he'd unbuttoned the dress shirt. "Hey, Z."

Dev walked to the bar and poured himself a drink. He came back with two glasses. I tried to refuse, but he pressed the vodka into my hand. "You're going to need it, sweetheart."

"Just get this over with." I wasn't some spoiled child to be called in for chastisement. Maybe I had made some mistakes, but I made them honestly. I couldn't help the fact that I loved them. I hadn't meant to hurt anyone.

"Daniel and I have been talking it over, and we've come to a decision," Dev explained, taking a short sip of what looked like Scotch. I was surprised because he hated Scotch.

"Do I get any say in this?" I asked, knowing I didn't.

"Of course. You can accept it or not." Dev sounded so calm and reasonable. I really wanted to push him. I wanted to get rid of the politician and fight with the man.

"Well, that seems fair." For the first time, I thought seriously about walking out on both of them.

"Z, just listen," Daniel said. "It's not what you think, but it is serious. It's your choice."

"Fine. Hit me, Dev." I had things to do anyway. I would get this deeply painful conversation over with and concentrate on finding Neil. Halfer was still out there and I had no doubt he would show back up, but I would put all my efforts into finding Neil and bringing him home. Felix said he needed time, well, he could spend time healing here in Dallas. I tried to think about anything but the choice they were going to ask me to make.

Dev smiled for the first time, and it was filled with a sexy promise. "She really thinks this is going to be bad, doesn't she?"

"Dude, we've strung her along for days." Daniel shrugged. "You can't expect her to take that for long."

"There were things we needed to negotiate, Zoey," Dev explained, looking slightly amused. It threw me off balance, which I think was his point. "We can't go into this lightly. Daniel and I had to work some things out between us before we made our proposal to you."

"What is this proposal the two of you have come up with?" I wanted to hear the words. I wanted to know it was all right to keep dating both of them. I would be respectful and try to keep our worlds as separate as possible.

Dev's lips curled up in a sexy grin. "We want to make our ruse into truth. The rest of the world believes we are a happy, settled *ménage à trois*, and Daniel and I have decided we can make it work."

"What?" The word sounded dumb coming out of my mouth.

"We're going to share you, lover," Dev explained, his eyes already heating up at the thought. "Do you remember what we did in Vegas? We'd be doing it on a regular basis. That's not to say you wouldn't be sleeping with us on an individual basis as well, but there will be an enormous amount of sharing. We liked it, Zoey."

I looked at Daniel for confirmation. He smiled slowly, and I caught a glimpse of fang. "It was hot, Z. I have to admit it. I liked watching you."

He also liked the power that had come from Dev's magic. If he fed from it regularly, he might be able to daywalk on a permanent basis. There was so much more to this proposal than mere sex. Dev was right. I needed the vodka.

"Marcus called me your Lancelot, Zoey, and perhaps there is some truth to it," Dev said quietly. "But maybe Camelot would have stood a little longer if Arthur and Guinevere and old Lance had been a bit more sexually liberated."

"How is this supposed to work?" I tried to catch my breath.

"We've decided to live here," Dev replied. "All three of us will share these rooms. I've already ordered a bigger bed and some light-tight drapes. The staff knows that you and Daniel are to be treated as residents not guests. The two of you will have access to everything. Daniel and I will continue to work together. You should think about this, Zoey. We'll more than likely be very demanding. We consider this a committed relationship. Any sex we have is with you, and I, for one, am going to want a lot of sex."

Daniel held up his hand. "I will, too, Z. I'm done with denying myself. I want to fuck you daily, and I'm not going to walk away like a gentleman after you feed me. We've also decided that Dev is going to donate on a regular basis. His blood really is fairly close to yours. I want you both to take my blood at least once or twice a week. You're aging, Z, and I'm not. I can stop that. I can stop it for both of you."

Dev shrugged out of his jacket and laid it over the couch. He started in on his dress shirt. "If this proposal is acceptable to you, we would like to consummate our arrangement tonight. I've been miserable sleeping by myself." Dev tossed his shirt over the jacket. "Come with us, Zoey." He leaned down and kissed me. His tongue was insistent, and I let him in. I was drowsy with wanting by the time he was done with me. "I'll be in bed waiting for your answer."

Dev walked off toward the bedroom, and it was Daniel's turn to persuade me.

"You're really okay with this?" I asked as he pulled me into his arms and against his chest.

"We're stronger together than we are apart, Z." Daniel's hands cupped my ass. He growled a little as he kissed me, letting me feel just how all right he was with the arrangement. "We need each other. The last few weeks proved that to me. We're not going to get a white picket fence and two point five kids, but we can still be happy." Daniel pressed his lips to mine once more and pulled away. "I love you. I'm going to go to bed. Don't leave me waiting too long because two dudes in bed gets gay after a while, even if we are waiting for a girl."

Daniel was tossing off his clothes as he walked to the bedroom.

I took a really long breath. I was stupid. There was so much more to this than simple love and lust. There always would be with these two men. They were ambitious and could be cruel and ruthless when it came to fulfilling their well-thought-out plans.

If I walked into that bedroom, I would be walking into a relationship where I had to fight not one but two men. I would have to fight to maintain my freedom because they were already working in tandem to curtail it. I would have to fight to be more than a pretty face and a soft body in bed. It would be so much harder because they were already presenting a united front.

Daniel wanted that power he could only get from Dev. Dev wanted to play the game, and more than that, he wanted to belong. He wanted a brother to replace his own, and Daniel could be that person for him. I would be the conduit to bring them together. This was so complicated, and I knew it was going to be far harder than either of them could imagine.

I knew all of that. I knew the best course of action was to grab the key from Dev's jacket and march myself right back down to Ether. They would come around eventually. I could keep them both and maintain my control.

So why did that seem like a sad half-life compared to what they were offering me?

By the time I reached the bedroom, I'd gotten rid of those pesky clothes. I didn't need them with my loves. I let Daniel pull me into bed, and Dev's hands were on me before I hit the sheets.

I tried to kick my stilettos off, but Dev playfully slapped my hands away. "Leave them. We like the heels."

Daniel was in full agreement as he wrapped those heels around the small of his back and his fangs found my neck.

It was the longest time before I managed to get out of those damn shoes.

Zoey, Daniel, and Dev will return in *Steal the Moon*, coming January 2014!

Steal the Moon

Thieves, Book 3
By Lexi Blake
Coming January 2014

When an ancient artifact enslaves every werewolf on earth, humanity's only hope is a thief...

Zoey Donovan should be happy. Her love life couldn't be better, her demonic nemesis is on the run, business is booming, and no one has tried to kill her in seven whole months. But without her best friend to share it with, it all seems a little hollow. Neil, her fabulous furry wingman, is missing and two grumpy werewolf bodyguards have taken his place.

Undaunted by her humorless babysitters, she intends to track Neil down even if it means risking her newfound romantic bliss. But someone else has plans for Zoey, and they don't intend to play nice. Lucas Halfer is desperate for revenge, and he knows just how to get it.

An ancient Roman legend tells of an artifact that will grant its possessor the power to control all wolves. No one, including Daniel and Dev, believes the Strong Arm of Remus is real but Zoey thinks Halfer might have already located it. With every werewolf pack in North America gathering in Colorado, the demon could enslave an unstoppable army.

To save the day, and possibly the world, Zoey will have to find a way to steal the Strong Arm of Remus from one of the most powerful demons in existence. Then again, impossible is kind of her specialty.

* * * *

Dev reached out and suddenly I was no longer wearing that towel. He tossed it aside and took a moment to let his eyes roam my body. "I believe we had an arrangement before, lover. Do you remember it? I was more than willing to concede the reins of our relationship to you as long as I maintained a certain level of dominance in one very specific place."

Dev liked to be in control in the bedroom. He liked to play certain games and we hadn't done anything like that since bringing my husband into the relationship. I have to admit everything female in me tightened at the thought of Dev taking control again. Sex had been good the last six months, but Dev had allowed Daniel and me to explore what we were willing to do together. The boundaries had yet to really be pushed. As I looked into those green eyes, I realized he was done with going with the flow.

Dev was going to take charge.

Dev stood up and before I could protest, he tossed me on the bed. I tried to scramble up but found myself tangled in green vines that shot out from the walls to hold my arms and legs. The lush ivy held me tight, and I couldn't stop the startled cry that sprang from my lips as I was spread in a very wanton fashion across the bed.

"Now, my goddess," Dev drawled as he and Daniel looked down at my body. Dev's eyes were hot, and there was no mistaking the erection he was sporting. "You were a very bad girl today. You caused an enormous amount of trouble. Did you think you could get away with it? It's time to discuss your punishment."

"God, she looks hot," Daniel said with an expectant grin as he looked down at me.

"She does indeed," Dev said, watching me struggle against the bonds. They caused me absolutely no pain but they held me tightly. I wouldn't be going anywhere. My skin was already getting hot under the boys' scrutiny.

Dev walked to the side of the bed and ran a single finger against my pussy, testing it. I sighed against the light pressure, wanting so much more. My Faery prince smiled down at me satisfied I was already responding. He drew the saturated finger directly into his mouth and sucked the cream off. He turned back to Daniel, who was more than interested in the proceedings now. There was a very large tent in those sweats.

"I have never had a lover get so fucking wet, so fast. It's intoxicating," Dev commented, shaking his head.

My vampire smiled. "I spent most of my youth with my face in her pussy, so I have to agree with you. It's my happy place."

"I'm sorry, sweetheart," Dev said as though suddenly noticing I was writhing on the bed. He walked up to me and gave me a slow, sexy grin. "Was there something you needed, my mistress?"

I held my head up so I could look at them. "You know what I want, Dev."

He sighed. It was the sound of true contentment, and I knew he meant business. If I had busted out of my funk today, then Dev was right behind me. "I know exactly what you want. I know what he wants, too. I also know it will be a while before either one of you gets it."

"What does that mean?" Daniel was used to getting straight to the fun.

Cupping my breast, Dev sat on the edge of the bed. He played lightly with my nipples, allowing the tips of his fingers to dance softly across the peaks. They hardened and I tried to press up, needing a much firmer touch. I would have preferred his mouth there, but I was going to have to take what I could get.

Dev looked thoughtfully at Daniel. "It means that I am ready to move this relationship forward. It means I am done with merely participating. You've trained me to be a better fighter. I've listened to your advice and allowed you to be the master. In this room, I am the master. Up until now our sex has been what I can only call somewhat circumspect."

Daniel looked confused. "Dude, we fuck the same girl in the same bed. How much freakier can it get?"

Dev laughed. "You have no idea, Daniel. Until tonight, I've been content for the most part to wait my turn and allow you to have yours. We've watched as the other pleasured our lover. This is not true sharing. Tonight we're going to play a little game, and I'm going to take us places you haven't even thought of yet."

"Oh, I've thought of it, Dev," Daniel admitted, his voice tight so I knew his fangs were out. "Are you kidding me? It's all I've been able to think about for months. I just don't know if Z's ready."

"Do what I tell you and I assure you, she'll be able to handle it." Dev looked down at me his face serene even as I knew mine was tight with need. "Do you trust me, sweetheart? Will you let me lead you?"

"You know I trust you, Dev." I trusted him implicitly. "Please, please fuck me."

I was already going crazy. I was worried this little game of his just might kill me with wanting, and he hadn't really touched me yet.

"Why don't you find your happy place," Dev ordered softly, looking at my husband. "But Daniel, long, slow strokes of the tongue. This is meant to tease, to torture in the most exquisite fashion. We don't want her to come too soon. There should be some work behind a truly good orgasm. Make her beg for it."

"Dev, that's not fair," I managed to say before Daniel took my breath away with that first sweep of his very talented tongue. It ran the length of my pussy, and I could feel every inch of that stroke. Daniel's big hands spread my legs further as he settled in and started to torment me with the light caresses. I tried to push down, to force him to fuck me with his mouth, but the bonds held too firmly.

"Will it help if I promise you'll be completely satisfied with the experience?" Dev asked as he rolled a nipple between his thumb and forefinger. He leaned down and touched the puckered nipple with the tip of his tongue. Teasing the nipple to a hard point, he finally pulled it into his mouth. He lightly sucked on it, the sensation making me want so much more. I nearly came off the bed when he gave me just the slightest edge of his teeth. I wanted to cry, to beg, to plead with him to give me more.

"Dev, please." I gave in to the need.

Love and Let Die

Masters and Mercenaries, Book 5
By Lexi Blake
Now Available!

A Tragic Love Story

Charlotte Dennis's mission was clear: distract and misdirect CIA operative Ian Taggart by any means necessary. If she failed, she would never see her sister again. With her training, it should have been simple, but after one night in Ian's arms, she knew that saving her sister would mean losing the man of her dreams.

Ian was tracking a terrorist when he met the beautiful American daughter of a Russian mobster. His instincts told him Charlotte was trouble, but his body craved her like a drug and his heart would not be denied. She took his ring and his collar. For once he was truly happy. But as he closed in on his target, her betrayal cost him his mission while her sacrifice saved his life. As she died in his arms, Ian vowed he would never love again.

A Dangerous Reunion

For five years, Charlotte has thought of nothing but returning to her husband, her Master. Working in the shadows, she has devoted herself to earning a chance to reclaim her place in Ian's life. But forgiveness isn't a part of Ian's vocabulary.

Nothing is more important to Ian Taggart than his new mission. But the information he needs is firmly in the hands of the woman who betrayed him. To catch his most dangerous prey, Ian will have to let Charlotte back into his life. As the hunt takes them to some of the world's most exotic locations, the danger grows and their passion reignites.

Will Ian forgive his wayward submissive…or lose her again?

* * * *

"Who?"

Charlotte frowned as though the whole meeting wasn't going quite the way she'd planned. She'd no doubt expected him to give in to instinct number one. "What do you mean who?"

He liked the fact that she was off balance. She couldn't seem to get a handle on his calmness. He couldn't blame her. He'd always been a dipshit passionate idiot around her. She didn't know the real Ian Taggart, the one he'd been before he'd married her, the one he'd found his way back to after long years of mourning. He was cold, calm, collected. He was a professional. "Who shot you, Charlotte?"

She stilled. "You're not going to like it, Master."

"Ian, please. I'm not your Master, sweetheart. I would prefer you use my given name. I keep the honorary title for the submissives I top." He kept his voice at the same even keel, but the word "Master" did something to him when it came out of her mouth.

"You're always my Master," she said, her voice sweet and a little sad. "And I'm your submissive."

"We'll have to agree to disagree on that." Or he could shove her over his knee, work those jeans off her hips, and slap her ass silly. Charlotte could take it. Charlotte craved it.

Who had been smacking her cheeks and tying her up and fucking her until she screamed? Because there was no way she went without.

"Master, I need you to listen to me." Her blue eyes fairly pleaded with him. Those eyes were what had gotten him in the first place. Oh, he'd loved her breasts and her hips. She was solidly built, and that just did it for him. He wanted a woman he could fuck for hours and not worry about breaking, but her eyes were striking. Ocean blue, like the waters of the Caribbean reflecting a crystal sky. He'd been drawn into those eyes.

"I'm listening, Charlotte." A thought occurred to him. "Is that the name you're going by now or should I call you Kristen? I have no idea what your real name is."

Her hands made frustrated fists. Ah, she hadn't changed her little tells. Those fists always made an appearance when she thought he was being stubborn. Her hair might have changed, but he could still tell when he was getting to her.

"I'm Charlotte Dennis and you damn well know it. You checked me out the first time. I never lied about my background."

He raised a single brow.

She bit into her bottom lip, her eyes sliding submissively away. "I apologize, Master. I shouldn't have cursed."

He shook it off. It was just a habit. Disciplining her had been a habit, the same way her sinking to her knees at his feet and rubbing her cheek to his leg had been a habit. The way he'd been able to relax and think as he'd petted her hair and enjoyed the contact before he would inevitably pull her into his lap and start to make love to her.

Yep. Just a habit. He could break habits. He hadn't had her in five years and he'd survived perfectly well. "Curse all you like. I probably would if my boss had shot me and then dosed me up with puffer fish toxin. Do you think he expected you to live?"

He tamped down the panic that flared at the thought of someone shooting her and dosing her up and leaving her there on the floor of their flat like a sacrifice. The protectiveness was a habit, too. She wasn't his to protect, and she never had been. She hadn't really been his sub. She'd been his opponent, and the first round had gone to her.

But she wasn't going to win this one.

"He wasn't my boss, babe. He had something I needed, and I thought he was the only one who could do the job. After I met you, I realized just how stupid I was." Her eyes were cloudy with tears, and she started to reach out for him. He moved his hands and leaned back out of her reach. "I should have talked to you but by then the man I was working for had Chelsea. After he killed my father, he took her as insurance that I would do the job. I couldn't risk Chelsea."

"Of course not." He had no idea who Chelsea was. Probably her dog. "I would like a name, Charlotte."

Her jaw tightened, and she looked down at her hands. "Chelsea is my sister's name. I know I didn't tell you about her, but she's younger than me. She's more…fragile. You remember how I told you about my father?"

Her Russian mobster dad. Yes, Vladimir Denisovitch. He had a rap sheet about twelve miles long in twenty-two different countries. If he'd followed the Russian mob practice of tattooing his crimes on his body, Ian was sure there hadn't been an inch of skin left on Vlad's flesh. But his crimes against Charlotte were even worse. However, Ian no longer cared. "I asked for a name. I don't need to know about your sister."

"You're going to be difficult."

He shook his head. “Not at all. If you don’t want to talk, you should feel free to leave. There’s nothing at all difficult about it.”

She took a long breath before speaking. “I’ll tell you, but I want you to stay calm.”

Everything fell neatly into place. There was only one name he could think of that would truly enrage him. Or would if he really gave a shit about her. “Then it’s Eli Nelson.

From USA TODAY Bestselling Author Carrie Ann Ryan

An Unlucky Moon

A Dante's Circle Novel

Hunter stood in front of Dante's Circle, the sunset beating down on him. He narrowed his eyes, the brown contacts he wore irritating them. He hated wearing the damn things, but yellow eyes seemed to scare the humans. He hadn't worn them the last time he'd been here, but he'd forgotten.

After spending four years battling demons and doing things that would haunt his nightmares for years to come, putting a thin film over his eyes to keep from scaring the little humans hadn't occurred to him.

People milled around in the early evening sun, talking and going about their day. Most of them were humans so they didn't realize they were venturing around a walking shadow of death. A pixie passed him and froze, her eyes widening. She blinked then scurried off, as if too afraid of what he *could* do rather than remembering that, to most predators, prey running away only egged them on.

Hunter wasn't one of those predators though. Despite his name, he didn't feel the need to hunt after prey when the one he truly wanted was within the walls in front of him. It had been a month since he'd seen Becca. A month since she'd lain in his arms, her body pale, healing.

He could still remember the howls echoing off the walls. It hadn't been until later that he'd realized those howls of anguish had been his own. Though he hadn't known much about Becca—still didn't—the wolf within him knew everything he needed to know.

Becca Quinn would be his mate—*was* his mate.

Now he just had to convince her of that.

Leaving for a month to let each other heal and work his way through the labyrinth of lies and betrayals within the Pack might not have been the best idea in retrospect. From what he knew of females, he was pretty sure leaving without any form of communication wasn't the smartest thing.

He'd have to court Becca—something he had *no* idea how it worked or what it entailed. Maybe Ambrose and Balin would help him. Even in hell, the angel and demon had known how to make Jamie smile. Hunter was pretty sure Ambrose had messed something up before they'd gone to hell in the first place. Hunter took that to mean that if the eons-old warrior angel could make mistakes and come out of it okay, surely he could.

Hopefully.

Hunter was the Beta of the Nocturne Pack, yet right at this moment, he didn't know if he had the strength to face her. He'd never had a mate before, let alone a human one—or whatever Becca was. He wasn't exactly sure, and the triad hadn't exactly been forthcoming with details.

Most wolves within his Pack mated other wolves. That was just the way of things. Wolves had one true mate—sometimes two if they were in a triad. That was it. Sure they could mate others and have children, but it wouldn't be a true mating. All other supernaturals had the same idea of true bliss.

Finding one's true half was a blessing.

A rare one.

The moment he'd stepped into that alley and had seen the red-haired goddess, he'd known she was the one for him. It had hit him like a freight train. Where most men would have thought it was crazy, Hunter had welcomed it.

He'd known she was his.

Now he just had to figure out what to do about it.

His Pack wanted him to mate—at least the ones who wanted him alive anyway. He had a true mate, but she wasn't part of the Pack. Hunter knew this would be an issue, but he really didn't care. All he wanted was the sweet-scented woman who drugged him like an elixir with her presence.

A human bumped into him and gave him a dirty look, presumably for standing in the middle of the sidewalk. He didn't blame the human for being annoyed, so he blinked at him rather than growling. The human's eyes widened, and fear seeped from him before he took off at a brisk pace in the other direction.

"Scaring people again?" Balin asked as he walked toward him from the parking lot.

Hunter shrugged but nodded toward the demon who had become his friend. "I didn't growl or bite him. I thought I was doing well."

Balin shook his head and chuckled. "You were. I don't really get it up here either." Up here being the human realm rather than the hell realm that Balin had lived in for three hundred years.

Though Hunter's own Pack was dark, gritty, and slightly demented, he still preferred it to hell.

Balin gave him an odd look then shook his head again. "We haven't seen you in a while. Did you get things taken care of?"

Hunter thought back to the looks of pity and fear within his Pack. "Not fully, but I've been away long enough."

"You're not going to tell me what you needed to do, are you?"

"I can't." It was true. Though Balin had helped save Hunter's life, he wasn't Pack. Some secrets needed to remain within the confines of their own species—something the demon should understand.

"You're here for Becca, aren't you?" Balin crossed his large arms over his chest and glared.

Not that Hunter knew exactly why the demon happened to be glaring, but it didn't sit easy with him. Hunter's hackles rose, but he toned them down. It was good that Becca had people to take care of her—even if the warnings were misplaced.

"Yes. She's mine," he answered simply.

Balin narrowed his eyes. "Remember that these women are not like those you know." The demon looked around at the humans who were oblivious to the rising tension. "Let's go inside. We can talk a little more freely there."

"You'd stand in the way of a bond?"

Balin shook his head and led them to the front door. "No, but I will stand before her to ensure it's what she wants. You left her high and dry and confused as hell a month ago. Don't think you can just prowl in and think everything will be okay."

Hunter frowned. "I know I will have to court her. I plan to ask you and your mates for help."

Balin blinked, his hand on the door. "You're going to ask for help? I thought you were an Alpha wolf."

"I'm the Beta of my Pack, but I'm a dominant. That doesn't mean I don't know how to ask for help when it's necessary. Becca isn't of my Pack, and I want her to remain safe. Bringing her into my Pack right now would be dangerous without all the facts, and I don't plan on forcing her to be with me."

Balin snorted then opened the door, leading them into the bar. "You're saying all the right things, but I have a feeling you'll act all wolf and think she should bend for you."

Hunter clenched his fists. "I'm not as enlightened as some. Fate made her for me, and the course has been set. I will not break from that."

The sweet scent of mate and woman filled his nose, and he turned to see the goddess of his dreams. She'd put her curly red hair in a tangle on the top of her head so little ringlets fell down her neck. Those pieces seemed to beg for his touch, and he had to remember not to reach out to her just yet. Her long neck would be perfect for his tongue, as would her ample breasts. There were more than a handful, and he wanted to know the color of her nipples.

Would they be a dusky rose or a dark red when he licked and sucked them so they became pointed peaks? Her waist was a tiny thing that flared out to hips that would be perfect for his hands as he gripped her, pummeling into her heat from behind. Her ass was perfect, not those small ones that women seemed to love, but with enough meat on her to make his mouth water. He couldn't wait to see her naked and wondered if those freckles that dotted her nose were anywhere else. He had a feeling he'd love licking each and every one, learning her curves and her taste.

Those jade green eyes bored holes into him as they lit fire. She tapped her foot, then raised her chin. It seemed his mate wasn't happy to see him. He'd known this would be the case, though the wolf within him seemed disappointed she didn't immediately rush into his arms and declare her undying love and need.

No worries. That would come.

He ignored the other patrons as he strolled toward her. He knew he moved more like an animal than man, but he didn't care. Becca would have to learn he was a wolf, not the man she might have dreamed of.

Fate wouldn't give him a mate who couldn't accept the animal within him.

It had already been cruel enough.

He stood in front of her, their bodies a whisper apart. Her scent enraptured him, holding him close.

She tilted her head and blinked at him. “You’re back.”

About Lexi Blake

Lexi Blake lives in North Texas with her husband, three kids, and the laziest rescue dog in the world. She began writing at a young age, concentrating on plays and journalism. It wasn't until she started writing romance that she found success. She likes to find humor in the strangest places. Lexi believes in happy endings no matter how odd the couple, threesome or foursome may seem. She also writes contemporary Western ménage as Sophie Oak.

Connect with Lexi online:

Facebook: Lexi Blake
Twitter: www.twitter.com/@authorlexiblake
Website: www.LexiBlake.net

CPSIA information can be obtained at www.ICGtesting.com
Printed in the USA
LVOW08s1812260214

375274LV00004B/857/P